SECRET
HUNGER

Amy,
It's never too late to
follow your dreams!
Satin Russell

SECRET HUNGER

SATIN RUSSELL

To my loving husband, who encouraged me to reach for my dreams and supports me as I do so. I love you beyond measure.

Acknowledgements

Thank you to my mom and sister for your insights and excitement throughout this past year. I couldn't have done it without you. Also a big shout out to my WriNoShores writing group, most especially Lynne Favreau and Sara Leahy. Thank you for all the inspiration, write-ins, commiseration, and writing advice. Thank you to my editor, Debbie, and my beta readers for your invaluable input.

Lastly, to all the readers out there willing to take a chance on a new author like me, "Thank you!"

Prologue

Detective Mason Clark looked up from the file in his lap and watched the scenery pass by his window. Multi-family homes with peeling paint and sagging porches slumped alongside cracked sidewalks. Even the sky looked gray and dingy, as if it, too, suffered from the same socio-economic forces as the neighborhood it watched over.

Amidst the monochromatic backdrop, colored strands of lights were haphazardly draped in windows and interwoven between the slats in some of the fences. Mason turned to his partner of five years and grumbled, "It's not even Halloween or Thanksgiving yet, and people already have their Christmas lights up. When did everybody start rushing through the holidays?"

Detective Ryan Miller shrugged and laughed at his best friend. "I don't know, man. You'd think people would want to savor one holiday before rushing to the next. It's not as if post-holiday winter holds some great prize. Late January and February are the worst, all the bad weather and none of the good stuff."

He thought about that and nodded. "Speaking of which, you and Shauna getting along any better? She gonna let you see your kid for the holidays?"

Mason knew they'd been having some problems and had recently separated. He also knew Ryan was still hoping to work things out. He looked over at his friend, who now had a pained look on his face.

"Sort of, I get the day after Thanksgiving with her and will be stopping by for Christmas Eve. They're heading over to Shauna's parents' house on Christmas Day." Stopped at a traffic light, they stared out of the windshield as a wrinkled, drunk, old man stumbled past them on the crosswalk.

He chuckled, ruefully. "She told me she wants a MacBook."

Ryan pulled the car to the curb. They paused a moment, taking in the details of the run-down, faded house sitting before them. At one point, Mason thought, it might have been blue, but the building had slowly become a faded gray over time. The color fled long ago, abandoning the inhabitants much like hope and prosperity had done before it.

Mason set the papers on the dash and removed his seatbelt. "So, this is where the bastard lives, huh? You want to take point on this, or should I?"

"I've got it. Something about this guy stinks. I think about scum like this stalking and hurting women and it makes me physically ill. All I can think is, what if someone like this got close to my Jenny? If he's our guy, I'm hoping we can throw him away for good."

"Alright, you get point, but don't get overeager. Remember, we don't have any solid evidence on him yet. They tried to get him for stalking over in Ohio, but couldn't get anything to stick."

Ryan sighed with exasperation. "It doesn't help that stalking is so hard to prosecute. A woman practically has to be assaulted or kidnapped just to get any attention. By then, it's usually too late."

Mason agreed, "Well, hopefully, it's not too late for this woman."

They both swung out of the car and scanned their surroundings. The sun was just beginning to break through the clouds, but Mason could still see his breath coming out in little puffs.

Gray patches of snow cowered in shadows, remnants of the last snowstorm.

Leading the way, Ryan walked up the steps in front of the door and rang the bell. "Mr. Mendez? Are you home? We need to ask you a few questions."

Robert Mendez barely cracked the door open. He stood between it and the frame, his body blocking any view of the gloom behind him. He wasn't very tall—only about 5'10" or so—but his shoulders were broad and it was obvious he kept himself in good shape. Mason noticed he was dressed completely in black: black cargo pants, combat boots and a black shirt buttoned all the way up to his neck.

"Officers," Robert looked at the two men standing before him and scowled. "What do you want?"

In his most official tone, Ryan inquired, "Robert Mendez? We're in the process of canvassing the area and have reason to believe you may know something about the disappearance of a young woman from this neighborhood. May we come in and ask you a few questions?"

Just then, they heard a thump, like something, or someone, falling and a soft, muffled cry from one of the back rooms. Mason watched Robert's shoulders tense and his eyes give a quick flick before immediately smoothing his face back to an inscrutable expression.

"Sir, are you alone in the house? Who do you have back there with you?" Raising his voice, Ryan took a small step forward, lifting his hand to push the door further open...

Shock and surprise registered on Ryan's face as his chest exploded in a sea of red. His expression seared itself into Mason's memory just as a bullet slammed into his own body, slightly off-center since his partner shielded most of him.

The weight of the other detective stumbling back threw Mason off balance, sending both of them tumbling down the stoop.

Mason struggled to see past the black spots beginning to form in his eyes and managed to whip his gun from its holster.

Desperately, he pulled the trigger, aiming towards the man now dashing out the front door towards them. The doorframe splintered as he took his only shot.

A second slug created a fiery trail of pain along his arm, grazing his shoulder. Gasping, he began to hear screams from across the street.

With adrenaline rushing through him, he attempted to get up, but his left arm didn't seem to be working very well and he couldn't get enough oxygen into his lungs. Each breath speared him with searing pain. For a moment, the entire world centered on his next inhalation.

With a feeling of detachment, almost as if he were watching a movie, Mason crumbled to the ground and lay there while the suspect bounded over him and Ryan, rushing towards his car. A woman with large, haunted eyes and a nest of stringy brown hair peered out from the shadows within the house.

Her mouth formed a hollow oval, reminding him of an Edward Munch painting. Her scream echoed throughout his soul, mirroring the one in his own head. As he succumbed to the blackness dragging him under, his last thought was of Ryan.

Chapter One

Olivia struggled to balance her purse, umbrella, and a large bag of baked goods as she unlocked the door to the restaurant. Fumbling for the lock, she quickly made a mental note to replace the bulb that had blown out at the back door... again. Didn't she replace it just recently?

Coming in from the damp, she dropped everything on the counter and switched the kitchen lights on. *First things first*, she thought, and turned to the coffee maker, pouring a healthy dose of coffee beans into the grinder. The loud crunching and whirring from the grinder woke her up nearly as much as her alarm clock had earlier. Savoring the moment, she took a deep breath and inhaled the aroma.

Really, was there anything as wonderful as the smell of freshly ground coffee beans? She pondered the question for a moment. Well, unless it was the smell of bacon, she thought.

Shaking her head at her silly musings, she began her usual routine of checking the restaurant, making sure everything was ready to open. The Three Sisters Cafe was a popular morning stop in the charming town of Bath, Maine and she knew that it would probably be busy, despite the storm coming in later.

She loved these first few minutes to herself before things got busy. It was a moment when she could take stock and be proud of the little café she had built from the ground up.

The café was on the corner of Main and Centre Street, and she could practically see all of downtown from her vantage point. Big bay windows graced the front of the eating area and looked out onto the quaint street with its older store fronts. She loved the picturesque effect that white Christmas lights and pine boughs had on the small town. It looked just like the front of a holiday card, even with the dark gray clouds and overcast skies above.

Inside, the café boasted cheerful, pale yellow walls that brightened up the space even on the gloomiest days. A bakery counter inhabited the back corner of the waiting area, full of muffins, scones, and bagels for the people who were in a bit more of a rush and just wanted to pick something up quickly.

A bank of coffee pots was placed along the right wall where guests could come in, grab a mug, and select from a number of roasts—from light, medium, or dark, to flavored, or decaf. Granted, she could have chosen to stick with just regular or decaf, but in a small town with limited options, the added luxury seemed to go over well with people.

The coffee counter was a part of a small reception area with benches along a half-wall, just in case there was a line. On weekends, when the demand was high, people didn't mind coming in, getting a mug of coffee and chatting while they waited for a table. In the summertime, she also made sure to have some benches out front so people could enjoy the warm weather and sun.

Not that it's an issue today, she thought, giving a little shiver. This morning had been particularly frigid with a cold front coming in from the north, and they were due to have a bad Nor'easter sweep through later that afternoon.

To the left, past the half-wall separating the front waiting area and the dining room, were a number of two-and four-top tables with cheerful little bud vases - currently filled with bunches of autumn leaves. Even though Christmas lights had already been strung up around town, Olivia insisted on decorating for Thanksgiving until after the holiday. All the tables were light and easy enough to be re-arranged and were regularly moved around to accommodate larger parties during the holiday season.

Along the back wall of the dining area was a breakfast counter where people could perch on black and chrome stools and enjoy the activity in the kitchen, observe the people in the dining room, or just watch the morning talk shows from the large screen TV hanging on the wall. To the left was a hallway running to the bathrooms, a storage area for paper goods and various sundries, and Olivia's shoebox of an office.

After making her usual rounds through the dining room, straightening a chair here and there, Olivia headed back to the kitchen to check on the coffee and start the prep work. One of the things she was most proud of was the way the kitchen looked and functioned.

She had remodeled it the first year she had gotten into the space, and now it had an expansive open griddle, a six-burner cooktop, and plenty of counter space. There were metal shelving units long one wall that held large covered bins of dried goods, each clearly labeled and dated. A modest sized walk-in fridge took up the back corner and had produce on one side, meat on the other. Everything was stainless steel, spotless and gleaming.

She liked that she could stand at the griddle and see the people sitting at the breakfast counter, all while handing plates laden with delicious, steaming breakfast food through the pass-through window. It made it easier to keep an eye on things and get a feel for how the shift was going on any given day.

From the kitchen, she heard the bells on the front door jingle, indicating her best friend and manager, Jackie, had arrived.

"Hey, you back here?" Jackie poked her head back into the kitchen. "Happy Birthday!"

The greeting made Olivia grin. "Well, technically, it's tomorrow."

With a flourish, Jackie presented her with a little box, beautifully gift-wrapped.

"Aww, you know you didn't have to get me anything." She gave her friend a quick hug and tore open the paper. Lifting the lid, she revealed a pair of sparkling, dangly earrings. "These are great, thanks!" Most of the time, she forgot she even had her ears pierced, but with the reminder, she promptly began to put them in.

"How do they look?" At her friend's approving murmur, she kept them in and tossed the box. "It's hard to believe I'm actually twenty-seven now. I feel like I should be older, somehow."

"Oh, now," Jackie gasped, "let's not get ahead of ourselves. My birthday is still a few months after yours and I'm already quivering at the idea that I'll only be a few years from thirty. I'd rather not think about that milestone just yet, if it's all the same to you."

She glanced at her friend and thought she didn't have to worry. Jackie was one of those people who would always look younger than she was. Partly because, at 5'3", she was so petite. Olivia noticed her friend's cute, blond, angled bob was mussed from the hat she'd been wearing and wondered how her friend's cornflower blue eyes could be so sparkling and awake at this early hour. Then again, that was just like her—pretty, vibrant and always full of energy.

Not for the first time, she was thankful her high school friend had agreed to help her run the café all those years ago. It had been shortly after her parents had passed away and not only had she needed someone she could trust, but also someone who would be able to see her vision and believe in her. Her friend's natural charm with people and her innate organizational skills had been a bonus.

Granted, offering her the job of café manager had helped Jackie out, too. When she'd floated the idea to her, Jackie had been a young, single mother with a little girl just under two years old.

After discovering she was pregnant, the baby's father had run as fast as he could to the nearest exit and never looked back. She never mentioned it, but Olivia suspected that was why her friend had such trust issues when it came to meeting men now.

Not only that, but her strict, religious parents had disowned her when they'd found out what had happened, and had left town shortly thereafter. That had left Jackie juggling two part-time jobs and just barely paying the bills for a studio apartment, lacking both financial security and sleep.

It had been tough times for both of them, but together they had managed to power through. If leaving that all in the past required her getting older, then she would gladly greet her birthdays with a smile.

After admiring her present, Olivia said, "I got the first coffee pot going. I think it's nearly finished. Tom will probably be here any minute. I'm just going to load up these baked goods in the case and then get started on the specials menu."

"Sounds good. I'm assuming you already did your usual run through the dining room and made sure everything is in order. Do you know if Becky was planning on coming in today?"

"Yeah, she's on winter break. She said she'd be in to help out for a few hours."

Tom came in from the back door and nodded his greeting at the two women. Jackie rolled her eyes and shared a smile with Olivia. They knew it was the most interaction they'd get from him until he'd had at least two cups of coffee, and even then, it wouldn't be much more than that.

He was an Army vet who had served three tours in the Iraq and Afghanistan wars. His long, dark hair barely brushed his shoulders and was just beginning to streak with gray. He had it pulled back into a ponytail that accented his high cheekbones. It was obvious he had some Native American in his family lineage, but how much was hard to say. His nearly black eyes looked like deep pools, full of past memories and secret things left unsaid. Not for the first time, Olivia was reminded of that saying, "Still waters run deep."

He'd shown up at her café about a year after it had opened, looking for a job. By that point, business had been taking off and she'd been struggling with the workload of running her own café, as well as raising her two sisters. She'd jumped at the chance to have a second pair of hands in the kitchen.

He wasn't much of a conversationalist, but one got the feeling he noticed everything around him. More importantly, he was good under pressure, which was essential during the morning breakfast rush on weekends. It didn't hurt that he made the best hash browns in town.

The two ladies watched as he pulled out a bin and started peeling the mountain of potatoes they would need for the next few hours.

Olivia heard the coffee maker start to spurt and sputter, indicating it was done, and turned to fix cups for her and Tom. "Jackie, you want one?"

"Sure. I'll come back and get it in a minute. I think I see Mrs. Crowley standing out there in the cold. I'm going to let her in a little early."

Olivia laughed. "Between her and Mr. Harrington's little contest to see who gets here first, we're going to be forced to open earlier and earlier!"

Jackie grinned. "Tell me about it. Hey, at their age, whatever keeps them ticking. I think it's sweet to see them flirting with each other. I hope I can be like that when I'm in my eighties." She shot her a rueful grin. "Of course, it would be nice to meet a man *before* I reach that age."

"I hear that. If all else fails, we can drink wine together when we're gray and tottering. I'm sure I'll be available to keep you company."

Tom shook his head and grunted, the potato peeler never

pausing in his hand. Both of them looked at him, then at each other, and started laughing. "Don't worry, Tom. You can join us," Jackie said with a wink, before heading to unlock the front door.

For the next few hours, the Sunday morning crowd kept Olivia and Tom busy filling order tickets. Whole rashers of bacon popped and sizzled on the flat tops and pancakes bubbled into golden discs as she stuffed and flipped a steady array of omelets. It was a constant and precise kitchen ballet that they both performed with perfect harmony and synchronicity.

After a while, she glanced at the clock and was surprised to discover it was already after 10 a.m. There was a slight break between the early birds and the people coming in from after church or those who had just slept in late and were now ready for brunch.

Sensing a lull in the breakfast crowd, Olivia turned to Tom. "I think I'll head back to the office and work on my supply order. Hopefully, I can get it finished without having to stay any later this afternoon."

"Yeah, that works. I'll let you know if it gets too busy."

"Great."

She sent silent thanks for having a right-hand man like him working for her. He may be a man of few words, but no matter how busy the kitchen got, he always managed to be the calm in the middle of the storm. Between him and Jackie, she knew her business was in good hands.

As she made her way down the back hallway to the little storage room she'd converted into her makeshift office, her phone rang. "Hey, Liz, what's up?"

Eliza, or Liz, was Olivia's younger sister. She worked at the mechanic shop a few blocks down the street, the same one where their father did when he had been alive. "Just wondering how the crowd's doing over there. Thought I'd try to pop in for a quick breakfast before I get started on this next car."

"It's a bit busier than usual. I think most people are getting what they need early and planning to hunker down before the storm blows in. What would you like? I'll let Tom know."

"Just my usual and a side of bacon, please. I should be there in about ten minutes or so."

"I'll be in my office; come on back when you get here." Hanging up, she detoured back towards the kitchen to put Liz's blueberry pancake order in before putting on another pot to brew.

* * *

There was such a feeling of satisfaction in being able to pay the bills for another month. She loved knowing the roof above her head was paid for, the people who worked for her would still have jobs, and her guests would be able to come in for a good meal and good company. A knock on the door interrupted her just as she started delving into the process of making sure everyone would be paid that week.

Liz opened the door and poked her head in the room. "Hey, Livvy, do you think my food is ready?"

"Yeah, I put the order in when you called. I'll go check and see if it's in the window. I need a warm-up for my coffee, anyway. Why don't you sit back here and keep me company while you eat?" She gave her seat to her sister and went to grab her food.

A few minutes later, she leaned against the desk and took a sip from her mug. Liz slanted her a look as she poured an obscene amount of syrup on her pancakes. "So, how does it feel to be twenty-seven, birthday girl?"

"About the same as it did when I was twenty-six, I guess. I don't know why people make such a big deal about getting older. I can honestly say I feel fine about it."

She smiled, watching syrup pool on Liz's plate. How her sister managed to maintain such a lean, athletic build was beyond her. Where she was curvy, her sister was straight and slender. Her short brown hair was usually styled into an edgy, pixie cut that perfectly framed her startlingly pale green eyes. However, Olivia noticed it was currently standing on end from the cold wind outside.

Liz just nodded and took a bite, chewing thoughtfully for a moment. "I can see why you'd feel like that. If you think about it, you've been in this stage of your life since a lot earlier and for a lot longer than many of your peers. When they were out hitting the happy hours and clubbing, you were home making dinner, doing laundry, and checking that we'd done our homework.

"Most of them are just now starting to enter a stage of their lives where they are responsible for running a household and raising families. You've been taking care of Fiona and me for years now, along with running your own business. There probably isn't that much of a difference between this time of your life and the last four years prior to it."

Olivia tilted her head and looked at her, watching as she chased a blueberry across her plate. Leave it to her sister to be able to cut directly into the heart of a subject. "You know, I never thought about it like that. It kind of makes sense when you put it that way."

Liz shrugged and took a swig from her coffee. "It makes me wonder, though. Do you think you'll wake up one day and wonder what you missed during that stage? It's not too late, you know. Have you thought about the fact that since Fiona and I are out of the house, you could go sow a few wild oats?"

She laughed. "Wild oats? Um, no. I don't think that's going to be much of an issue with me. Playing the field is not appealing." She thought about it a little more. "Besides, I don't regret the choices I've made. The only thing I would change is the fact that our parents died at all. I still miss them; I know we all do. But, I'm happy that I was old enough to take custody of Fiona so that she didn't have to be put into a foster home. Going out partying really isn't that important when compared to keeping the three of us together."

She straightened up from where she was leaning on the corner of her desk. "At any rate, I need to get back to the kitchen and see how Tom is holding up. The brunch crowd should be filtering in by now. Will you lock the door and bring the plate back to the kitchen once you're finished?"

Liz nodded and popped the last of her pancakes in her mouth.

"Oh! Have you heard from Fiona today?" Olivia asked. "She said she was going to drive down from school and stay in town for the weekend."

"I haven't talked to her today, but I remember her mentioning it."

"I hope she gets an early enough start to be off the road by the time the storm hits. Will you give her a call and see when she plans to leave?"

"If I was to guess, she probably woke up and promptly forgot everything else with her nose buried in another one of her books." They both laughed with warm affection for their youngest sister. Liz rose from the chair. "I'm almost done at the shop for the day, anyway. I'll give her a call on the walk back."

"Alright, thanks. We're still on for the birthday dinner tonight, right?"

"Absolutely. I thought I'd ride out the storm with you two and just spend the night in my old room. We can have dinner, drink some wine, and make a sister party out of it."

"Sounds perfect. I'll try to stop by the grocery store and pick up a few things for a nice meal. I meant to do it earlier, but lost track of time. It's been awhile since I've made my Chicken Marsala and I've been craving it."

Liz grinned and rubbed her hands in anticipation. "Make sure you leave a bit early, too, okay? The weather is supposed to start getting pretty nasty around two o'clock."

After giving her sister a quick hug, Olivia made her way back to the kitchen to take over the grill. She scanned the restaurant as she passed through the dining room, noting that everything was running smoothly and there was a small crowd of people in the front of the lobby waiting for a table.

Suddenly, the back of her neck began to prickle with the feeling of being watched. Looking around quickly, she spotted a man sitting at the breakfast counter with sharp, blue, brooding eyes, a strong—slightly stubbled—jaw, and a dark fall of hair across his forehead. Instantly, her cheeks flushed. Her pulse stuttered, and then began to race.

Speaking of wild oats, she thought.

Flustered, she turned slightly away, put her hair up in a quick bun, and headed back into the kitchen. Curiously, she contemplated the man sitting at her counter, as well as her own immediate response to him, while she pulled down the next ticket.

They didn't get a lot of strangers in town during the off-season, and it had been a long time since she'd felt so completely stripped bare by just a look. Not altogether comfortable with her reaction, or train of thought, she began cracking eggs onto the grill.

It was probably just as well she remained back behind the scenes, Olivia thought. She didn't have time for these sorts of distractions in her life.

Chapter Two

Mason flagged the high-school girl down for another cup of coffee and hunched over his breakfast plate. Idly, he rotated his shoulder to ease the stiffness in his left arm. He had to admit, the food was pretty good in this little café. Much better than he would have expected from the usual small-town greasy spoon.

The bubbly, dark-haired girl gave him a grin as she topped off his coffee.

"How is everything?"

"Good, thanks." Mason grimaced as the girl gave him a big smile. She kind of reminded him of Ryan's daughter, Jenny.

She cocked her hip and leaned on the counter, practically batting her eyes at him. "Did you need anything else?"

Was she actually trying to flirt with him? With a long look, he replied, "Just the check, please."

He watched her cheeks turn pink as she straightened up and pulled the bill from her apron pocket. Mason felt kind of bad. He hadn't meant to embarrass her. "Here you are, then. Let me know if you change your mind."

He took a sip of his coffee and nodded agreement. Ryan's little girl wasn't much younger than the waitress. Who was going to be there to watch her back while she learned how to navigate the process of becoming a woman and how to make good choices?

His mouth twisted at the thought. *Don't go there. Stop that train of thought before you go any further.* Glancing down at the plate, he sighed and pushed it away. The stray thought had made him lose his appetite despite how good the hashbrowns tasted. Actually, he was surprised his plate was half empty, considering it'd been weeks since he'd felt hungry or eaten more than a few bites.

No, it wasn't a bad little café, he thought, as he took another look around. Judging by how busy it was, it seemed to be a hot spot for the locals. He watched as a well-dressed family, obviously just out of church, was seated across the dining room.

He liked how bright and cheerful the place was with the large windows looking out on the town. People stood at the front, holding white mugs filled with coffee and chatted with neighbors as they waited for a table. His seat at the counter gave him a glimpse, through the pass-through window, at the organized chaos of the kitchen.

As he looked around, he noticed a young woman make her way into the room from the back hallway. Something about the way she moved was utterly alluring. There was an unselfconscious grace in the way she held herself; shoulders back, head up, and a fluid gait that flowed straight down from her hips. She couldn't have been more than 5'5", but the way she walked gave the impression that her legs went on forever.

As Mason watched, she didn't go to join a table in the dining room, but instead made her way behind the counter and pulled a white chef's jacket down from the hook by the kitchen door. He appreciated the way the pale coat contrasted with the toasted-almond color of her smooth skin.

She deftly wound her long, mahogany-colored hair into a bun at the nape of her neck. His fingers itched to feel if it was as silky as it looked. Mason couldn't help but notice the gentle slope of her breasts, barely visible under the shapeless frock.

For crying out loud, he needed to get it together. Granted, it had been awhile since he'd seen or dated anybody, but that was no reason for him to start acting like a gawky teenage boy who had never been with a woman before.

Truth be told, catching the interest of a beautiful woman had never been a problem for Mason. Many would have been considered more attractive than the lady behind the counter in her baggy chef's coat, faded jeans, and serviceable sneakers. So, what was it about her that caused such an instant, visceral reaction? Maybe it was because it was so obvious that she hadn't tried to enhance her natural beauty, and yet it still managed to shine through.

About the time he reached this conclusion, he realized he'd been staring. Mason quickly went to take another sip of his coffee, but it was too late. She must have sensed his attention, because she suddenly turned and looked directly at him.

He paused with his mug halfway to his lips, and forgot to breathe. Her eyes reflected the pale sunlight filtering in through the windows and glowed like bits of amber. For a split second, everything else faded into the background. Then, just as quickly, she turned away and swung through the kitchen door.

Mason watched as the woman pulled down the next ticket. He could tell she was clearly in her element as she easily fell into the rhythm of working the grill with the other cook, a man. Every action seemed to be fluid and competent.

He lingered over his half a cup of coffee for another ten minutes and enjoyed watching the easy way the two of them worked. He knew what it was like to work in sync with a partner. He missed that feeling of knowing someone well enough to practically predict their next actions before even they knew what they'd do.

The swift sting of loss caused his fascination and enjoyment of the moment to pop like a soap bubble. He berated himself for his preoccupation. Dammit, his partner hadn't been buried for even a month, and here he was mooning over some random woman who, truth be told, hadn't done anything to encourage his wayward thoughts.

What the hell was wrong with him? The last thing he needed was to get involved with somebody, given his current state of misery. He could barely stand his own company, let alone subject someone else to his surly moods. It was bad enough that his sister had to see him like this as he recuperated.

Besides, he knew first-hand how deeply it hurt to lose someone close. He wouldn't wish it on anyone. If he chose to stay in this line of work, the best thing he could do is keep his distance. Mason suspected the intriguing woman would want more than just a casual arrangement.

Shaking his head and firmly deciding it was time to go, he laid some cash on the counter to pay the bill and told the girl to keep the change. Resolutely, he strode towards the door and out into the cold, refusing to allow himself even a quick – tempting – glance back at the golden-eyed kitchen goddess.

Chapter Three

By the time Olivia managed to finish her next supply order and close the restaurant, it was four o'clock in the afternoon. The storm had rolled in earlier than predicted and snow had already been coming down for nearly four hours.

Close to a foot of snow had piled up along the sidewalks and mounded in the gutters along the road. Pulling her collar up and bending her back against the wind, she silently scolded herself for not following her own advice and heading home earlier.

The fan belt gave a squeal of protest as she started her car. With a sigh, she made a mental note to have Liz take a look at it. She threw her purse into the passenger seat and grabbed her ice scraper.

Luckily, the heater had a chance to kick in once she'd cleared her car off, and the interior was toasty when she climbed back in. She was grateful that although her Toyota Camry was twelve years old, it still worked like a champ.

Before pulling out from the space behind her building, her chilled fingers quickly dialed Liz's number and got her voicemail. "Hey, it's me. I got out a bit later than expected but I'm heading to the store now and will be home soon." She hung up and carefully navigated her way across the road and into the grocery store parking lot.

She promised herself she was just going to quickly stop in the grocery store to pick up what she needed for the Chicken Marsala and make her way home. Thankfully, her sisters were probably already out of the snow and safely inside the house.

At least there was one good thing about the storm, she thought, pulling into the parking spot closest to the doors. As she walked towards the entrance, a group of young women were coming out of the store. They looked like a flock of bright tropical birds that had taken a wrong turn north. All of them were about her age, maybe a few years younger, and looked like they were going out for a night on the town.

She cringed inwardly at how cold they all looked. They must not have felt a coat matched their outfits, because none of them wore one. She glanced down at the pretty heels they all wore and wondered which one of them would fall first. It was hard enough to balance on high heels; she couldn't imagine trying to walk through snow and ice on them.

She walked up to the automatic doors, catching her own reflection in the store windows. She'd changed out of her sneakers and into some sturdy, blue Merrell snow boots with rubber soles. Her jeans were so worn that the seams had begun to turn white. She was thankful that her long, black coat came halfway down her legs. Her long hair was gathered and tucked up under a dark-gray knit hat. Overall, she may look a bit old and frumpy, but at least she was warm.

Olivia gave the women a final glance as they piled into the car, laughing and shivering. She honestly couldn't remember ever being that young. The thought came out of nowhere and had a depressing effect on her. The conversation she'd had with her sister earlier echoed in her mind. Telling herself it was just a small case of birthday blues, she shook off the moment and headed into the warmth of the store.

Stomping her boots at the door, she had to resist the urge to take a detour down the international food aisle. Ordinarily, she could spend hours checking out new products or comparing labels, but now wasn't the time to linger.

Where some people might like to go to cafés or the library to hang out, she found solace at the grocery store. Her sisters thought it was funny, but she liked being inspired by new recipes and thinking about all the different things she could make.

There was always some strange fruit or vegetable when she went through the produce aisle, and she loved discovering a new kind of cheese, or a product she'd never seen before. For her, it was like being able to go on an adventure without ever having to leave her small town or spend lots of money on a trip.

"Hey Olivia. You're lucky you got in when you did. Think we're going to close up early today." The grocery store manager — a slightly balding, portly man, in his mid-fifties — greeted her. He was used to seeing her wander through the aisles of his store, and had even special ordered quite a few items for her over the years.

"Hi, Herb. Yeah. I was hoping to be home by now, too. Unfortunately, I got held up on the phone, placing my supply order. I'm glad I made it before you closed. I promised my sisters Chicken Marsala tonight to ride out the storm."

"Sounds good. How's it looking out there?"

"There's at least a foot already on the ground and it doesn't look like it's going to let up anytime soon."

"Hmm, I think I'll inform the rest of the staff to finish up and get ready to go. We'll probably close in about half an hour or so."

"Okay, I won't be but a minute." She strode through the aisles, quickly gathering what she needed before heading back towards the last open register. There was a gangly teen standing at the counter waiting for her.

She greeted the young man with a nod and set the basket down, beginning to unload it. "Are you new here? I don't think I've seen you before."

"Yes, ma'am, just started this last week. I'm hoping to earn a little extra money for the holidays."

Olivia gave him an encouraging smile, but inside she cringed. *"Ma'am?!" When on earth did I become a "ma'am?"*

Just then Herb showed up. "Wow. I think you set a new record for fastest visit."

She grinned at his teasing as she pulled out her nylon grocery bags. He loaded the bags himself. Despite the fact that he had mentioned closing early, he didn't seem to be in a particular hurry. As he chattered away about how long and tough winter had been this year and how it was probably going to affect the cost of food, it was all Olivia could do to politely converse, silently wishing she could get going and head home.

Finally, her items were all rung up and bagged, and she could swipe her debit card through the machine. Thanking them both for their help, she pulled her hat further down on her head and quickly left the store. Her sisters and a good glass of wine were waiting for her at home, and it was about time for her to get there.

Chapter Four

Robert gripped his steering wheel and cursed the fickle bitch that was Mother Nature. All women were worthless bitches until they were trained, why would Mother Nature be any different? If he could get his hands on her, guaranteed he'd get her to do his bidding.

Okay yeah, so maybe he should have been watching the weather a little more closely. Sure, it had been awhile since he'd been in Maine during the winter, but still, he should have known better.

The problem was that he didn't have much choice after shooting and killing that cop down in Boston. It had been all he could do to gather his emergency stash of money and clothes and cross the state lines without being caught.

Even then, it had been a close call. He probably wouldn't have managed it if that guy hadn't picked him up from the side of I-95. No way would he have been able to drive through the toll booths and up to Maine in his own car, not with all the cameras around.

The memory brought a sick grin to Robert's face. The poor idiot had been only too happy to have help with the gas and toll expenses. He probably didn't think it was worth the cost now that he was lying dead by the side of the road, under the brush Robert had piled over him. But, hey. What could you do?

That's what you get for being a Good Samaritan. With that thought, he pounded on the dash, trying to get the heater to kick back on. Too bad the guy hadn't had a better car, though.

Preoccupied, his attention divided between the road and the dash, he didn't see the hill until he'd already started to head down it. The car picked up speed rapidly and he struggled to keep it under control, praying the old sedan didn't have bald tires to go with the beat up heater.

Suddenly, a pair of headlights speared out of the white wall of snow. Robert managed to shift the wheel, just barely preventing the two cars from colliding. Cursing the other driver, he quickly regained control over the car, sliding the rest of the way down the hill without incident.

No way was he going to be able to make it up to the cabin tonight, he thought. He was going to have to hole up in the area until the storm passed and the roads were plowed.

If he remembered correctly, there was a little motel just outside of town. Maybe they'd still have a vacancy for…Robert reached over and grabbed the wallet he'd taken from the previous owner of the car…Samuel Wellfleet. Caucasian male with brown hair? Chuckling, he thought, *close enough.*

After another twenty minutes of navigating the storm, he finally pulled into the rattrap motel. The vacancy sign flickered in the wind, cautiously catering to passing motorists as the long, one-story building huddled against the blowing snow and elements.

With a resigned sigh, he flipped the collar of his coat up and pulled his hat lower on his head, letting the brim shadow his eyes. Reluctantly, he climbed from the car and headed into the office.

The counter stood prominently across the back of the room and was unattended. He could hear the droning voice of a news anchor coming from the room behind the check-in area. Impatiently, he slammed his hand on the bell a couple of times to let them know he was there.

He heard the squeak of an office chair and the heavy footfalls of a man making his way towards the front, and gave a curt nod to the large man who appeared through the curtained doorway.

"Wasn't expecting anybody else to come in tonight. Have you been out driving in this storm the whole time?"

Putting on his best "Aw shucks" face, he gave the man a sheepish grin and nodded. "Yeah, unfortunately. Got worse than I thought it would on the roads. Can I get a room?"

"Looks like you're not the only one who was caught by the storm. You're lucky we have one room left. Fullest we've been in a while."

Robert pulled out the dead man's ID to procure a room for the night, almost forgetting to sign with the other man's name. Luckily, the proprietor didn't look too closely at the license that had been handed to him and seemed more interested in getting back to his TV program. Ten minutes later, Robert set his bag down in the threadbare, dingy room.

Shuddering, he glanced around the sparse surroundings. The TV was bolted to the dresser, and the remote tethered to the nightstand with a thin cable. He hated places like this. He sat down on the bed, grimacing at the way the springs squeaked and groaned with his weight. He'd be lucky to get any sleep on that thing.

Next he poked his head into the tiny bathroom. The tile floor was cracked in one corner, and the once white bathtub had faded to a dingy yellow. He supposed he should be grateful, though. In spite of the unfortunate color, it looked relatively clean.

An old familiar sense of panic welled up in him. He'd spent so many years of his childhood in places just like this. Too often, he'd be huddled in the bathtub with the door closed, trying to block out the sounds of his mother and whatever man was willing to pay her to make the springs creak.

How many times had he woken with his cheek pressed against the porcelain, a crick in his neck, and drool running down his chin? When he was old enough to realize what was going on, he'd promised himself he'd never settle for a used bit of trash like his whore mother.

Agitated, he sat down on the one chair by the window and worked to compose himself. He pulled out a lock of hair from his pocket, a memento he'd taken from his latest lady. Fingering the silky length of it, he remembered how shy and frightened she'd been when he'd taken her. He'd felt omnipotent when she'd stopped her begging and struggles, finally succumbing to his dominance. Just thinking about it made him hard.

Shifting in his seat, he tried to find a more comfortable position for the aching bulge in his pants. His thoughts turned back to his latest conquest and his eyes darkened. Who knew the woman had managed to retain a bit of fight in her after all? In the end, she'd been a whore just like all the rest of them. He regretted not being able to take care of her before leaving town.

He clenched his fists thinking about the two cops coming to his door. If it hadn't been for those bastards, he'd be having fun between that bitch's thighs, not sitting on some damn squeaky bed in a rundown room reliving the past.

What a rush it had been to pull the trigger on them! He still couldn't get over the look of surprise on that first guy's face when he'd blown his chest wide open. He knew he'd shot the second cop, as well. Too bad he'd heard on the radio that he was expected to live.

If things hadn't gotten so hot for him, he may have stuck around to finish the job. Would serve them right for ruining the good thing he'd had going on. Frustrated, he began to stroke the length of silky hair again.

It'll be okay, though. Once he got up to his cabin and settled in, he'd find another lady to train. And this time, no one would be able to find him.

Chapter Five

The headlights cut a swath through the hypnotic swirl of flakes coming down as Olivia hunched over her steering wheel. The squeak-swish of the wipers kept pace with her heart as they struggled to keep up with the storm. Luckily, the snow plows had been hard at work and the accumulation on the roads wasn't too bad.

At the end of Centre Street, she took a left and made her way up the hill and out of town. The roads were icier here, the reason she always hated driving this hill in the winter. Olivia knew she'd have to accelerate to have any hope of making it up the slope, and mentally crossed her fingers.

The good news was she was used to Maine's storms, having lived in the area all her life. The bad news was she was driving her 4-door sedan with no four-wheel drive and very little tread on her tires. She'd been saving up money to replace them, but hadn't gotten around to it yet.

Just before she reached the crest of the hill, another vehicle came flying over the rise, sliding around the curve. Olivia had just enough time to take her foot off the gas and turn the wheel, barely missing being side-swiped by the reckless driver. Her car began to lose its forward momentum up the slope.

"No, no, no...come on!" She muttered as her car started to

slide down the slope backwards. She pressed on her brakes and could feel the tires spinning without purchase as the backside of her car slid, angling towards the ditch on the side of the road.

"Ugh!" she pounded her hands against the steering wheel. "This is NOT what I needed right now."

She climbed out and looked at her car lying canted sideways in the ditch. At least she wasn't blocking the road, she thought ruefully. Olivia climbed back into the driver's seat and pulled her cell phone out of her pocket.

"No bars. Of course. This afternoon just gets better and better," she grumbled. It was already nearly full dark due to the storm, and the last thing she wanted to do was to wait until someone came along to help her out. Most sane people would already be cozied up in their homes by now. Who knew when the next person would be by?

With that thought in mind, Olivia secured her hat on her head, fastened her coat, and gathered her grocery bag from the passenger seat. It wasn't too long a walk back to the house. Besides, she was already halfway up the hill. She'd just have to get Liz to pull her car out and tow it back to the shop tomorrow after the storm. Reluctantly, she locked the car, and with a final backwards glance, started the trek up the hill to her house.

About twenty yards from her car, she wondered if she'd made the right decision. The whole world felt cold and desolate. The sky was already gray, and growing darker by the minute. Soon she'd feel like the last person left in a frozen, lonely world.

Maybe she should have just stayed in her car. At least she'd be able to have the heater on. She briefly debated pulling her phone out and checking for service, but pulling her gloves off to use the phone seemed unbearable in the wind.

Just then, a Ford pickup truck pulled up alongside her and the passenger window rolled down. "Hey! I'm guessing that was your car back there. Need a lift?"

Sighing with relief, she smiled and turned towards the truck, surprised to find herself facing the man she'd noticed earlier at the diner. *Oh wow*, was her first thought. He was even better looking up close.

He leaned across the cab and popped the door open. "Here, get in. It's way too cold, let alone dangerous, for you to be walking alongside the road like that."

Gratefully, she lifted her grocery bag onto the seat and crawled up into the cab. She briefly fought the wind to close the truck door, and then just sat back with her eyes closed and breathed for a moment. The man let her take a second to get her bearings, but she could feel him watching her and discreetly looked back over at him.

He was dressed in a Carhartt coat that did amazing things for his shoulders. Black, tousled hair was in disarray, probably from the knit hat that was on the console beside him. His jaw had a couple of days' worth of scruff, which just worked to make him seem even sexier. He had a high brow and straight nose, but really, it was his eyes that stole her breath away. They were clear and as blue as a distant summer's day, and at the moment, looked more than a little concerned.

"Are you okay? How long were you out there?"

"Not long, maybe fifteen minutes. I was actually thinking I might have made a mistake about leaving my car. When you drove up I was debating whether or not I should go back and just wait until someone came along."

"Yeah, the visibility is really bad out here. You're lucky I saw you at all. I could have just as easily run you over, especially now that it's getting dark."

"I tried to call my sister, but there's no service here because of the storm. Some car ran me off the road and…well, you saw where it ended up. I really appreciate you stopping for me."

"No problem." He proffered his hand. "My name is Mason Clark. I think I saw you earlier today at the café."

"I'm Olivia Harper, and it's nice to meet you. Yes, I saw you sitting at the breakfast counter this morning." He noticed how delicate her hand felt in his, and that even though her fingertips were chilled, her grip was firm and sure. Mason took in her smooth, tawny skin and the long, chocolate-brown hair that had managed to work its way out from under her beanie. Now that he was closer, he saw that her eyes were still gold, like the color of warm honey, but they also had little green flecks in them.

She felt a catch in her throat as she looked into his eyes and swallowed. The unruly tuft of stray hair didn't detract from the intensity of his gaze. Her fingers itched to reach up and run her hands through the errant strands. "I don't usually see many unfamiliar faces in the off-season. You're from out of town?"

His mouth quirked up at the corner in a little half-smile and set off a slew of shivers in her system. He shot a glance towards her. "I'm visiting my sister for a few weeks."

"That must be nice. She lives up this way? Who is she? I might know her."

"Melody Clark. She owns the La Luna Vista Bed and Breakfast."

At that, Olivia gave him a dazzling smile. "No kidding? That's the gorgeous Victorian on top of the West Chops Point with the big wrap-around porch, right? Oh, I admire it every time I drive by there! The views must be incredible from that vantage point."

Mason sat, stunned by the transformation caused by Olivia's smile. Her face was already beautiful, but when she smiled that way, it was as if the sun had come out from behind a puffy white cloud to make everything seem better and brighter. "Yup, that's the one. You should stop by. I'll give you a tour of the grounds, if you'd like."

"Do you come to visit your sister often? What do you do?"

A shadow crossed over his face. "I'm a Boston police detective.

I'm actually on disability at the moment, recovering from an injury." He pulled away slightly and turned back towards the steering wheel. "Okay, where do you live? Let's get you home."

Sensing his discomfort, she said, "Oh, I'm sorry to hear that." *Way to open mouth and insert foot, Olivia.*

He shrugged, but didn't expound any further. She was briefly caught off guard by the abrupt change in subject, but quickly recovered. "It's not very far. At the top of this hill, you'll want to take the first right."

Mason deftly pulled the truck back onto the road and made his way up the slope, taking a right into the middle-class neighborhood. The silence in the cab filled the space between them.

She wasn't sure if she was just imagining things, but one moment Mason had seemed warm and personable, and the next he had grown removed and distant. She hadn't expected that asking him what he did would bring about such a change in him.

"I'm the house at the end, on the right." Olivia directed him to the small, white Cape Cod with black shutters and the ubiquitous New England red door. There was a warm, welcoming glow coming from the windows, and a Jeep in the driveway.

She let out a breath that she hadn't even known she was holding. "Looks like my sisters made it here okay, at least." Olivia turned to him and shook his hand. "Well, it was very nice meeting you. Thank you again for helping me out."

She glanced down at their joined hands and then back to his eyes. A flicker of disappointment made her wish the ride hadn't been so short. Shaking off the feeling, she climbed out of the truck. Mason awkwardly reached across the bench and handed her the grocery bag. She got the feeling that the cold and exertion were starting to affect whatever injury he had.

Just as he was about to back out of the driveway, she paused. Catching his attention, she jogged back to his truck. Mason rolled down the window with a question in his eyes. "Oh, sorry. I just had a thought…um, you should stop by the café sometime and I'll make you breakfast to repay you for the rescue."

"It really wasn't any trouble." He hesitated, and then looked directly into her eyes. "But that sounds great. Maybe I'll come by in a day or so to see how you're doing."

Olivia's stomach did a funny little flutter-flop. Being on the receiving end of such focus made her wonder what else he could do with that kind of intensity. She watched as he pulled out of the driveway and, with a little wave, drove off. She caught herself letting out a sigh. What was wrong with her? She was acting like a sex-starved, half-crazed, mad woman!

Well, sex-starved may not be that far off the mark…how long had it been? Don't answer that, she silently admonished herself. Hmm, maybe there was something to Liz's earlier remarks.

Shaking that unwelcome thought from her head, she adjusted her bags, and headed towards the house just as Fiona poked her head out the front door. "Hey, birthday girl. You going to stand in the driveway holding those bags all day? Who was that? And where's your car?"

"It's lying in the ditch along Centre Street."

"What?!?" Fiona exclaimed. "Oh my God, are you okay? What the heck happened?"

Olivia regretted the way she said it the minute it came out of her mouth. Of the three of them, Fiona was the most sensitive. Especially when it came to car accidents. "Yeah, I'm okay," she soothed. "I'll tell you all about it while I'm making dinner. First let me get out of my coat."

She handed the bags to Fiona, who took a look inside, "Oooh, Chicken Marsala? My favorite."

Olivia grinned at Fiona's enthusiasm and sat down on the chair by the door to take off her wet, snowy boots.

Liz came into the front entryway. "Hey, what took you so long?"

She gave her a quick hug. "Long story. I'm going to go change into something comfortable and get dinner started and then I'll tell you what happened."

Fiona called from the kitchen, where she'd started unloading the groceries. "I'll pour you a glass of wine."

Olivia smiled. She loved it when all three of them were here in the house like this. Granted, it wasn't like they lived that far apart, but she missed the warmth and easy camaraderie they had shared on a nightly basis before first Liz, and just recently Fiona, had grown old enough to move out and get their own places.

She climbed the stairs to the master bedroom. At first it had seemed strange to take over the bedroom her parents used to share, but her sisters had insisted it made sense for her to switch rooms, since she was the new head of the household. She hoped they were looking down on them and smiling at how the three of them had turned out.

Olivia rummaged in her drawer for a pair of yoga pants and her favorite CIA sweatshirt, and considered the direction her life had taken. She'd always wanted to be a chef and had been halfway through her second year at the Culinary Institute of America when their parents had died and she'd assumed custody of her two younger sisters.

Even though she never once doubted whether she made the right decision, she'd sometimes catch herself wondering how things might have turned out if the situation had been different. For the most part, she had to admit she was pretty happy.

It helped having The Three Sisters Cafe. Sure, it may not be the higher-end, fine dining establishment she'd always envisioned, but she still got to make delicious food and provide people with a charming experience.

As she made her way back downstairs, she admired how the expanse of marble countertops and white cupboards made the kitchen look clean and bright. The room was Olivia's favorite place in the house. Her parents had remodeled it a year before they passed away and every time she entered the room, she remembered the joy on her mom's face when she had seen it for the first time.

The kitchen was spacious, with an island in the middle that invited people to sit and visit. There was a window over the sink that overlooked the deck, back yard, and the trees beyond. The gleam of the stainless steel appliances and brushed chrome pendant lights hanging over the island looked fresh and modern, while the hardwood floors kept the atmosphere warm and homey. As far as Olivia was concerned, this kitchen truly was the heart of their home.

Fiona was at the sink rinsing off mushrooms, and nodded towards the glass sitting on the counter. "Thought you might need that before you get started."

"Mmm, thanks." She twirled her glass and admired the deep ruby swirls of Chianti as they caught the light from overhead. The first sip tasted dry and tart on her tongue and left a warm trail down her throat. "Where's Liz?"

"Oh, she's in the living room getting a fire started."

"Perfect. Thanks for starting the prep."

"No problem." Fiona dried her hands and took a seat at the island. Liz came into the kitchen and sat down beside her. "So, tell us what happened. Who dropped you off, and where's your car?"

Olivia described her near accident, lack of cell service, attempt to walk home, and subsequent ride with the newly met and gorgeous Mason Clark, all while she put water on to boil and pulled the chicken out of the fridge.

Then she told them about her observations at the store, of the group of women not much younger than her, the way she'd been called "ma'am" by the guy at the checkout, and the strange onslaught of feelings about getting older.

"Oh, honey, that must have felt so awkward." Fiona sympathized. Although, Olivia suspected her sister was too young to fully relate to what she was saying, she was so sensitive and empathetic that Olivia knew it was easy for Fiona to imagine her dismay.

Liz sighed with exasperation. "Old, my ass. You are a gorgeous grown woman and a successful small business owner. Now that the two of us are out of the house, there is nothing preventing you from getting out of this rut and exploring your options. What's holding you back?"

"I know, I know…you're right. Honestly, I don't know what's come over me. Maybe I'm just experiencing my first bout of the birthday blues."

Liz held up her glass. "Well, here's a toast to our beautiful birthday girl. May she find adventure and love this next year and remember that she's not too old to pursue her dreams."

Fiona clapped and raised her wineglass. "Here, here!" After taking a sip, she leaned forward eagerly. "So, tell us about this Mason Clark. I didn't catch a very good look at him, but from what I did see…"

Instantly she blushed. "Oh, he has dark, unruly hair, a scruffy beard, and the bluest eyes…I swear you could sink right into them."

Her sisters cast each other significant looks. Neither of them could remember the last time she'd paid enough attention to be able to even describe a guy in years…probably since her freshman year in college. Definitely not since their parents had died. They both hoped this was a sign that she was ready to get on with her own plans. As much as they appreciated all she'd done in the past years, they worried that she may never get a chance to live her own life.

Olivia turned back towards the stove and poured Marsala wine into the pan. A plume of heavenly aroma wafted up and Fiona groaned. "Oh, that smells so good." She hopped up from the bar-stool. "I'm going to set the table."

Liz also stood. "I'll grab another bottle of wine."

Ten minutes later they gathered at the dining room table and lifted their glasses. "Cheers! Here's to sisters, snowstorms, warm fires, and good food."

Liz added, "And wine."

"And birthdays!" Fiona exclaimed.

They all got quiet as they took their first few bites and enjoyed the meal. Eventually, Liz turned to Olivia. "Okay, so we've established this guy is hot. Who is he? Did he move here recently?"

"Well, apparently he's a Boston police detective. He said he's taken a leave of absence and that he's on disability. He's currently staying with his sister, so he probably won't be here for very long."

Fiona shot Liz a disappointed look, but Liz just shrugged and said, "Well, there's nothing wrong with a little fling, right? A girl can have fun."

Olivia thought about it, but then shook her head, "I suppose, but it's not really my style. He seemed pretty nice, but kind of clammed up when he mentioned his job. It felt awkward to ask how he got hurt or how long his recuperation would be."

"Who is his sister?" Fiona asked.

"Her name is Melody. She owns that cute bed and breakfast at the top of the hill on West Chops Point. You know, the one overlooking the bay? I couldn't believe it when he told me."

"No kidding? Oh, I love that place! I have daydreams of sitting and reading on their porch and looking out at the view. Hm, maybe we can finagle an excuse to go up there and take a look around."

"Actually, he offered to give me a tour, sometime. Maybe you can tag along."

The storm grew louder as their meal progressed and they could hear the wind whip around the house, making the timbers creak a bit. Just as they finished washing the dishes, the lights flickered off and on. Twice the power came back, but the third time the house stayed dark.

"Well, there goes our plan for a movie marathon. At least we have the fire going." Olivia pulled some candles out of the junk drawer in the kitchen before they all moved into the living room.

"Hm, it's too dark to read. Why don't we play Scrabble?" Fiona suggested.

Olivia and Liz groaned. They both knew she was a fiend at Scrabble and usually kicked their butts. "Okay, okay, but just one game."

The three of them wound up playing two games, finishing their second bottle of wine and then turning in. Overall, Olivia thought, as she slipped under her covers, other than having a nice warm man to cuddle with, it was the perfect way to pass the storm and celebrate her birthday.

Chapter Six

The flash of a muzzle…

His partner's weight falling back on him…

Losing his balance and the sensation of tumbling backwards as the world faded to black…

Mason jolted awake, his brow and palms damp with sweat. He lay there trying to catch his breath.

"Mason? Are you up yet?"

He groaned and pulled the pillow over his head as his sister came into the room and opened the curtains. Even though it was overcast, the dull light that flooded in was still offensive.

He tried to roll over on his side and promptly cursed. It'd been nearly a month since the shooting and he kept forgetting that it still hurt to do that. Relegated to his back, he pried one eye open to give her the evil death stare from under the pillow.

Melody was not impressed.

She stood at the end of the bed with her hands on her hips and glared right back. "Your captain called again. He said that Dr. Patel still hasn't heard back from you. He wants me to remind you that you will not be cleared for duty until you have at least a few therapy sessions and they can determine you're mentally healthy. You need to call him today."

He responded with a muffled grunt and pulled the pillow off

his face. Man, he felt like shit. He scratched his jaw and tried to think back to the last time he had shaved, or even taken a shower, for that matter.

Struggling to a sitting position, he caught his breath as pain tightened his lungs. For the most part his shoulder was recovering fine - it had only been grazed along the outer arm - but his chest was still uncomfortable with certain movements. He considered the fact that he had probably overdone it yesterday, being out in the cold for so long. After his breakfast at the café, he'd been feeling restless and had ended up walking around the small town for a few hours.

"Yeah, yeah. Ok, give me a moment to pull myself together."

His sister's eyes softened as she looked him over. He could tell she was worried about him, but he couldn't seem to work up the energy it would take to ease her mind. It sucked, and he felt like an ass about it. Hell, pretty much everything sucked nowadays.

"Good. Thank you. Make sure you take a shower first. I can smell you from over here." Now, there was the bratty little sister he remembered.

He tossed the pillow at her, allowing himself to wince after her back was turned and she'd walked out the door. Sitting on the edge of the bed, he did a couple of deep breathing exercises that his doctor had taught him to help his lung recover.

Slowly, he got to his feet, stood up straight, and tried to will the old man feeling from his bones. Maybe a hot shower would feel good after all.

He padded into the bathroom and paused to appreciate the heated floors and plush towels. Thankfully, when Melody had opened her bed and breakfast, La Luna Vista, she hadn't spared any expense. He was glad to see that their father's trust fund had been put to good use.

After filling a cup with water and taking the handful of antibiotics and various other prescribed pills, he started up the shower.

For a while, all he could do was stand under the hot spray and lean his forearm up against the cool tiles. Water sluiced down his face and neck. Images from that day invaded his mind.

Wood splintering...

The shock in Ryan's eyes...

A pool of red blossoming across his partner's chest...

With a jolt, Mason fumbled for the shampoo bottle. He washed and turned the tap off. As he reached for the towel, he realized his hands were shaking, and decided he'd rather keep the scruff for another day than cut his chin again.

He laughed at himself mockingly and turned away from the mirror in disgust. Who the hell was he fooling? How could he expect to go back to active duty and handle a gun when he couldn't even trust himself with a razor?

After dressing, Mason picked his phone up off the desk and stared at the number of missed calls.

The problem was, he didn't really know what to say to his Captain. On one hand, he was eager to get back to work. The need to hunt down the guy who shot him and killed his partner was so overwhelming that he couldn't breathe at times. It was the single point that kept him focused on his recovery and fueled his determination to get back to full health.

However, in those quiet moments at three in the morning, when he was awoken by nightmares and drenched in cold sweat, he had to admit to himself that he had doubts about his ability to perform at a high level. It was hard to imagine working cases without his partner there with him.

He shoved the uncomfortable thoughts back into his subconscious. Bad enough they plagued him in his sleep; he wasn't about to let them deter him from his goal.

Resolutely, he hit the speed dial.

"Detective Clark, I was beginning to think you'd forgotten about us. How's the recovery going?"

"Slowly, sir, but I am improving."

"Glad to hear it, son. So, I'm sure you know why I called you. Dr. Patel tells me you haven't spoken to him yet to make an appointment. You do realize you need to meet with him at least three times and be cleared by him before you can come back, don't you?"

"Yes sir. Look, I'm not trying to be a pain about this, but right now I'm in Maine, staying with my sister. We just had a big snowstorm drop over a foot of snow and it's not a good time to make the drive down."

"This wouldn't be another one of your excuses to avoid meeting with him, would it?"

"No, sir." He ran a hand through his hair and let out a sigh. "Well, maybe. All I'm saying is, with the holidays coming up, I'd just like to wait for a few weeks. I've been focused on getting my body healed up right now. I can meet up with him first thing after the New Year."

He could hear the familiar squeak of the other man's chair as he stood up and shut the door to his office. The noise of the bullpen in the background grew muffled over the phone.

"Mason, I'm worried about you. I know how close you and Ryan were. Anytime a detective loses his partner it's hard, but you guys went to the academy together, were officers together, became detectives together…" There was a pause as he waited for a response.

Mason looked down, realized his hands were clenched into fists in his lap, and forced himself to relax his fingers. There was nothing he could say around the lump that had suddenly formed in his throat.

He heard the Captain sigh over the phone. "Okay. You win. I'll let the doc know you're going to keep working on your physical recovery and to expect a call from you after the holiday. The Christmas holiday, not the New Year's holiday."

"Remember, your mental and emotional recovery is just as important - maybe even more so. There are three of these meetings that you have to go to. If we time it right, you'll be ready to start back at the first of the year."

"Thanks, Cap. I know I've been difficult."

"I just want you to remember we all lost a good detective that day. You may have been closest to him, but Ryan was loved by all of us. If you ever need to talk, don't hesitate to give me a call."

"Will do. I really appreciate your understanding and how much you've done for me. I'll get in touch with you in a few weeks."

After hanging up, he sat for a moment and just stared at the phone in his hands. He really needed to get his act together and find a way to screw his head on straight. These nightmares and lack of sleep needed to go. Until that happened, no way was he going to be considered fit to serve.

He liked being a detective and had worked damn hard for his position. Yet, every time he thought about getting back out there, his heart started to pound, his hands began to sweat, and he started experiencing a panic attack. He hated the idea of talking about what had happened to some guy who couldn't possibly understand.

Then again, the thought of that bastard getting away with murdering his partner had him seeing red. Like hell was that going to happen. He would just have to find a way to convince the shrink he was okay, preferably without baring his soul.

Mason let out a self-deprecating laugh, mocking his thoughts.

Who was he kidding? At this point he was still jumping at every loud noise. Just the other day, he had practically thrown himself down in the street when a truck had backfired. Being jumpy with a gun would only exacerbate the problem. The last thing he wanted was to be the cop who shot some unarmed kid because he thought he'd seen a weapon instead of a pack of cigarettes.

But, what were his other options? Accepting that Mendez was

walking free on the streets was not an option. Especially now there was a woman who could testify that he stalked, kidnapped, and raped her. Add to that the fact that he shot and killed a cop, and getting charges to stick on this guy would not be a problem. They just had to find him first.

Mason wouldn't be surprised if even now he was out there stalking his next victim. If he hadn't picked out his next target yet, it was just a question of when. Men like him would never voluntarily give up their pursuits. He felt women were there for his use and disposal, about the same as toilet paper.

He put the phone back on his desk and reminded himself that he wasn't the only person on the force looking for retribution. The department was full of good people, good cops. He knew they wanted to catch the bastard almost as badly as him. He could afford to take the time to make a full recovery. He'd bought himself this time during the holidays to focus on getting better, and that's exactly what he'd do. After the holidays were over, he'd be ready.

Mentally shoving the issue aside, he put his boots on and headed downstairs.

Glancing out the kitchen window, he noticed his sister was already shoveling the front walk and felt a quick pang of guilt. Logically, he realized she was perfectly capable of running this place by herself. In fact, that's what she usually did. Still, he couldn't help feeling bad for not being out there helping her.

Just as he was turning to put his coat on and head out, he heard her start cussing under her breath. He made his way up the shoveled part of the walk to where she was standing. She had a handle in one hand, and the head of the shovel was lying on the ground in front of her.

She glanced up at his approach. "Shovel broke. Dammit. I was hoping to get the whole walk cleared before my guests arrive later today. Do you think you could head into town and pick up another one? I still have to get some cookies baked and the soup started."

"Sure, no problem. I remember seeing a hardware store downtown. Think they'd have what you need?"

"Frank's Hardware. Yeah, Frank is usually pretty good about staying stocked up."

"Did you need me to grab anything else while I'm there?'

"I'm all set. Did you return that phone call?"

"Yeah."

She gave him a long, assessing look. "And...? How did that go?"

"I told him I'm still trying to recover physically and that I'd call to make an appointment with the shrink after Christmas."

She nodded. "Ok, that works. It'll be nice to have you around for the season. It's been awhile since we've had a chance to spend it together."

"Yeah, it's been awhile. I'm usually working during the holidays. You'd be amazed by how many freaky things happen this time of year."

"To be honest, I'd rather stay in my little bubble and believe that this is the season for peace on earth and goodwill towards men."

He gave her a wry smile. "Don't worry about the walk. I'll finish it when I get back."

Impulsively, she gave him a hug. "You know what this means, don't you? Now you really won't have an excuse for forgetting to buy me a Christmas present."

He laughed and wrapped his good arm around her shoulders. "Oh, I'm sure I could come up with some reason to forget."

She shot him a pout. "You'd better not!" With that, she made her way back to the front door.

He watched her enter the house before letting his smile slip from his lips and heading to his truck. His hands and nose were already beginning to tingle with the cold, and he took it as a cue to get his errand done quickly.

Well, not too quickly. Maybe he would duck into a few stores and see if he couldn't find something special to pick up for Melody. She really had been amazing through this whole ordeal and he didn't know what he'd have done without her.

With that idea in mind, he threw his truck into gear, turned on the heat, and cranked up the music. The Black Keys' pounding beat kept him company and almost managed to drown out his doubts and memories on the ride into town.

Chapter Seven

Sunlight patterned across Olivia's ceiling as she slowly opened her eyes to the morning of her actual birthday. Thank goodness the café was closed on Mondays and she didn't have to worry about rushing from the warm, comforting cocoon of her bed. She allowed herself the luxury of lingering and dozed for another fifteen minutes before her bladder insisted she get up and start the day.

As she exited the bathroom, she peeked out her window and was dazzled by the pristine shimmer of newly fallen snow blanketing the world around her. There was nothing as glorious and pure as that first morning after a big snowstorm, with the air scrubbed clean and crisp. Snowy diamonds glinted from the fields and icicles dripped and sparkled from roof eaves and tree branches.

If only it could stay like this and not turn muddy and brown, she thought. She slipped into her robe and slippers and made her way downstairs, adding to her list of desires; *less cold would be nice, too.*

Liz turned from the coffee machine as she shuffled into the kitchen. "Oh hey, Livvy. Just started a fresh pot of coffee. I've gotta get going. Paul said there are a bunch of cars needing tows, and I'm guessing we're going to be busy today."

"Speaking of which, I'm one of those people that needs to call for a tow for my car. Ugh, not exactly what I wanted to have to deal with on my birthday."

"Already on it. I told him where your car was and he said he'd call it in. We're going to have it taken to the shop so we can check it out and make sure nothing else was messed up. I noticed the tread on your tires was starting to wear. I think that was probably a factor in your accident. We might have a set of tires in inventory that'll fit."

Paul was co-owner of the mechanic shop with Liz. He had gone into business with their dad twenty years ago and was like a favorite uncle of theirs growing up. Since the accident, he'd taken on the role of mentor and benevolent father figure.

"Wow, thanks. Tell him I appreciate it and will pay you guys back as soon as possible."

"Don't worry about it. Anyway, I'm off. Fiona said she could drive you in to pick up your car later today, if you'd like."

She strode towards the door, her boots clomping against the hardwood floors, and shrugged into her winter coat, then pulled her ear-flapped hat down over head. With a jaunty toss of her hand, she slipped out the door.

Olivia shook her head and admired her younger sister's energy and purpose. She turned to pull down a mug from the cabinet, fully intent on lingering over her first cup of coffee and then making breakfast before doing anything nearly so strenuous herself.

She grabbed a bowl from the cabinet and set it on the island. Then she checked the contents of the fridge and loaded her arms with bacon, bread, eggs, and milk. She had just finished with the bacon and was in the process of placing the first slice of cinnamon French toast into the pan when Fiona came into the kitchen.

"Good morning." Fiona leaned over the pan and inhaled deeply. "One of the best things about staying overnight is waking up to your breakfasts in the morning. Need help?"

"Nah, everything's almost finished. Why don't you pour yourself a cup of coffee and set the table."

The two girls fell back into the morning rhythm they'd established growing up over the years. Easy mornings like this were Olivia's favorite. As she watched her sister tuck into her breakfast she was once again struck by how much she missed having them around the house.

I'm too young to be experiencing empty nest syndrome . She shook her head and felt silly. It wasn't as if Fiona had gone off to some far away college. Despite receiving many acceptance letters, she'd decided to stay close to home and chose Bowdoin College, which was only about fifteen minutes away in Brunswick, Maine.

"I'll probably head back to school after dropping you off at the shop," Fiona informed her. "Any big plans for this afternoon?"

"Not really. Just to get my car working and pick up a few things in town. I've been playing around with the idea of keeping the café open for dinners and want to start putting together a potential menu."

"That's a great idea. I had no idea you were thinking about doing that." She took a tentative sip of coffee, still hot enough to make her wince. Setting the mug down, she asked, "If you stay open, won't you be crazy busy? I mean, you'd be waking up super early for the breakfast crowd and then trying to stay late for the dinner people. Don't forget to keep some time for yourself."

"No, I know you're right. I haven't really figured that part of the equation out yet. It's just something I've been considering."

"Well, I think it's good you're going to try something new. I know how you've always wanted to pursue your cooking career. Liz and I half wondered if you were planning on going back to culinary school now that we're both out of the house."

"I'll admit, the thought crossed my mind." She sighed. "I don't know. A part of me is tempted to do exactly that, but then I get this feeling like that ship has already sailed."

"Don't be silly. People go back to school all the time. You're not even thirty yet. There's still plenty of time for you to pursue your dream if you want."

"True, but don't forget, I also have employees at the café who count on me to keep it going. I feel like I'd be letting them down."

"I understand your concern for your employees. I love Jackie and Tom as much as you do. I'm sure if you talked to them, you guys could figure out a way to keep it running while you took classes."

She leaned forward and laid her hand over Olivia's. "Sweetie, we just want you to be happy. We both know everything you sacrificed to take care of us. Whatever you decide, just know we're behind you one hundred percent."

Olivia looked at her baby sister across the table and was struck once again by Fiona's innate grace and beauty. Of all them, she was the one with the kindest heart and gentlest nature.

Deciding it was time to change the subject, she asked, "So, tell me how your classes are going. What's college life like?"

Knowing her sister needed the distraction, Fiona bemoaned the fact that she had to take remedial math before she could move on to earn college credits. She discussed the irony in having a myopic English teacher, with coke-bottle-thick glasses, who could barely read the text from their required reading list, but wrote so small that nobody could read what he put on the board.

She also talked about her work-study program working in the Hawthorne-Longfellow Library, and how she loved the wall of arched windows looking out onto the lawn. She'd met a lot of her fellow students while working the reference desk. As she listened, Olivia could tell that her sister was really happy with the transition to college.

Finished with her meal, Fiona gave a satisfied sigh and pushed away from the table. "We should probably get going soon. Why don't you head up and get ready, and I'll take care of the dishes."

As Olivia trotted up the stairs, she considered what her sister had said earlier. It WAS time for her to start thinking about where she wanted to go from here. Should she fully commit to the café and the life she already had, or go back and try to pursue her previous dream?

She'd always wanted to go into fine dining. If she started serving dinner at the café, would that sufficiently fulfill her vision? She shook her head. One thing was clear. She'd have to figure out what she wanted before she had any chance of making it come true.

Chapter Eight

Olivia hopped into her car, flipped on the heater, and danced a happy little shimmy in the driver's seat. She patted her steering wheel as if consoling it for the trauma it had gone through. Glancing up, she noticed her sister heading towards her.

The moment the window rolled down, her breath puffed out in short little streamers and the tip of her nose began to numb. The storm from last night had left the air scrubbed clean and the sky sparkling blue, but the day was still sharp and frosty. She could see little flakes of snow caught up and shimmering in the light breeze.

"Livvy, we replaced the tires and made sure they were aligned. You should be good to go, but please be careful!"

Smiling at her, Olivia realized last night must have scared Liz more than she had realized. It wasn't like Liz to be the worrier. That was usually her department.

"I really appreciate you getting it done so quickly. I promise I'll be careful," Olivia reassured her. "Since this took up half my day off, I think I'll just run a few errands and then spend a quiet afternoon relaxing back at home. Did you want to come over again tonight?"

"Nah, I'll probably just crash upstairs after work. We've got quite a few cars still waiting in the shop, so it's going to be an extra-long day around here." She sighed and glanced back at the garage.

Olivia laughed. "Well, at least you've got the shortest commute around. Paul couldn't have found that house just outside of town at a better time."

"Tell me about it. Yeah, owning an apartment above where you work has its advantages. But don't forget, it also means people think you're always on-call. Anyway, I should probably get back. Just wanted to see you off. Love you, Livvy."

"You too. Don't work too hard." Giving her sister a final smile, she pulled out of the lot. She reminded herself to make a stop at the hardware store to replace the backdoor light bulb.

Just as she spotted a parking space in front of the hardware store and began to turn the wheel, a beat-up sedan going in the other direction pulled a U-turn, swooped across from the other lane, and snatched the space from her.

Jerk! "Hey! I was parking there!" She yelled from her window as the man climbed out of his car.

The guy barely glanced up, shrugged his shoulders...and kept walking.

What a snotty, self-centered, prick. After finding a spot a couple of blocks away, she glanced irritably at the offending vehicle. *He's lucky I'm not the kind of person to key someone's car...even if they DO deserve it.*

Maybe it was just as well she had gotten this spot, since she found herself parked just outside the coffee shop. *Might as well go in and get a cup.*

Chapter Nine

Robert chuckled as he stepped out of the restroom, thinking about the indignation of the woman outside. Ordinarily, he would have tried to keep a lower profile and not draw attention to himself. However, he'd had to piss so badly that he'd have cut off anybody short of a cop.

He walked up to the counter to order a drink and was surprised to find himself standing behind the woman who'd just yelled at him on the street.

He listened to the dulcet tones of her voice as she ordered an almond latte. Interesting how her shrieking voice had morphed into smoke and honey. He wondered what else would create that kind of transformation.

Dark fantasies began to flood his mind of taking her smart mouth and putting it to good use. He'd have her learning her place within a day. In a week, she'd be begging him for mercy.

He noticed the way her worn jeans lovingly hugged the curve of her ass. Her long, dark hair flowed down past the middle of her back and his fingers clenched with the need to wrap the strands around his fist. Cautiously, he leaned forward and caught the faint scent of honeysuckle.

Just then, she stepped back from the counter and practically into him.

"Oh, excuse me!" Olivia exclaimed as she turned, startled. She stopped dead when she saw who it was. He watched with fascination as her initially warm expression cooled considerably while looking at him.

"You shouldn't stand so close behind someone. You're liable to get stepped on." She moved around him towards the pickup side of the counter.

"My apologies," he responded, with a mocking bow. One sardonic eyebrow shot up as his eyes raked down the front of her. Inwardly, he laughed at the way she shuddered in reaction to his look. Her emotions were so easily read as they flitted across her face.

Oh yeah, this woman would have been a perfect replacement. Suddenly this little town had become very intriguing. He sighed. Too bad he was headed up to the cabin.

He watched as she turned slightly, effectively trying to cut him off. After giving his order to the girl behind the counter, he took a few steps back towards her. Leaning a little closer, he propped his hip against the wall and took a moment to regard her profile as she studiously looked down at her phone, actively trying to ignore him.

After a moment, Olivia blew out a puff of breath and shot him a glance. She shifted uncomfortably and looked away, scanning the café.

Robert followed her gaze and inhaled sharply when he spotted the man watching them from over by the window. Quickly, he lowered his head and turned slightly away.

What the hell? How on earth could that damn cop be here? Robert's pulse raced, his hands becoming clammy. Calmly, he reassured himself there was no way that bastard would be able to recognize him.

Hell, Robert would barely even know himself. The face that

had stared back at him from the mirror this morning had not been his own.

It had taken him over an hour to apply the prosthetics to his nose and chin, making sure that the alterations were subtle and looked natural. It had only taken him a few days to grow out his beard enough to obscure his jawline. With those changes plus the brimmed hat he wore and the collar turned up on his coat, there was no way Detective Mason Clark would be able to recognize him from across the room.

Still, though. It was a shock to see him sitting in the same little café.

"Olivia." The barista called out to the woman standing by him. With a final, nervous look back at him, she stepped to the counter and grabbed her coffee.

Startled, he watched as she made her way over to the cop's table. He watched her whole demeanor change as she drew nearer to the other man. Her gait grew longer and more confident, and a warm smile now graced her face. From the way they greeted each other, it was obvious they had met before. He could tell by the way Mason followed her with his eyes that he was attracted to her.

Disgusted, he couldn't help but feel a pang of jealousy deep in his gut. What was it with guys like that? How did they always manage to attract women?

A seed of resentment burned in his chest. Just another dumb whore like his mother. Then it struck him. Fate had just handed him the perfect opportunity. He'd be able to replace his previous angel *and* get his retribution on the cop bastard who had caused him all this trouble.

Of course, it would require him to delay heading back to the cabin. But, in good weather, the drive was only a few hours. He'd be close enough to create havoc and still get things set up for when it was time to take her.

"Hey, mister." The barista called over to him. "Do you want

your coffee? It's been sitting here." Pulled out of his reverie, he stepped up to the counter and grabbed his cup. "Thanks," he mumbled and allowed himself to take one final casual look over at the table where the two were still talking.

He felt a familiar rush of excitement, having found his next lady friend. Only, this time was going to be even sweeter because he'd get his revenge as well. With a pleased little smile, he hurried back out the door. There was plenty to do before he could put his plan into motion. Best to get started right away.

Chapter Ten

Mason watched Olivia interact with the man standing behind her in line. He could tell by the way she kept sidling away from him that she was uncomfortable. From where he was sitting, it seemed like the guy was standing too close.

Just as he was about to stand up and walk towards her, she saw him sitting by the window. The way her face lit up at the sight of him was breathtaking. He followed her progress over to his table, being sure to keep one eye on the guy still waiting for his coffee.

"Hi." She greeted him warmly.

He gave her a grin. "Hi, yourself. Was that guy giving you a hard time?"

She waved his concern away. "It's nothing. He was a jerk and stole the parking spot I was pulling into a few minutes ago. Luckily, I've never seen him before and know he's not from around here. I doubt I'll have to deal with him again."

He nodded. "Okay. So, I see you're out and about; did you get your car fixed?"

"One of the benefits of having a sister that's a mechanic." She shrugged. "I get VIP treatment."

"Convenient. That's cool that your sister is a mechanic. How'd she get into that?"

She shot him a grimace. "You're not one of those guys who

doesn't think a woman can be a mechanic, are you?" He shook his head, quickly denying any such misconceptions.

Satisfied, she said, "She's always been into fixing cars. My dad and Liz were two peas in a pod like that. She's a whiz at puzzles and putting things together, and can fix just about anything."

"Ah, and you?"

At that, she laughed. "Me? Oh no. I take after my mom, mostly. Put me in a kitchen cooking any day. Everything else and I'm all thumbs." She took a sip of her coffee, taking a moment to inhale the aroma. The way she savored her drink had him shifting in discomfort. She opened her eyes. "So, what's up?"

The question brought a number of possible answers springing forth in Mason's mind. "Excuse me?"

"What brings you into town today?"

He pulled his mind from the direction it was taking. "Oh, I'm headed to the hardware store. My sister was clearing the walks this morning and the head on her shovel broke. I told her I'd get a replacement and finish the job when I get back."

"Yeah, the snow was really wet and heavy this storm. I'm actually on my way over there, too."

He stood up. "Great. Why don't I walk you over?"

Frank's Hardware was a pillar of Main Street. Anything a person could want or need for home improvement lined the shelves and walls of the store, from nails, wall hangers, paint and wood putty to power tools, and everything in between. It was also a main hub for local information and small town happenings. Nothing occurred in town that Frank didn't know about or talk about.

"Hey, Frank. Did you make it through the storm okay?"

"Olivia! I did ok, but I heard what happened to your car. How are you doing?"

She gave him a warm smile and assured him, "Thankfully, I'm fine. I'll admit, I was pretty shaken after it happened, but luckily, this gentleman stopped and helped me out.

"Mason, this is Frank. Frank, Mason." She turned to the stor-eowner. "He's staying with his sister up at La Luna Vista."

Mason reached over the counter and they shook hands. "Pleasure to meet you."

Frank waggled his eyebrows up and down at her before nodding at him. "Thanks for taking care of our girl."

Olivia blushed and rolled her eyes at his antics. "I need to grab some lightbulbs and some deicer."

"Go ahead, dear. I'll be here when you're ready to check-out."

She pointed down one of the aisles. "The shovels are down that way."

Mason watched as she turned down one of the aisles that pre-sumably held lightbulbs. Giving the other man a nod, he made his way towards the snow shovels. It was nice the way she seemed to know everybody in town. Although, he supposed it wasn't hard con-sidering how small it was.

He wondered what it would have been like to grow up here. It seemed like such a far cry from his childhood of carefully con-structed and monitored playdates, sanctioned activities, and politely distant interactions. He remembered hating how everything about growing up had seemed so pristine - and fake.

Maybe that's why he'd decided to live in Boston after leaving the house. He'd yearned for the grit and noise of the city. Those first few years, the masses of humanity, exhaust fumes, and dirty alleys had seemed so much more real to him than the pampered life he'd led up until that point.

How could he have known his life would wind up so god-damn messy? He really should have been more careful about what he wished for. Perhaps a small town like this was a happy medium between those other two extremes.

Shaking his head at the direction his thoughts had taken, he quickly grabbed a shovel from one of the hooks. After setting the item at the counter, he decided to see where Olivia had wound up.

Chapter Eleven

Olivia knew the aisle she needed. Frank's cheerful banter filtered back through the store, along with Mason's deep-timbered voice, the one that had her heart skipping a beat. The very same voice had played a prominent role in her dreams last night.

Blushing at her errant thoughts, she quickly set the replacement bulbs for her back door light into her basket and, headed towards the rear of the store, where she knew the deicer was kept. It wouldn't pay to have her customers falling down and hurting themselves outside her café tomorrow morning. Especially since she knew Mrs. Crowley and Mr. Harrington would probably be up to their usual antics bright and early the next day.

Plus, she could take a moment at the back of the store to regroup and calm the butterflies in her stomach. Something about Mason put her whole system on alert. It left her breathless and edgy.

Spotting the bag she was after, she bent at the knees and hefted it up to her shoulder, then turned and nearly fumbled it as she ran into Mason's chest.

"Whoa! Easy there." He put one hand on the bag and one on her shoulder to steady her. She could feel the heat of his fingers seeping through her jacket, her sweater, and the long-sleeved shirt underneath. How was that even possible?

"Looks like it's becoming a habit of yours to save me from one accident or another," she said. It was all she could do not to stare at his smile. The corners of his eyes crinkled and his eyes filled with warmth. It was dazzling, and all too brief. She must have been staring because his expression slowly began to turn puzzled.

"Did I hurt you?" he asked, concerned.

Startled, she stammered, "What? Oh, no."

"Here, let me take that," he offered, but as he reached to grab the bag, his arm resisted, causing him to wince.

"I hurt *you!*"

Embarrassed by his inability to help a lady with a bag, he tried to reassure her. "No, no, it wasn't anything you did. Remember I said that I was taking some time off to recover from some injuries? I'm just a little stiff from all this cold air, that's all."

He shrugged and rotated his shoulder, trying to loosen the muscles a bit. "Ordinarily, I'd offer to take that bag from you. Unfortunately, my arm isn't feeling very chivalrous today."

"Don't worry, I've got this. I do this multiple times every winter. I'm just going to head up to the counter with it, since I have everything I need."

"I'll walk up with you," he offered, and took her basket of lightbulbs. "I'm pretty sure I can manage this, at least."

She smiled her thanks and headed up the aisle, wondering once again what had happened to him to cause such an injury. She wanted to ask him, but their previous conversation had given her the distinct impression that he didn't wish to discuss it.

The bag of deicer dropped to the counter with a thud as she looked up at Frank, who had a cat-ate-the-canary grin on his face. She noticed Mason had already left his snow shovel by the register.

She furtively shook her finger at Frank, telling him to behave himself, but he looked entirely too mischievous for her peace of mind.

Sure enough, as Mason stepped up to the counter, the older

man leaned forward. "So, has Olivia offered to repay you for your kindness last night? I don't know if you know this, but she's quite a good cook."

She gave an inward groan at Frank's matchmaking antics just as Mason turned toward her, and caught her in the act of rolling her eyes. He raised an eyebrow, his blue eyes twinkling. "Well, I've been to her café for breakfast, but wasn't aware she's a bona fide chef."

"Oh, yeah. Our Olivia went to school for it and everything. I'm surprised she didn't mention it." Frank turned to her. "Even knights in shining armor have to eat well, you know."

Mason gazed steadily into her eyes. "I get the feeling she is very rarely a damsel in distress, so it was a true privilege to be of service in her time of need."

Her cheeks began to turn pink. When was the last time she had teased and flirted with a man? She couldn't even remember. With an inner shrug, she thought, what the hell?

"I did appreciate your help yesterday. The offer of breakfast still stands."

Mason glanced at Frank, releasing her from the spell of his gaze. He shifted towards the older man, as if to let him in on a secret. Frank eagerly leaned as far over the counter as his big stomach would allow. Conspiratorially, Mason asked him, "I'm not sure breakfast is quite enough sustenance for a knight in shining armor. What do you think?"

Chuckling, the shop owner smacked the counter with his palm. "Oh no, a man your size would definitely need a good steak dinner to feel satisfied after such hard work."

Lips twitching, she fought back a laugh. She knew Frank was thrilled to have plenty to talk about for the rest of the day.

Mason nodded approvingly at him, then turned to her and gave a wink. "What do you say, Olivia? Would you be interested in coming out to a nice steak dinner with me?"

What on Earth was she getting herself into, she thought. Followed closely by the thought, *and who on Earth could resist an invitation like that?* She stared up at his handsome face.

"Well, how could I possibly say no to that? I am, after all, forever grateful." She gave him a few bats of her eyelashes just to play along.

A gleam appeared in his eyes as his look wandered down to her smiling lips. There was a charged heat underlying the teasing that neither one of them could quite ignore. She found herself leaning in towards him, her body helpless to resist his gravity.

Frank glanced between the two of them and cleared his throat. Sheepishly, she stepped back to give herself a bit of room to catch her breath.

"You know..." he added, slyly, "You two might as well make it a real date and plan some entertainment while you're at it. Did I mention my niece is in the holiday school concert?" He pulled a beat up, metal box out from under the counter. "I happen to have tickets for sale right here."

At that, she broke eye contact with Mason and turned to Frank. "Oh! Actually, I've been meaning to pick up a ticket. Didn't you mention she's got a solo this year?"

Frank's chest puffed out with pride. "Yup, she sure does. I heard her rehearsing in the living room when I went to visit my sister last week. Think she's going to really impress everybody with her talent."

Mason reached back and pulled his wallet out. "Well, now, that doesn't sound like something we should miss. Why don't I get two from you? That is, if Olivia will agree to accompany me to the performance as well as a steak dinner?"

She felt her cheeks warm again, but wasn't sure if it was due to anticipation of her date with Mason, or the fact that Frank had witnessed the whole scene. Regardless of how the story would play out in the town's gossip mill, there wasn't any way she was going to miss out on an evening with the gorgeous man standing in front of her. "I'd be happy to. Thank you for the invitation."

After the tickets and their respective items were paid for—and they assured Frank that he would be the first to know what they thought of the holiday production—they both stepped outside the store and glanced around.

"Looks like you're parked a few blocks down. My truck's right here. Why don't I give you a lift so you don't have to carry that heavy bag of deicer so far?"

"Thanks, I'd appreciate that." They placed the shovel and bag into the bed of his truck and climbed into the cab.

When he turned the ignition, music blasted from the stereo, startling them both. He gave her a sheepish grin and quickly turned the volume down. "Sorry, I was playing it kind of loud earlier."

She laughed, "Hey, I get it. Sometimes you just have to let it out, especially if it's the Black Keys."

He seemed pleasantly surprised that she was familiar with the music he was playing. He shot her an approving look, before putting the truck into gear and driving the few blocks to her car.

Mason sat companionably by her side. "This seems like a pretty and peaceful small town. It looks like you really fit in here." As an afterthought, almost as if to himself, he added, "I'd forgotten life could feel so simple and good, with very little worry in the world…"

"I imagine it probably feels slow for a big city homicide detective like you, but you're right. I love it here."

"Well, I admit, there are benefits to living in a city. For one thing, I like being able to step out my door and have my pick of a dozen types of cuisines. Want Chinese food? No problem, they can deliver. Indian? Two blocks down the street. Thai, Mexican, fine dining, standard American fare…all within walking distance.

"Plus, there's the entertainment. Bars, bands, theater shows, art galleries…it's nice having that kind of variety outside your door whenever you want it.

"But," he continued, "You also have to deal with the negatives, too. Drunken bums and homeless people asking for spare change on the streets. Alleys that smell like piss, muggings, pollution, and a constant state of too much traffic and not enough parking. I never thought I'd say this, but it can get to be tiresome."

She nodded her head in understanding. "You've probably been exposed to a lot more of the negatives in your line of work."

"Yeah. It didn't use to bother me as much. I mean, it was awful, don't get me wrong. Homicide is the worst. Even before that, there were the domestic disputes. Some lady getting the crap beat out of her, insisting she was just clumsy as her face turned three shades of purple while you're talking to her. Junkies passed out in their own vomit, lying in back alleys. People's homes being broken into, windows smashed, electronics ripped out of the wall…

"You don't get the best impression of humanity working on the force. It used to be that I could get off shift, maybe grab a beer at the bar with a couple of the guys, and shake it off." He shifted his focus back to the windshield. "It's getting harder for me to do that lately."

She could feel her heart being squeezed. He looked so pensive talking about his work. "Well, it sounds like you needed a break. I'm glad you could find it here in our quiet town, even if it's only temporarily"

He nodded and pulled in behind her car. "So, it looks like the school concert is this Friday evening and starts about six. Would you mind if I made dinner reservations for afterwards, or will that be too late?"

"I think dinner after will be fine," she agreed. "I'll arrange for Tom to open the café the next morning, so I won't have to be there at five in the morning, as usual."

He winced. "You get up that early every morning? That has to be hell in the winter."

"I'll admit it can be tough getting out of bed in the dark and cold, but most of the time it's not so bad. Don't you usually keep odd hours with your job?"

"Yeah, sometimes I'm up that early and I haven't even managed to see my bed yet. Criminals don't seem to keep normal business hours."

She laughed. "If only they could be more accommodating."

"Yeah, if only…" Something dark flashed in the depths of his eyes before quickly being suppressed. He seemed to pull himself out of whatever thought had crossed his mind. "So, I'll pick you up at 5:30 Friday night for our date, Ms. Olivia."

"Sounds good. Um, thank you for the ride…again."

"Not a problem. Do you need help getting the bags into your car?"

"Nope, I think I can manage." Olivia climbed down from the cab, and wrapped the handle of the bag holding her bulbs through her arm, then walked to the back of the truck and hauled the bag of deicer over her shoulder. "Talk to you later, then."

After making sure she got into her car, and got it started okay, he gave her a nod and drove off. Dazed, she sat in the driver's seat and waited for the heater to kick in.

A few minutes later, she found herself humming as she entered the house, closed the door, and stood in her entryway staring into space with a goofy grin on her face.

Realizing she was standing and smiling at nothing, she shook her head and laughed at herself.

She couldn't remember the last time since she'd had a date to look forward to. Sure, she'd gone on a few dates back when she was in college, but after she took custody of her sisters, there had never seemed to be enough time for stuff like that.

Besides, most guys her age hadn't been ready for the kind of commitment it would have required to date a woman who's taking care of two younger girls. Most people in their early twenties were more concerned with going out to the clubs, drinking, and hooking up.

She had sort of skipped that step. Now that her sisters were out of the house and successfully living their lives, there was nothing stopping her from making up for a little lost time. This was a good thing.

Ugh, why am I standing here justifying this to myself? I have every right to a romantic pursuit, she thought. Liz and Fiona were right. This was exactly what she needed.

She put a hand to her stomach to dampen the dancing butterflies. She was just feeling nervous. After all, it *had* been years since she had even thought about a date, let been tempted to go on one.

With that thought, she groaned. Oh man, what was she going to wear? She didn't have anything remotely resembling date clothes.

Honestly, there hadn't been a point. Most of her wardrobe consisted of clothes she didn't mind getting dirty while working at the café. Jeans, t-shirts, maybe a few skirts, a ton of chef coats…but not anything worthy of a first date. She needed to call her sister, Fiona, and get some help.

Grabbing her phone, she headed into the kitchen to make some tea. "Hey, Fiona. How was your day?" she asked.

"Pretty busy. Finals week is coming up and everybody and their dog is at the library studying. What's up?"

"You'll never guess what happened to me today…" and with that she told her about running into Mason and walking away with a date.

"Olivia, I'm so happy for you! Of course I'll come over and help you pick out a good date outfit. Tomorrow is my night off, let's get together then. I know you don't have much in your closet, so I'll bring over a few things you might like. Do you think Liz would like to come too?"

"I don't know, but I'll ask. Thanks so much, Fi."

"Are you kidding? This is going to be fun!"

She gave Liz a quick call and confirmed she could also come over the next night. Happy to share her good news with her sisters, she thought it was funny they were so excited for her. Their energy was infectious and helped alleviate the nervousness that threatened to creep in.

Plans made, she spent a couple of hours looking up recipes and working on her upcoming dinner menu. Afterwards, she took a nice, long, hot bath, and finished the book she'd been reading. As she lay in her bed, drifting into sleep, she couldn't help but think she was starting her next year off right.

Overall, it had been a really great birthday.

Chapter Twelve

*T*oday is not a good day, Olivia grumbled to herself.

It had started as a bad morning. First, she managed to trip and fall up the steps while letting herself in the back door of the restaurant. Sure, she'd *bought* a new lightbulb, but hadn't actually had a chance to replace it yet.

That had left her with a scraped palm and a bruised knee, along with half a bag of baked goods lying on the concrete slab around her. Then, Jackie – who is *never* sick – called in sick.

This left her trying to cook in the kitchen with Tom as well as working the front of the house with Becky. Of course, the one day she was short-handed, the entire town decided to show up for breakfast.

Apparently, Frank and the rumor mill had been busy. The recent storm wasn't the only popular topic circulating around the coffee counter that morning. She'd been fielding questions about her forthcoming date with Mason from at least a dozen folks, including Mrs. Crowley and Mr. Harrington.

Not, she reminded herself, *that I should be complaining about too much business.* She would have asked Fiona if she could drive over and help cover tables, but she'd been called in to the library to haul books out from under a leaky spot in the roof.

At eleven o'clock, Olivia was cleaning up a table where a

five-year old boy had decided his eggs would be better on the floor than in his belly. Suddenly she felt an eerie, prickling sensation on the back of her neck.

As she looked up, she spotted the weird guy from the coffee shop sitting at the breakfast counter, watching her. "Great, just what I need," she muttered, and blew hair out of her face. He just smiled and raised his mug in a toast.

Quickly, she finished putting the table back in order, dropped off the place settings and headed to the door for the next party in line. All the while, she could feel the man's eyes following her. What could he possibly want? She didn't have time to deal with a creepy jerk today.

Any thoughts she had about his intentions were quickly forgotten as she worked to keep up with the rush. By the time she remembered him, he had disappeared. Puzzled, she glanced around the dining room, but didn't see him. Ah well, she mentally shrugged. He probably just got frustrated with the wait and left.

Feeling relieved that he was gone, she threw herself back into the rhythm of working a busy shift. After another couple of hours, business started to slow down. Finally, it was two in the afternoon and time to close the café. Tom had filled the last ticket; Becky was just wiping down the last few tables.

"Phew! We haven't had a mid-week rush like that in a while." she exclaimed.

"Tell me about it. For a moment there, I felt like I couldn't catch my breath. I swear I spilled more orange juice than I served this morning," Olivia glanced distastefully down at the front of her shirt.

"In fact, I think I have a spare shirt in the back. I'm going to go change real quick and then we can get the dining room put back in order."

"Okay, I'm almost done wiping the tables down. Really it's just the side work that needs to be tackled."

"How about this. You get everything sorted out here and I'll do the side work. You did a great job today. I couldn't have done it without your help this morning. Thank goodness you're off this week for winter break."

Becky beamed with pride. "We both did well. I just hope Jackie feels better soon."

"Me, too." Olivia smiled at the younger woman and headed down the hall to her office. As she passed the kitchen she called out, "Great job this morning, Tom," and heard him grunt his response.

After quickly changing into a fresh shirt, she headed back to the dining room and started gathering the ketchup bottles, salt and pepper shakers, and sugar containers, stacking them on the breakfast counter to begin refilling them.

As she struggled with a stuck ketchup bottle top, she heard the bell at the door ring. All it took was a second to glance up, and sure enough, red suddenly exploded across her chest.

Of course Mason would be standing in the doorway and watching right as I squeeze a huge glob of condiment down my shirt, Olivia thought ruefully. However, embarrassment quickly turned to concern as Mason's face turned sheet white and he began to breathe heavily. Bent over, he started to shake and gasp for breath.

Concerned, she rushed to him. Recognizing the signs of a panic attack, she murmured in low, soothing tones. Gently, she rubbed her hand in slow, calming circles over his back until he managed to get his bearings again.

After a few moments, he raised his head. The dark, raw, look of anguish in his eyes speared her to the core. It was hard to see such a strong man with such dark shadows in his eyes. It made her ache to hold and comfort him.

She could sense his embarrassment as he glanced away. "Sorry about that." His deep voice was rough with emotion.

"It's okay." She gave him one, last rub on his back before stepping away.

Straightening, he gestured to the ketchup splattered down the front of her.

"Uh, yeah," she glanced down at herself, "not exactly the most graceful thing I've ever done. I don't think I could be any more embarrassed at the moment." Her laughter helped to dispel any lingering awkwardness. "Talk about timing."

Mason broke into a reluctant grin. "Here, let me help you with that." He reached out with his finger and grabbed a bit from her chin.

Entranced, Olivia gave an inward groan. How is it possible to be utterly embarrassed *and* turned on at the same time?

"Great, I even managed to get it on my face? I think that answers my question about whether I could be any clumsier. Sheesh! I think I need to go back to bed and start over again tomorrow."

He walked over and wiped his hands off. "Rough morning?"

"You have no idea." Olivia grabbed a handful of napkins and started mopping up the mess, unaware of the way her breasts strained against the tight cotton of her t-shirt.

Gulping, he said, "I was going to try to grab lunch, but it looks like you're closed."

Startled, she glanced up from her shirt, "Oh! Yeah, sorry about that. We close at two." Gesturing towards the kitchen, she added, "I can make you a sandwich if you'd like…"

"Oh, no, that's okay. I can grab something at my sister's." He looked around. "I didn't tell you this before, but your café is great. You put this place together yourself?"

Olivia found herself pleased to know he liked it. "Yup, for the most part."

"Frank mentioned you were a chef. What made you open a café?"

She sighed and gave up on making her shirt any less of a disaster. Setting the napkins down, she resumed filling the little table holders with multi-colored sweeteners.

"Well, after I graduated high school, I went to the Culinary Institute of America in New York. At the time, I wanted to become a top-rated chef and eventually open my own high-end restaurant, preferably in the Boston area.

"After my parents died, I put all that on hold to come back and take custody of my sisters." She shrugged. "I figured I might as well put what I'd learned to some use, so ended up opening the café."

"I'm sorry about your parents. I can't imagine how hard that must have been. Hell, when I was that age, I think I was busy partying and drinking my way through college. I didn't even have the discipline to study, let alone take care of two other people. That must have been quite a challenge."

"It wasn't easy, but it could have been worse. We were lucky to have a good community of people helping us out."

He nodded. "Listen, since I missed lunch here, would you be interested in coming up to the bed and breakfast with me? We could have a late lunch. You could meet my sister and get the grand tour of La Luna Vista. You mentioned you always wanted to check the place out. Here's your opportunity."

"That sounds like a great idea. I'll have to stop by my house first, to change my clothes, though."

While she finished up her side work, he offered to replace the lightbulb in the back. Half an hour later, she stepped outside with him and locked the door behind her.

This was one of the benefits of only being open for breakfast and lunch, she thought, as she walked towards her car. She liked having the late afternoons and evenings to herself. Of course, if she decided to go forward with her plans to start serving dinner that would all change.

He was parked next to her. "I'll follow you back to your place. I was thinking we could just take my truck and I'll bring you back home later. Does that work for you?"

"Sure. See you at the house," Smiling, she climbed into the

car. With the prospect of a great afternoon ahead, she left her bad morning in the parking lot.

Minutes later, he followed her through the front door and into the entryway. There was a little bench along the wall, with hooks on the wall for outerwear, and a small rack for shoes. Everything was neat and orderly, yet still managed to feel welcoming.

Through the arched doorway to the left was a dining room with big bay windows overlooking the front yard. There was a tasteful table and chair set made of mahogany, inlaid with what he thought was bird's eye maple. The open floor plan enabled Mason to see towards the back of the house and into the kitchen with its granite countertops and gleaming stainless steel appliances.

The living room was in the right front of the house and had a sleek flat-screen TV hanging on the wall over a large fireplace. At the other end of the room, he noticed a pair of French doors leading into an office, or a study, with a wall of bookshelves taking up one end of the room. In front of him was a staircase leading up to where the bedrooms must be. Just to the right of the staircase was a door leading to a bathroom.

"Feel free to make yourself comfortable. Would you like something to drink?" Olivia hung her coat on one of the hooks.

"No, thank you, I'm fine."

"Okay, then. I won't be long." With that, she headed up the stairs towards her bedroom. Mason wandered into the living room.

He was struck by how warm and cozy her place was. It was obvious this was a home, well-tended and loved. The couch looked comfortable enough to sprawl out and read a good book, or tempting enough to convince a person to take an afternoon nap. There was a throw draped along the back of it and soft pillows tucked into its corners.

She had chosen muted, neutral tones for the furniture, but had used reds and oranges in the accent pieces. He walked towards the mantel and noticed a framed picture—set in a place of honor—of a smiling family of five.

Instantly, he recognized the younger version of Olivia. Her head was thrown back and she was laughing, her arm was wrapped around the waist of a curvy and slim older brunette who had the same amber-colored eyes and radiant smile. The woman, presumably Olivia's mother, was sheltered in the crook of a taller, wiry-framed man's arm.

The younger girl hanging around his neck had the same slim athletic body and green eyes as her father. That must be Olivia's sister, Eliza. *The tomboy mechanic,* he thought. Standing arm in arm with her was an even younger girl with soft, dreamy eyes and a shy smile. She'd be her youngest sister, he deduced.

"That was a good day," she said softly behind him. "It was the summer after I graduated high school, a couple of weeks before I left for college."

He carefully placed the frame back in its proper place and turned away from the mantel. He saw that she had changed into another dark, V-neck t-shirt, this one long-sleeved.

Funny how, even when she was dressed in casual clothes, she had a way of standing out. He knew some women spent hours hoping to achieve her kind of effortless beauty. Yet she never seemed to try to draw attention to herself.

Shaking the wayward thought aside, he asked, "When did you lose them?"

"I was twenty-one, nearly twenty-two, and about halfway through my second year at the Culinary Institute of America. Liz was going to be graduating high school that year, but Fiona was just a sophomore. I ended up dropping out and moved back home to take care of them."

"How did you manage to do it?"

She laughed. "I'm not going to lie, it was scary. Technically, I was old enough to take custody of Fiona, but felt so ill-prepared to do so. Added to that, we were all dealing with so much grief at the time."

She traced the edge of the frame with her finger. "I think it was hardest on her because she was the youngest and still in the middle of high school. Her situation felt the most vulnerable to us. There was no way I would leave her to the foster care system. Not after the kind of loving childhood I'd had. She deserved the same opportunity. Besides, even Liz, who was technically able to live on her own, would need support."

"I'm sure your parents would be very proud of you."

She gave him a smile. "Thanks. I'd like to think so. We were lucky. Mom and Dad had been very organized with their finances. Their wills and beneficiaries were in place for all of it. They also had made a few modest investments, which really helped out when I decided to open the café.

"Plus, we had a good network of family friends and were surrounded by people who knew us and wanted to help. Mom had stayed at home with us kids, but as we got older she did a lot of volunteering at the public library and used to lead the reading hour for little kids in the afternoons. Dad had been known to cut deals or delay payments for people who were hard up and needed car repairs.

"They were both so well-loved by the community that when it came time to pitch in after the accident, people were coming out of the woodwork. Added to that, Dad's business partner, Paul, was invaluable during those early days. I honestly don't think I could have made it work without all the help."

While he appreciated her modesty, he doubted it. He had a feeling she would have figured out a way to make things work, no matter what. In fact, when it came to her family, he had a feeling she'd walk through fire to see they were safe.

"You still miss them," Mason said, sensing her melancholy.

"Terribly," Olivia agreed, giving Mason a poignant little smile.

"I don't think you ever fully get over something like that. You just kind of have to push on and learn how to live in spite of it."

Mason nodded. He could understand that. Wasn't he trying to figure out how to do the same thing with the loss of his partner?

"Have you ever considered going back to school?"

"Sure, I've thought about going and trying to finish the program now that my sisters have both moved out, but it's been four, almost five years, and I've got the café now. I feel a sense of responsibility to my employees. They took a chance on me when not many people would have. Jackie has been my best friend since high school and she's just as invested in the café as I am. I owe it to her and Tom to keep it going." She gave a wistful sigh. "It just doesn't feel like school is the direction I'm headed anymore."

He watched as she shook the darker thoughts from her mind. "Anyway, enough about that, I think. Are you ready to go?"

They both headed towards the entrance. As she put her coat on, he tugged the lapels on her collar and slowly drew her up against his body. His eyes had taken on their familiar intensity.

Gently, he raised his hand and stroked a thumb along her cheek, then tucked a strand of hair behind her ear. Her skin heated under his touch. Tension and yearning filled the air between them.

His blue eyes pierced her golden ones. "I admire the hell out of you and what you've done with your life and for your family, Olivia. I don't think you realize what a remarkable woman you are." Her eyes grew round as she flushed with his compliment.

He continued, "I've been attracted to you since I've laid eyes on you. I'm not sure where that's going to lead us in the long run, but I wanted you to know. Regardless of anything else that may or may not happen, I find you amazing."

Thinking it was best they get going before things got out of hand, he carefully drew back and turned towards the door. "So, that being said, ready for a tour?"

Chapter Thirteen

Mason's words had left her feeling flustered, and Olivia found she was grateful for the fifteen minutes it took to reach Melody's place. She caught glimpses of the water between the trees as they drove steadily upward. La Luna Vista was set perfectly on top of a hill overlooking the Merrymeeting Bay.

The house itself was set off of the road a bit. Mason pulled onto the drive that led up towards the shining, white house on the hill. Windows sparkled and reflected the weak winter sun.

She admired the big wrap-around porch, black shutters, and iconic New England red door. Somebody, presumably his sister, had decorated in the region's typical autumn extravagance. There was a leafy wreath hanging from the door and pumpkins along the porch railing. Large, brightly-colored potted mums graced the steps up to the door.

About halfway up, the driveway forked and led to a large white barn sitting off to the right side. She could smell the salt of the ocean and hear the wind and waves crashing along the steep slope down below.

"It's so charming."

"She'll be happy to hear you say so. I know she's put a lot of time and hard work into making this place successful."

"I can't wait to see inside." He had barely parked the truck before she jumped out of the cab. Grinning, he hurried to catch up with her. Just as they approached the door, Melody opened it in greeting.

"Hi. You must be Olivia. I'm Melody. So happy to meet you."

Right away, Olivia could see the family resemblance between the two siblings. Although she was shorter than Mason, Melody was taller than her. Probably about 5'8" or so, if she had to guess.

She had the same dark, black hair as her brother, only hers was longer and had been woven into a French braid that hung down to the middle of her back. Her eyebrows arched gracefully over eyes that were a slightly softer shade of blue than his. She had the same high cheekbones, but her mouth was wider and fuller – more feminine. There was an unmistakable, easy air of class about her that Olivia instantly recognized and admired.

"Come in! Come in. Mason tells me that you own the café in the middle of town. I've been meaning to stop in for ages, but I'm usually too tied up around here in the mornings to make it in."

"That's right, The Three Sisters Cafe. Looks like we're both in the business of feeding others their breakfast. This place is beautiful! Thank you so much for agreeing to let me see it. My sister is going to be sorry she missed it."

"Oh, well, she's more than welcome to visit. Mornings are usually busy, but it tends to quiet down in the afternoons after the rooms are finished. Even then, things can get quiet around here, especially during the off-season. Sometimes I feel like I'm cut off from the rest of the world."

Olivia stood in the front entryway and admired the space around her. Melody had placed a beautiful, burgundy Oriental rug down on the dark, hardwood floors that had vines and flowers woven into it. The wood gleamed along the large staircase leading upward.

The room to the right appeared to be a large formal dining room with a fireplace. To the left was a cozy living room, also with a fireplace. Mason took her hand, threading his fingers through hers. "I was thinking we could do a quick tour around the house and then maybe have a bite to eat. Does that work for you, Mel?"

"Sure, go ahead and show her around. Just so you know, there is an older couple staying in the Snow Room on the second floor, so try to steer clear of there. They're in town at the moment, so you probably won't run into them."

"Snow Room?" Olivia inquired.

"As you can imagine, we have an amazing view up here on the cliff. The moon, in particular, is a pretty spectacular sight, especially when it's full. Hence the name, La Luna Vista - or the moon view.

"I decided to continue with the moon theme and named my rooms after various full moons throughout the year. I have the Wolf Room, Snow Room, Pink Room, Flower Room, Strawberry Room, Buck Room, Harvest Room and Hunter's Room named after January, February, April, May, June, July, September and October's full moons, respectively."

Olivia laughed, delighted. "What a clever idea. I love that."

Melody grinned. "Thanks. I have my owner's apartment on the fourth floor and privately refer to them as my Blue Rooms. It's a good thing I only have the eight rooms, or else I'd ended up having to call one of them "The Worm Room" for March.

"Why don't you guys take a look around? I have some soup on the stove. When you're ready we can have a late lunch, sit, and visit for a bit."

Mason gave his sister a quick smile, and led Olivia through the doorway to the left. The living room had a warm, comfortable feeling to it. It had cream colored walls that glowed softly in the firelight and there was another beautifully woven Oriental rug on the hardwood floor. In one of the corners by the window was a lounge chair and lamp that practically invited someone to sit and indulge in an afternoon of reading.

There was a fire going in the hearth and a beautiful swag of fall leaves along the mantel with candlesticks strategically placed throughout the boughs. A conversation area with a dark leather sofa and two large chairs placed in front of the fireplace welcomed anybody passing to make themselves comfortable and stay awhile.

She noticed a little banquet bar along one wall stocked with a decanter of whiskey and crystal glasses. Every detail seemed thought out and accounted for.

"Oh, this room just makes me want to curl up, pour a finger of whiskey, and while away the rest of my day reading a good book." She was utterly charmed.

She turned to him. "I have to say, I've never actually stayed in a bed and breakfast, but I've seen pictures online. They always appeared too flowery and overwhelmed with clutter. I love how she's kept things welcoming, but minimal, letting the house speak for itself."

He nodded in agreement and opened the door on the far side of the fireplace. It led them to another sitting room. This one had a wall of windows looking out over the slope and to the water. She gasped. "Oh! Look at that view."

Here, Melody had kept the room lighter in color. The walls were a pale yellow and the creamy couches sat facing out, towards the bank of windows. Olivia noticed there was a pair of French doors at the end that led out to the porch. She could imagine sitting here in the summertime with the windows tossed open, the cool breeze coming up the cliff from the water, sipping her morning coffee, and just enjoying the magnificent view.

Mason seemed to enjoy her reactions as she wandered through the room discovering things. His sister had set up a table surrounded by four chairs at one end of the room and lined the walls with books and board games. She wondered what it would be like to sit with him one afternoon and have nothing more pressing on her mind than who would win the next chess game.

As if sensing the direction of her thoughts, he walked up to stand beside her, casually draped his arm across her shoulders, and looked out the windows with her. Idly, his fingers began to lightly brush the skin where her neck and shoulder met, causing her whole body to go on alert. She wondered if he even realized the effect he was having on her. "Let me show you the rooms upstairs." He spoke softly in her ear.

Shivering, she nodded in agreement. Being with him certainly kept her system in a constant state of need and anticipation. There was a low-grade thrum throughout her body whenever he was near.

They walked back to the entrance and up the stairs. As she climbed the steps, she ran her fingers along the banister and admired the workmanship of the wood. "This house really is beautiful. What made her decide to come out here and open a bed and breakfast?"

He shrugged. "I think my sister has always wanted a warm, inviting place to call hers. It's not that we didn't have a nice place to live when we were growing up, but it was always a little too perfect, too clean, and too hard to relax.

"My mother liked to decorate all in white. White couches, white carpet, white walls, white everything. As kids growing up, we were constantly on alert about leaving things messy. We didn't dare track dirt in from playing out in the yard, or leave our clothes on the floor… in the end, I think Melody simply craved a place that she could relax and be comfortable in."

Olivia thought about what he said. It sounded so different from the kind of childhood she had experienced. She had memories of messy cookie decorating sessions in the kitchen with her mom and two sisters, and her father coming home with stained overalls and grease under his nails. Disorganized chaos was just another part of life growing up in the Harper home.

They headed down the hall and to the first door on the left. "What does your mother do?"

"For the most part, she goes to the country club, plays tennis, volunteers on a few charity boards and does everything expected of her as the much younger, beautiful wife of an older, wealthy, and very successful international businessman."

He shot her a look. "Don't get me wrong; when we were growing up, she was kind, in her way. It was important to her that we got the best training and education money could buy. She made sure that we went to the best schools and signed up for all the appropriate after-school programs. Dad was away a lot on business, so most of the work of raising us fell to her and our nannies."

As she listened to him describe his childhood, they made their way down the hallway. She noticed that each of the bedroom doors had small, brass plaques with their name on them. The next one she came across, she read aloud, "The Wolf Room."

Together they opened the door and looked inside. She noted the gray walls and darker wood. There was a chaise lounge in front of the fireplace with a fur throw along the back of it. She ran her hands through the softness. Even though it wasn't real fur, it felt plush and luxurious.

She poked her head into the attached suite and sighed at the Jacuzzi style tub and beautiful, sleek finishes. It reminded her of a very high-end spa.

"Wow. How many fireplaces does this place have, anyway?"

"Six, if I remember correctly. Basically there are two chimneys on either end of the front of the house, so all the front rooms have one, including four bedrooms, the front living room and dining room. The back rooms have the views, but no fireplaces."

"Oh, I get it. So the rooms named after winter months are in the front with the fireplaces, and the summer rooms are in the back with the views. Seems like a pretty nice set-up. Every room gets to have something special going for it, and it still leaves the fourth floor for Melody's private space. She's really thought this out."

"Melody has been pretty successful with it. Plus, she seems to love it, which should count for something."

Olivia nodded, and made her way back out towards the hallway. The door across the way was the occupied Snow Room, so she wandered back towards the other summer rooms.

After poking her head into each, and taking note of the comfortable, tasteful décor, she turned back to Mason. "Your sister is really talented. She has a great eye for design and color, but manages to make it still feel comfortable and welcoming. What room did she put you in?"

"I'm in the Hunter Room on the third floor. I think she thought it suited me."

He did look like a fierce hunter, with his unruly, slightly long hair, intense eyes, and broad shoulders. Not quite tame, she mused. Power, and the control to leash it. She could see him hunting the streets for bad guys, relentlessly pursuing justice. She thought his sister had chosen well.

Together they climbed the stairs to the next level and walked into Mason's room. Here she found dark, gleaming, wood floors and a big, polished sleigh bed that took up most of the space. There was a deep-cushioned leather chair in front of the fireplace and a lushly woven rug in front of the hearth.

The walls had been painted mocha brown and Melody had used forest greens in the bedding. Butter yellow accent pillows brightened the space and gave the effect of sunlight filtering through the trees. The room was unashamedly masculine and smelled of sandalwood and Mason. Other than some change on top of the dresser and a pair of shoes outside the closet, the room was neat.

She could feel him watching her as she explored his room. His intense gaze caused her to feel restless and needy. Unsure of herself, or the emotions he was stirring up, she wandered aimlessly towards the windows and found herself looking out at the view again.

Gently, his hands settled on her shoulders and he turned her towards him. The desire she saw in his eyes set her blood on fire. Before he could do anything but tilt her head back, Melody called up to them. "Mason? Olivia? Lunch is ready!"

With a half-groan, he gave her a grin before dropping a kiss on her nose. "My sister has the worst timing."

Flustered, she pulled back and ran her fingers through her hair, hoping doing so would help put some semblance of order to her thoughts, as well. She was surprised to find her pulse racing and a slight tremor in her hands. "I'm afraid I completely lost track of where I was for a moment."

"That's a good thing." He shot her a smug, supremely cocky, male look before taking her hand. "Come on, let's go see what she's cooked up."

"Ah, there you are." Melody greeted them as they walked into the kitchen. Olivia took a deep breath and detected the comforting aromas of sage and thyme. "I made homemade chicken noodle soup. It's been so cold; it seems like a good soup day."

"It smells delicious," Mason said as he turned to grab some bowls from the cupboard. "Thanks for going to the trouble."

"Oh, it's no trouble. I have some fresh bread I made this morning to go with it. Olivia, did you want something to drink?"

"I think I'll stick with water for now. You've done incredible work here. I absolutely love how you've decorated the rooms."

Beaming, she flushed with pride. "Thanks. It's a lot of work, but it's been so much fun putting everything together. There was a point when I was younger that I thought I'd like to be an interior designer. This gave me the perfect place to focus some of that natural energy."

"Did you have any official training or go to school for design?"

"I took a few classes, but it wasn't a part of my official curriculum, no. Although, my business degree has come in handy making sure this place pays the bills and stays afloat. I'm lucky I managed to find something that satisfies both my interests and my training."

Olivia laughed. "The business degree probably served you better in the long run. I ended up having to take a few crash courses at the community college after I opened my café. Those were long days. I'd wake up at 5 am, work mornings and afternoons, commute down to Portland for a late afternoon class, head home, feed Fiona and Liz, study, do homework and pass out. Then, wake up and do it all over again."

Melody shook her head. "I'm impressed. That's a lot of work." They all sat around the kitchen table. Olivia appreciated how warm and natural the familial setting was with Mason and his sister. Conversation flowed smoothly as they enjoyed their meal and got to know each other better.

She laughed at the childhood stories Melody told her about Mason. She could see him as the rambunctious little boy, from running around with his water gun hollering, pretending to catch bad guys while playing cops and robbers, to scaring off her boyfriends in high school.

"It must have been hard raising your two sisters after your parents died," Melody said, after hearing her story.

"Oh, I don't know if I'd say I raised them, really. Liz was already a senior at that point and had made plans to take over the mechanic shop long before Dad passed away. Fiona was a sophomore and pretty self-sufficient. She ended up staying with me for her first two years of college to help save money, and only just recently moved into her own apartment. I'll admit, the house feels really quiet without them."

"So, do you have any new plans now that they're out of the house?"

She hesitated. "To be honest, I'm not sure. I've been playing around with the idea of staying open later and serving dinner at the café. I've always wanted to have a fine-dining restaurant. Right now I'm still trying to figure out what the menu would be. If I do end up extending the hours of the café, I'm hoping I can figure out a way to make it a bit nicer for the evening business."

"I think it's a great idea. We don't have very many high-end options in town. There are a few seafood places along the waterfront, and of course you can always drive down to Portland or up to Bar Harbor…but I think our town could use another really nice place for more formal dining. I've even considered trying to get the barn out there remodeled and open an establishment myself," Melody replied.

"Oh, I could see that working really well. You could keep a lot of the integrity and charm of the old barn, but open up one of the walls and get the benefit of the view."

"Exactly. You should see some of the wood in there. There are some beautiful, big beams in the rafters that would be really magnificent once cleaned up. You know, you can't get them like that anymore. The structure itself would have to be secured, and it needs a new roof, but the foundation is still solid."

"So, what's stopping you from doing it? It sounds like you've given it quite a bit of thought."

"I'm not sure I'm up to tackling it right now. I've got a lot on my hands just running this place and I know I wouldn't be able to handle both businesses on my own. Basically, it's just a nice idea to think about."

"I can understand that. Like I said, I'm still in the planning stages, myself. After I put together the general idea for the menu, I'm hoping to get in touch with some of the local farmers around here. I'd like to keep as much of the food locally sourced as possible and help support the community, if I can."

"I feel exactly the same way. Actually, I know quite a few of the farmers around here. I usually get my eggs and vegetables from them, and I belong to the local co-op. If you'd like me to help you with introductions, let me know."

"Thanks, I will."

After finishing his second bowl, Mason sat back with a satisfied sigh. "Mel, you really outdid yourself. This was outstanding and perfect for the weather." He got up and gathered the used dishes. "Why don't you ladies relax in the living room? I can do the dishes and clean up."

Olivia raised her eyebrows and slid a glance towards his sister. "Is he always this great, or is he just on his best behavior because I'm here?"

She laughed. "Oh, I don't know if I'd say he's ALWAYS this great, but he usually does pretty well at keeping chores evenly distributed."

He rolled his eyes, grabbed a dish towel and started winding it up. "You ladies better stop talking about me like I'm not here, or you're going to feel my wrath."

Laughing, they both hopped up from the table and moved their dishes to the sink. "Did you want some more water, or would you like to join me in having a glass of wine?" Melody asked.

"Ooh, I'll have a glass with you..." As they started heading out of the kitchen, Mason smacked Olivia's butt with the dishtowel.

"Hey!" she cried, with mock indignation.

Flushed, she laughed and headed into the living room with Melody, not catching the look of surprise and joy on the other woman's face at her brother's antics.

Chapter Fourteen

An hour and a half later, Mason turned into Olivia's neighborhood. She glanced over at him. He hadn't talked much that afternoon, but seemed to enjoy watching the two women interact with each other. Liz's Jeep was sitting in the driveway and the soft glow of lights filtered out from the front windows.

"Looks like my sisters are already here," she murmured, turning to face him as he pulled into the driveway. "Thank you. I had a really good time this afternoon. It was so great meeting your sister. She's done an amazing job with the bed and breakfast."

"I'm glad you could join me today. I knew it was last minute and wasn't sure what your schedule is typically like."

"Afternoons tend to be pretty open for me, other than the usual errands and bookkeeping…" She let her sentence trail off as she felt him begin to run his fingers through her hair. His thumb circled the spot on her neck where her pulse had quickened at his touch, as if relishing the way he affected her. With his other hand, he released both seatbelts and tugged her across the bench seat towards him.

She gave a small gasp as she tumbled into his lap, her hands bracing against his chest. She curled her fingers into his muscles, being careful to skirt the bandages she could feel beneath his shirt, and laughed a little breathlessly as she tipped her head back. The piercing heat of his gaze stopped her in her tracks. She watched as his eyes took in her face and then focused on her mouth.

He paused, giving her a moment to pull back or indicate that he wasn't welcome, but instead, she met his eyes and let him see her own desire reflecting back at him. With slow, deliberate determination, he lowered his head and claimed her lips with his own. His left hand curled back around her head, gripping her hair and drawing it back to the perfect angle.

She moaned as his tongue swept past her lips and explored the sweet, dark depths of her mouth. All thought fled her mind as sensations swirled into her system. Slowly, his fingers began to lightly trace the side of her waist, following the line down to the curve of her hip and back up again.

Emboldened, she moved to kiss along his jawline, but as she tried to snake her arms around his neck, her body twisted and her elbow slammed against the wheel. The blare of the truck's horn sliced through the stillness of the neighborhood and seemed to echo off the garage door, startling them both into half jumping out of their skin.

Instantly, their eyes clicked and they both collapsed into laughter. Reality came crashing in, quickly dispelling the air pressure in the cab. He leaned his forehead against hers as they both fell silent and took a moment to just savor the breath between them.

Carefully, he cupped her cheek, and gave her a self-deprecating grin. "I don't think I've felt this flustered and anxious in the cab of a truck since I was a seventeen year-old just starting to figure things out." After a soft brush of his lips, he reluctantly pulled away from her and let her settle back into her seat.

With a half self-conscious laugh, she cast a glance over at him, and then noticed that one of her sisters must have heard the horn and turned on the front light at the door. "Me neither. I also forgot how illicit it could feel to see the porch light come on,"

She puffed out her cheeks and blew a breath out, willing her heart rate down to something less than a jackhammer. "I should probably get going."

"Okay. I had a good time with you this afternoon. We're still on for Friday, right?"

Olivia flushed with pleasure. "I'm looking forward to it."

"Great. I'll see you then." At that, she climbed out of the cab and headed to the house, knowing she was going to be hearing from her sisters the moment she unlocked the door.

Liz was lying in wait in the foyer as she let herself in. She tried to keep the goofy grin from her face, but couldn't quite stop her lips from quirking up at the corners.

"Oooh, looks like someone has had a good afternoon. Rumpled hair, blushing cheeks…what have *you* been up to I wonder…?" Liz teased Olivia as she hung up her coat and sat down to take off her boots.

"All right, all right, get your kicks in while you can. I don't think anything could pull me down from this good mood." She stood up and padded into the kitchen. "Sorry I'm a bit late. Mason stopped by and took me up to meet his sister, Melody.

"I'm telling you, Fiona would absolutely flip over the bed and breakfast she has up there. The place is everything you would want it to be. Romantic, comfortable, whimsical…perfect."

Liz gave her sister an appraising look. "I don't think I've ever seen you look this flustered before. Let's pop open a bottle of wine and you can tell all the details while we raid your closet. Fiona said she was running late and should be here any moment."

Fifteen minutes later, Fiona stepped through the doorway. "We're up here!" Olivia called down to her.

She came up the stairs and stood, gawking at the clothes piled on and hanging from every surface. "Wow. This place looks like a tornado hit it." She hefted an overnight bag full of clothes onto the bed. "I see you got started without me."

Olivia glanced at her sister in the reflection of the mirror. "I can't believe how bad I've let my wardrobe get. It's nothing but t-shirts, jeans, and sneakers. I just found this dress shoved in the back of my closet." She held it up and tilted her head at herself in the mirror, "What do you think?"

Fiona walked up to get a better view of her sister. "I think that has got to be the ugliest dress I've seen in a very long time. Why on earth would have you purchased it?"

Sighing, she tossed it on the pile of discards in the corner of her room. "You know dressing up was never a strong suit of mine. Besides, there always seemed to be something more important to spend money on. It doesn't make sense to buy nice clothes when half the time I wind up ruining them at work."

Fiona hugged her back. "Well, I think it's about time we cleaned some of this stuff out. I'd suggest donating it, but I'm not sure I'd wish that dress on anyone."

Olivia laughed. "Oh come on, it's not that bad."

"Shows what you know." Fiona fished another faded shirt out of the closet and unceremoniously tossed it onto the same pile in the corner. "We are not going to allow you to dress up as a brown paper sack from the eighties for the first date you've had in years."

Liz piped up from where she leaned back on her bed. "I have to agree with Fi. I'm sure we can do better than that."

Olivia rolled her eyes. "Oh, come on, as if you're any better." She turned back to Fiona. "Okay, okay. I realize I've never been much of a fashion plate, which is exactly why I asked you to come over. So, what'd you bring for me?"

"I brought a few options you might like, but first I need to know a little bit more about this date."

"Well, he's going to pick me up at 5:30 and then we're going to go to the high school holiday concert. He said he's going to make dinner reservations for afterwards."

"How quaint," Liz commented drily, rolling her eyes.

Fiona admonished her sister, "Hey, I think it's sweet. Did he say what restaurant he's going to take you to?"

"He didn't mention the place specifically, no."

"There are only a few places that would need a reservation. I think it's safe to say it'll be a fancier place if he needs one," Liz pointed out.

"Right. So, we need something that will be flattering, somewhat sexy, but still subdued enough to wear to a high school production." Fiona started to rummage through the bag she'd brought.

"I think this will be perfect for you." She handed Olivia a hunter green sweater wrap dress.

She held it up to her cheek. "It's so soft."

"Cashmere." At Olivia's shocked look, Fiona shrugged, "It was a killer deal. Sixty percent off. Try it on."

Quickly, she stripped and pulled the dress on, taking a moment to smooth the fabric over her hips. Fiona and Liz both sucked in a breath.

"It's perfect!"

"Wow, you're good, Fiona." Liz gave her younger sister an approving look.

Rushing back to the mirror, Olivia was surprised to find that the dress fit exactly right. "I'm not used to seeing myself in a dress," she said, half to herself, as she adjusted the sleeves and hemline a bit. "Are you sure it's not too much cleavage?"

"Absolutely not. You've got the curves, might as well put them to good use once in a while. Stop fidgeting," Fiona instructed, batting her hands down. "The color brings out the green in your eyes." She sighed. "You may as well keep it. That dress was meant for you."

"What about the rest of her?" Liz asked, getting into the spirit of things.

"Well, the fact that it's a sweater dress and has long sleeves should keep you warm enough. I'd probably pair it with some opaque tights, and wear your boots. Gold accents would work well with that color."

"Thanks, Fi, I really appreciate it. I don't know the last time I went out on a date."

"I know it's been a long time. I don't think I can even remember you ever going out," Fiona began to dig through her bag again, looking for the pair of gold hoops she'd brought with her. "So, tell us about this guy. What's he like?"

"Judging by the way her cheeks were flushed coming in, he's a good kisser," Liz interjected before she could answer.

"Really? Olivia!" Fiona teased, with a mock scandalized expression.

Blushing, she conceded, "Well, actually…yes, he is." Olivia took the earrings her sister handed to her and moved to the mirror to put them on. "I don't know. He has a focus about him. He's very intense, but he can also be quite charming and goofy when he forgets to be sad…"

"What do you mean, sad?" Fiona asked, watching her sister's face in the mirror.

Olivia's reflection met their eyes. "Did I mention he was a police detective down in Boston?" When they nodded, she continued, "Well, something happened to him down there, something bad, and recently. He's up here staying with his sister while he recuperates."

"Do you know what?" Liz asked.

"No, but I can tell that whatever it is, it haunts him. When he doesn't realize anybody is watching, he walks around with shadows in his eyes. Earlier today he had a panic attack at the café when I accidentally sprayed ketchup down the front of me. It was only later, when I was thinking about it, that I began to wonder what had instigated it."

"It must have looked like blood for a second…" Liz observed.

"That's exactly what I was thinking," she nodded.

"How awful!" Fiona exclaimed. "You know, we could look it up, if you want. Find out what happened."

Olivia shook her head. "I thought about that. I'm not going to say I haven't been tempted, but I feel like this is something I should let him tell me when he's ready."

"Are you sure? What if he's not emotionally stable? I'd hate for you to get hurt."

"Thanks." Olivia turned and smiled at her sisters, shaking off the pensive mood creeping over her. "But, it's just a date, right? Nothing says we have to let things get too serious. I think I'm just going to take things as they come and not worry too much about where they're headed."

Her sisters both exchanged a long look with each other. She laughed, "Oh, come on. Liz, weren't you the one who said something about me sowing my wild oats?"

"You're right, I did," Liz conceded, "but just be careful. I know I was teasing you, but you're not really one to play games. You're the kind of woman who invests in the people she cares about and commits. Don't sell yourself short. You deserve to get that back."

Olivia was touched by what Liz said, and wasn't sure how to respond. Sensing her discomfort, Fiona changed the subject, "So, you went up to the bed and breakfast this afternoon? Tell me all about it."

Two hours later, she waved good-bye to her sisters and watched as they pulled out of the driveway. Liz's words echoed in her mind. She didn't want to be cautious and responsible this time. For once, she was going to live in the moment and let the future take care of itself.

With that thought in mind, she closed the door and went back upstairs to stand in front of the mirror. She could hardly wait to see the look on Mason's face when he came to pick her up.

Chapter Fifteen

Robert sat on his usual stool at the breakfast counter, idly checking to make sure the mustache he was using as a disguise was secure, and watched as Olivia put another order up in the window. He'd been coming in every day this week and enjoying the way she moved in the kitchen.

He didn't even mind her interactions with the other townspeople. Most of the men seemed too old or already married. He noticed she had a way of talking to people and yet still keeping herself slightly apart. The only exception that he'd seen had been with that damn detective from Boston.

Luckily, after that day when he'd first spotted her, he hadn't seen any further sign of Mason. A part of him wondered if it had just been a coincidence that they had talked to each other that afternoon.

It didn't matter, she was his now. He'd seen the way she had appreciated the flowers he'd left for her, tucked under her windshield wiper for her to discover after work yesterday. He'd left her a note the day before telling her he'd be seeing her soon. Robert knew women liked a lot of attention.

She didn't know it yet, but tonight, he was going to take her out on their first date. He couldn't wait to see the joy and surprise on her face when he came by her house to pick her up. He could already tell his little gifts had pleased her. Just wait when she found out what his plans were for this evening.

"Is there anything else I can get you?" The unwelcome inquiry broke into his reverie.

He stared at the young girl who was looking at him with barely concealed distaste. He clenched his fingers around the handle of his mug. She was lucky she was too young for him. Otherwise, he'd feel obliged to teach her a lesson in respect. "I'll take another refill of coffee."

The girl turned to get the pot, but not before he saw her mouth twist in disdain. "Be right back."

Moments later, she filled his cup again and, with a pointed look, left the check on the counter before heading back to the kitchen. He could tell that whatever she said had to do with him, because, for an instant, Olivia's head came up and she cast a quick look over at him.

Thinking it was probably best to leave before he became too obvious, he took a final swig of the still steaming coffee and left a few bucks by the ticket. He smirked as he headed out the door. Damned if he was going to leave a tip for that upstart little bitch.

Chapter Sixteen

The rest of the week seemed to fly by for Olivia. With Jackie still out sick, the hours her café were open smeared into one big blur. At night, she pored over cookbooks and tested out various recipes for her dinner menu.

By the time Friday morning had rolled around, Jackie was finally back, recovered from the bug she'd had. Olivia was relieved to be working the grill beside Tom again.

She hadn't seen Mason all week, but had been surprised to find the little gifts he'd left her. She wouldn't have thought he'd be the type to leave notes and flowers. His style had seemed more straightforward than that.

And where was he, anyway? He'd asked her out for a date on Friday and then practically disappeared. Couldn't he have come in to say hi when he left the flowers on her car yesterday?

She was baffled. Maybe he was just trying to build up anticipation, she thought. Hell, it had been forever since she'd dated anyone. What did she know? Maybe this was how it was done now.

Thinking that must be it, she finished plating the order she was working on and tossed it up into the window, calling out for pick up.

As she did so, she felt the heat of someone's gaze on her. She didn't even have to glance over to know that Mason was sitting at the counter. Her eyes collided with his and everything else stopped. The clink of silverware, the murmur of voices, the sizzle and scrape of Tom flipping bacon, all faded into white noise.

Speak of the devil, she thought. Olivia could feel her heart lurch. "Tom, I'm taking a quick five minutes."

"Okay, I got this."

She swung out of the kitchen door and headed towards him, relieved to see that it wasn't too busy. Flipping a mug over, she poured him coffee. "Hi."

"Hey. Sorry I haven't been in to see you this week. I went into Boston for a few days to check on my partner's daughter and drop off a few Christmas presents."

"Oh, that's sweet of you."

"I just wanted to make sure we're still on for tonight?"

"Yes!" Inwardly, Olivia cringed and reminded herself not to sound too eager. "Yes, of course."

"Okay, great. So, I'll be by to pick you up at 5:30, then. I'm hoping you know where the play is going to be held."

"Oh yeah, don't worry about that. It's held at the Chocolate Church. You can't miss it, since its right in the middle of town. Be prepared, though. You're probably going to end up meeting everybody tonight."

He flashed a smile. "I'm looking forward to it." He got up from his seat and left some money to pay his bill. "Don't work too hard."

She smiled and watched him leave the café, catching herself before she sighed out loud.

"Well, well...I seem to have missed quite a lot this week." Jackie said, from behind her. She leaned on the counter and watched her watch him leave the café. "Who is that intensely sexy hunk?"

"His name is Mason. Remember me telling you about my car breaking down and getting a ride home after the storm last week?"

"Lucky woman. Is it weird that I'm now wishing my car would break down?" She laughed. "Of course, with my luck it would be some backwoods hillbilly with missing teeth stopping to pick me up." Her eyes wandered over to Tom and she gave him a saucy wink. He just shook his head and stacked another plate with breakfast potatoes.

Olivia laughed and gave her a hug. "I'm glad you're feeling better. I missed you."

"So, what's the deal? Did I hear him say he's going to pick you up tonight?"

"As a matter of fact, you did. I haven't had a chance to fill you in, but I happen to have a date with that very sexy man tonight."

Jackie clapped her hands with excitement. "Details! I need details. Where's he taking you?" Just then, a woman called out, "Ma'am?"

"I'll be right there." She turned back to Olivia, "We have a date after shift and are going to talk, missy. We have some catching up to do."

She smiled and gave Jackie another quick hug before heading back to the kitchen. "You got it."

That afternoon, the two friends chatted over sandwiches. Olivia told Jackie about her date with Mason, the impromptu afternoon she'd spent with him, touring his sister's bed and breakfast, as well as the supercharged kiss they'd shared when he'd dropped her off. She also described how she'd been finding flowers and notes left for her all week, but hadn't seen him since last Tuesday.

"Life must be so tough for you, Livvy. Here you have a hot guy leaving you romantic gestures and you're wondering if it's normal."

Olivia rolled her eyes. "Oh, come on. You know me better than that. I'm just not used to this kind of attention."

"At least you're getting some. I say count yourself lucky and have fun with it."

"You're right. How about you? Anybody catch your eye lately?"

"There aren't a lot of good men in this town looking to start a relationship with a single mom. And, to be honest, I'm too busy to worry about it that much…" she hedged. "The only man I saw this whole week was Tom when he dropped off some 'get well soon' soup."

Olivia was so caught up in her own situation that she didn't catch the hesitancy in her friend's answer. "I completely understand. Well, who knows? Maybe some hunky guy will come into town and sweep you off your feet."

"I think the hunky guy already came into town, only it wasn't my feet he was sweeping." Jackie glanced at her watch and got up. "Speaking of being a single mom, I've gotta go pick up my kid from school. I expect to hear all about how the date goes tomorrow."

"Will do. Oh, by the way, I have Tom opening for me, since I'll be up later than usual tonight. Would you mind coming in a bit early just to make sure he doesn't need any extra help?"

"Not a problem. But, like I said…details! I'm fully planning on living vicariously through you."

"Agreed," Olivia got up and began clearing the table. "Don't worry about the dishes. I'll take care of them. Say hi to Abby for me."

With a little wave, Jackie took off, leaving Olivia to clean up. Now, she'd just have to figure out how to fill the next few hours without going crazy.

Chapter Seventeen

Olivia rushed to finish her final brush of mascara right as she heard the doorbell ring downstairs. Nervously, she took one last look at herself in the mirror. She wasn't used to seeing herself all done up like this. Most of the time, she didn't wear more than a swipe of lip gloss. She liked how the gold eye shadow made her eyes shimmer in the light.

With a final toss of her hair, she headed down the stairs and took a deep breath before opening the door. Instantly, she noticed that he had trimmed his beard, but was secretly happy he hadn't decided to shave it off. She wondered how the scruffy texture would feel against her skin.

How he could make a simple V-neck sweater look so good was beyond her. She liked the way the dark blue set off his eyes. He wore a bomber jacket and dark wash jeans. Even though he'd cleaned up, he still had an air of danger to him. Her blood thrilled as she watched him rake a glance up and down her body and take in her appearance.

"You look gorgeous."

She stepped back to let him in. "Thank you. I could say the same about you."

She quickly grabbed her purse, but before she could head towards the door, he shifted and wrapped his arms around her waist, gently drawing the length of her body against his. His eyes sharpened into twin blue lasers. It was all she could do to grab hold of his hips and hang on.

He held her there, staring into her eyes, like he was making up his mind about something. Slowly, he brought his mouth down and brushed his lips ever so gently to hers. Just the barest of touches, but it sent electricity streaking through her bloodstream.

Her eyes fluttered closed and she leaned in towards him, but he didn't deepen the kiss. Just teased and savored all the potential in that smallest of caresses. Idly, he stroked his thumb along her jawline and down her neck before releasing her.

Dazed, she opened her eyes and stared up at him for a moment before gathering her wits. "Well…" she didn't know what to say after that. How could a kiss be so light and gentle and pack that kind of heat? Desire was already beginning to curl low in her belly.

"I've wanted to do that all week. I hope you don't mind." Gently he pulled away from her. "Shall we?"

Just then, he glanced up through the archway and noticed a vase holding a dozen roses on the kitchen island. Light shining from the pendant lights highlighted the crimson blooms, causing them to be prominently spotlighted and displayed.

"That looks nice."

"Oh! How rude of me. I forgot to thank you for the flowers and note you sent this week."

Mason's attention swung back to her, giving her a blank look. "Flowers? Note?" At her nod, he said, "Olivia, I didn't send you anything this week. Remember? I was down in Boston all week."

Startled, her brows furrowed at the revelation. "Huh. I just assumed they came from you. It's not as if I'm routinely receiving gifts like these. I can't imagine who else would have sent them." She gave Mason a little shrug, beginning to feel self-conscious, "I wonder who they could be from."

Curious, he walked over to the vase. "Where were they left for you? Did they get delivered directly to the house?"

"Well, the flowers were placed on the windshield of my car. The note was left in my mailbox."

He cast a disturbed look at her with that tidbit of information. "In your mailbox? Maybe they're a belated birthday present. Was there an envelope or any kind of postmark?"

"Nope, just the note. I didn't think much of it because I figured you must have dropped them off." Olivia watched Mason closely, trying to figure out why he seemed so disturbed by the innocuous gifts…unless, maybe he was jealous?

"I'm sure it's nothing. It's probably just my sisters giving me a hard time and teasing me since they knew I was going out on this date tonight. Speaking of which…we should probably get going if we're going to make it on time."

He nodded and followed her out, waiting for her to lock the door. As she mutely followed him to his truck, he seemed to be preoccupied, lost in thought. She wished they could recapture the feeling from when he first came to pick her up. Her lips still tingled with the memory of his.

As they turned the corner into town, Mason admired the impressive architecture of the church rising up into the dark sky, its brown gothic spires lit from within. Snow coated the roof and created a nimbus effect at the top of its tower.

"Wow, pretty impressive for a high school concert."

"They call it the Chocolate Church, although it isn't used as a church anymore. Now it's an arts center. It was almost torn down at one point and turned into a parking lot. Luckily a group of town members got together and saved it, back in the seventies. Wait until you hear the acoustics."

As impressive as it was, Mason was surprised to find there wasn't a parking lot. He had to circle around a few blocks before he could find a spot.

Walking back towards the building, he was once again struck by how wholesome everything seemed in this town. Families with younger siblings, high school kids, and teachers all streamed towards the double doors.

At that moment, a familiar prickle of sensation ran down the back of his neck. He surreptitiously scanned the crowd of people making their way into the church, trying to figure out why he felt like he was being watched.

He spotted a lone figure about a block and a half down, leaning against the wall. It was too far to get a good look. All he could make out was the soft glow of the end of a cigarette.

"Is something wrong?" Olivia asked, craning her neck to look in the direction he was focused on.

Shrugging, he turned back to her. "It's probably nothing. Just a guy trying to get a smoke in before the performance. I must be a little jumpy, that's all."

She wound her arm through his. "I'm afraid your city instincts are wasted in this small town."

With a final glance, he thought she was probably right. As they made their way through the doorway, he noticed there was a display for the upcoming holiday events posted at the front of the building.

"I have to admit, this is a first for me. I've never had occasion to come to a high school concert before."

"So, I take it no kids?"

"No kids, no ex-wives."

"No nieces or nephews?"

"Melody is my only sibling, so no nieces or nephews, either."

"Well, then I can understand why this would feel so weird to you."

"What about you? How are you so familiar with all of this?"

"Fiona liked the theater when she was in high school, and I got into the habit of coming here. Besides, I try to support the town and school whenever I can. I figure the cost of a ticket once in a while won't kill me. I think you'll be surprised. They tend to put on a pretty good show."

Olivia liked the way he gently placed his hand on the small of her back to help guide her through the crowd as people were funneling in the door. She wasn't used to being escorted by a gentleman.

That must be one of the differences between dating now and in the past. Back then, the few college guys she'd gone on dates with had felt showing up in a clean shirt was an accomplishment.

She watched as he scanned the crowd and his surroundings. His eyes never seemed to stop for too long. It wasn't that she got the impression he was restless, just constantly alert.

"Olivia, Mason. I'm so happy to see you could make it." Frank called out to them as they were turning in their tickets and being handed a concert program.

"Frank, great turnout tonight. How's Rosie doing? Any first night butterflies?"

"She had the jitters earlier."

"Aww, well, I'm sure she'll do great."

As they both entered the auditorium, Mason appreciated the way the ceilings soared above him. The dark wooden beams and arched entrances created a sense of drama. She checked their tickets. "Looks like it's open seating. I see a couple of spots over there."

As they weaved through the crowd, he noticed she was greeted by a number of people and seemed well liked, and was comfortable in the room. Most of them had probably eaten at her café in the past week. He noticed quite a few of them cast him curious glances as they chatted with her.

Again, he got the uncomfortable feeling of being watched. As casually as possible, he continued to search the crowd, trying to pinpoint what was causing it. He had just spied a man in a baseball cap a handful of rows back that seemed to be looking in their direction when the auditorium lights started to dim. Reluctantly, he shook off his concern, chalking it up to having spent the past week in Boston and feeling jumpy.

Making the conscious decision to relax, he reached over and wove his fingers through hers. This had to be one of the most original first dates he'd ever been on. High school holiday concerts weren't his usual scene. He could only hope they were as talented as Olivia had led him to believe.

* * *

An hour and a half later, Olivia wound her arm though his as they made their way back to the truck. "So? What did you think?"

"I'm impressed. Actually, they weren't bad."

"I thought the a Capella version of Carol of the Bells was the best."

"That was good. Rosie did well with her solo for Silent Night, too. Frank looked very proud."

"We'll have to be sure to let him know we enjoyed it." Suddenly, her stomach growled and he laughed.

"Good thing I made reservations for dinner."

She blushed. "I don't usually eat so late. Most of the time, I'm in bed by 9:30, 10 at the latest."

"Well, don't worry. The place we're going isn't too far from here. I hope you like Italian food."

"I love Italian food. Actually, I'm pretty adventurous when it comes to trying all types of food. As a chef, I think it's important to be open to new flavors and taste combinations."

"Have you always wanted to be a chef?"

"Ever since I was little. My mom and I used to spend hours in the kitchen together trying out new recipes. When I was younger, she'd let me wash the vegetables, stir the pots and lick the spoons, but as I got older, we'd try more complicated things."

She laughed in remembrance, "We used to pick a country or

region as a theme and try to cook a whole week's worth of recipes from that area. One week we'd eat all Spanish food like paella and various tapas. The next week it would be French food. You should have seen us after we made our first successful soufflé. You'd have thought we'd won the lottery. It was our time to bond. I got my love of cooking from her."

"She sounds amazing."

"She really was. Even though we lived in a small town, she managed to make the whole world feel accessible and brought it to us. I wasn't a very popular kid growing up. With all that cooking, I was a bit chubby and shy, but I always knew I had a place to go that I was understood and loved."

He reached across the seat and grabbed her hand. "Looks like you grew up well to me."

She laughed. "That's because after I graduated high school and left for college, I finally came to the realization that if I was going to keep cooking and eating the way I wanted to, I had to learn to love exercise just as much. I started running every week and have never stopped. How about you? Have you always been fit?"

"Well, I was always into sports and physically active, so yeah. It came with the territory."

"You were probably one of those guys in school that everybody loved and all the girls crushed over, huh?"

He shot her a look. "I didn't do too badly for myself."

"Now, why do I think that's an understatement?"

He pulled up to the restaurant and parked the car. "That kind of stuff never seemed like a big deal to me. I'm old enough now to realize it's probably because I wasn't on the other end of the social spectrum and didn't have to worry about it. I liked playing sports. I'm pretty competitive by nature. The rest of it was just a bonus.

"As long as I kept my grades up, my parents left me alone, but there weren't any warm family dinners. My sister and I are close, but other than that, I have a pretty cool and distant relationship with the rest of my family."

As they headed in, the host greeted them and showed them to a romantic little table by the windows overlooking the water. She sighed out at the view and fingered the white linen tablecloth. Candlelight made her eyes glow a deep, warm amber. Mason took a moment to enjoy her beauty.

"Do you mind if I choose a bottle of wine?" he asked her.

"Please do."

"Would you prefer red or white?"

"Red would be nice."

After the waiter told them about the specials and took their orders, she turned back to him. "I feel like I've been talking about myself all night. Tell me more about you."

He watched her from across the table. "What do you want to know?"

"Well, did you always know you wanted to work in law enforcement?"

"When I was younger I used to pretend I was a detective and run around trying to solve 'mysteries.' My dad always assumed I'd grow out of it. He would have preferred I use my MBA and take over the family business. But, I knew from a pretty early age it wasn't for me."

"What does your father do, exactly?"

"Did, he's passed away now. He was in international corporate finance, specializing in mergers and acquisitions. He did a lot of traveling when I was growing up."

"I'm sorry to hear he's gone. That must have been hard to have him away so much. You weren't interested in following in his footsteps?"

"I felt like I could make a difference by going into law enforcement. It felt like I was serving a purpose higher than myself. Besides, I've never wanted to be stuck behind a desk and working in an office environment." He gave her a lopsided smile, "Although, a large part of my job right now is filling out reports. I guess no one can ever really run away from paperwork."

"Well, there's that. Although it sounds like finance would be safer," Olivia gestured towards Mason's shoulder.

Her words were a cold wind instantly blowing out the warm light in his eyes. The humor in the corners of his mouth vanished and his face settled like stone. Quietly, he placed his wine glass down and became intensely interested with the oil and vinegar on his bread plate.

"Damn, I never should have brought it up," she stuttered, feeling her cheeks grow warm.

On an exhale, he looked up. His eyes held long shadows in them, as if a cloud had crossed over the summer sun. "No, I'm sorry. I shouldn't have tensed up on you like that. I thought I was moving past it a little bit, but apparently it's still raw."

At that moment, the waiter discreetly delivered their meals and then, sensing they didn't wish to be disturbed, quietly left. Mason picked up his fork and looked down at his food. Glancing back up at her, he could see the unasked question in her eyes.

She just looked at him, her eyes filled with compassion. Impulsively, she reached across the table and laid her hand on his. He turned his hand over and threaded his fingers through hers. Sighing, he began to tell his story.

"It was just a couple of weeks before Halloween. My partner, Ryan, was grousing about how his daughter had asked him for a MacBook for Christmas and basically bemoaning the fact that his little girl was growing up too fast. He and his wife had recently split, and this was going to be the first time that he wouldn't be able to see her opening presents on Christmas morning.

Anyway, we're going to check out this real scumbag of a guy. He'd previously been brought in on stalking charges, and had a couple of restraining orders out against him. We suspected him of abducting a woman who had disappeared a block away from his house. We were going to take a look around, ask him a few questions, and kind of get a feel of the place.

"He was a real sleazeball, but he had no history of confrontational behavior that we knew of. Guys like that tend to be more inclined to run than fight when faced with an actual opponent. So, Ryan and I walked right up to the front door and asked if we could talk to him. He must have had the woman close enough that she could hear us at the door, because suddenly there was a loud thump that sounded like a person falling off a bed. The next thing we knew, the guy had whipped a gun out and started shooting."

Olivia gasped. All the color drained from her face and she gripped his hand tighter. Their meals sat, forgotten.

"I got shot twice, a sucking wound to the lung and graze on the outside of my shoulder. But, I was lucky. Ryan was standing in front of me on the stoop and took the brunt of the attack."

He set his fork down. "He didn't make it."

Her other hand covered her mouth, "Oh my…I can't imagine."

"I was in the hospital for a few weeks. For the most part, my shoulder has healed up. The muscle still twinges a little, but it's not too bad. My lungs are taking longer. I have to do these breathing exercises, and the cold air makes them feel worse, but even they are getting better. I've started adding cardio back into my workouts to help strengthen them back up."

He looked up at her stricken face and came out of the swirl of his tortured memories. Belatedly, he noticed how hard he was gripping her hand and self-consciously released her, reaching for his wine glass instead.

"So, now that I've completely dispelled any feel-good date feelings…"

She reached for her own glass and took a healthy gulp, letting the memory of sun-ripened grapes sooth her. She thought about the fact that if a bullet had gone just another inch to the left, she may never have had the chance to be on this date with such a charismatic, interesting, *let's not forget gorgeous*, man. "I'm sorry you had to go through something so tragic. It sounds like you two were quite close."

"We were. He really was the best."

"How is his daughter doing?"

"It's been tough, as you can imagine. Especially during this time of year. I've called her a few times and have been trying to keep tabs on her from up here. I get updates from her mom."

"It's hard losing a parent when you're young. I know how difficult it was for me at my age, and I was quite a few years older. I can only imagine how much harder it must be for her."

"Thankfully, she has her mom looking out for her. It's been hard on both of them, but at least they have each other."

"So, how long will you be on leave? What's the recovery time for something like this?"

"I was in the hospital for about two weeks while they had me on oxygen, antibiotics, and pain meds, and kept me under observation. There was some concern about infection, since they had to go in and remove bone fragments. Actually, my ribs seem to be taking the longest to heal, but overall, it could have been worse. I was told the faster these types of injuries are treated, the shorter the recovery time. I had an ambulance get to me within ten minutes of being shot.

"That being said, all I can think about is getting back to active duty and helping to find this guy."

"You mean he's still out there?"

Mason gritted his teeth. "The bastard got away. It's one of the reasons why I'm so anxious to get back. I won't be able to rest until Ryan and his family have some sort of justice."

"When do you think you'll be able to do that?"

"I spoke to my Captain yesterday. I'm required to go in for a couple of psych evaluations before I'm allowed to return to active duty. He's giving me until after the holidays to have them all finished, but said my first appointment should be sometime after Christmas."

He sighed, picked up his fork, and twirled a few strands of pasta around the tines. "To be honest, Olivia, I don't have any idea what my long term situation is going to be." He shrugged. "Maybe it was unfair of me to ask you out tonight, since I don't know how long I'll be in town.

"I do know that I won't rest until I can get some resolution for my partner. Ryan and I came up through the academy together, we worked the streets together, and we became detectives together. He was a good guy and deserved better."

She thought about what he had said as she began to cut into her chicken primavera. "Well, I don't think we need to make any big decisions just yet. You've been through some serious trauma. It's okay if you don't know what's going to happen next. The most important thing you can do right now is focus on healing physically, and take it one day at a time."

"I just wanted you to know where things stand with me in my life right now. I'm attracted to you and enjoy your company, but I can't tell you if I'll be sticking around or just how far things can go with us. I don't want you to feel like I haven't been honest with you or upfront about that."

Olivia smiled. "I appreciate the candor. To be honest, I haven't dated in a really long time and I'm not exactly sure what I want, either. I don't think we need to have any expectations in order to spend time together. Let's just enjoy each other's company and see how things go."

The two of them sat and ate in contemplative silence for a few moments, each steeped in their own thoughts. Gradually, as if by some quiet consensus, they began to move on to other—easier—topics.

She already knew they shared a similar taste in music since

the other day, although he tended to listen to it much louder than her. It didn't come as a big surprise to her that he gravitated more towards action movies, but she was pleasantly surprised when he got her Firefly reference.

They finished their meals. As the waiter took their plates away, Olivia was startled to realize it was nearing midnight.

"Should we get some coffee and dessert?" Mason asked.

"Yes to the dessert, but I think I'll pass on the coffee. If I drank it now, I wouldn't be able to sleep at all tonight. I might take some herbal tea, though."

She liked the intimacy of sharing something sweet together. Philosophically, she thought a person could tell a lot about a man by the way he shared dessert with a woman. Some men ate it quickly. They were so eager to get as much as they could that they forgot to enjoy it. Others made sure to take the choicest pieces, or refused to share altogether.

After admiring the generous slice of triple-layer, chocolate mousse cake placed in front of them, she watched to see what Mason's first reaction would be. He gestured to her. "Ladies first. Let me know what you think."

He watched as she cut through the layers of various dark chocolate and ganache and slid it silkily into her mouth. His stomach clenched as she closed her eyes to savor the flavors on her palate.

She couldn't help but moan with the pleasure exploding on her tongue. "Ohhh, this is *sooo* good. Wow, this is really rich. I'm glad we're splitting it." She opened her eyes and found him staring at her. "Uh oh. Did I get some on my face?" Cautiously, she lifted her fingers to the corner of her mouth.

It was such an unexpected question and so far from what he'd been thinking that Mason burst out laughing. She frowned and began earnestly rubbing her cheek until he grabbed her hand and threaded his fingers through hers.

"You're absolutely beautiful. I can assure you there is nothing on your face. I was just admiring you." He reached out with his fork and took a bite for himself, never breaking eye contact with her. "Delicious."

She felt herself tremble under such scrutiny and wondered what other ways his intensity manifested itself. Even with his warning that this may only be temporary, she was tempted to find out. So what if all it became was a hot fling? With a man this enticing, why should she refuse? She was a perfectly healthy, hot-blooded woman, wasn't she?

He had taken his time with dessert, sipping his coffee between bites and giving her the only strawberry. To her, it was a good sign and showed that he was open to sharing and enjoying what he had. The two of them lingered another half hour, savoring their dessert and each other's company.

After paying the bill, Mason escorted her out into the chill, night air, and she shivered, despite the warm dress and coat she was wearing. She blew on her hands, huddled deeper into her coat collar, and paused in the alcove to put her gloves on. From the corner of her eye, she caught a flash of movement to the left. Turning, she peered into the trees, trying to get a closer look.

"That's weird," Olivia muttered under her breath.

Mason stopped and looked in the direction she was facing, casually positioning his body in front of hers. Growing very still, he took a moment to scan the deep shadows. "What'd you see?"

Brushing it off, she waved the odd feeling away with her hands. "It's nothing. For some reason I thought I saw a guy standing there, but it must have been some animal moving through the brush."

"A man? About how tall was he? Did you get a look at his face? Was he wearing a baseball cap?"

"What? Mason, no. I'm sure it was nothing. Forget I said anything."

"Are you sure? I got the sense I was being watched earlier."

She laughed and began walking over to the passenger door of his truck. "That's because you were. The whole town was taking a good look at you." She climbed up into the cab and turned to face him. "I warned you, it's a small town. People are going to be talking about seeing me out on my first date in years for at least a week."

Noticing he still had that tense, hyper-aware look about him that she'd seen earlier, she sighed. "I shouldn't have said anything. I'm sure it was nothing. We're probably both just a bit jumpy from the conversation we had earlier."

Reluctantly, he started the ignition and, with a final glance towards the surrounding trees, nodded. "I'm sure you're right. Let's get you home."

They sat in comfortable silence on the way home. She watched the moon play peek-a-boo between the trees outside her window as she mulled over the conversation they'd had over dinner.

Her porch light greeted them cheerfully as they pulled up to the front of the house. Mason got out of the truck and walked her to the door. She was surprised at how jittery her nerves were. He took the keys from her and unlocked the entrance.

She turned and looked up at him. The pale, yellow light left his face shadowed as he looked down at her and all she could see was the blue gleam of his eyes. "Did you want to come in for a moment?"

He reached up and brushed his thumb gently across her cheek. "It's pretty late. I should probably let you get some sleep before you have to be at the café tomorrow."

A flicker of disappointment streaked through her. Just as she opened her mouth to respond, his descended on hers; firm, masculine lips claiming and molding her mouth to his. This wasn't the soft, teasing kiss from earlier. This kiss shot her right out of a rocket and sent her soaring towards the stars. She heard a groan of relief and longing and wasn't sure if it had come from her or him. His tongue swept between her lips and sampled the taste of her.

She smelled like honeysuckle and tasted like wine. It was the only coherent thought in his mind before he dove under her spell again. His hands ran up the collar of her coat and delved into the thick tresses he'd been dying to run his fingers through all night. He cupped the back of her head and tilted it into a better position, kissing her even more fully. He would have been perfectly happy to devour her right there in her doorway.

Olivia wrapped her arms tightly around his waist and ran her hands up his back. She pressed her breasts to his chest, trying to get closer. *More*, was all she could think. She wanted so much more of this man that she'd only met a couple of days ago. All the passion and heat that had been lying dormant in her for years burst alive throughout her body. Every nerve ending felt electrified with need. She could feel his arousal through his jeans and instinctively ground her pelvis against him.

Her hands couldn't stop exploring. She admired the width of his shoulders and twined her arms around his neck. Her fingers played with the hair at the nape of his neck. His hands travelled down and around to cup her ass and lift her more fully to him, making her gasp at the friction and contact. Her head fell back as he trailed kisses down the creamy column of her neck and then back up to tease her earlobe. She could feel her nipples harden and peak in desire.

A deep growl started in the back of Mason's throat, and he realized he needed to slow down or they really were going to make use of the bench in the entryway. Gently, he made his way back to her mouth and lightened the kiss. Each pulled back slightly as he continued to nibble at her lips. They were both breathing hard and he was feeling entirely too hot.

"I had a really good time with you tonight," his voice rasped. Slowly, he bent down and gave her bottom lip another nibble.

With a sigh, he leaned his forehead against hers. "I should really go now, otherwise, I might change my mind about not coming in. If that happened, I can't guarantee you'd make it into work tomorrow at all."

She wound her arms tighter around his neck and gave him another lingering kiss. "I know you're right. Thank you for taking me out, I had a great time." Reluctantly, she stepped through the doorway and flipped the hall light on.

With a final, wistful look, Mason said, "I'll call you," and made his way back to the truck, giving her a little wave before pulling out of the driveway.

She watched him leave as she stood hugging herself. Gradually, she came out of the haze his kiss had left her in and realized she was standing in the doorway, out in the cold, like a lovesick loon. Laughing, she locked up and made her way to bed. She could only imagine what kind of dreams she was going to have tonight.

Chapter Eighteen

B eep!
   Beep!
   Beep!

"Euuurrrrggggh! Alright already!" Olivia slammed her hand down on the alarm clock and flopped face first into her pillow. She briefly debated the merits of hitting the snooze button one more time against the need for a quick shower before heading into the café. Sleep vs. clean hair…hmmm.

In the end, it was her bladder that forced her to roll out of bed and stumble blearily into the bathroom. Ten minutes later, with her wet hair in a bun, she managed to make her way downstairs and out the front door.

Thank goodness she'd had Tom and Jackie open the café this morning, she thought. Even with the extra hour of sleep in the morning, she was having a hard time functioning. Of course, it hadn't helped that she had tossed and turned practically all night.

If it wasn't unfulfilled desire keeping her up, it was remembering Mason recount the incident with his partner. His eyes had been so tortured. She wished there was something more she could do to help him combat those demons.

Shaking her head to clear it of that unpleasant thought, she pulled into the lot behind the building and slipped through the backdoor. Surprised, she listened to Tom whistling as he worked the grill. Well, at least one of them was chipper this morning. Maybe she should have him open more often.

"Hey, Tom, I'm here." she called, pulling her chef coat down from the hook by the door.

"Hey, Olivia. No rush, take your time and have some coffee. It's not too busy just yet."

"Thanks. I appreciate you opening for me. Jackie's out front?"

"Yup."

She poured herself some coffee and made her way into the dining room, hoping she could take a moment and talk to Jackie about last night's date. She was happy to find only a few tables occupied.

Jackie greeted her from behind the breakfast counter. "Livvy, let me just make sure everybody is topped off, and then you and I can have a little chat."

Cautiously, she blew on her hot coffee and watched as Jackie swung by two tables, topped off a few mugs, laid a bill on one of them, and then made a beeline back to where she was standing.

Dumping the pot back onto the burner, she turned to Olivia, "So…? How'd it go?"

"The kids put on a good show…" Olivia answered coyly.

Jackie hit her friend on the shoulder. "I don't care about that! Well, I mean, I'm glad to hear they did well, but you know darn well that's not what I want to hear about. How was Mason?"

"Sexy, intense, wonderful…Oh my goodness, Jackie, the man can KISS!" She fanned herself.

"A man looks like that, I would certainly hope so."

"On one hand, I felt so comfortable with him. We never ran out of things to talk about and actually seem to have a lot in common. But, then there was this underlying tension and heat between us. Every time our eyes met, it was like he was stoking a fire in my belly. I have never felt that kind of chemistry with someone before."

Jackie shivered in delight. "Please tell me you did something about it."

"Well, there were a couple of pretty heated kisses, but that's about it. He came right out and told me he's not sure how long he will be in town. I think he was trying to give me a chance to make up my mind about how far I wanted to let things progress with him."

Her friend made a face in disappointment. "Well, how long does he think he'll stick around?"

"To be honest, I'm not sure. I don't think he even knows for certain. He's been through so much recently. There's a part of him that's really struggling right now…" She gave her a brief version of what had happened to him and his partner.

"That poor man!"

"Suffice it to say, it's knocked him off kilter. I get the feeling he's at a crossroads in his life right now. I don't know if it would be fair of me to make things more complicated for him."

"Well, what about you? How do you feel about getting involved with someone temporarily?"

She stared down into her mug and pondered the question. "I don't know. When I'm around him, all I can think about is experiencing as much as I can with him and letting tomorrow sort itself out. On the other hand, it could open me up to a lot of heartache in the near future."

"True, but then again, any relationship has its risks. You don't get a guarantee when it comes to that kind of stuff."

"Exactly! Which is what makes me want to say, 'to hell with it' and just go for it."

"Especially if by 'it' you mean really hot, toe-curling sex with a hunky man."

Olivia laughed. "Right."

Jackie drummed her fingers on the counter and pondered the situation. After a moment, she sighed. "In all seriousness, Livvy, you're the only one who's going to know what's right for you. However, if I were in your shoes, I'd probably go with my instincts. Feel more, think less, and don't worry so much. You're young, have fun. Trust me, it's not every day a hot man comes along and wants to make your pulse sizzle."

Downing her coffee, she gave Jackie a hug, "Thanks. I'll think about it. But, for now I'm going to go back to the kitchen and see what Tom's up to."

Despite her best efforts, Olivia couldn't get Mason out of her head all morning. Unfortunately, her preoccupation kept leading to mixed tickets and incorrect orders. By the third incident, Tom's good mood had evaporated. He was his usual cantankerous self again, with some extra grumbling.

"Wheat toast! This plate gets the English muffin. Olivia, the eggs were supposed to be scrambled, not your brain. What's going on with you this morning?"

"Sorry, I guess I'm not all here right now."

He grunted. "Don't you have some bills or inventory you could be doing in the back office? I can handle the kitchen; it's not too busy."

She protested. "It's really not necessary. I'll get my head in the game."

"Please. I insist. I'll call you if I need you."

Reluctantly, she started to take her chef coat off. "Okay, but be sure to grab me if it gets too busy. I'll just be back in my office."

Spatula in hand, he gave her a final shooing motion and turned back to the griddle.

Olivia refilled her coffee mug before walking back to her office and shutting the door. How pathetic. One date left her this flustered? She knew she was out of practice, but still. She'd never been a simpering female before, and she would be damned if she'd start now.

Resolved to set the whole matter out of her head and get

something productive done, she turned to her books and started to fill out her next inventory order. Fifteen minutes later, there was a knock on the door.

Fiona poked her head in. "Hey, Jackie told me you were back here. Mind if I come in?"

"Not at all. You didn't have to work today?"

"I'm covering for Sarah this Saturday so she can go visit her grandchildren. She's taking today for me instead. So? How'd last night go? Did the dress make his eyes pop out?"

She laughed. "Oh yeah. It was perfect. I had a really good time last night."

Sensing she was holding back something, Fiona prodded her, "But…?"

"But, I'm not sure if there should be anything more than that." She put her head in her hands for a moment, and then looked back up. "Don't get me wrong, he's hot. When I'm with him, sparks fly. But, he also lives in Boston and is only here temporarily. Why set myself up to get hurt like that?"

"Have you thought about just enjoying the moment for what it is? Not everything has to be a long-term commitment."

"I've thought about it, but that's just the thing. I think I could really like this guy. I mean, other than his good looks, he's kind, considerate, funny, heroic…thoughtful. And, we have a lot of interests in common. I'm afraid if I let myself get close to him physically, I'll get too close emotionally. Then, when he's healed up, he'll be gone."

Concerned, Fiona asked, "I know you mentioned he was here recuperating, but is he really that badly injured?" Olivia explained the circumstances of what had brought him to town.

"Wow. That's pretty insane. Okay, so he's going through a tough time right now. I can see why you're hesitant…" She leaned over and put her hand on Olivia's shoulder, "but, you have to realize, no matter what, there are always going to be risks. Opening up, being vulnerable, that's a part of it. You can try to keep your-self safe emotionally, but you'll just end up keeping yourself alone. At some point, you're going to need to decide which way has the bigger risk."

"Have you and Jackie been reading the same books? You've both basically said the same thing to me this morning." She gave her sister a hug, "How did you get to be so wise?" She took a step back. "Thanks for your help. I think I'm going to set it aside for now. I'm tired of thinking about it."

Olivia turned back to her computer. "Besides, I should be concentrating on my plans for changing this little café into a fine dining experience during the evening. I'll probably need to hire at least one new employee to help cover the added shifts."

"How's that coming along?" Fiona said, allowing her to change the subject.

"Well, I've been trying a number of new recipes and experi-menting with flavors. I really want to source most of my produce from the local farms if I can. I came up with a really great crab cake recipe the other night."

"That's great. When are you thinking of having your 'Grand Opening?'"

"Probably after the holidays. I'm hoping I can find a way to consolidate the items on both menus to help defray costs. I'm also thinking about limiting the start of evenings to the weekend only. Kind of have it be a soft opening of sorts. Hopefully, it won't be too hard to adjust the atmosphere in the dining room for both purposes. I'll order some nice little candles and new linens to dress up the tables. I might have to close the restaurant for a week to repaint and hang some new art that can work for both night and day."

"Yeah, somehow I don't think the cheerful sunflower motif is going to cut it for a romantic evening atmosphere."

"Right. So, you can see, I still have a lot of things to work through. Really, the last thing I need is to get distracted by romance."

Fiona scoffed, "Oh, come on, Olivia. Now you're just hiding behind excuses. Lots of people manage to function and fall in love at the same time. There's no reason you can't do the same."

"Woah! Who said anything about falling in love? I've had one date with this guy. I'm just trying to keep things in perspective here. Maybe I do think he's interesting and charismatic. Who knows? Maybe I will have a fling with him. But, the fact is, in all likelihood, he's going to heal up and head back to Boston and I'm still going to be here. The café, and my goals for it, is still going to be here. My priority has to be here."

Sighing, her sister conceded the point. "Okay, but that's still no reason not to enjoy life and be open and willing to enjoy opportunities as they present themselves. You've always been the responsible one. It's time to have some fun."

"You make me sound like a stick in the mud. I have fun!"

"You know what I mean…" She got up and gave Olivia a hug. "Whatever you decide, I'm sure it will be right. Just try not to make your decisions based on fear."

"Thank you, Yoda. I'll be sure to keep your wise words in mind."

Laughing, Fiona left her sitting at her desk, pondering life and love, and wishing there was a recipe for it all.

Chapter Nineteen

That afternoon, Olivia got home and dropped her bag on the bench by the front door. She glanced around, feeling at odds with herself and not really sure what she was in the mood for.

Wandering into the living room, she sat down on the couch and picked up the remote control, but after clicking through a few channels, quickly turned it off again.

With a sigh, she grabbed the cooking magazine off the table and started to flip through it. Five minutes later, she realized that she'd been reading the same paragraph over and over again and still didn't know what it said. It was weird to hear the house so quiet.

Exasperated with herself, she finally stood and headed upstairs to her bedroom. "This is crazy. I just need to go for a run and clear my head. Maybe once I get rid of all this pent up energy, I can go back to thinking like a normal, rational woman."

Catching her reflection in the mirror, she grimaced. "Great, I'm even talking to myself like a crazy woman. Now all I need are a few dozen cats and I'll be all set."

Turning away, she pulled off her shirt and dug into her drawer for a sports bra. Suddenly, she heard something clatter and thud downstairs.

Her head jerked up and she froze. "Hello?" Craning her neck, she paused and listened. "Liz? Fiona? Are you down there?" Feeling vulnerable without a top on, she grabbed the first shirt on the pile and whipped it over her head.

Feeling a bit more confident, Olivia cautiously padded down the stairs, all the while straining to hear any more unusual sounds.

As she reached the bottom of the steps, she took a moment to scan the front entryway and poked her head into the living room. When she didn't notice anything out of place, she shook her head. "I'm getting as paranoid as Mason."

At that, she brushed off the eerie feeling and made her way into the kitchen to grab a glass of water…

And stopped.

There, on the kitchen island, were the mysterious flowers she'd received and placed in a vase. Their stems were all broken, blooms drooping down towards the counter, as if in mourning.

They reminded her of beautiful broken dolls with snapped necks.

Inhaling sharply, she quickly scanned the rest of the room. One of the stools by the kitchen island had fallen over and was lying on its side in the middle of the floor. That must be what she had heard a moment ago. Her pulse spiked. No way could that have tipped over on its own.

Alarms went off in her mind. Spinning around, Olivia darted back out towards the entryway, grabbed her purse, and lunged to unlock the front door, but halted just before running out of the house.

What if whoever broke into her house was still out there? She'd just heard that sound coming from the kitchen…they could be lying in wait for her right now, hoping she'll run out and into their arms. Carefully, she replaced the latch and peered out the window, trying to make out any figures in the late afternoon shadows, her mind racing with possibilities.

She'd just come from her room and master bathroom and

knew the upper level was safe. With that thought in mind, she changed course and sprinted up the stairs and through her room, and locked herself into the bathroom.

Fumbling through her bag, she quickly dug out her phone and dialed 911. While waiting for the cops to arrive, she shuddered to think that the whole time she'd been sitting in the living room someone must have been in her house, maybe even watching her.

That thought caused another full body shiver. A couple of minutes later, she was relieved to hear the sound of sirens gradually filtering into the room.

Thank goodness for small towns and their ability to respond quickly. Cautiously, she poked her head out of the bathroom before making her way to the front door to let the cops in.

After checking through the window, she opened the door and gave the officer a relieved smile. "Brad, or should I say Officer Brad? I'm so glad you're here."

"Hi, Olivia." Brad made his way into her house and gave her a brief, comforting hug before getting down to business. "We got a call that there was a break in at this address. I thought I remembered this was your home. Are you okay?"

"Yes, but someone else was definitely here." She quickly relayed what had happened.

"Let me take a look," he said, and made his way into the kitchen, stopping just inside the threshold. "Did you touch anything?"

"No, I just turned and ran. I didn't know what else to do."

He turned to look at her. "You did exactly right. You got yourself to a secure location and gave us a call."

Exhaling, she nodded. "It was only after I locked myself in the bathroom that I thought I should have grabbed one of the kitchen knives or something. I looked around up there, and all I could find for a weapon was a can of hairspray and a nail file."

He gave her a comforting pat on the arm. "We don't get too

many break-ins around here. I'll have a forensic team come in here and take a few fingerprints, see if we can find a match. In the meantime, why don't we go into the living room and take some notes for the report..."

"Olivia!"

The alarmed, frantic voice caused both Olivia and Brad's heads to swing towards the man standing in the doorway. "What's going on? Are you okay? Why is there a police cruiser outside with its lights on?"

"Everything's okay now. I had an intruder and was just about to answer a few questions..."

"An intruder?" Mason walked into the kitchen and took the scene in at a glance.

"I'm sorry, sir, don't step any further," Brad raised a hand to him, indicating he should stop.

Mason shot him a look. "I'm not going to contaminate your scene. I just wanted to take a look at what's going on in here."

She stepped between the two men and gently placed her hand on Mason's chest. "Brad, this is Mason Clark. He helped me out the other night when my car was run into a ditch. Mason, Brad and I went to high school together. He's the best cop we have in town."

At the introduction, he eased back slightly and took a position next to Olivia. Brad shook his hand. "Well, I don't know about the best, but I'd like to think I do a good job. You know how it is with small towns like this. You pretty much can't help running into a classmate or a cousin anywhere you go." He gave Olivia a fond look. "Some of them might be biased."

Mason nodded and turned to Olivia. "Have you filed your report yet?"

"We were just about to do so in the living room."

"Do you mind if I stick around?"

She shook her head. "I'd be glad if you did."

He gave her a reassuring look before once again addressing the officer. "I may have some information that might pertain to this, but I want to hear her version of events before mentioning anything further."

Curious, Brad nodded. "Well, okay, then. Let's get started."

As they all made their way into the living room she realized that Brad was nearly as tall as Mason was, she'd guess about 6'2." However, where Mason had broad shoulders and a solid chest, Brad was long and lanky. His legs practically folded in half as he sat down in her armchair.

She and Mason both took the couch, sitting close enough for their knees to touch. Once again, she described the events that had happened since she first came home. Mason's hand tightened when she got to the part about finding the vase of flowers on the kitchen island.

"And you say you don't know who gave you the flowers?" Officer Brad asked.

"No, they were just out on my car windshield when I got off of work this past week." She slid a look at him, then back to the officer. "Originally, I thought they'd come from Mason, but he was in Boston."

Brad focused on him. "I know you're new to this area. Is that where you're originally from?"

He nodded. "Actually, I'm a police detective with the Boston PD. I'm just up here for a short while to recover from an incident on the job."

A flash of recognition entered the other man's eyes. "Ah, right. I thought you looked familiar. That's a rough break. I'm sorry to hear about your partner."

Mason's eyes grew more shuttered, but he met Brad's look steadily. "I appreciate that. In fact, the incident here may have something to do with that."

Brad's face grew more serious. Olivia was startled to notice he had the same expression in his eyes as Mason's. It was a focused, direct, and shrewd gaze. She could see the heightened awareness in them as they regarded each other.

"The pattern she's describing, with the flowers and the note…"

Instantly, swinging his gaze back to her, Brad interjected, "There was a note?"

"Oh, yes. I'm sorry, I didn't mention it. I didn't think it was related to this."

"Do you still have it?" At Olivia's apologetic look, he turned back to Mason. "Okay, go on."

"Well, the pattern is the same as we saw before, on the stalker case my partner and I were working on when we both got shot."

"So, you're afraid this isn't due to some punk kids in the neighborhood and that it's somehow related to your previous incident?"

Exasperated by the other officer's dubious tone, he ran a hand through his hair. "Look, I know how it sounds. If I were in your shoes, I'd be thinking I was paranoid, too.

"But there's something that doesn't sit right with me about all of this. And the timing… I keep thinking I missed something, and I've got an itch in the back of my neck. My instincts are telling me something's wrong."

Brad gave him a long, assessing look, and closed his notebook. "Okay, we'll keep a close eye on this situation. I'll see if we can get any fingerprints from the kitchen and, if so, we'll check it against your guy. If it's a match, we'll have something to work with. Unfortunately, that's all I can do for now. I'm not saying I question your instincts, but they aren't proof."

She watched resignation and relief war on Mason's face. Brad got up from the chair, causing them to stand as well. "Be on the lookout, Olivia, and pay special attention to your surroundings. Regardless of whether or not this is the same guy, it's obvious that you have caught the attention of someone willing to break into your home to make contact."

She shuddered as his words hit their mark. He continued, "Make sure to replace the lock on that door, but not until after my team gets here. In fact, you should probably replace all the locks and add a few deadbolts while you're at it. Who knows? He may have found a spare key while in your house."

"I will. I can't thank you enough for getting here so quickly." She walked him to the front door.

He turned to Mason and shook his hand. "I'll keep you in the loop as a professional courtesy and let you know if we get a match. I'm assuming you're still in contact with Boston and keeping tabs on the search for the asshole that shot you and your partner. If you come across any new information from your department, I'd appreciate you returning the favor. Especially if it turns out he's on my turf."

"You have my word."

Satisfied, Brad cast Olivia a final smile before heading out the door. "Take care of our girl."

She closed the door after he left and stood there for a moment, taking the afternoon's events in. Sensing Mason's presence behind her, she leaned back into him, his arms wrapping comfortingly around her shoulders.

She just stood in the foyer for a moment and soaked in the relief he provided by just being there. This event had been completely out of the realm of her experience and she was grateful to have someone help her navigate through the situation.

"You really think this has to do with that guy, Robert Mendez?"

She felt him put his chin on top of her head and squeeze her tighter. "I don't know. I'm afraid to think it might. No matter what, I'm not going to let anything happen to you. Whether it's him or some other jerk who thinks he can come in here after you."

At that, she turned in his arms and faced him. "Why'd you stop by, anyway? I don't remember making plans…" She threaded her fingers through the hair at the nape of his neck.

"Oh? Can't a guy just stop by and see how your day went?"

"Yeah, I suppose," she gave a little shrug. "I'm just not used to it."

"Well," Mason's voice lowered as he bent his head down. "Maybe you should get used to it." With that, his firm lips captured hers and he pulled her even tighter against his body.

Everything else that had happened fled her mind as she let the sensation of his kiss wash over her. His tongue traced the seam of her lips, silently asking for passage. With a sigh, she opened her mouth to his, thrilling as he probed the deep recesses.

A warm ache quickly began to spread between her thighs as she pictured him delving into even more intimate depths. With a groan, he raised his head at the knock on the door behind her.

"That must be the forensics team."

"Huh?" He looked down at her and cast a satisfied – supremely male – look at her bewildered expression. "Get the door, Olivia. I think the forensic team is waiting to be let in."

"Oh, right." She raised cool fingers to her overheated cheeks, gave her head a quick shake to clear it, and then turned around to let the gentleman in. Her lips felt swollen by his kiss, and she was sure she probably looked flustered.

She left the cop to do his work after showing him the way to the kitchen. Five minutes later, she ended a phone call with the town's only locksmith and walked back into the living room where Mason was standing by the window.

"Well, the locksmith says he can't come in to install the new locks until tomorrow. I think I'll call Liz and see if I can stay with her tonight."

He turned to her. "Don't do that. Didn't you say she lives in a one bedroom apartment over her shop? Why don't you come with me and stay at the bed and breakfast? My sister has plenty of rooms and I'm sure she won't mind."

He raised his hands as she cast him a long look. "No pressure. Whatever we have between us, I want to let it happen naturally."

He walked towards her and wrapped his arms around her waist. "However, I also want you to be safe. There's no reason for you to sleep on a couch when there are six perfectly good empty beds up at the house."

She gave him a tentative smile. "You're right. As long as you don't think Melody will mind."

"Are you kidding me? She'll be glad to have company that's not her grumpy brother, I'm sure."

"Okay, let me just go upstairs and pack a bag real quick. I should probably drive my own car so I can open the café tomorrow morning."

"Alright, I'll stick around here and leave with you. I'm guessing it won't take that guy very long to finish up in the kitchen. Then we can head out."

With a final hug, she pulled away from his arms and climbed the stairs while he got on the phone to call his sister and let her know to expect a guest for the night.

Chapter Twenty

Olivia quickly grabbed her overnight duffel, her last pair of clean jeans, a t-shirt for work the next day, the usual pajama pants and cotton tee she wore to bed, her toiletries from the bathroom…and then paused. She glanced back at her dresser and considered.

Quickly, before she could change her mind, she put her perfectly serviceable pajama pants back in the drawer and grabbed the silky, sexy nightie Fiona had gotten for her a few Christmases ago, one that she'd never worn. When she'd tried it on, it had come to about mid-thigh and the burnished gold had done great things for her eyes, but it had seemed silly to wear just for herself, and there hadn't been anyone since.

Trying not to overanalyze her actions too closely, she zipped her bag up with more determination than she really felt. She glanced around her room with a wistful sigh. She'd never felt unsafe in her home before, and didn't like that she didn't feel comfortable enough to stay the night.

This house had been their family's warm, welcoming nest during the good times growing up. It had also been their safe harbor through all the tough times after her parent's death.

A surge of raw anger filled her. She would be damned if whoever was behind this would ruin her family's foundation. She would install new locks, and even get a security system if she had to, but she was NOT going to be made to feel unsafe in her home like this. Never again.

Fortified with resolution, she grabbed her bag, turned off the light, and headed down the stairs.

"Are you ready?" Mason asked, as he got up from the couch.

"Yeah. I really hate feeling like I'm being forced to leave my house because of this jerk."

He wrapped his arms around her shoulders and held her comfortingly. "I know. Just think of this as a little mini-vacation. People pay good money to stay at Melody's bed and breakfast, y'know."

She offered him a tepid smile, and squared her shoulders, "You're right. I'm grateful. Are you sure she doesn't mind?"

"Are you kidding? She was thrilled. It means she's going to have better company than just her older brother." He winked, and grabbed her bag. "Is this it?"

At her nod, he headed towards the door. "Have you called your sisters yet, to let them know what happened?"

"Not yet. I was going to do that when I got up to your place."

"I think it's a good idea. The sooner the better. This guy probably won't be showing up again today, but just in case, I wouldn't want them to stop by and not know what was going on."

A chill raced down her spine and she felt dread land like an iron ball in the pit of her stomach. "Oh jeez, you're right. I can't believe I didn't think of that. I was so focused on not worrying them, it didn't even cross my mind I could be putting them into danger."

He cast a look back over his shoulder at her as they both walked out to their vehicles. "No need to panic. Like I said, the guy is probably not going to show up again tonight. I'm sure calling them when you get to Melody's will be soon enough." He opened her car door and tossed her bag into the back.

She climbed into her seat and smiled when he ducked down to give her a quick kiss before shutting the door and making his way to the truck. Despite his assurances, the first thing she did was put her earpiece in and call Liz.

"What? What do you mean some guy broke into the house?!"

"I'm okay, Liz. I'm going to be staying up at the bed and breakfast tonight."

"You're a lot calmer than I would be, I can tell you that."

"Oh, trust me, I'm pretty shaken up. There were definitely some hairy moments while I was sitting, locked in the bathroom, waiting for the cops to arrive. I'll admit it, I'm still freaking out a little bit."

"I bet. I'm glad you're not staying in that house tonight, Livvy."

"Me too. It kills me to say it, but I wouldn't want to be there alone." She sighed. "I don't know what to do about this. The whole situation feels so unreal. Who would have thought I could have a stalker? Can you believe it?"

"I'm sure that's what every woman who has ever had to go through this has thought at one point. We have to take this matter seriously. What does Mason say about it?"

"He's being incredibly supportive, but I think he's pretty shaken up, too. He's convinced himself this is the guy from his previous case."

"Really? Do you think he's right?"

She glanced in her rearview mirror at the old sedan behind her, "I don't know. A part of me would like to think he's wrong and this is all just a carryover from his earlier trauma...but, that doesn't seem like Mason. From everything I've read, he was really good at his job and he seems to have good instincts. It's hard to say."

"Well, I suppose, it doesn't really matter, does it? No matter what, you need to stay safe. You said you have new locks getting installed tomorrow?"

"Yeah, I'll have to make sure you and Fiona get a new key. I'm also going to look into security systems, so there may also be a code needed to get into the house."

"Whatever it takes. I'm glad you're okay. You want me to call Fiona and let her know what's going on?"

"That'd be great. I'll call you again tomorrow."

Fifteen minutes later, she parked alongside Mason's truck and grabbed her bag. Melody was already standing at the door to greet them.

"Hello, again. Welcome." She gave Olivia a quick hug. "I know you've had a rough day, but tonight, I want you to think of yourself as a guest. Here, let me get your bag."

Mason walked up behind her. "Thanks, Mel, I've got it. What room did you put her in?"

"I made up the Harvest Room for her." Olivia remembered the room. She had admired its warm, autumnal color scheme. She also recalled its position directly across the hall from the Hunter Room — Mason's room. Apparently her sisters weren't the only ones trying to play matchmaker.

"Thank you so much for taking me in."

"Really, it's no problem. I have a rosemary chicken roasting in the oven for dinner that I couldn't possibly have eaten myself, anyway. I don't know why, but it just sounded too good to pass up. I'm glad you're here to help us, or we'd be eating leftovers for a week."

Melody led her into the front living room, and they sat down on the couch. Olivia noticed she'd already opened a bottle of red wine and had it breathing in the decanter. Wine glasses stood beside the beautiful, crystal container, waiting at the ready.

She could learn a thing or two about hospitality from Melody, she thought, as she sank into the plush cushions. Mason returned and sat in the armchair beside her. Together, they relayed that afternoon's events.

"And, you have no idea who it could possibly be?"

"I don't," she cast a glance at him, before continuing, "Mason said he thinks it may be the guy they were investigating earlier, but I have my doubts."

Alarmed, Melody turned to her brother, "Do you really think it could be him?"

He shifted in his seat, uncomfortable under both women's scrutiny. He rubbed his hand on his neck and shrugged. "To be honest, I don't know. I'm trying not to jump to any conclusions." He looked up and pinned Olivia with his gaze. "However, there are some very real similarities to this and other cases I've worked on involving Mendez. Plus, something about the timing has me uncomfortable." He looked back at his sister. "I've got a bad feeling, Melody. When I get a feeling like this, it very rarely leads to something good."

Somberly, she nodded her head and took a sip of wine. "Well, I've known you long enough to trust your instincts, even when you don't fully trust them yourself. So, we'll err on the side of caution and keep an extra eye on Olivia here."

With that, she got up and headed towards the kitchen. "I'm going to finish making dinner. Why don't you two relax here for a bit? Sounds like you both could use a little downtime. Olivia, do you remember where the Harvest Room is?"

At her assurances that she did, Melody excused herself. Silence filled the air between them. Olivia twirled and fiddled with her wine stem while Mason brooded. Finally, she couldn't stand the quiet and looked up. "I wasn't trying to imply that you don't know what you're doing, or that I don't trust your judgment. I think I'm just really hoping you're wrong. Do you truly think it could be this guy?"

He took a moment and thought about the question. "I know there isn't any proof, but, yes, I think it could be." He leaned forward. "Even if it's not, it doesn't matter. You have a guy out there who's willing to break into your home, and – judging by the way those flower stems were snapped – he doesn't seem to be too pleased with you at the moment."

Throughout the evening, despite the delicious meal and the efforts Melody had gone through to make sure she was comfortable, Mason's words kept ringing in Olivia's mind. Shortly before nine, citing the fact that she had to wake up early in the morning, she excused herself and headed to bed.

However, even the charming room and comfortable bed weren't enough to calm her thoughts. Slowly, she watched as the numbers on the bedside clock ticked later and later. It was almost surprising the ceiling didn't have two holes in it where she'd been staring at it all night. Finally, exasperated, she got up and put on the robe that Melody had left hanging from the bathroom door.

Quietly, she slipped from her room and padded down the hallway, wincing as the stairs creaked at her passing. Hopefully, the sound didn't disturb anybody.

A small, dim hall lamp had been left on in the entryway to light the way. Olivia carefully picked through the shadows and made her way into the kitchen, hoping that a cup of tea would help calm her enough to sleep.

She flipped the light on and grabbed the kettle off the burner. As she stood at the faucet filling it up, she stared out past her reflection and into the night, thinking about the events of the last day.

This whole experience was completely beyond the scope of anything she'd had to deal with before. She'd never been one to attract a lot of attention. Her beautiful sister, Fiona, caught people's notice more often.

But her? She was the one in the ratty clothes, sweating over a hot stove in the back of the café. What could this guy possibly see that caused him to fixate on her?

For that matter, what could have caught Mason's attention? Granted, it was a far more welcome kind of attention, but this was the most she'd received of either kind in ages, both wanted and unwanted.

Olivia sighed and turned to place the kettle on the hot burner. She admitted to herself, a part of her wished she could go back to her quiet existence before all this stuff had started…

Just then, a pair of hands was placed gently on her shoulders. Yelping, she quickly turned to find Mason standing before her in a pair of sweatpants and a t-shirt. She noticed his hair was mussed up again.

"Aah! You scared me!" she admonished, heart racing. She fought the urge to sweep the hair back from his forehead.

"Can't sleep?"

She turned around and pulled the whistling kettle off the stove. "Sadly, no. I think I'm just too wound up after what happened today. Care to join me for some tea? It's herbal, so there's no caffeine."

At his nod, she moved away and reached up, grabbing two mugs from the cupboard. "Sugar?"

She could feel his regard following her as she bustled around the kitchen, but didn't feel quite ready to meet his eyes. "Olivia."

At the sound of her name, she stopped. Once again, she found herself looking at her reflection above the kitchen sink window. Quietly, he walked up behind her. They looked good together. The errant thought crossed her mind before he turned her towards him.

He pinned her with his gaze. "I'm not going to let anything happen to you." He ran his fingers carefully through the hair at her temples, massaging her scalp, and tilted her head up to him.

Yearning filled her and she leaned into his body, silently pleading with him to make her forget to be afraid. Slowly, with his eyes trained on hers, he lowered his head and brushed his lips against hers.

Back and forth, once, twice…

Impatiently, desperately, she craned her neck up and opened

her mouth for a deeper kiss. With a groan, he complied, sucking her under his spell and silencing all the bothersome thoughts that had kept her awake.

Backing her up to the kitchen sink, he pressed the full length of his body against hers. She could feel his arousal through the thin barrier of his sweats and ground her achy, needy core against him.

As the kiss deepened, one of his hands released her hair and cupped her breast through the terry cloth robe, squeezing with just enough pressure to make her squirm. He broke off the kiss and trailed his lips down the slim column of her neck, while his clever fingers began to release the sash around her waist.

With a growl, he lifted his head when he discovered the silky material beneath. Olivia could see the passion burning in his eyes. She shivered along the path his finger made as he traced the lacy border of her chemise, her skin breaking out in goosebumps with his faint touch.

He followed the strap up, across her collarbone and dragged it down, bending his head as he did so and kissing the sensitive spot where her neck and shoulder met. Gradually, his mouth made his way down to the slope of her breast, where the garment tenuously clung to her skin.

Panting, she arched her back, her nipple thrusting up through the flimsy fabric, begging for attention. His hot breath stoked her passion, as she felt the tip of his tongue dip beneath the edge, exposing her breast to his mouth. He wrapped his lips around the tip and gently nipped it with his teeth before sucking it into his mouth.

She could feel the tug all the way down to the juncture of her thighs. Silky, liquid heat pooled at her core. Her whole body ached to be filled.

Abruptly, a car alarm came alive in the darkness beyond, it's wailing sound screaming for attention. Startled, she jerked, her breast popping from his mouth. They both looked up and out into the pitch black, straining to see beyond their reflections in the window.

"Stay here," he commanded gruffly, his voice hoarse and roughened with desire. Nodding, she hastily pulled the strap of her nightgown up and quickly wrapped the robe around her.

With a regretful glance at the very rumpled Olivia, he released her and dashed out the door into the night.

The car siren rang in his ears, spurring him to move faster. His bare feet took the brunt of his sprint as the asphalt from the driveway scraped into his heels and soles. Warm breath streamed from his mouth as he quickly rounded Olivia's car. No one was there.

Frustrated, he spun around and stared out into the darkness beyond the pool of light the front porch fixture provided. In the distance, he could hear an engine start. Twin headlights speared the darkness farther down the slope.

The bastard must have parked just at the mouth of the driveway, he thought, as the car beside him chirped twice and the alarm cut off. Silence filled the atmosphere around him, nearly as deafening as the sirens had been a moment ago.

Mason glanced back at the house and noticed that both his sister and Olivia stood in the doorway, silhouetted from behind by the hall light. If anything happened to either one of them...

Quickly, he shut that train of thought down. "Stay in the house. I'm going to see if he managed to do any damage."

"Here." Melody called out to him. "Take the flashlight."

With a nod, Mason bounded up the steps and grabbed the light from his sister. "Thanks." He looked down at Olivia and noticed the way she had her arms wrapped tightly around her waist. She looked so young and innocent wearing the fluffy, white robe with her hair flowing loose down her back.

He couldn't resist dropping a kiss on the crown of her head before slipping on his shoes and heading back outside. This time, he tried to take care where he stepped and watched the ground closely for any signs of their intruder.

It was difficult to spot anything on the driveway's blacktop. There certainly weren't any footprints that he could see in the dim light. He jogged down the length of the driveway, ignoring the way his lungs twinged as he inhaled the cold air. He hoped there might be tire treads out by the entrance, since the shoulder of the road was just dirt.

Unfortunately, when he reached the place he'd seen the lights turn on, he noticed the ground was too frozen to have been impacted by whatever vehicle had been there. Shivering and frustrated, he ran his hands through his hair and stared down the road into the empty distance.

After Mason walked back to the house, he slowly circled Olivia's car for the third time that evening, this time checking for damage to the actual vehicle and not just for clues around it. He noticed the vehicle leaned drunkenly to one side, and got down on his knees to inspect the tires a little closer. Just as he suspected, they had been slashed.

With a resigned sigh, he got up from the ground and jogged back towards the two women waiting for him.

"Anything?" Olivia asked.

He shook his head. "He did a number on your tires, but other than that, it looks like the ground was too hard to get any kind of indentations. Looks like I'm driving you to the café in the morning. We'll also call Brad tomorrow and let him know what happened. There isn't much he can do for us tonight."

They all walked back into the entryway, Mason shutting and locking the door behind them. His sister let out a breath and looked first at Olivia, then Mason. "Well, I think it's safe to say somebody is determined to get to you. So, what do we do?"

"I'm so sorry... I had no idea it would come to this. I never would have come here if I thought it would be putting you in danger."

Her bruised, haunted look bothered him more than anything else had leading up to that point, and he wrapped his arm around her shoulders, hugging her closer to his body.

Melody rolled her eyes and quickly reassured her new friend. "Nonsense. It was better that it happened here where we could help you out, rather than down at your house. I can't imagine how much more terrifying this whole experience would have been if you'd been alone."

She continued, "The question is, what are we going to do about it? I think it's fair to say that this whole situation is unsustainable. Obviously, you're going to want to have your house back at some point. Mason? Do you have any ideas?"

He felt the attention of both women turn to him. "Well, unfortunately, each state has its own set of stalking laws. I'm going to have to do some research and see what the state of Maine has to say on the matter. I also think it's important for us to keep a healthy, working relationship with the local PD here, and make sure they're aware of every incident. It will help to have a record of everything that has occurred if this ends up going to court."

He directed his attention to Olivia. "It helps that you and the officer assigned to the case already know each other and have a friendship. I'm hoping that will make it easier to include me and keep me in the loop as things develop."

"As far as whether or not this is Mendez—gut instincts aside— I know technically speaking it's too early to say. However, you know I've been keeping track of the investigation down in Boston and they've been keeping me informed of any new developments."

The three of them stood there in the foyer and looked at each other for a split second, each of them lost in their thoughts and thinking about the ramifications of the night's events.

"Well," Melody finally said, coming back to the present, "I

doubt there's going to be any more excitement tonight, and there really isn't anything else to be done right now. The best thing we can do is try to get some sleep and tackle the whole situation in the morning."

Olivia nodded, her eyes straying towards Mason before quickly gliding away again. Her cheeks took on a slight blush. The recent stolen moments they'd shared seemed so long ago in the wake of everything that had happened. They all headed back upstairs, Melody saying her good nights as she continued up to her own private quarters.

Silently, they both stood awkwardly across the hallway from each other, remembering the passion that had occurred in the kitchen. Their gazes held the knowledge of where they were headed before they'd been interrupted.

"Well…good night." she said, slowly turning the knob on her door.

"Olivia…wait," She turned back to face him. "Listen," he took a step towards her, but stopped as she shifted slightly away. "I meant what I said earlier about keeping you safe. I'm not going to let anything happen to you."

Hesitantly, she nodded. "I'm just not sure I should get you or Melody any more involved in this messy situation. I can't tell you how terrible I'd feel if something were to happen to either of you."

He raised his hand and gently traced the side of her face, wishing he could bridge the gap between them and gather her into his arms. However, he sensed she was feeling overwhelmed by everything that had happened and was holding herself back.

Reminding himself to go slow, he let his hand drop. "What time should we leave for you to open the café tomorrow?"

"Oh! Probably no later than 5:30." Olivia gave a little wince at the thought of having to get up so early.

With a groan of commiseration, he glanced down at his watch.

"Well, then, I guess we should get some rest. I have a feeling it's going to come a lot earlier than either of us wants."

With a thin ghost of a smile, she cracked her door open and slipped inside, but before she closed herself in, she stopped. "Mason?"

Pausing, he looked back at her. "Thank you. I really appreciate you helping me out with this situation tonight and earlier today."

He nodded and watched as she shut the door, the click of the latch sounding final in the now silent hall.

Well, hell, he thought. Not exactly the way he was hoping this night would have ended. With a sigh, he let himself into his room and fell back into the bed. Tomorrow was going to be a long day.

Chapter Twenty-One

Robert sat in the shadows and huddled deeper into the collar of his jacket. He stomped his feet and blew on his gloved fingers, trying to get feeling back into his hands and feet.

This afternoon had been too close. He knew he shouldn't have lingered over the photo albums in the office, but they'd been too tempting to resist.

He couldn't believe it when he'd heard her walk through the front door. It was only his quick reflexes that had caused him to dive under the desk. And what if she had come back to her office to work on her menu items?

He'd found the file of recipes she had left strewn on the top of her desk, along with all sorts of useful information in the drawers, such as bank accounts, social security numbers…it had been a gold mine.

Ohhh, but to be able to watch her relaxing on the couch like that! Completely unaware that she was being observed through the French doors. The arch of her bare foot as she'd stretched her leg out onto the table…he'd nearly been overcome by the need to stroke her there.

Now, light from the kitchen window spilled out into the darkness around him. His pulse quickened as Olivia came into view. He watched as she stood there and stared out into the night. It was as if they were connected on a deeper level and she could sense his presence.

Instantly, the hours of waiting in the cold for just a glimpse of her all became worth it. His eyes eagerly soaked in the image of her framed in the golden glow of the window. It was almost as if she was an otherworldly being. An angel, sent down to Earth to save him.

Right as the thought crossed his mind, another figure stepped up behind her. He watched as the other man's hands came down on her shoulders, possessively, turning her towards him. Furious, he stared as their lips met.

Damn them! Damn them! Robert's hands shook in rage as he watched the two of them kissing. The light became a sharp, piercing spotlight for the act, as if they were blatantly mocking him.

He watched as the little tramp's robe slipped from her shoulder. Oh, that bitch was going to pay for her infidelity. In fact, he would enjoy showing her just what to expect when she crossed him.

His stomach clenched as he watched Olivia's head drop back, that pig of a cop slowly making his way down the column of her slender neck.

Why? Why couldn't she have just taken the hint from the flowers earlier? Why did all women insist on being such whores? Even his own mother had been a failure.

He dropped his head into his hands before raising it again to the scene in the window. He'd had such high hopes for this one, but he should have known better. Instead, she was just like all the rest of them.

Maybe he just needed to get his hands on her. He could teach her the lesson she obviously needed. He could make her learn how to be a lady. Make her yearn to live up to his exacting standards.

The darkness that was always there inside him began to roil and writhe in his breast. Visions of himself carving through that silky soft skin filled his mind and his fingers ached to do damage.

He wanted to penetrate her in as many ways as possible. He wanted her to see red just like he did when he watched her with another man.

He wanted her to pay.

Feeling the need to lash out, he quickly dug through the pack he always carried with him and fished out the knife he kept there. Then, with a final glance at the activity in the window to spur him on, he slunk through the shadows towards her car.

Robert carved out his anger in black rubber. As he made the first slashes to her tires, he imagined it was her flesh he was transforming to his will.

Chapter Twenty-Two

Olivia's alarm clock began its incessant beeping entirely too early for her taste. Bleary-eyed, she automatically tried to hit the snooze button, only it wasn't in its usual place. Confused, she lifted her head, and only then remembered she was not in her familiar bedroom, but staying at Melody's bed and breakfast.

With a groan, she dragged herself out of bed and across the room to where the alarm clock continued its harassment. All of the previous night's events came rushing back to her, including the fact that she wouldn't be able to drive herself into work because her tires were, once again, out of commission.

Stumbling into the bathroom, she briefly debated taking a shower before deciding to simply splash cold water on her face. After brushing her teeth, and slipping into her worn, but clean, work clothes, she opened the door to her room.

Mason's door across the hallway was firmly shut, and she wondered how he'd slept the previous night. She shivered. Not everything about last night was a bad memory. Who knew? If they hadn't been interrupted, she may have found herself slipping out of his room this morning.

She lightly jogged down the stairs and into the kitchen,

surprised and relieved to find the aroma of coffee greeting her in the entryway.

"I hunted up a couple of travel mugs for us to use on the way into town," Mason said, hearing her enter the room. "You take yours black, right?"

Eagerly, she reached for the mug and inhaled deeply. "I do, thank you. This is a lifesaver."

"I take it this morning was rough for you, too?"

Nodding, she rolled her eyes and took her first tentative sip. Mason smiled, watching her. "Careful. It's still hot. You have all your things packed?"

"Yeah. I left the bag in the foyer. Thank you for taking me in this morning. I know it's a pain at this early hour."

He shrugged. "I don't mind. Besides, it will give me a chance to get an early start on my day. I'd like to go talk to Brad and make sure he adds last night's vandalism to his file of events."

"Okay, that makes sense."

"I'll also call your sister and arrange to have your car picked up."

"Oh, you don't have to do that."

"Really, it's okay. I don't mind," He walked up to where she was standing and gently wrapped his arms around her. "It's not like I have a lot on my schedule, at the moment. I want to help." He bent down and gave her a kiss. "Let me do this for you."

She took a moment, curving her body against him, relishing his strength and the feeling of having someone willing to help carry the weight of a bad situation. "Okay. Thank you, I could use the help."

"Good." He glanced over at the clock on the stove. "We need to get going if you're going to be there on time."

The two of them climbed up into the cab of his truck and sat in silence on the way into town, neither one of them awake enough to make decent conversation. She thought it was nice that they could be comfortable enough not to break the quiet between them.

The world outside had taken on a slate gray appearance, and there were frost crystals fringing the windows of parked cars. She'd heard another cold front was supposed to be coming through that day, and already, she could feel the temperature take on an edgy bite.

"You can just turn into the back lot," Olivia directed absently. "I usually let myself in through the back door. Jackie or Becky will unlock the front doors closer to opening."

Mason nodded at her direction and pulled into the lot. "Why don't I come in with you and make sure everything is okay?"

"Oh, that won't be necessary. Tom's car is already here." With that, Olivia opened the door to hop out of the cab, but he reached over and touched her elbow.

"Hey."

She turned towards him with a question in her eyes. That is, until he snagged her lips with his, giving her a deep kiss and setting her senses instantly alert. Dazed, she looked up at him. "Have a good day."

Giving him a quick nod, she jumped out of the cab with a smile dawning on her lips. "You, too."

She could feel him wait for her to let herself in before he took off.

"Hey, Tom. You're here early."

"Not too early, boss. Just got here."

"Um, Olivia? Can you come here for a second? There's something I think you need to see…"

Surprised by the odd tone she could hear in her friend's voice, she headed into the dining room to where Jackie was staring out the windows.

"Hey, you don't usually get here until just before opening. What are you doing here so early…?" Her question trailed off as she caught sight of the bright red paint splashed all across the windows. "What the hell?"

"Whore!"

"Slut!"

"Bitch!"

The vulgar words shouted to the public from her windows, screaming out into the frozen dawn.

Aghast, she strode out the front door, but could do nothing but stare at the words for a minute. Her mind reeled from the shock of such terrible vandalism.

Jackie joined her outside and put an arm around her. "Sweetie, do you have any idea who could have done something like this?"

Numbly, she nodded her head, her hand to her mouth. Quickly, she recounted the events from the previous day and last night, along with Mason's suspicions of who may be behind them.

She allowed herself the luxury of another moment to wallow in the shock, and then squared her shoulders. "Well, we obviously can't leave it like this. I'll go get a bucket of water and some scrapers. Jackie, you finish getting the dining room ready, and tell Tom he's unfortunately going to have to get the prep done on his own."

"Are you sure, Livvy? We could have him do the windows for you, so you don't have to look at it."

She looked directly into Jackie's eyes, her gaze blazing with fury. "Oh no. I'm going to look directly at it, and stare and stare at it while I clean it off. Up until this point, I've been feeling timid and scared by whoever is doing this. First my home, now the café? No more. Now, he's just managed to piss me off."

"Well, okay! Don't let this asshole cow you. I'll try to hurry up and then come out to help." With a final hug, she ran back into the kitchen to let Tom know what had happened.

Wrapping her arms tightly around herself, she shivered and stood looking at the writing. Then, with a resolved look, she lifted her head and went inside to grab a bucket.

Forty-five minutes later, she was just wiping off the last of the red paint along the doorway. She had worked like a demon, rushing to get the filthy language removed before the rest of the town had a chance to wake up and see it. She would be damned before she'd let that happen.

Watery, red paint had dripped everywhere; down her arms, on the back of her neck, all along the front of her…she even had it in her hair! With a look of distaste, she glanced at her reflection in the now clean windows and grimaced. Her arms, neck and shoulders all ached from the strain of scrubbing above her head.

Plus, despite the fact that she'd refilled her bucket multiple times with warm water, she'd quickly started shivering in the frigid morning air.

"Isn't it a little cold to be cleaning your windows, Olivia Harper?"

At the older woman's voice, she let out a squeal and spun around. "Mrs. Crowley! You startled me!"

The older woman gave her a shrewd once-over, "What's going on here? Don't you know better than to be washing your windows in freezing temperatures like this? And why are you covered in all that red stuff?"

She sighed and barely stopped herself from running her dirty hands through her hair. "Oh, I'm sure it's nothing, just some kids playing pranks." She gathered up the bucket and dirty cloths she'd been using. "Do you mind getting the door for me, Mrs. Crowley?"

Obliging, she exclaimed, "A prank? You have to be kidding me. Kids these days…I tell you what, they ought to be bent over somebody's knee and taught a lesson!" Olivia walked her to the usual booth and, after giving her a weary nod, left her muttering about the way things used to be.

With a nod to Jackie, she headed back to the bathroom to clean up before more people came in asking questions. Thankfully, she'd managed to get the front windows cleaned before she had to open.

A few hours later, Becky slipped in the back door, looking for her.

"Olivia?"

"Becky, I didn't think you were working today."

The younger woman stepped all the way into the kitchen. "Well, I'm not. Actually, I wasn't planning on coming in at all today."

"Oh? What's up, then? Everything okay?"

"Do you pay attention to the online review sites at all?"

She cast a quick glance over her shoulder and shot Becky a puzzled look. "Well, I don't know if I would say I keep track of them, but I know about the sites you're talking about…."

"Well, I'm on them pretty regularly. I like to write reviews and there are some pretty entertaining ones. Most of the time, I'll also check for the Three Sisters Cafe while I'm at it and just see what's being said.

"Olivia, somebody left some really nasty reviews last night. Not just on one or two, either. They took the time to post to all of the sites, under multiple profiles."

"What?!" She flipped the pancake she was working on before it burned, but she could feel her hands begin to shake. "What kind of things? What do you mean by nasty?"

"Well, things like they got food poisoning by eating here and that there were cockroaches that could be seen scurrying in the corners and down the hall."

Tom and Olivia looked at each other with weighted expressions. "Why? Why would someone be doing this? Tom, could you…?"

Nodding, he took the spatula from Olivia's hand. "I can handle it here. Go see what she's talking about."

With a grateful smile, she turned back to the younger woman. "Come back to my office with me. I need you to show me."

Fifteen minutes later, Becky cast her a final apologetic look before leaving. Sitting in her old, beat-up office chair, she shook with fury as she read the slanderous reviews before checking the contact and posting policies for each website, and sending off emails to the webmasters. She didn't hold out much hope, though. Who knew what they could do, when they'd get to it, or whether they would even try to discover the truth?

Wearily, she dropped her head down into her hands and contemplated the consequences of the damage this attack would cause. This was her livelihood. Her very reputation as a chef was being called into question and decimated by the whim of…who? Some madman? Some sicko who had decided she was his? How could something like this happen in this day and age? More importantly, what – if anything – was she going to be able to do to fix it?

Keeping that thought in mind, she opened a new window in her browser and began looking up "State of Maine stalking laws." Just as she was about to click the first link, a light knock interrupted her.

"Yes?"

Jackie poked her head in the doorway. "Becky told me what happened before she left. I know it's already been a rough day, but unfortunately, I don't see it getting any better…"

Closing the browser, she sighed. "What is it?"

"Health inspector is here to do a surprise inspection."

Well, the hits just keep on coming. She stood up and straightened her chef's jacket, thankful that the jacket at least covered up most of the red stains she'd gotten on her shirt earlier. "Okay, I'll be right out."

Her friend put a hand on her shoulder and gave it a squeeze. "Hang in there, Livvy. You and I, we've gone through worse times than this. We'll get through this one, just the same as all the others."

Encouraged by the thought, Olivia thanked her and made her way down the hall to greet the pale, tweedy man waiting for her at the breakfast counter.

Of course, two hours later, he still hadn't found anything. At his disappointed look, she was almost tempted to feel badly for him. Almost…except that he'd gotten more and more determined as the time had gone on. Now, she was not only exhausted, but had also run late enough that she'd been forced to reschedule her appointment with the locksmith for later in the afternoon.

One spot of good news was that Liz had called and let her know that her tires had once again been replaced and her car was ready to be picked up. As she was closing the café and saying her good-byes to the health inspector, Mason walked through the front door and gave her a hug.

Gently, he bent down and dropped a kiss on her lips, before handing her a latte. "Thought you might need this. How was it today?"

With a sigh, she told him about her day. It was still hard to believe someone had actually gone through all the trouble of creating multiple profiles and posting to so many review sites. Whoever was after her was determined to make her life hell.

"I'm sorry this is happening to you. I hate to think I may have been the one to bring his attention to you…"

"This guy's sickness, assuming it is actually him, is not your fault, Mason."

"Still, if you don't mind, I'd like to follow you back to your place after I drop you off to pick up your car. I want to be there when the locksmith comes in to install the new locks."

She locked the back door and followed him out to his truck, "That actually works out well. All I can think about doing right now is getting out of these paint-stained clothes and taking a shower, but I don't want to do that in the house without new locks. Would you mind standing guard while I get myself cleaned up before the guy comes?"

"Sure, I can do that."

As they pulled up to the garage, she noticed her car sitting in front of the mechanic bay doors and turned to give him a relieved smile. "I'll only be a minute."

"No problem. Say hi to your sister for me."

Liz came out of the garage as she approached. "There you go. Two more tires and it's good as new again. I double checked the rest of the vehicle just in case, but I didn't see anything else he may have messed with. The car alarm must have startled him."

"Either that or seeing Mason sprinting out the front door in his sweats and with bare feet had something to do with it."

Liz shot a glance at Mason sitting in the cab and gave him a little wave before turning back towards her. "Oooh, lala! Please tell me there's something going on with you two."

She blushed and shrugged, trying not to make it obvious they were talking about him. "Well…nothing too serious, yet. We seem to keep getting interrupted."

At that, her sister's eyebrows shot up. "That implies that there was something to interrupt."

"Maybe…"

"Olivia, do NOT be coy with me."

Surreptitiously, she glanced over her shoulder and then back at her sister. "Let's just say, he's a fabulous kisser, and if it hadn't been for that damn car alarm last night, I may not have been waking up in my own bed this morning." She looked down at her hands.

"Okay, so…what's the problem, then?" At her look of surprise, Liz tossed her hands up in the air. "Oh, come on. I can tell when you're over-thinking something. What's going on?"

"I don't know…I just, with everything that's been happening, I'm not sure now is the right time to get caught up with anyone."

"Do NOT let this asshole prevent you from living your life. He does NOT deserve it. Besides, by keeping yourself back, you're only allowing him to win."

Olivia shot her a confused look, so she continued. "I've been doing a little reading up on stalking, and a lot of the sites mention they try to isolate their victim, get them to sever ties with their loved ones and remove themselves from their everyday, normal interactions.

"It's a form of control, Livvy. All it does is serve to fray the victim's support system and make them more vulnerable. You can't let that happen to you. I won't let that happen between us, and you shouldn't let it happen between you and Mason, either."

"Okay, okay…you have a good point. I'll think about what you said, I promise." She held her hand out. "Now, can I please have my keys so I can take my car home? It's already been a really long day, and I still have to deal with the locksmith."

Liz gave her sister a hug, then handed her the keys. "There you go. Want me to come by later tonight?"

Olivia gave her a smile. "Thanks, but no. I think what I'd really like is to just spend a quiet night at home and go to bed early. I'm exhausted. Maybe we can do something tomorrow? Or this weekend?"

"That works. Let me know if anything else happens or if you find out anything new."

"Will do."

Once in her car, she pulled out of the parking lot and checked the rearview mirror to make sure Mason was behind her. As she pulled into her driveway, she noticed the locksmith's truck was already waiting across the street.

Chapter Twenty-Three

Mason pulled up and parked behind the locksmith's van. He quickly noted the company and snapped a picture of the license plate. It wouldn't hurt to make sure the guy was legitimate—just in case.

He walked up to where Olivia and the man were talking. She'd already begun explaining to him what she wanted done.

"Okay, so you want me to replace the locks on both this front door and the kitchen door, and then install new deadbolts?"

"Yes, please. About how long do you think that will take?"

The balding, rotund man shrugged and stroked his chin. "Shouldn't be too long, maybe an hour or two."

She cast a look at him. "Ok, great. This is Mason, he's going to keep an eye on things," She looked down at the red splattered across the front of her shirt. "I really need to get myself cleaned up. If you have any questions, just ask him."

Mason watched as she trudged up the stairs, and then nodded at the man standing in front of him. "Hi. I'm going to be in the living room if you need anything."

"No worries, I've got this. I'll let you know if there are any problems."

With a final nod, he moved into the other room and pulled out his phone. First thing he did was check the website for the locksmith. Satisfied that everything was as it seemed, he called his captain in Boston.

"Mason. Wasn't expecting to hear from you until after the holidays. What's up?"

"Hey, Captain. I wanted to see if there were any new developments on the Mendez case. Have you guys been making any progress with it?"

"Actually, it's been going pretty slowly. You really shouldn't be worrying about it, though. You're not on active duty right now, remember?"

Mason winced a little at the warning tone in the other man's voice. "Yeah, I kind of had a feeling you'd say that. Actually, there's a reason I'm bringing it up…" He took a moment to catch his captain up on the events that had been occurring in Maine.

"Sounds like quite a situation you have up there." The older man hesitated. "And you said there hasn't been any evidence that can help support your suspicions this is him?"

He moved over to the front of the living room and looked out the window at the quiet street. He noticed the day was already slowly turning to twilight. "Other than the similarities of the flowers and the speed with which this situation has progressed, all I have is my gut telling me it's somehow related."

Captain Fields sighed, "Well, Mason, you know I used to work the streets, just the same as all of you guys, and if there's one thing I've learned, it's that a good cop should trust his gut." He hedged, "Of course, if there's no evidence, then my hands are tied."

"I know. I just wanted to make sure you're aware of the situation. I was hoping you'd be willing to pass on any information you do have to the local PD here. Officer Thompson is the guy working the case, and he's a good cop. Not to mention, he's personally motivated to help solve this since he and Olivia are old high school friends."

"Sure, I can do that. Give me his number and I'll get in touch with him. Am I safe in assuming you're keeping tabs on his progress with the case as well?"

"Yeah, he offered to keep me in the loop when he found out about my ties to Boston."

"Fair enough. If we find anything out, I'll let you know. Strictly off the record, of course."

"I appreciate it. I'll keep in touch."

"Do that. Mason, don't let this impede your recovery. I fully expect you to be back here in Boston at the first of the year. No excuses."

"Right." He hung up and pocketed his phone. With that out of the way, he felt a little bit better about the case. Maybe with both departments working together they could finally get a break and catch this guy.

He wandered back into the entryway, feeling at odds with himself, just as Olivia came wandering down the stairs. He noticed that she'd changed into another pair of jeans and a t-shirt. He was beginning to think of it as her daily uniform and suspected that the dress she'd worn the other night had been the first she'd worn in a long time.

She was carelessly winding her wet hair back into a bun, and it was a mystery to him how she could still manage to look so elegant, despite her casual style. *Probably something about her I'll never understand*, he thought as she stopped in front of him.

He noticed that without makeup she had little freckles scattered across her nose, and wanted to kiss them. In fact they made him want to find and kiss all of her freckles. He struggled to keep the errant thought from taking over.

"I thought I heard you on the phone."

He pulled her into his arms and told her about the conversation he'd had with his captain.

"Well, I'm glad they'll both be working together, just in case it is this guy."

He looked down into her eyes. "Did you want me to stick around for tonight, just in case?"

She hesitated, looked down at his chest, and then back up into his eyes. "I appreciate the offer, but…"

He gave her a little squeeze. "No pressure. I wouldn't mind sleeping on the couch."

At that, she blushed and looked away, giving a little laugh, "Oh, come on, Mason. You and I both know where our night was headed if that car alarm hadn't interrupted us." She gently pulled out of his arms and took a step back. "And, to be honest, I'd be lying if I said I didn't want to go there with you."

"Well, then…"

"But I think there's been so much happening these last few days that I kind of need to take a breather tonight before I make any big decisions." She gestured at him. "I mean, you're already going through so much with your recovery… I don't want to drag you into whatever this situation is, on top of everything else."

Exasperated, Mason exclaimed, "Drag me in? Drag me in?! Olivia, for all we know, I'm the one who dragged YOU into this mess."

"We don't know that for certain." She bit her lip. "That's another thing I'm a little worried about. You seem so fixated on the fact that it's this guy, but who knows if that's accurate? You could just be…" Quickly, she snapped her mouth shut.

He stalked towards her, speaking in a very quiet, intense voice and said, "I could just be…what? I could be over-reacting? Crazy? Seeing things?"

She took a step backwards, and another one, until finally her back bumped against the wall. All she could do was stare up at him as he loomed over her. His fists were clenched down by his sides and his eyes burned like twin blue flames.

"Mason…" She raised her hands, placating.

"Oh, no…I get it. You think I'm still too emotionally unstable.

That I could be jumping at shadows that aren't there. That some part of me needs for this guy to be Robert Mendez so I can see it through. You don't think I haven't had all those same doubts, Olivia?"

He spun away and stood with his back to her. She ached to see the way his shoulders curved as he raked his hands through his hair. "Fine. I admit it." He shrugged. "Maybe you're right."

Pulling his keys out of his coat pocket, he turned back towards her. "Alright, I'll go. Take your night and get some rest. I know it's been a long couple of days for you."

He stopped on his way to the door and turned halfway back towards her. "Just do me a favor, would you? Don't do anything stupid. As soon as the locksmith is done, lock the doors. Don't go off by yourself anywhere, and just…be careful, okay?"

Silently, she nodded. A part of her was screaming for her to just reach out, apologize, and ask him to stay, but in the end, all she could do was stand there. He cast her one final look, and then opened the door and strode out.

He didn't go far, though. He sat in the cab of his truck and watched the house from across the street. Even frustrated, he couldn't just leave her until he knew she was safe. Some part of him said he should just go back inside and assure Olivia he understood her concerns.

For an hour and a half, he resisted the urge to go and knock on her front door and try to smooth things over with her. The problem was, he did know where she was coming from. He *had* all of those same doubts that she had expressed.

And, so? Now what? Here he was outside, in the cold, observing her house from across the street. He was nearly as bad as the stalker, he thought, disgusted.

He watched as the locksmith stepped out the front door and Olivia thanked him. Satisfied that at least she had new locks on her doors, he reluctantly turned the key in the ignition and pulled away from the curb.

It was probably just as well, he thought, as he rotated his shoulder and tried to ease the stiffness from his joint. He hadn't gotten a lot of sleep, either. Maybe they could both stand to take a night off and do some thinking.

Keep telling yourself that, buddy. He cranked the music up, once again trying to drown out his thoughts.

Keep telling yourself that.

Chapter Twenty-Four

Olivia buried her head under her pillow and groaned. She was really beginning to hate her alarm. It didn't used to be so hard to wake up this early to open the café, but that was before Mason had started making a habit of commandeering her thoughts and leaving her tossing and turning at night.

Resigned, she got up and shut the infernal noise off. Last night had been tough. Even with the new locks, she'd been uncomfortable in her own home. She'd been tempted to call and see if he'd come stay with her, but had managed to resist the urge. It wasn't fair of her to drag him into this situation when he had so much going on in his life as it was.

Besides, his single-minded focus on Robert Mendez was bordering on obsession. She knew how much it meant to him to be able to go back to active duty in Boston after the holidays. He wasn't going to be able to do that unless he passed the psych evaluations, and adding to his stress wasn't doing him any favors.

Bleary-eyed, she splashed cold water on her face and winced at her reflection. Hard to believe anybody would be fixated on her, looking like this. She quickly wrapped her hair up in a ponytail and changed into her usual work clothes.

On her way out the door, she practically tripped over the box of roses sitting on her step. For a moment, her heart skipped a beat as she reached for the card tucked in amongst the blood-red petals. Maybe Mason had left them for her as a way of making up!

"*Good behavior deserves a reward.*"

Not Mason. Her stomach dropped and she raised her head to scan the neighborhood around her. The air was still sharp and cold against her cheeks. At this hour, nothing moved. Even the birds were silent in the winter morning. There was a light on in the house across the street where someone was up and getting ready for work, but otherwise, no sign of life.

Feeling exposed, Olivia debated leaving the flowers there on the steps. She didn't want any part of whoever was harassing her to be allowed to disturb the sanctuary of her home again. Then she recalled what Brad had told her. In order to make a case that she was actually being stalked, they would have to create a file and record all the events that occurred.

Reluctantly, she picked them up and brought them inside. These would have to be added to the file she'd already started.

Resigned, she unceremoniously dumped them onto the kitchen counter and dug her phone out of her pocket to call Tom.

"Hello?" his gruff voice greeted her.

"Tom? Hi, I'm sorry to have to call you so early."

"It's fine. What's wrong?"

Suddenly a lump formed in her throat, and she struggled to swallow past her frustration.

"Olivia? You there?"

"Yeah. Hi, I'm here. Sorry, I know I've been a little flaky lately…but I'm going to have to ask you to open the café again without me."

"Sure. It's no problem. I'm up already, anyway…"

"Is that Olivia? What's going on?" Olivia was startled to hear Jackie's sleepy voice in the background and wondered what was going on between the two of them. For the past couple of weeks, she'd been so caught up in everything that was going on in her own life that she'd completely missed what was happening under her nose.

Vowing that she'd stop being so self-absorbed and be a better friend, she made a silent promise that she'd ask Jackie about it first chance she got.

She tuned back into what Tom was saying, "…let me know if you need me to come and get you."

"Oh, no, thank you. Although I appreciate it. I'm going to call the cops as soon as I hang up with you. I'm hoping it won't take me very long to file a report. I just found another little gift this morning waiting for me on the front step and need to get it on the record."

"Okay, don't worry about the café. Jackie and I can handle it for now. Just do what you can to get this situation resolved as quickly as possible, and keep us posted."

"Thanks, I will. I really appreciate it."

With relief, she hung up the phone, thankful to have good friends that she could rely on. She needed to get this whole thing over with. It was not only affecting her, but everybody else in her life…and that was just not acceptable.

Resolved, she dialed the police station and asked for Brad. The faster they could catch this guy, the sooner she could move on with her life.

It was nearly ten o'clock before she could finally make it into work. The smell of bacon and coffee greeted her as she slipped into the kitchen and pulled her chef coat down from the hook. Jackie gave her a quick look on her way to take an order, "Hey. You made it. Everything okay? We need to talk, but it's too busy right now! Think we can take a minute after closing to catch up?"

This, at least, was still the same, Olivia thought. "Yeah, we do. Was that you I heard in the background this morning?" Surprised, she watched Jackie blush. With a little, secret smile, she said,

"Maybe…" Her friend made a shooing motion with her hands. "This afternoon!"

With a nod, she took up her usual spot on the grill. Tom spared her a quick look, and in his usual subdued manner asked, "Everything okay from this morning?"

"Yeah, it's taken care of for now." She sighed. "I really need my life to get back on an even keel again."

Nodding, he kept working. Curious what was going on with him and Jackie, she cast him a surreptitious glance.

"Quit looking at me like that," he said gruffly, then looked at her and gave a wink.

Setting aside her worries, she beamed. "What look? I'm not giving you a look." Giggling, she noticed his ears had started to turn pink, and nudged him with her shoulder. "'Bout time you spoke up about how you were feeling."

He gave her a grunt, but couldn't quite hide the smile as he turned back to flipping pancakes. Happy to be back in her familiar setting, she lost herself in the rhythm of cooking and filling tickets. It was just busy enough that, for a few hours, all her concentration and focus was needed to keep up with the rush.

Before too long, she looked up and realized that it was already close to two o'clock, and started scraping down and cleaning the grills. She tried not to think about the fact that she hadn't seen Mason all day, even though she knew it wasn't fair to him. After all, she'd basically pushed him out the door herself, and now she was pining for him.

Talk about mixed signals. The problem was that, what she should do was not the same as what she wanted to do.

"Hey, missy. You almost finished up back here?" Jackie poked her head into the kitchen. Instantly, Olivia could feel the air between her and Tom electrify.

"As a matter of fact, I am."

"Well, come on out here, then. How is it I can see you almost every day and feel like I have no idea what's going on in your life right now?"

Olivia dried her hands off on a dishtowel and removed her chef coat, happy to have the time with her best friend. Maybe she could help shed some light on everything that had been happening.

"Before you ladies get started, I'm going to take off." Tom focused in on Jackie and calmly walked across the kitchen to where she was standing in the doorway. Olivia watched with wide eyes as he curved his hand around the back of her neck, bent down, and kissed her deeply.

After a moment, he lifted his head. "Would you like me to pick Abby up at the daycare so you can take a little time for catching up?"

Jackie just looked up at him. Olivia chuckled at the dazed look on her face, but then stopped. She suspected it was exactly the same as the look on her face after one of Mason's kisses.

"I'm sorry?" Jackie stuttered.

He just gave her a smile and dropped another kiss on the tip of her nose. "Abby? You know, your daughter? About yea high…?" With that, he let her go and gestured with his hand about thigh high.

She laughed. "Yes, if you don't mind. Can you pick her up for me?"

"Not a problem." With a nod to Olivia, he walked out of the back door. Jackie cast her a glance, her cheeks turning a bright red. She laughed a bit self-consciously. "So, um, I might have a few things to tell you, too."

It was good to see her friend so happy.

The two women poured themselves something to drink and then sat at a table in the dining room. Neither one of them seemed very hungry, despite it being mid-afternoon.

"So…tell me about you and Tom." Olivia said, without preamble.

Jackie's cheeks once again turned a light pink as she fiddled with the handle of her mug. "Well, remember that week I had to take off sick?"

"It was just a few weeks ago, I think I can remember."

She stuck her tongue out at Olivia. "Do you want me to tell you the story, or not?"

Contrite, she gestured for her friend to continue. "Tom came by one of those days to drop some soup off for me, and check to see how I was doing." She gave an embarrassed laugh. "You should have seen me, Livvy. I was a total wreck when I opened the door. My nose was bright red from blowing it all day, my hair was standing on end, and I was wearing my rattiest sweats, an old t-shirt with a hole in the armpit, and my bunny slippers!"

Olivia laughed, having seen the infamous pair of slippers, and could absolutely picture her friend in such disarray.

"Ohhh, and there he was, standing in my doorway, with his dark hair and sexy eyes...I'm telling you, I felt like sinking straight through the floor."

"Hm, sounds like you've been harboring a little something for him for a while."

She looked down and picked at a corner of her napkin. "Well, I don't know about that...but, come on. You have to admit, the man is HOT! And mysterious...the way he's always so quiet, but you get the feeling he'd be there in a heartbeat if you needed him..." She gave a delicate little shudder.

"Okay, okay, I think I get the picture." She laughed. "So, how did you get from bunny slippers to that kiss I saw a little bit earlier?"

"Well, you know how I've pretty much given up dating ever since I've had Abby? It's not like I've had a lot of time or the inclination to go looking for anybody. But, that afternoon, I was feeling like hell, and he offered to pick her up from daycare for me so I could get a little bit more rest. I must have passed out on the couch, because the next thing I knew, I could hear the two of them in the kitchen, Abby giggling and sounding like she was having the time of her life. I walked in, and there they were, drinking hot cocoa and making funny faces at each other. Tom had done my dishes and had even started dinner."

"Wow!"

"Yeah…" Her eyes turned dreamy, "You should have seen him, Livvy. He had the biggest smile on his face. Do you realize that in all the time I've known him, I don't think I've ever seen him smile like that? It was so open. And, then, he caught sight of me standing in the doorway, and the look he gave me…it was like, something just …clicked."

Jackie became very serious and looked her directly in the eyes. "It was as if a door had sprung open up in my mind and let all the sun in. As if, for the first time, everything was focused and I could see with clarity. I thought, well, duh…! How could I have been so blind not to see what was right in front of my nose?

"I have to tell you, I think my heart just fell out of my chest and landed at his feet then and there."

"Aww, Jackie."

"I know!" Jackie took a sip of her coffee. "Anyway, come to find out, all that time I was thinking he was cute but couldn't possibly be interested in a single mom like me, he was thinking I'd be intimidated by his past history."

"Well, he is pretty intense."

"True, but don't you see? That's why he needs me and Abby. He could use a little more joy and light in his life. We've always suspected he went through some pretty difficult times during the war. I think he's just now starting to make his peace with some of the things he did and saw over there. Besides, Abby just loves him."

"Well, good. I'm so happy for you two." Jackie smiled broadly before changing gears. She gave her friend a concerned look from across the table.

"Enough about me. What's going on with you, Olivia?"

The smile faded from her lips and she groaned, dropping her head in her hands. "Oh, Jackie, I didn't want to admit it, but I think I really do have a stalker on my hands."

Jackie gasped. "Are you sure? Has it really gotten that bad?"

"I think so, yeah. Both Brad and Mason seem to think so... what with the flowers, and the note...and now last night with my tires. Then, this morning, finding even more flowers outside my door."

"Creepy!"

"I know, right? I mean, not only does this guy know where I live, but he's obviously willing to break into my house. Last night, I had to wash everything in my top drawer because who knows if he pawed through it? I couldn't bear the thought of putting anything he may have touched against my skin. And forget about sleeping. I tossed around all night."

"You mean you didn't have Mason stay with you?"

She slumped down in her chair and gave her friend a glum look. "Mason and I kind of had a spat yesterday." Under her breath, she admitted, "It may have been my fault."

She relayed to her friend her concerns about Mason's obsession with Robert Mendez and how she wasn't sure it was healthy to be dragging him into the whole stalker situation she found herself in.

"...but, Olivia, what if he's right and this really is that Mendez guy?"

"Come on. What are the odds the two of them would be in the same small Maine town at the same time? Everything I've read indicates they think he's holed up somewhere and laying low, trying to avoid the heat from the cops."

"I don't know. Stranger things have happened."

"True." She threw her hands up in the air. "Like the fact that I even have a stalker. This whole situation feels completely ridiculous. Honestly, if I hadn't been so scared the other day, I'd think it was a joke."

Jackie gave her a pointed look. "But it's not, Olivia Harper, and you'd better start taking this whole thing more seriously, or you could wind up getting really hurt."

As her friend filled her ears with caution, Olivia's gaze slid away and spotted the tall, handsome man striding across the street towards her café. Jackie's eyes widened as she followed the direction her friend was looking.

"You're awfully lucky I figured things out with Tom, or I might have decided to give you a run for your money with that man."

Olivia laughed at her, and got up to unlock the front door and let Mason in. The fact was that she was relieved to see him, especially after what had been said the previous day.

"Hey," he greeted her as he stepped through the door.

"Hi."

"Well, I hate to break up this scintillating conversation," Jackie said as she walked up to the two of them, "but, I have to get going. Who knows what kind of trouble Tom and Abby have gotten into without me?"

She gave Mason a smile. "I'm Jackie, by the way. I hear you've been helping my best friend with her little situation."

He couldn't help but smile at the sunny, petite woman standing in front of him. "I'm certainly trying to. She doesn't always let me."

She patted him on the shoulder. "You just keep trying. I have a feeling you're helping her a lot more than you know."

With that, she gave Olivia a wink and then paused, her face growing more serious. "Be careful, okay? And, let me know if anything else happens or if there's some way I can help."

Giving her best friend a hug, Olivia said, "Honestly? The best thing you can do is keep yourself and Abby removed from the situation as much as possible. I couldn't stand it if I thought I'd somehow dragged you two into this mess with me."

"Don't worry. I'm not any kind of wimp or anything, but I know for a fact Tom will keep us safe."

With a final squeeze and a nod to Mason, she let herself out the front door. He watched her as she climbed into her car, parked out on the street.

"That's some friend you've got there."

Olivia nodded. "The best."

For a beat, neither one of them said anything else. Silence filled the space between them.

"Look, Olivia…"

"Mason, about yesterday…"

They both stopped and looked at each other. He gestured for her to go first.

She nervously swallowed and began again. "About yesterday, I'm sorry about what I said. I know all you're trying to do is help protect me, and I shouldn't be so quick to dismiss your instincts."

A ball of tension and anxiety began to loosen in his chest. It had hurt more than he'd realized that she had been so quick to doubt him.

"I can't tell you how much that means to me." He ached to reach out and pull her into his embrace. Something about this woman made his arms feel empty without her in them.

Instead, he stuffed his hands in his pockets and tried reason. "Look, I know this situation sucks. And you're right; there is still the possibility that this isn't even Robert. I went by the police station today to talk to Brad. He'd gotten the forensic report back."

She raised her eyebrows. "Oh! That's good news, right?"

"Unfortunately, they didn't find any fingerprints. They did, however, find some traces of light powder, the kind you find on the inside of plastic or latex gloves. They think the guy was wearing them when he was in your house."

She sighed. "So, we're back to square one, then."

"Well, not exactly. Not that I ever thought this was likely, but I think we can rule out the possibility that this was just a prank done by some neighborhood kids. They wouldn't have thought to take forensic countermeasures."

She thought about that and nodded. "That's true. Okay, so, now what?"

"Well, I don't know about you, but I didn't get any sleep last night. I was so worried that I was half tempted to drive back to your house and sit out in my truck, watching."

She felt a twinge of guilt for causing him more distress. "I know what you mean. I had a restless night, too."

"I really don't like the idea of you being alone with this guy out there, *whoever* he his. I'd like to propose that, for the time being, you use me as your bodyguard. I promise, I will stay on the couch, and nothing else will happen unless you want it to, but please, Olivia. Let me do this. I need to be sure you're okay."

Maybe it was the fact that she was still so tired from the night before, or the tone of his voice and the earnest way he looked at her. Or, maybe it was just the way her heart began to race when she'd seen him crossing the street, and the sense of relief that had filled her when she realized she hadn't completely messed things up between them. Whatever the case, Olivia knew she wasn't going to be able to say no to him. Not again.

Cautiously, she nodded, and felt any residual tension between them melt away. He took a step towards her and folded her into his arms.

"Great! I can't tell you how happy that makes me. I really wasn't looking forward to spending the nights in my truck if you'd said no."

She gave him a startled look. "You mean, you really would have done that?"

He smiled and gave her a light kiss. "Yes. I told you, I intend to see you safe. I keep my promises."

A sense of warmth and well-being filled her as she gave what he said some thought. "I appreciate that, but Mason, I have to tell you, I don't see how this situation is going to be very sustainable. I don't want this guy making me feel like I'm a prisoner in my own life. What if the cops never catch him? What then?"

She pulled out of his arms to head back towards the kitchen. He followed her. Pulling her coat down off the hook, she began getting ready to leave. "I mean, even you are going to need to get back to your own schedule after the holidays. You are still planning on going back to active duty down in Boston, right?"

He caught her hands as she put her hat on and tugged the cap snugly over her ears. "Look, I realize this is a temporary solution. I didn't say it was perfect. But, for now, I think it's the best we can come up with.

"Who knows? Maybe we'll catch this guy. Or maybe when he sees we're constantly together, and you're always escorted, he'll move on. Don't get me wrong. That's not Mendez' style. Once he fixates on someone, his obsession takes him over completely. However, you said it yourself; there really hasn't been any proof that it's him, for sure. So, if it's just some fly-by-night, amateur stalker with a fancy for golden-eyed, sexy cooks, maybe he can be convinced to move on."

He sighed. "The point being that we can tackle the rest of it when we get there. Okay?"

She got the feeling he was talking about a lot more than just the stalker situation with that last statement. But, hadn't she already been entertaining the idea of just enjoying the time she had with him, regardless of whether it was only for a short time?

"Okay."

Bundled and prepared for the cold outside, they both walked

out the back door. He stood to the side as Olivia locked the café for the day. "So, what's next?"

"Well I was planning on heading over to the grocery store to pick up a few things. How do you feel about root vegetables?"

He gave her a grin. "With you cooking? I feel pretty good about them."

"Great, because there's this new recipe I've been wanting to try..."

Chapter Twenty-Five

An hour later, they were walking in her front door. He chuckled as he juggled the cute, reusable nylon bags of food. "I don't think I've ever been to the grocery store quite like that before."

She cocked her head at him as she made her way into the kitchen, and started unloading her finds. "What do you mean?"

"Well, first off, when I go to the grocery store, I don't get personally greeted by the manager."

She laughed and took a moment to admire the small pumpkin she set on the counter. "Herb? Of course he's happy to see me. I certainly spend enough time and money in his store."

"But the real difference was that it was like an adventure. I've never stepped down half those aisles before. I know I've never bought a whole pumpkin for the purpose of actually cooking it instead of carving it."

"It's just a little one." She shrugged and turned to put her eggs in the fridge. "What can I say? You just got to see me in my version of a toy store."

"It was nice." He stepped around the kitchen island and reached for her hand, tugging her into his arms.

She looked up at him and wrapped her arms around his neck.

"Hey, I figure if you're going to be my bodyguard, I might as well feed you properly."

He bent his head down and began to nibble on her ear. Little shivers raced down her neck and she tilted her head to give him better access. "Mmm, I'm starting to feel very hungry."

The way his voice had roughened and thickened with desire caused her to melt a little more. She struggled to keep her senses with his mouth trailing down her neck. "Mason…" Was her voice really that breathy? It should be illegal the way this man addled her brains with a kiss.

"Hmmm?"

She gave a little laugh that somehow became a moan as she felt his tongue dip into the hollow of her neck. "Mason…if you want dinner at all tonight, I need to start putting things together…"

He raised his head and looked her in the eyes. Reluctantly, he loosened his hold on her and leaned his forehead against hers. He sighed. "I suppose I should call my sister and let her know I'm staying here tonight anyway." He carefully released her, but not before giving her a final kiss on the lips.

Self-consciously, she tucked her hair behind her ear and moved to pull out her cutting board. "Go ahead and make your call. I'm just going to get this pumpkin in the oven and start making the pasta for tonight."

"Wait, you're going to *make* pasta?"

"Oh yeah! It's not that hard, and it tastes so much better. Just wait. You'll see." Now that they were back on the subject of food, she was feeling more confident again. She didn't know what it was about him, but somehow he always had her feeling slightly off-balance and on edge.

"You're going to spoil me."

"Pretty much. I guarantee you'll never be satisfied with store bought again."

He just grinned at her and went to make his call in the living room.

Left to her own devices, Olivia quartered and scraped her pumpkin, placed the pieces on the baking sheet, and popped them in the oven. Then she grabbed a mixing bowl and began making the pasta dough. She knew she'd have to let it sit for about half an hour before she could cut it.

After rolling it into a nice round ball and putting the dough back into the mixing bowl, she began working on the various root vegetables. She was so lost in the familiar rhythms of cooking that she didn't even notice him standing in the doorway.

"You know you hum when you cook?"

Startled, she nearly dropped the knife she'd been rinsing at the sink. "I'm sorry?"

"When you cook, you hum. I never noticed before. Probably because it's usually too loud at the café, and you're tucked back behind that kitchen pass-thru window."

She could feel her cheeks warm. She hadn't realized that he'd been watching so closely. He moved further into the kitchen and took a seat at the island. "You have this easy confidence about you when you're cooking. You seem to flow…it's very graceful."

"Oh…well…"

He laughed. "Ah hell, now I've done it. I wasn't trying to make you self-conscious. Just telling you I like to watch you work. It's obvious you love what you do."

"Well, thanks." Hoping to move on to a more comfortable topic, she asked, "So, what did your sister say?"

"Not much. Just that she was glad I was here to keep you safe and for me not to worry about her."

She turned from checking the pumpkin pieces in the oven. "Do you think she's in any danger? I don't like the idea of her being up there at the bed and breakfast by herself."

He took a moment to consider. "Most stalkers tend to only

focus on one victim at a time. Whoever this guy is, we know he's fixated on you for the time being. She should be okay… but, just in case, I also called Brad and asked if he wouldn't mind taking a drive out there and checking on her at some point tonight."

"Oh good, that was a smart thing to do. I'm going to need to get him a thank you gift or something after all of this blows over. He's been so patient and helpful throughout this whole situation."

He nodded. "Yeah, it's been convenient that you two know each other." Pausing, he added, "So, what's the story between you two? Did you guys ever date?"

She laughed. "Who? Brad and me? Yeah, for a short time back in high school we did. We went to junior prom together. He was always a nice guy, but we quickly realized we were better off as friends."

"What happened?"

"Nothing really, just no chemistry. He took one look at this new girl, Jenny Masterson, and fell head over heels. They ended up dating for a few months that summer, but…you know how it goes. I think she ended up going to college somewhere out West."

"Ah, young love."

"Exactly." The whole time they'd been talking, she had steadily been peeling and dicing veggies. She piled everything into a bowl, and turned to take the pumpkin out of the oven.

"Wow, that looks great. What all is in there?"

"Oh, just a few carrots, a sweet potato, parsnips, and some shallots."

"Huh, it's very colorful. I don't think I've ever eaten parsnip before."

"Oh, really? Well, they're good. I think you'll like them." She pulled out the package of pancetta she'd gotten from the deli, diced it into small cubes, and then set it aside.

"What are you going to do with that?"

"I'm going to fry it up so it's crisp, then sauté the veggies in the rendered fat and a little bit of olive oil."

"Kind of like bacon?"

"Yup, it's basically like Italian bacon. Before I get started on that, though, I need to get the peels off this pumpkin and pop it in the food processor to puree it. By that point, the dough should be about ready to start rolling."

He got up and grabbed the pasta dough, leaning over her shoulder to place it on the counter in front of her. "So, how does the pumpkin and pasta come into play?"

"I thought I'd make little pumpkin tortellis—basically small pockets of pasta filled with pumpkin—and serve it with prosciutto and root vegetables in an herb butter sauce."

"Sounds amazing."

She smiled at his enthusiasm. "We'll see. If it turns out as well as I'm hoping, I may have another item for my dinner menu."

"Great. Is there anything I can do to help? I feel kind of bad about sitting here watching you do all the work."

"You could open a bottle of wine."

"I can do that." Turning, he pulled a bottle from the wine holder. After opening a few cupboards, he grabbed two wine glasses and poured a generous amount for each of them.

Meanwhile, she began rolling out the pasta. After it was flattened and thin enough, she began indenting the pasta into squares. She showed him how to take a spoonful of the pumpkin puree and place it in the middle of the pasta squares, then separate them and fold the edges so that they looked like little purses.

They made about a dozen before she paused. "I think that's more than enough." She set them aside to be cooked at the very end and threw the pancetta into the hot pan.

"Are you finished with the cutting board?"

"Oh, yes, thank you."

As he stood at the counter, she was struck by how warm and

cozy it felt having him here with her. She enjoyed being able to cook dinner and talk with him while they shared a glass of wine. It would be so easy to forget everything else that was happening, forget about all the things that were still up in the air, and just overdose on the feeling of domestic bliss.

Just then, she noticed the pancetta was starting to get a little too crisp, and rushed to pull it off the burner.

"Something wrong?" he asked as he turned back towards her.

"What? Oh, no, I just have to get this out of the pan and toss the veggies in. Dinner won't be too long now."

He dried his hands on a dishtowel. He'd caught sight of her dreamy, contented look in the reflection of the window above the sink and wondered what she'd been thinking about. "Well, I have everything pretty much straightened up over here. Why don't I get the table set while you finish things up?"

"That'd be great, thank you."

As she finished up the sauce, Olivia plopped the pumpkin pasta pockets into the pot of boiling water she'd started a few minutes before. Five minutes later, she took the two dishes he'd set out for her and plated them.

She took a moment to add a final flourish of fresh sage over the top, and wiped the rim of the plates before bringing them into the dining room.

Mason had found her candles and lit them. The room was awash in a warm, romantic glow. Eagerly, she sat down and waited to see what his first reaction would be to the meal before him.

"This looks great." Mason leaned forward and savored the aroma, then picked up his fork and carefully cut one of the pumpkin filled pillows in half. She gave a little shudder as she watched his lips slowly wrap around his fork.

He let out a sensuous groan as the warm fall flavors took over his senses. The butter sauce was silky and decadent and felt elegant on his tongue. He could taste the smokiness of the pancetta and appreciated the crunch and texture it leant to the dish. The unfamiliar, slightly fibrous, sweet flavor must have been the parsnip he had been curious about.

Mason hadn't even realized he'd closed his eyes, until he opened them to find her watching him with a small, secretive smile on her lips.

"This is incredible. I can't believe you made it all from scratch like this. You really have a gift."

Satisfied, she took her first bite and chewed contemplatively. "Pretty good, I must say. I think we have another winner."

He speared the next forkful. "I know I'd be willing to make a special trip for a dish like this, that's for sure."

He winced. The subtle reminder that he'd have to travel in order to enjoy future meals like this sat on the table between them.

Delicately, she bridged the silence that had begun to fill the space. "So, I've been thinking…"

He nodded for her to continue, relieved to move past the awkward moment.

"You said you've worked these kinds of cases before, right? Maybe you could tell me a little bit more about stalking in general so I have an idea of what to expect."

He was surprised by the change of topic. It seemed almost a shame to let such ugliness into the otherwise intimate setting. However, he could see the barely concealed nervousness in her eyes, and knew she'd feel better if she had an idea of what she was up against.

Besides, who knew? Maybe something he told her today would give her the tools she'd need to survive tomorrow.

He took another bite of pumpkin tortelli while he gathered his thoughts, and then sat back with his glass of wine. "Okay. Well, I guess we should start with the basics. Stalkers can generally be placed in two main categories. The most common type of stalker is one that is usually known by the victim. I'm sure you've probably heard about ex-husbands or boyfriends stalking their former wives and girlfriends. A lot of times, stalking is just one part of the abuse found in these types of relationships. And while many of these types of cases can end tragically, it's not the same kind of stalking you're dealing with."

Olivia was so engrossed in what Mason was saying, she'd set her fork down. She gave a little shudder and grabbed for her wine glass to quickly take a swallow. "How terrible. Just the thought that someone I had been close to, maybe even thought I'd loved at one point, turning like that."

Mason nodded, "That's one of the risks to those types of scenarios. The victim makes excuses and refuses to accept what's really happening to them until things have escalated so much, that it's too late to change the outcome."

"Okay. You said there were two types of stalking?"

"Right. So, the second main category would be when the victim doesn't know her stalker. Technically, you could say there are two main sub-categories to this type. The first has mainly to do with celebrities and well known public figures and doesn't apply to your situation. The second, however, can be happen to anybody.

"Maybe the stalker had a chance encounter and she smiled at him, or made random eye contact…maybe they didn't meet at all, and he just happened to see her walking down the street. Whatever the case, that stalker has fixated on his victim and begins to spin an entire fantasy life and love relationship with that person."

"You said, 'he.' Is it always a man perpetrating this type of stalking?"

"Oh, no. However, since I know we're relating it to what's happening to you, it's just easier to refer to the stalker as he."

"But that's one thing I don't get about this whole situation. I mean, all I do is go to work, hang out with my sisters, and go home…it's not as if what I'm doing could be considered terribly exciting."

He gave her a tender smile. "I think you sell yourself short, Olivia. However, I get the point you're making. It doesn't always have to make sense. Something about you has caught this guy's eye. If it's Mendez, as I suspect, it could simply be your interacting with me. However, even if it's not, it really could have been something as innocent as holding a door for him on the way into a store."

She sighed. "Okay, that's just scary. It's almost enough to make you not want to smile or interact with anybody."

"Well, unfortunately, that's one of the symptoms that victims suffer in these types of cases. Because they don't know who their stalker is, they tend to become suspicious of everybody. They have a tendency to cut themselves off from all of the people around them and avoid public interactions. Instinctually, it makes sense, but it also has the effect of isolating them and making them even more vulnerable to their stalker."

"Well, obviously I can't do that. I have my sisters. I have a business to run…"

"You have me." He pinned her with an intense look and reached across the table to catch her hand in his. "I'm not trying to upset you. Do you want me to stop?"

She tamped down the rising anxiety that threatened to crawl up her throat and shook her head. "No, no…please continue. If I'm going to have any hope of getting through this, I need to know what I'm up against."

He gave her hand a little squeeze before going on, "I think it's important to understand, that all stalkers suffer from some type of mental disorder that encourages this type of behavior. For the stalkers who are complete strangers, it's usually what we call 'erotomania.' In essence, they've convinced themselves that they have a very intense, loving relationship with their victim. Eventually, they try to make contact, but because the affair is all in their head, they are disappointed by their victim's response towards them."

"So…what? You're saying it's better to play along?"

"If you find yourself alone with them, it may be a good option to buy yourself some time. However, it can also be risky, because a lot of times, they want more than you'll be willing to give. No matter what, it's going to be a fine line."

"There's really no good choice, is there? I mean, how do situations like this usually end? If this is a mental disorder, it isn't as if they can just be talked into stopping, right?"

"Unfortunately, that's true. Just about every stalking situation ends up escalating, and most become serial stalkers. The somewhat good news is they tend to be identifiable by the patterns they establish."

All the information and the enormity of the situation became overwhelming. She pushed back from the table and began pacing the dining room. "I can't do this. I can't let that happen to me, and yet, at the same time, I can't be a prisoner in my own life. What am I supposed to do? What about my sisters?! How is this going to affect them? What if it does?" She stopped and turned towards him. "Mason, I'm scared."

He stood up and held her close to him. He could feel the slight tremor running through her body, and her shoulders were tight with stress. Silently, he berated himself for speaking so baldly. "Shhh, shhh. It's okay," He pulled her back so he could look her directly in the eyes. "You *will* get through this. I am not going to let anything happen to you, okay? No matter what."

She clung to the assurances and determination in his gaze. After another second, she gathered herself together by sheer force. A solid ball of courage settled in the pit of her stomach. She reminded herself that she'd been through bad things before with the death of her parents and raising her two sisters at an early age and somehow had made that work. This jerk, whoever he was, was not going to take her down without a fight.

Mason nodded at the renewed will and the resolve he saw in

her face and felt another surge of protectiveness towards the brave woman before him. Gently, he brushed her hair back and tucked it behind her ear.

He hazarded a glance at their half-eaten dinners on the table. "I hate talking about this and ruining such a lovely meal." He cast her a rueful glance, and was rewarded with a cautious smile.

"It was good, but I think I've lost my appetite." She gave him an apologetic look.

"I have an idea. Why don't I refill your wine glass, and you relax while I take care of the dishes and clean up."

"That sounds really nice. I think I may take you up on that offer and go run myself a hot bath. Are you sure you don't mind?"

He carefully massaged the back of her neck. "Not at all. I can feel that your muscles are all knotted up. Go ahead and do your thing. Pretend like I'm not even here."

She gave a little laugh at that and shot him a dubious look. "I doubt that's possible," she gave him a fleeting grin, "but I'm willing to give it a try." Turning, she grabbed her glass, and gratefully made her way upstairs. She could already hear him stacking the plates in the kitchen as she entered her bathroom.

She set her wine down on the counter and made the conscious decision to put everything Mason had said out of her mind. She began running the water and pulled the bottle of luxurious bubble bath she rarely used down from the cupboard.

As she gratefully sank into the inviting hot water, her mind wandered. It felt like it had been forever since she'd had a moment to just sit and relax. So much had changed in the last few months, with her sisters moving out, meeting Mason, and now this whole stalker situation.

Thanksgiving was this week, and she still hadn't even gone shopping for it. Every year, she hosted dinner for family and friends, and she would be damned if whoever was following her would get in her way this time.

At the thought of the coming holiday, she could feel herself getting worked up all over again. *Breathe. Just, breathe…*she reminded herself to relax and let it all go. Gradually, she could feel her muscles release their tension.

Forty-five minutes later, with her fingers wrinkled and her thoughts smoother, she stepped out of the water. She stroked lotion on her freshly shaved legs and let her hair down from its bun. Finally, after slipping into her pajamas and wrapping a robe around herself, she headed downstairs.

Glancing into the dining room, she noticed everything was straightened up and neat again. Olivia could definitely get used to having someone else do the dishes after she cooked. Wondering what Mason had gotten up to, she turned towards the living room.

He was sitting on the couch with his laptop open in front of him. The pale blue glow of the screen lit his face in ghostly light. The only other illumination in the room was the soft, yellow glow of a small table light in the corner. She stood and watched him, unobserved for a moment. Her eyes traced the line of his jaw and his broad shoulders. It crossed her mind that he looked perfectly at home…and perfect in her home.

Suddenly, he glanced up. The blue flame of his eyes met her golden ones and scorched her. He set the laptop aside, stood up, and began slowly walking towards her, all the while pinning her in place with desire in his gaze.

There would be no interruptions this time. They both seemed to acknowledge that fact as they let the breath between them stretch. Finally, when neither of them could stand it anymore, they both reached for each other at the same time.

His mouth descended on hers, urging her to open for his delving tongue and lips. She tilted her head, gripping his shoulders in desperation as her knees buckled and the world spun out and away from her.

A needy whimper bubbled up from her as he traced his lips

down the slender column of her neck. One strong hand firmly cupped her breast as she arched into him. She could feel his desire, and wantonly ground herself against his hard length. She needed to feel him between her legs, filling her spaces with his heat and strength.

He cursed. He didn't want to take her on the living room floor, but that was where they were headed if they didn't move soon. Her startled gasp set his blood on fire as he grabbed her ass and boosted her up, wrapping her legs around his waist. Quickly, desperately, he began to climb the stairs. She vaguely gestured towards her bedroom as she nibbled on his ear and sent shivers down his back.

Suddenly, the world was turning on its axis once again and Olivia was laid out on the bed looking up at him from her back.

She watched as he tore his shirt up over his head. Her hands ached to run over the contours of his chest and shoulders. She could see the two round scars where the bullets had torn his flesh. He looked like a battle-torn warrior from the past, come home to claim his woman.

She watched as he hastily peeled his jeans down over his hips, catching his black boxers on the way down.

Olivia lost her breath just looking at him. His penis jutted out proudly and she could feel her body clench with need. She reached for him, her arms craving to hold him. Finally, he climbed onto the bed with her and settled his hips between her thighs.

He unwrapped her robe and pulled her camisole up over her head, letting her breasts spring free. She could feel her nipples pebble under his gaze and ached to feel his mouth on them. As if sensing her thoughts, he bent his head towards them and slowly circled the tip with his tongue before closing his lips over her and suckling.

She could feel the draw all the way down between her legs and arched up, begging him to take her more fully. Pressure began to build up inside her and she writhed with aching need.

Mason felt his balls clench at the soft mewling sounds she made. He doubted she even knew she was making them. He looked up and admired the way her head was thrown back, her eyes closed, mouth open...her hair spread out behind her as the graceful line of her neck created an arc of abandon. Her skin was smooth and creamy, the color of café au lait.

With both hands, he grabbed the waistband at her hips and pulled her pajama pants down the length of her legs.

He could live a thousand years and never tire of her body.

Lifting one smooth, long leg up, he began nibbling the delicate bone of her ankle. Gradually, he licked and kissed up the length of that tempting stem. Reveling in the curve of her calf, pausing at the hollow in the back of her knee. Her thigh was like silk against his stubbled jaw.

Olivia's legs fell open and she mindlessly strained to feel his mouth where she needed it most, but just as he drew closer to that spot that throbbed for his attention, he pulled back and started the whole process again on her other leg. All the while, his hands kneaded and traced her body. The under curve of her breasts, the line of her waist, her thighs...

Her hips lifted up from the bed, a silent plea to relieve the tension built up in her very core. Finally, finally! His mouth hovered at the juncture of her legs. He opened his mouth and exhaled over her mound, hot breath setting her to shivers.

The tip of his tongue delicately traced the inner petals of her folds before concentrating on her needy little bud. Pleasure tore through her, hips bucking at the first shock of his touch. His strong hands wrapped firmly around her ass as he held her in place. The very center of her a willing sacrifice, as if spread out on an altar, and open to his questing, plundering mouth.

The world ceased to exist as pressure built and built within her. Ratcheting up further and further to the point where there was no air, there was no pride, there was nothing but Mason's tongue, lips, teeth and her own excruciating need…

Just as she wondered how much pleasure she could hold, he lightly traced his finger around her entrance and then delved two fingers into her heat. The entire universe burst forth from the center of her being. Every nerve ending stretched and quivered. She could feel the vibrations of her orgasm to her very soles, unable to do anything but succumb to the demands of her body.

Watching Olivia's unbridled response was humbling and thrilling at the same time. He loved the way her skin flushed, the way her nipples begged for his attention, the way she melted into liquefied heat at his tongue and fingertips. It was all he could do to keep his own desire reigned.

Suddenly, it was too much.

He needed to sink into her hot heat and feel her sheath close around him. He spread her legs and once again settled himself between her thighs. The velvet tip of his penis brushed up against her entrance, seeking access. He could still feel her quaking, and gently brushed the hair back from her face, urging her to look at him.

Her golden eyes were dazed and dilated. Just as they met his searing blue, he plunged into the sweet depths of her body.

Instantly, he could feel her inner muscles tighten and grip the length of his cock. "Ahhh, Olivia…you feel *so* good…" He thrust his hips, burying his length to the hilt. Beneath him, she panted and writhed, her legs wrapped tightly around his waist, her heels digging into his ass, urging him to go even deeper.

Trembling, he grasped the last remnants of his control and clung to them by sheer force of will. Slowly, painfully slow, he withdrew from her body. Out, to the very tip, and hovered there on the edge of sanity before once again plunging his thick cock into her welcoming warmth. Already, he could feel her unraveling, her inner walls milking him.

He snapped.

Every molecule of his being was overwhelmed by the need to take her and fill her with all of him. She bucked and strained towards him, as equally lost as he, her head once again thrown back, her eyes closed, as she strove for that one point where their souls would be completely merged.

With a shout and a final thrust, they both launched themselves over the cliff and soared. For half a beat of eternity, nothing else existed but the two of them. Gradually, they came shuddering back to earth, their breaths intermingling.

Olivia reveled in the way Mason's weight pressed her down into the mattress as he collapsed into her arms. She loved the way his muscles rippled and responded to her stroking fingers along his back. She could still feel him inside her and marveled at the intimacy.

Raising his head, he gave her a lopsided grin. Finally able to act on the impulse, she savored the indulgence of sweeping the fall of hair from across his forehead before allowing her hand to land limply back down on the mattress.

"That was…"

"…incredible!" They looked at each other and laughed. Mason propped himself up on his elbows and looked down at their bodies, both slicked with sweat and cooling desire. Reluctantly, he began to pull himself out of her. She gave him a little frown at the void he left in his wake.

With a chuckle, he leaned down and kissed the small furrow between her brows. "Let me get you something to clean up with."

At her nod, he went into the adjoining bathroom and brought back a damp washcloth. She supposed she should feel hesitant or shy at the way he carefully bathed her most intimate places, but the warm glow of the experience they'd just shared wouldn't allow it. Instead, she stretched languorously.

Finished, he tossed the cloth into the hamper and once again laid down alongside her, pulling the covers up over them, and taking her into his arms. She couldn't resist stroking her fingers along the muscles of his chest, her fingers gently circling his scars, reassured by the steady beat of his heart under her ear.

Mason rubbed her arm and felt the moment she gave way to sleep. Now, more than ever, he felt the pressure to resolve the terrible situation she was in. He knew what Mendez was capable of. The consequences of not taking him seriously enough were carved into his skin. He'd be damned if he'd allow anything like that to happen to Olivia.

As her breathing deepened and took on a steady cadence, his thoughts chased their tails, running in circles through his mind, until he could no longer sustain them. His body was too sated— his arms too content holding her—to harbor the concerns best left for the morning. His last thought was that he should head down to Boston while she was at work tomorrow and see if he could find out anything new. At peace for the first time in a very long time, he gently joined Olivia and dropped off to sleep.

Chapter Twenty-Six

Robert sullenly shifted his weight on the cold, hard curb where he sat and watched the house across the street. Not for the first time, he wished he could have risked staying in his car where he'd at least have a heater.

Unfortunately, this was the type of street where the neighbors all looked out for each other and noticed when something was off. Besides, he didn't want to risk that cop she was hanging out with recognizing a strange vehicle parked in the quiet neighborhood.

He'd been watching her all day, waiting for a chance to make contact and reassure her he was still there. He knew she had loved the flowers he'd left for her that morning when she'd gone directly back into the house to put them in water.

Excited, he'd decided that today would be the day he'd try to make contact with her and give her the chance to thank him for the generous gifts. However, when he'd rushed to the café, he was surprised to find she wasn't there.

Although he'd lingered over a few cups of coffee, and tried to ignore the looks he'd received from the waitress for taking so long during the rush hour, she still hadn't arrived by the time he'd left.

With a frustrated sigh, he ground the butt of his cigarette under the heel of his boot and dug out another one from his dwindling pack. He hunched over the flame and sucked in quickly until the tip glowed coal red.

By the time she'd shown up at the café, it was too busy to pull her aside. One thing was for certain, when she was his woman he'd make sure she stayed home where she belonged and could focus on him.

He exhaled, a plume of smoke wafting up into the air before him. That hadn't even been the worst of it. He'd seen the cop pick her up after the café had closed, and followed them to the grocery store. Robert had been sure she'd finally wised up and gotten rid of that bastard for good. Hadn't she sent him packing just last night?

It had been a huge risk, going into the store after them, especially since he hadn't been wearing his disguise, but it had been irresistible. From a distance, he'd watched them interacting in the grocery store, talking and laughing comfortably with each other.

He'd been mistaken. They seemed to be getting along just fine, after all. What was it with this guy? Everywhere he turned, the man kept getting in his way.

Why did women have to be such fickle whores?!

And now? Here he was, once again out in the cold, with another man's truck parked outside his woman's house. Robert jumped up, no longer able to sit with so much anger and frustration running through his veins. Tossing his cigarette on the ground, he made his way across the street and carefully snuck through the side yard.

He knew from previous visits that he'd have a limited view through the windows in the back, but he had to try to get one final glimpse of her before calling it a night.

Cautiously, he made his way to the office windows and peered in. He could barely make out the living room through the closed French doors. There was just the barest glow of light in the room beyond, and it was difficult to make out the details.

Suddenly, there was movement from the couch. He watched

Mason stand up and turn towards where the stairs were. Robert instinctively flinched, and resisted the urge to duck down, knowing it was unlikely he'd been spotted.

Riveted, he watched her enter the living room, and clenched his teeth when he realized she was inappropriately dressed in nothing but her robe. Dirty tramp! Hadn't he been the one to give her the flowers that morning? Hadn't he been the one sitting out in the cold watching over her?

His hands unconsciously fisted as he watched the two of them come together and kiss. His vision turned red with rage until he couldn't stand it anymore and turned away in disgust. It was obvious he needed to step in before the asshole was allowed to sully her any further.

And her...the little slut. He'd tried to play nice, but apparently she hadn't learned her lesson, yet. He pulled the slightly crumpled photo from his pocket and stared down at the picture in his hand. He had removed it from one of the photo albums when he'd broken into her house. It was of the three sisters laughing.

Resolved, he realized it was time to hit her where he knew it would hurt the most and make sure she understood just how serious he is. He was the one who controlled her. Every aspect of her life was subject to his will. Every relationship susceptible to his discipline. She belonged to him. The sooner she realized that and fell into line, the less he'd have to hurt the people around her.

Carefully, he made his way back to his truck parked a few blocks away and headed to the dingy motel room to set his plans in motion. All the personal information he'd taken from her office were in files on the bed. He'd have to access them in order to accomplish the next step.

Olivia may not realize it yet, but she was already his.

Chapter Twenty-Seven

Olivia woke up with a warm, hard, male body curled around her and strong hands busily exploring the curves of her stomach. She could feel his arousal pressing against her buttocks and couldn't resist wiggling to adjust herself more fully against him.

His clever fingers delved between the apex of her thighs and he groaned when he found her already hot and damp for him. Shifting his body, he spread her legs, and quietly sank into her depths.

The ride was a long slow fall, as if back into a dream. He rocked his body into hers, his hands stroking her sides, her belly, and breasts. Every touch, one smooth glide. Gently building, both of them caught in the upwelling of sensations and emotions until, united, they gradually crested the wave together. She cried out as the surge of feelings overtook her. With her back arched, she could feel him deep in the very core of her.

Shuddering, they collapsed onto the bed. She reached behind her and stroked his face, loving the feel of his arms around her waist as they both fought to catch their breath.

"Well, if that's any indication of how today is going to go, I think it's going to be a good day."

He chuckled and pulled out of her body. "I wish we didn't

have to get up and could just stay in bed. Now, *that* would be a good day."

Groaning, she buried her head under her pillow, "Ohhh, why did you have to remind me?" Suddenly cold air accosted her backside. "Hey! Don't take those covers away from me."

He swatted her butt. "Come on. Gotta get up! I don't want to be the reason your café goes out of business."

With a final grimace, she sat up in bed and petulantly tossed her pillow at him. He just smiled. "You know, for the proprietress of a breakfast establishment, you sure don't seem to like mornings very much."

Rolling her eyes, she got out of bed, "Exactly why I will be working the dinner shift once I start staying open for evenings."

"Ahh, so that's the real reason for the change."

She cast him a smile and headed towards the bathroom. "That's right, you figured me out." She stopped in the doorway and gave him a saucy wink. "I'm going to take a quick shower and freshen up a bit. Care to join me?"

Twenty minutes later, fully sated, and having worked up an appetite, she wound her still damp hair into a bun. There may not be enough time left to dry it, but at least the start of her day had been worth the slight discomfort of having wet hair on a cold morning.

Mason had already gotten dressed and left the bedroom by the time she emerged from the bathroom. She looked out the front window and spotted him outside, intently inspecting something on the ground.

As she watched, he carefully tucked a small baggie into his pocket, before straightening from his crouched position. He jogged back from across the street as she stepped out of the house and locked the door.

"What were you looking at?"

"How well do you know your neighbors, Olivia?"

"Pretty well. We've been living in this neighborhood for quite a while. Why?"

"Do you know if the person across the street from you smokes, by chance?"

"The Andersons? Oh no. I know neither of the parents do, and they have two small boys who are way too young to smoke. Why are you asking?"

"There was a pile of cigarette butts in the gutter over there, almost as if someone had been sitting for quite some time watching the place. I just wanted to see if there might be a logical explanation. Maybe Mrs. Anderson doesn't know Mr. Anderson likes to sneak a smoke once in a while…?"

She shook her head. "In all the time I've been here, I've never known either one of them to be smokers. But you don't really think it was one of my neighbors, do you? You think the stalker was here last night."

He nodded and gestured for her to get into the truck. "I think it's a likely possibility, yes. I went ahead and grabbed a few butts. Maybe we can get them DNA tested."

He watched her as she climbed into the cab of his truck. "Listen…" She turned towards him, the pale morning light casting a glow on her face, and he was struck once again by how naturally beautiful she was. If anything were to happen to her…he stopped his train of thought and swallowed past the lump that had formed in his throat.

"I'm thinking about heading down to Boston today to meet up with the Captain and see if I can get any more information out of him."

She nodded slowly. "Do you think he'll have anything new to tell you?"

"I'm not sure, but I know he's more likely to share what he does have if I'm standing there face to face with him." He gently stroked her cheek with his thumb before turning the key in the ignition and starting his truck. "The thing is, I don't really want to leave you alone right now, either. Not until I can get some kind of handle on this situation, anyway. Can you do me a favor?"

She admitted to herself that she'd been shaken up pretty badly these last few days, but had been feeling more hopeful this morning. Now she remembered that nothing had really changed as far as her stalker was concerned. "What would you like me to do?"

"Promise me you won't be alone until I get back from Boston. It's only a couple of hour's drive, so I shouldn't be too late getting back. Maybe you can call your sister to come by the café and pick you up after your shift, or something."

"You really think it's necessary for me to have a babysitter?"

"It's hard to say for sure. You said it yourself, we're not even positive this is Mendez. However, I will say that it would make me feel a whole lot better and help put my mind at ease while I'm out of town."

She mulled it over. It was still hard to accept that these types of steps were truly necessary. On the other hand, the consequences of not doing it could be far worse. "Okay, I'll give my sister a call and ask if she can come over this afternoon."

He felt a little bit of the pressure ease in his chest and gave her a smile as he pulled into the back parking lot of the café. "Thanks. Now, why don't I walk you in and make sure everything is okay before I take off? The sooner I get going, the faster I get back."

He stopped her from crossing the threshold and silently indicated she should stand behind him. A part of her hoped his actions were a little extreme, but she admitted that she felt better with him there and let him enter the building first.

Methodically, he walked through every room, making sure to check the walk-in freezer, her back office, and the utility closet where she kept her broom and vacuum. He even paid close attention to the dark shadows behind the bakery counter.

By the time he had satisfied himself that everything was in

order, Olivia had a pot of coffee brewed. She poured him a to-go cup right as Jackie came in the back door.

"Where's Tom?" Olivia asked.

Jackie sighed. "Remember how I mentioned he came over when I was sick? Well, now he has it."

"That stinks. I hope he feels better soon."

"Hm, I was hoping he would be here until your sister came over later," Mason said.

Olivia looked at him. "I'm sure it will be fine." She wound her arm through Jackie's. "You don't mind keeping me company for an extra ten minutes after work while Liz heads over here, do you?"

Jackie gave her arm a squeeze. "Of course not! We can finish the gossip session we started yesterday."

Satisfied that she would be as safe as she could be while he was gone, Mason figured it was time to go. He walked over to her and gave her a final kiss. He looked down at her and tucked a loose strand of hair back behind her ear. "I'll be back early this evening, okay? Be careful."

Her cheeks flushed from the kiss, she nodded. "Don't worry about me. Just drive safely and get back soon. Hopefully, your captain will have some new information we can work with."

After he left, Olivia began prepping for the breakfast crowd while Jackie checked on the dining room and made sure everything was ready for opening. Two hours later, she was relaxed and had fallen into a good rhythm in the kitchen.

Actually, despite her lack of sleep and everything that had been happening the past few weeks, she couldn't help but feel a little extra bounce in her step after last night with Mason. In fact, it was all she could do not to let her cat-ate-the-canary grin out. *Just another day at the office…*

Her phone began to vibrate in her pocket. Distracted, she grabbed it with one hand right as she finished the final plate for an order.

"Hello?"

At first, there was nothing but breathing. Confused, she glanced down at the phone, but the number was blocked. Putting the phone back to her ear, she raised her voice a little louder. "Hello? I'm sorry, I think we have a bad connection."

"Soon…" The deep, male voice could barely be heard over the other noises in the kitchen, but something about the sinister promise caused her to shudder. Instantly, she hung up the phone. Dammit. She'd almost managed to convince herself everything was perfectly normal.

She couldn't let this guy get to her. Mind games, that's all this was.

With a shake of her head, she peered into the dining room, wondering where the call could have come from. Disgusted with how easily this guy could rattle her morning, she was just about to shove her phone back into her pocket when it began to vibrate again. With a spark of anger, she jabbed the screen. "Look, asshole!"

A watery, tremulous voice greeted her. "Olivia?"

"Fiona! I'm so sorry, I thought you were…never mind, what's wrong? Are you crying?"

"Ohh, Olivia! They're not letting me register for my next semester's classes. They said we haven't paid them the tuition yet."

"What? I paid it weeks ago. Gimme a second, let me go back to my office where I can hear you better." She checked the dining room before swinging out the kitchen door and striding down the hall towards her office.

"I need to get these classes; otherwise I could have difficulty graduating on schedule."

"Okay, okay," she soothed. "We'll get this sorted, don't worry. I know I wouldn't have missed such an important payment. I just have to log into the bank account."

Hoping the orders would wait another minute, she booted

her computer and quickly logged into the bank's website, scrolled down to about three weeks, and checked the account history. Sure enough, the entries for tuition payments were there. "Well, they're right here. Why don't I give the office a call, and I can send them a copy of the statement."

Her sister sighed in relief. "I thought it was strange when they told me that. I'm actually standing at the counter right now, why don't I hand the phone over?"

Olivia spoke with the woman at the registrar's office and explained that she could immediately fax or scan a copy of the proof that the tuition had been paid.

The woman's deep foghorn voice filled the line. "I don't think you understand. Our records indicate that transaction had a stop payment placed on it."

"What?"

"Yes, ma'am. And, I'm afraid another personal check will not do in this case, since it's been an issue. We can accept a cashier's check or money order, but not a personal check."

She bit her lip, uncomfortable with going out by herself when she knew there was a stalker out there. In fact, she realized he was probably the one behind this whole situation. If he had access to her house, then he surely had access to her files and financials. There was no way she'd be able to head to the bank and then make the drive over to the college today.

She ran her hands through her hair. The lady's silence on the other end sounded like recrimination. "Unfortunately, I can't get away from the café right now to head down there. However, my sister really needs to be able to register today. Would you be willing to accept a credit card over the phone right now?"

She could hear the loud sigh as the woman let her know how put out she felt, but then she begrudgingly replied, "I suppose that will do."

She rolled her eyes, *Oh, you "suppose" you'll be willing to take my money?* Reminding herself not to think uncharitable thoughts, she infused her voice with warm cheer. "I appreciate that. Let me just read the numbers for you."

Ten minutes later, Fiona got back on the phone. "Thank goodness I could get a hold of you."

"Yeah, I don't know what happened. I'm sorry for the confusion, but you should be all set now. Do me a favor and get a receipt from her, okay?"

"Will do."

"I've gotta let you go and get back to the kitchen. Tom is out sick and I'm the only one filling the orders."

"Okay, thanks, Olivia. Talk to you later."

She wondered what the heck had just happened. She wanted to take a closer look through her bank accounts, but didn't have the time. Making a mental note to check with the bank later, she hoped to find a more benign explanation for the problem. Maybe there had been a mix-up or human error, somehow. She doubted it, but it felt good to hope it had been something less sinister, even if only for a moment.

Olivia made her way back to the dining room and noticed that everything was still under control. In fact, there hadn't been any new tables set in the time it took for her to handle the crisis. For once, she was happy that business was slow.

Impulsively deciding to take a moment, she grabbed the coffee pot and made her way around the breakfast counter. Too often lately, she'd felt the need to hide back in the kitchen, not knowing who or where her terrorizer could be. She was sick and tired of acting like a victim and being cowed. This was *her* place, dammit. If she couldn't feel safe here, surrounded by friends, then where else could she go?

Girded by her thoughts and resolve, she straightened her ¹ders and stubbornly pasted a smile on her face.

"Hello, how is everything going over here?" She warmly greeted one of her regulars, leaning over to refill a mug.

"Olivia. Everything is great, as usual! You ready for the holidays, yet?"

She grimaced. "Ugh, not even. I haven't started any of my shopping."

The young woman smiled. "I know, me neither. We'd better get on it, though."

Olivia nodded. "You're absolutely right. Well, enjoy your meal. Thanks for coming in."

Slowly, she made her way around the tables, taking a moment with each party to see how they were doing and touch base with her clientele.

Many of the patrons were familiar to her, but there were a few here and there that she didn't recognize. Although, with friends and family coming into town for Thanksgiving, she supposed that was to be expected.

Gradually, she began to feel more secure again. This wasn't just her place, this was her town. She'd grown up with these people; she knew them, knew their stories. No stalker was going to be able to take that sense of belonging away from her unless she let him.

Chapter Twenty-Eight

Robert watched as Olivia stopped at the table next to him and took a moment to speak to the patrons there. His pulse began to beat an unsteady staccato. He couldn't believe his good luck!

She rarely came out of the kitchen and here she was, so close. He probably could have leaned over and touched her. Maybe she had seen him sitting here in the dining room and fabricated some excuse for coming out to see him discreetly.

He scanned the café to see if Mason was anywhere nearby. All morning, he'd been keeping an eye out for the annoying detective, but hadn't seen him. It had been a pleasure being able to watch her without him interfering. Perhaps today would finally be the day he could make his move.

Suddenly, she turned towards his table. Frantically, he swallowed the bite he was chewing, coughing and sputtering as he swallowed it down the wrong pipe.

"Hi, are you okay?" The look of concern on her face had him turning red with embarrassment. He pounded his chest a few times, willing himself to stop hacking.

"Yeah, sorry. Food went down the wrong way."

"Don't you hate it when that happens?" Olivia smiled. "Need ‘ll on your coffee?"

He just sat, stunned. She smiled at him. At him!

He fought to remember what her question had been. "What? Coffee? Oh, yes please."

She leaned over the table in order to fill his mug. Subtly, he shifted so he could lean forward and inhaled deeply, memorizing the scent of her. He could just make out the curve of her tits. His fingers ached to reach out and test their softness.

Oblivious, she straightened. "How's your breakfast? Would you like anything else?" It was easily apparent to him she was looking for any reason to stay with him a little longer. He gave her a long, considering look. "I think you know what I'd like…."

He saw something flash in her eyes before she stepped back from the table and gave a hesitant half-laugh. He knew it. She *could* feel the connection between them. The little minx had just been playing coy. She probably couldn't even help herself, being a weak-willed female.

A sick thrill coursed through him at the way her nervousness filled the air between them. It was so obvious she was responding to him. He watched silently as she glanced towards the next table. Her skittishness made him feel powerful.

She quickly licked her lips and seemed to compose herself. Images of those lips wrapping themselves around his sensitive flesh as he filled her mouth flashed in his mind. "Well, if there's nothing else, I'll have Jackie come by with your check."

Such a little tease. He gave her a smug, knowing look and nodded. Was it his imagination, or did her hips sway a little more as she moved on to the next table? She wanted him.

Finally! He had the sign he'd been waiting for.

Today would be the day.

Chapter Twenty-Nine

The orange line of the speedometer crept past eighty. Mason gripped the steering wheel and reluctantly lifted his foot off the pedal. Slightly.

He couldn't complain. Overall, he'd made remarkably good time, despite the fact that he'd hit morning rush hour traffic. Still, the sooner he could be back in Maine, the better he'd feel. Leaving Olivia by herself was making him jittery.

As he passed the half mile sign to his exit, he let out a sigh of relief. Fifteen minutes later, he pulled into the parking garage about a block away from the police station.

The station's lobby wasn't very large, and was the standard issue, dingy, institutional beige that seemed to be found in every police station – small town or big city notwithstanding. After greeting the officer manning the front desk, he was buzzed through the security doors.

A wall of sound rose up and buffeted around him. It was the usual din of drunks yelling, victims weeping, and criminals threatening. There was the squall of perpetual phones ringing, the squeak of rubber soles on linoleum, conversations among peers, the occasional crash from someone giving the cops a hard time, and beneath it all was the barely perceptible clickety-clack of the keyboards as diligent cops and detectives hunched over their terminals and hacked out their reports. It sounded like a madhouse.

Mainly because it was one.

He took a deep breath, the corners of his lips involuntarily curling for just a moment as the constant cacophony assailed him. *Home…*

There was a glass-enclosed office at the back—the Captain's—and another room along the side for conferences or interviews. The aroma of stale, burnt coffee lingered in the air from the break room, through one of the doors on the back wall.

"Mason!" A beefy man, a little over six-foot tall, his muscular body just turning soft, came walking up and gave him a hearty slap on the back. "Good to see you, Detective. When you gonna get off your duff and stop milking the state for disability?"

He smiled. "Aww, come on, Smithy. We both know me being away is the only way you've gotten any attention around here. Are you really so quick to relinquish top spot?"

Detective Smithy grinned and gave his shoulder a warm squeeze. Mason was quietly relieved he was standing by the side of his good arm.

Smithy stopped and took a good look at him then dropped the smile. Mason keenly felt the other man's assessment as his astute detective's eyes quickly delved past the outer layers of his presence.

Uncomfortably, he shifted his stance, feeling slightly dissected but not wanting to break the other man's gaze. Smithy had been a veteran when he and Ryan had first become detectives and had taken them both under his wing, acting as a mentor to them. He owed a lot to the man standing before him.

With a sigh, Smithy let his arm drop to his side and gave him a wink. "Looks like you're really coming along. Glad to see you're up and about again. How's the chest?"

He shrugged. "Tight, achy in this damn cold…but getting better."

Smithy pinned him with a look. "You've got a couple of ten-pound bags under your eyes, man. You sleeping okay?"

"Mason. You gonna stand there and jaw all day, or are we gonna do this?" The captain's voice bellowed out of the office and above the bedlam. Instantly, the room hushed and heads swiveled to peer at the two men standing in the aisle before noise rushed in to fill the void once again.

With relief, he gave Smithy an apologetic look. "That's my cue. Hey, man, nice to see you."

"You, too. Take care of yourself, lad."

Mason strode across the room towards the man impatiently standing in the doorway and noticed the Captain looked a bit more haggard than usual. His badly wrinkled shirt appeared to have been slept in, and there was what looked like a mustard stain gracing his left cuff.

"Late night?" he asked, raising an eyebrow.

Captain Paul Fields just gave him a long look and sighed. "Aren't they all?" Mason nodded in commiseration. The older man had earned his respect a long time ago. He was a no-nonsense, extremely tough man, with exacting standards. Someone who wasn't afraid to get his hands dirty, and worked just as hard as any of the guys on the force. Mason knew he'd lost his wife to breast cancer a number of years back, which may account for his willingness to pull an all-nighter in the office just as often as anybody else.

He took a seat in the beat-up, slightly stained chair squatting across the desk from where Captain Fields' much more comfortable chair sat. However, instead of moving towards his own seat, his superior leaned a hip on the desk. "So, tell me what's going on with you up there. I know we've gone over a few things already, but why don't you start from the beginning and refresh my memory."

With a deep breath, he began categorizing the recent events leading up to his visit, ending with the most recent flowers on

Olivia's step and the pile of cigarette butts left in the street outside her door.

"I assume you brought a few with you for evidence?"

He pulled the plastic baggie of butts from his jacket pocket. "Yes sir."

Captain Fields nodded and opened the door, "Hey, you. Officer Reynolds!"

The eager, fresh-faced officer hurried to the door. "Sir?"

"Take these down to forensics, would ya?" He glanced back at Mason before instructing the officer, "Tell them to make it priority."

The officer took the baggie and rushed off to do the Captain's bidding. After watching him weave through the bullpen for a moment, the captain closed his door again. This time, he moved around the desk and sat down. The chair groaned and squeaked before finally giving up and accepting the familiar load. He leaned back in his chair, looking at Mason over his steepled fingers.

Mason caught himself bouncing his leg and had to consciously force himself to stop. Telling the sequence of events in their entirety had left him feeling antsy and filled with nervous energy. He didn't like being down here while knowing Olivia was up there with a madman in town.

The captain's voice redirected his thoughts to the business at hand. "Well, I guess that would help explain why you look like shit. I thought the whole point of you being up there was to get some much needed R&R and recover." He sighed heavily. "I take it you're seeing this woman."

It wasn't a question so much as a statement. Mason winced before schooling his features back into a relatively impassive expression. "Not that it's your business, but yes. I've been spend-ing quite a bit of time with her."

Captain Fields leaned forward in his chair. "Well, hell, that complicates things, doesn't it? No need to get defensive; I just like to know the lay of the land a bit before I go jumping headfirst into a situation."

Mason blew out a breath and ran his hands through his hair. "Look, I know I'm not back on active duty yet, sir, but I need to know if you guys have made any progress on this. Have there been any other breakthroughs, any ideas about where Mendez may have holed up? The guy couldn't have just dropped off the face of the earth."

The older man pulled a manila folder out of his top drawer and slid it across the desk. "As a matter of fact, we have. I don't think you're going to like any of the information we've discovered, though."

Mason pried the metal tongues apart and opened the flap. There were a number of reports along with a stack of crime scene photos. He looked up, surprised. "What's this? They've already found another one of his victim's?"

An odd mixture of relief and alarm balled up in his stomach. Maybe his instincts really were off. However, if that meant Olivia's stalker wasn't Mendez, then that was a good thing. For once, he'd be happy knowing he had been wrong.

"Well…not exactly."

"What do you mean not exactly?" Mason looked a little closer at the report in his hands.

"This was taken a little over a year ago…an unsolved case of a murdered woman in South Boston. She'd been bound, sexually assaulted, and brutally stabbed to death."

"Jesus," Mason flipped the top page up to read the second page. "They thought the fiancée did it?"

"Yeah, at first…but then they started doing the interviews with her family members and it didn't quite fit. They mentioned she'd begun to feel like someone was watching her. Had even made a few comments to them about flowers and notes being left for her – secret admirer shit. Only it persisted. Eventually, it started to affect her mood and actions. Friends said she stopped wanting to go out as often, had started declining invites to dinner, that sort of thing."

"Yeah, standard stalking stuff…sounds like a red flag."

Fields nodded. "Right. But then the family started talking about odd incidents happening to *them* up to the time of the woman's abduction. It was only much later, after it was too late, that they began to put together all the pieces and realize it must have been his way to separate and isolate the woman. She'd started to become estranged from her family, stopped returning their phone calls; you get the idea. Surprisingly, despite it all, the woman's boyfriend stuck around, and had recently proposed to her when she disappeared."

"No kidding."

"Yup. Unfortunately for the happy couple, the investigators suspect that was the catalyst. The detectives thought at the time—and I'm inclined to agree with them—that whoever was stalking her became enraged when he realized she'd gotten engaged." He gestured at the stack of gruesome pictures in Mason's hand. "Well, you can see where it led him."

Mason's lips twisted in a moue of distaste. He peered into the envelope and discovered a final piece of paper. It appeared to be a more recent printout. As he read it, he could feel his Captain's eyes watching him, assessing. After taking a moment to scan it, his eyes widened in shock.

"Are you shitting me?"

"And that's the link I wanted to tell you about today. I assure you, I am not 'shitting you.'"

"But this says the DNA at the scene of Robert Mendez' house—the scene of *my* shooting and Ryan's death—is a match for DNA at this woman's murder. How can this…? How did you even make this match?"

"We wouldn't have, to be honest. This case would have just sat in the unsolved murders cabinet and collected dust but for the fact that the head guy down in forensics just happened to have had a personality conflict with one of the guys working down there, and put in a transfer to move to Downtown. I honestly don't know how he paired the two together…but it's a match."

A match. The gravity of the situation floored Mason. It meant that Mendez had been violent long before his altercation with him and Ryan. That, in fact, he'd killed the women he victimized before. Who knew how many other poor murdered women were sitting in file cabinets waiting to be attributed to this guy?

Olivia.

A wave of restless energy had him jumping up from his seat and pacing the three steps of available space in the office. "We need to get those cigarette butt results *now.*"

The Captain watched from behind his desk as Mason stalked between the chair and the file cabinet. In all the time he'd worked with Mason, he couldn't remember ever seeing him quite so wound up and intense. He'd always been the calming force in his partnership with Ryan. Then again, he supposed recent events did have a way of changing a man.

As could falling in love.

He sighed. Maybe he really did lose two detectives that day. He wondered if Mason even realized it himself.

Trying to calm the younger man, he said. "They're working on it as we speak."

Mason whirled towards him, his hands fisted at his sides, his whole demeanor like a tiger caged and looking to pounce. "It's not fast enough." A deeper shadow moved across his face before he gritted his teeth and firmed his jaw.

Captain Fields once again stood and came around the desk towards him. "I know it feels that way." He put his hand on Mason's good shoulder. "Look, you'll be the first person I call when I get the results back from the lab. In the meantime, the best thing you can do is head back there, *focus on your recovery,*" at that he raised an eyebrow, "and reassure yourself that this woman of yours is safe."

With a grateful look, Mason headed towards the door, and then paused. "You'll call me?"

"As soon as I find out myself."

"Thank you, sir." Satisfied he'd done all he could, Mason wasted no time striding down the row of desks and back out into the lobby.

He pulled his phone out as he swung through the front doors and into the frigid afternoon air. "Come on…come on…" he muttered as ringing filled his ear. "Pick up the phone, Olivia."

He willed her to answer, but no luck. Leaving a brief message to call him, he hung up and checked the time. A little after noon…she was probably slammed at the café right now.

Luckily it was after the morning rush hour. It should only take him about two and a half hours to get back—two if he pushed it. Just in time to be there when she closed the café, or shortly thereafter. Feeling a little calmer, he climbed into his truck. He'd try calling her again in an hour or so.

Chapter Thirty

I t wasn't until after noon that Olivia realized she'd forgotten to call Liz and see if she could leave the shop a bit early today and keep her company. The tuition issues with Fiona had completely thrown her for a loop, and by the time she'd managed to get that sorted, the café had gotten crowded again.

"Jackie, I need to give Liz a call and see if she can keep me company this afternoon until Mason gets back. I won't be but a minute." She turned and headed back to her office. Surprised, she noticed she'd missed a call from Mason, but decided to try her sister first.

"Yo, Livvy, what's up?" Olivia could barely hear Liz over the background noise.

"Hey, Liz, sounds busy over there…"

"Yeah, we got a couple of new cars in the shop today."

"Oh." Her heart sank. She really hated feeling like an inconvenience. "Listen, I know it's probably a pain, but I was wondering if you'd be able to keep me company this afternoon until Mason gets back from Boston."

"Why, what's going on?"

"Well, you know how I've been having these stalker issues? Mason's worried about me being on my own for the time being. He's convinced himself it's this Robert Mendez guy. And after the home invasion and tire slashing…I have to admit, I'm a little hesitant myself."

"Shit, of course. I can't believe it's gotten bad enough he's afraid to let you be alone." She paused. "Yeah…I can move a few things around. I'll call and let one of my clients know their car won't be ready until tomorrow, and get over there a little after two."

"Thanks, Liz. If it's really too much trouble, I could just go over there and sit at the garage."

"No, I think I can make it work. There's not much I'll be able to do with the cars until some of the parts come in, anyway."

"Jackie said she has a few minutes she can hang out until you get here, so if it's closer to two thirty, I think it would be okay."

"Right. Well, I'd better get back to it, then."

Olivia hung up and stared at the phone for a minute. She hated feeling like this. With a sigh, she dialed Mason, and was surprised when it went to voicemail. *Huh, that's odd. I would have thought he'd be on his way back by now.*

Reluctantly, she sent a text letting him know everything was fine and she'd confirmed Liz would be by in a few hours. Tucking the phone in her back pocket, she headed back to the kitchen.

She was sick of having to deal with this whole situation.

The next few hours flew by with no further interruptions. It would have been so easy to pretend that nothing was wrong and all she had to worry about were plans for the upcoming holiday, but of course, the whole time her predicament niggled at the back of her head.

Thankfully, before she knew it, Jackie was saying good-bye to the last few customers as they straggled out into the blustery, cold afternoon.

Olivia had been straightening up the kitchen for the past thirty minutes or so, and there wasn't a whole lot left to be done.

She poured some tea for herself and Jackie and brought it into the dining room. Jackie looked down at the mug Olivia handed her. "Tea?"

Shrugging, she said, "I figured it was too late for more coffee. Besides, I'm probably too caffeinated at this point, anyway, and I refuse to drink decaf."

They sat down at one of the tables. Jackie leaned forward, her eyes twinkling. "So….?"

Olivia's lips quirked as she struggled to contain her smile, "So….what?" She gave her friend a wide-eyed, innocent look.

"Oh, my gosh. YOU DID! I want to hear all about it….well, not ALL about it, obviously…but you know what I mean. Was it good? Was it great?!"

She beamed, no longer able to keep the overwhelming joy from her face. "You have *no* idea…*I* had no idea. Sex has never been like that before." Her eyes became distant as she remembered the previous night. "Hot and steamy, with all this pressure building, and things climbing higher and higher, and yet, strangely melting at the same time…and, and…I can't even explain it."

An enigmatic smile filled with womanly knowledge entered Jackie's eyes. "Oh, don't worry, hon, I know *just* what you mean."

Sighing, she came back down to earth and stared morosely into her mug, idly stirring the steaming liquid. "It's pretty much the only thing that's been going right lately."

Jackie reached across the table and grabbed her other hand. "Oh Livvy, I'm sure all of this will work out soon enough. Remember what they say—'This, too, shall pass.'"

"Well, you know what? It can just start passing already." She chuckled and made a conscious decision to try and set it aside. She looked back up at Jackie. "There have been a few other things on my mind lately."

"You mean other than your raging hot sex life and stalker problems?"

Olivia cast her friend a wan smile. "Yeah…other than that. I've been meaning to talk to you about this for a while now, but with everything else going on, it slipped my mind." She took a deep breath. "I'm thinking about making a few changes to the café. Maybe keeping it open for a dinner shift. Not so much like a café or diner, but with more of an emphasis on a higher-end experience."

"Really? Oh, wow." Jackie leaned back and took a long look around the café, pondering the idea for a moment. "You know, I could see that working. What did you have in mind, exactly?"

"Well, I kind of thought you and Tom might like to take over the morning breakfast and lunch crowd, and then I could come in and take care of the evenings."

"Oh, that'd be perfect."

Olivia was reassured to hear her friend's enthusiasm at the thought, "Oh, good! I'm so happy you feel that way. I thought it would be ideal, since your schedule wouldn't have to change and you'd be able to pick up Abby after school just the same as always. And, to be honest, Tom probably doesn't need me back there with him, anyway. The man could handle the breakfast rush with his eyes closed. Of course, we can—and would—hire a second person to help him out, if he wanted."

"Well, obviously all three of us will have to sit down together and discuss the details, but I don't see why we can't make this change, Olivia. I think it's a great idea." Olivia let out a breath, relieved to find some of the pressure lifted from her chest.

Jackie glanced down at her watch. "Are you sure Liz said she'd be able to come over? I don't mean to be a pain, but I'm going to need to pick up Abby pretty soon. They charge me an extra dollar for every minute that I'm late."

Olivia checked her phone for the time, "I didn't realize it had gotten so late. Of course, you need to go pick up your daughter. Let me just give Liz a call." They both stood up from the table, Jackie shoving her arms into her coat sleeves.

Liz answered her phone on the first ring. "Hi, Livvy. I'm grabbing my coat now and just about to walk out the door."

"Okay, great. See you in a few minutes, then." Olivia hung up and gave Jackie a smile. "See? You know, since her garage is only three blocks down, it'll only take her a few minutes to get here."

"But I don't want to just leave you here by yourself. Mason made it very clear that you weren't supposed to be alone."

"I know. But, by the time I take care of our mugs, I'm sure she'll have arrived. Don't worry, I promise I'll stay here in the café until then." She gave her friend a quick hug, "I'm sure it will be okay."

Jackie cast her a dubious look, unsure of what to do.

Olivia laughed. "Don't be silly. I'm sure I can manage a few minutes on my own." At her friend's continued hesitation, she linked her arms with Jackie's and walked her to the door herself. "Go. Don't worry!"

With a laugh, Jackie pulled her hat down over her ears. "Okay, then, bye. Make sure to lock up behind me, at least. I'll let Tom know what you've proposed tonight over dinner."

"Thanks. We can talk about it more tomorrow. Tell him I hope he feels better." She stood in the doorway and watched her friend make her way to the car. "Hey! You guys are still planning on coming over for Thanksgiving, right?"

"We wouldn't miss it."

Smiling, Olivia closed the door and flipped the latch, then turned and looked at her café. What was usually peaceful suddenly felt eerie. A small shudder made her pause. If she were being totally honest with herself, the quiet *did* unnerve her a bit.

Shaking her reservations off, she grabbed the two mugs she and Jackie had been drinking from and headed back to the kitchen to wash them. Hopefully by the time she was finished, her sister would be here and they could go home.

Standing in front of the large, stainless steel sink, she sprayed the mugs clean and set them in the industrial sized dishwasher. A slight noise had her pausing and cocking her head to the side.

"Liz? I'm back here!" She waited, but didn't hear anything else.

She shook her head. This whole situation had her edgy and jumping at nothing. Grabbing a fresh dish towel from the drawer, she began wiping down the various surfaces.

The sound of the kitchen door swinging open behind her had her turning with a smile on her face. "Oh good, I was just..." She took a step back, bumping her spine against the unyielding counter.

"Wha...what are you doing here?" She gasped, alarmed to find a man standing in the doorway. Despite being a rather nondescript man, he looked vaguely familiar.

"Oh, hey. I didn't mean to startle you," the man said, raising his hands in a placating gesture. "The door was open. I just...I was here earlier and I forgot something in the booth I was sitting in."

She hesitated, but then remembered he was one of the guys she'd poured coffee for earlier that day. A tentative sense of relief began to creep back into her chest. "I could have sworn I'd locked the door." Silently, she berated herself for being so careless. It occurred to her that Mason would not have been pleased to know she'd forgotten.

At his silence, she continued, "Okay, well, did you find what you were looking for?"

The man shifted slightly to the side and took a step forward around the kitchen prep island. "You know...I DID!" With that, he lunged towards Olivia, catching her off guard.

She screamed as she felt his arms wrap around her shoulders, pinning hers down by her sides. "Get OFF of me!" His hot breath grazed her cheek as she struggled to pull out of his grasp and he fought to keep her in his grip.

Managing to get one arm free, she clawed at his face, remembering she'd read somewhere that going for the eyes was a good self-defense maneuver.

Unfortunately, she swung too wildly and clipped his chin instead. Confused, she recoiled at the sight of the damage she had wrought. A large flap of skin was left hanging from his face where his chin had been. *What the hell?* Desperately, she slammed her foot down on his.

He howled, "Stupid bitch!"

Next thing she knew, her face was pounding where his fist had connected with her cheekbone. Ringing filled her ears as she lost her balance and fell sideways against the counter. Her hands gripped the edge as she fought to stay standing.

Somehow, she knew that if she fell, it would be over. As her gaze lifted from the counter, she spotted the knife block in front of her. Wildly, her hand shot out and she latched onto the first handle her fingers touched.

Swinging with more force than finesse, she felt the sharp thud and give as the blade bit into the man's arm. He jerked back at the impact. Olivia kicked back with her foot with as much might as she could muster, hoping to hit his knee.

Her foot slid off his jeans-clad leg, and she sobbed as his fingers snaked their way into her hair and wrenched her head back.

"You little whore, playing your little games. I *know* you were flirting with me earlier." He made a grab for her arm and the knife while half lifting her up by her hair. Olivia swiveled, frantically trying to keep her knife hand away from him.

Her arm knocked against a canister on the counter and it crashed down to the floor. A blanket of white powder puffed up into the air, coating her and the assailant. She coughed and fought to gain her breath as her eyes rolled to the side, trying to get a look at the man behind her.

Abruptly, the man slammed her head forward into the counter in front of her. Her forehead exploded with pain as black spots began to edge into her vision. She fought to stay conscious. With a final, fierce bid for freedom, she stabbed behind her repeatedly, not aiming for anything in particular, but just trying to make any contact count.

The man jumped back, away from the sharp, steely point of

her knife, anxious to move before being cut again. She felt a large section of her hair being ripped from her scalp as she wrenched her head forward. Released, Olivia heaved herself towards the back door and blasted her way out into the damp, chilly, gray afternoon.

Without pausing, she dashed across the asphalt of the back parking lot, frantic to find anybody who could aid her. She could hear the door crash open and hit the brick wall and knew he was right behind her.

With tears streaming down her cheeks, she pumped her arms, pouring every ounce of energy she had into lengthening her stride. *I should have kept up on my running.* The thought, so out of place and unbidden, nearly had her laughing hysterically as she approached the edge of the lot.

Relieved, she spotted Herb's car just beginning to slow down and turn into the grocery store's lot across the street. Sensing rescue, she veered slightly to the right, hoping to catch him before he moved out of sight.

The sound of rubber soles slapped sinisterly behind her. He must have realized it was over, though, when she changed direction, because suddenly he began yelling epithets.

She got the feeling that he had dropped back, but didn't want to risk glancing behind her and possibly tripping as she ran. Wet, half-frozen patches of water and ice lingered in the dips and cracks of the pavement and it would have been easy to slide out.

Tires squealed as she rushed out into the street with her arms raised, begging Herb to stop. The look on the older man's familiar face reflected shock and she knew she probably looked half-crazed. She ran up to his driver's side door just as he opened it.

"Olivia? What on earth…?!"

"Herb!" She gasped between breaths. All at once, the enormity of what had almost just happened rushed at her and she burst into tears.

"Oh, my goodness, Olivia!" Herb scrambled out of the car and awkwardly wrapped his arms around her. Slowly, she sank down to the ground, fighting to catch her breath after the terrible fight, desperate run, and emotional outburst.

He crouched down, his bulk solid beside her. "Your face…" She felt Herb gently brush his thumb across her cheek and winced at how tender and swollen it felt. "Who did this to you?"

Liquid gold eyes, swimming in tears, looked up to meet his alarmed and questioning gaze. Her words came out in little hiccups and she could feel her nose running. "We need to call the police."

Nodding, he began to fumble his phone out of his pocket. He stood to make the call, but then his focus shifted to something happening behind her. A sinking feeling settled in the pit of her stomach as she watched his eyes widen in terrible fascination.

She turned her head back towards her café and inhaled sharply at the sight of thick, black smoke climbing towards the steel-grey clouds above.

Horrified, she pushed herself upright and stood beside Herb. The forgotten phone sat limply in his hand. She clutched at his sleeve. "Please! Make the call."

Snapped from his frozen state, he quickly dialed 911. Olivia listened impatiently as he reported what was happening, barely able to restrain herself from snatching the device out of his hand.

After giving him the exact street address to relay to the dispatcher, she turned and was horrified to see that the first few tendrils of smoke had morphed into great billowing flags of doom. Then the deep boom of an explosion rocked the air.

Sharp stabs of throbbing pain shot through Olivia's head as she watched the unfolding tableau with dread. Her eye had already begun to swell, steadily shrinking the scene before her down to a bare slit of vision.

All day she'd been trying to convince herself she could handle the situation, but she'd had no idea just how wrong she'd been.

Chapter Thirty-One

Robert slammed into the motel room, seething with frustration. He cautiously shrugged his jacket off and examined where the blood had seeped through his shirt. The flesh at his side flamed from where Olivia's blade had sliced him and he could already feel his face beginning to swell from the encounter.

What a little hellion. It probably shouldn't have come as such a surprise to him that she'd turn a kitchen knife on him. Hadn't he been watching her in the café for the past few weeks?

Wincing, he gingerly pried his shirt from the wound where the blood had already begun to clot, and took the shirt off. He scowled at his reflection in the mirror as cold water streamed from the faucet, inspecting the bruise slowly purpling under the skin on his cheek. He bent down and splashed water on his face.

Surprised, he found flour had gotten into his hair. It was then he remembered the bulk canister getting knocked off the counter and spraying forth a burst of powdery white as the lid had come off on impact.

Robert was disgusted with himself. How could he have let this situation get so far out of his control? Not only had he failed to take her, but now he'd also shown his hand. It was simply a matter of time before the cops realized he was in the area and began to look for him specifically.

Impatiently, he grabbed one of the threadbare towels from the rack in the bathroom and, after dampening it, used it as a compress against the wound in his side. Thankfully, it didn't look deep enough to require stitches. The angle would have made doing it himself difficult and he certainly wasn't able to go to the hospital to get it looked at.

He clenched his free hand into a fist, slamming it down onto the chipped porcelain sink. If only the bitch had behaved as she should have.

He paused.

He admitted to himself he'd underestimated her. If she'd come quietly, he wouldn't have had to take such drastic measures.

He chuckled as he headed back into the bedroom to grab another shirt. Oh, but he'd found a way to punish her for her insolence. Robert smiled in dark delight at the memory of those first few tendrils devouring the fryer oil, watching the red flames flicker across the counter's surface and over to the open flame of the gas stove.

Torching the place had been immensely satisfying. Too bad he'd had to leave before the gas had ignited. It would have been a pleasure to see the reactions flitter across her face as she watched her beloved café burn. He could imagine the flames reflected in her golden eyes, the way they'd be rounded in horror.

He hardened at the thought of her distress and idly rubbed himself with his hand. Really, who could have known she'd have so much fight in her?

The thought of taming her quickened his pulse.

For a moment he allowed himself to lay back on the bed, seeing images of her struggling beneath him, arms pinned at her sides, her hips bucking under his, and that moment when she capitulated to his dominance. Oh, he could practically hear her whimpering now.

Panting a little at the thought, he forced himself to stop. The outline of his hard cock pressed against the front of his jeans, arrogantly demanding release. Not yet…not yet, he reminded himself. Control, above all else, was essential. It was everything. He must master his urges and his body, or else how could he expect to gain the upper hand with Olivia when the time came?

He stood up from the bed and began packing his meager belongings into his duffel bag. Besides, he thought, the anticipation would make it so much sweeter once he did finally conquer her. For now, the best thing he could do was concentrate on getting out of town and up to the cabin. He'd lay low a bit and let her relax into a state of complacency, and *then* strike!

In fact, thinking about it further, taking a few weeks would be exactly what he needed to get the cabin prepared for Olivia's arrival. And won't she be so surprised by what he has in store for her?

Chapter Thirty-Two

"Olivia!" Liz's high, shrill, desperate voice, finally did what nothing else could have done. Olivia turned toward the frantic calling of her sister and watched as she came barreling down the sidewalk towards them. Detachedly, she noticed a number of other people had begun gathering, standing and watching the fire as it started to build momentum.

"Oh, my God, Olivia. I'm so sorry! Some lady with a flat tire drove up right as I was leaving the shop and I stopped to help her fill it up."

Liz searched her face and winced at the damage done there. "Shit, look at you." Gently, she grabbed both of her shoulders, turning Olivia away from the view of the smoke and forcing her to look directly at Liz.

Liz's eyes filled with tears as she gripped her in a hug. After a moment, she pulled back, disturbed by the lack of response in her older sister. "Olivia, honey, are you okay?"

Olivia's hollow eyes met hers before sliding back towards the ominous plumes. "The café. Liz, the café!" For a split second, her face crumpled around the edges before she managed to iron it out again. She couldn't seem to turn away from the sinister, sooty, black balloons of smoke.

Sirens pierced the frigid air around them, steadily growing

louder as they approached, but in her heart, she knew it was already too late. The damage was done.

"Oh, Livvy. I know…" Liz whispered, as she watched her sister's face, taking in the scene before her.

Anger, sharp and hot, pierced through Olivia. Trembling, she shot a quick look at her sister. "That bastard is going to *pay* for this."

"Wait, you mean…" Horror grew on Liz's face as she began to really assess the damage done to Olivia's face and body. Only then did Liz notice that Olivia couldn't seem to stop shaking. Her whole body was one big tremor as the adrenaline drained from her system.

"Ma'am?" Olivia flinched as a paramedic came up behind them. Liz wrapped her arm around her waist to help steady her. "Ma'am, I was told you had some injuries that I should see to."

What had started out as only slight trembling had quickly taken over her small frame. With her teeth chattering, she nodded her head at the young man. He held a warm blanket in his hands and gently wrapped it around her shoulders. "Why don't you come over to the ambulance so I can take a look at that cut on your forehead?"

Olivia raised her fingers to her head, only just realizing there was a robin-egg-sized lump beginning to form. No wonder her head was pounding so badly.

She gingerly sat on the back ledge of the ambulance. The paramedic dug a small light from his pocket and began to shine it in her eyes.

Liz stood just to his side and worried her bottom lip with her teeth. Olivia had a hard time concentrating on what she was supposed to be doing with the drama of the fire unfolding behind him. Her eyes kept drifting to the smoke.

She could see the burning red glow of the flames reflected against the windows in the stores across the street, but from her vantage point, couldn't actually see her café. Honestly, she wasn't sure that was such a bad thing given the circumstances.

"Okay, it doesn't look like any permanent damage was done, although you may have a slight concussion from that knock on your head." She focused on the man in front of her, but didn't know how to respond. *No permanent damage?*

How could he possibly say that as the inferno behind him blazed? Even if the fire could be stopped instantly, the damage would be extensive. Not to mention the feeling of violation, and the loss of security she was already experiencing. It all felt like permanent damage to her.

Dully, she simply looked away from the man and became aware of a uniformed officer standing to the side of the ambulance, patiently waiting for the paramedic to finish his tasks. After his assessment was announced, the cop stepped up. "Ma'am? Do you mind if I ask you a few questions?"

Liz came back over and sat down beside her, taking her hand for support. "Do we have to do this now? We really should call our sister, Fiona."

Olivia huddled a little deeper into her blanket and leaned into her sister's strength. After giving Liz's hand a reassuring squeeze, she nodded wearily at the officer. "Actually, I'd rather get this over with. However, before you start, you should know I already have a file related to this with Officer Brad Thompson. I've had a stalker harassing me for the past few weeks."

The young cop looked up from his pad. "A stalker did this?"

The weight of those words, and the knowledge that came with them, threatened to crush her. There was no getting around it now. No room for doubt.

"Yes." She whispered, barely audible over the sirens and excitement.

Just then Brad strode up and patted the younger man on his back. "Don't worry about this, I've got it."

Relieved, the cop gave him a nod and hurried back across the street to where some police tape was being set up.

Liz looked up at him. "Hi, Brad. Thank goodness you're here."

Brad nodded at her, then took a moment to really look at Olivia, as if cataloging her many injuries, both physical and otherwise. He sighed. "Well, this became a shitstorm, didn't it?"

His unexpected candor managed to break through Olivia's sense of shock. Startled, she looked up and offered him a wan smile. "That, I think, would be an understatement."

"Why don't you tell me what happened? From the beginning."

Haltingly, she began to relay the events that had occurred after the café had closed. Liz winced when she got to the part of her story where she was in the kitchen alone.

Brad was quietly intent and listened without interrupting. After she was finished, he asked, "Would you be able to recognize him again if you were to see him?"

An image of the man standing in the doorway flashed into her mind. She began to nod her head, but stopped when the pounding pain ramped back up to piercing, reminding her of the beating she'd just taken. Hot, sharp misery flashed behind her eyes.

"Okay, I know your head hurts, but I think we need to get at least a preliminary description of him before I let you go tonight. Your memory will be freshest right now. Are you okay with that?"

Olivia closed her eyes to better picture her assailant. "He's wasn't very old, or overly young. I'd put him about mid-thirties or so. He had dark brown hair. Brown eyes." She paused, trying to recall any other details.

"About how tall would you say he was?" Brad prodded.

Olivia got a flashback of him standing behind her and shuddered. Silently, Liz scooted closer to her and wrapped an arm around her shoulder. "Um, taller than me. I came to about his chin. Not as tall as Mason."

Brad looked down at his pad and added a few more notes.

"OLIVIA! OLIVIA!" The deep roar of a desperate man cut above the noise of sirens and the crowd. All heads turned towards the sound. Olivia instantly felt relief as she recognized Mason's voice.

"OLIVIA!"

Brad pivoted to look at where the panicked voice was coming from, and noticed the young officer valiantly trying to restrain Mason from entering the protected area.

He quickly got up and strode over to the cop. "It's okay. He's with me." Relieved, the younger officer gave him a harried nod and stepped back. Mason didn't even stop to utter thanks, but bounded over the tape and ran straight to Olivia.

"Olivia..." he slowed once he got a bit closer and could see the damage. "Oh baby, look at you."

Gently, he cupped her face in his palms, taking note of the lump on her forehead and her black eye, now swollen shut. "Can we get an ice pack here?" he yelled over to the paramedic. Instantly chagrined, the young man rummaged in his bag and broke a cold compress open.

After wrapping it in a bit of cloth, he handed it over to Mason. "Here." He held it to her face until she took it from his grasp and held it in place herself. He softly brushed her hair, trailing his fingers across her shoulders and down her free arm.

He held her hand and turned it over so the palm was facing up. The heel of her hand was scraped, her knuckles bruised, and a few nails torn down past the quick from when she'd fought the man off. He groaned and slowly lowered his head to kiss her poor, abused fingers.

Liz watched the two of them intently, taking note of the way they bent towards each other. Seeing the relief on her sister's face at Mason's arrival, she shifted and hopped down from the back of the ambulance to stand by Brad.

Now the full weight of what had transpired hit her. "I'm so, so sorry," she stammered brokenly.

"What do you mean, 'you're sorry?' How did this happen?" Mason's head jerked up to pin Liz in a stare before shooting a look back at Olivia.

Pulling her hand from his grasp, Olivia roused herself in defense of her sister. "It was *NOT* her fault. Don't you *DARE* give her a hard time!" She turned to look at her sister, who had lowered her head in shame and was staring at the ground at her feet.

"Do you hear me, Liz? Get it right out of your head that you had anything to do with this. If it wasn't today, it would have been tomorrow, or the next day, or the next…" Olivia's voice choked at the thought. The truth of her words reverberated through her soul.

She was trapped, as surely as if she were a prisoner in her own life. She turned haunted eyes back towards Mason and whispered, "This man is determined. It was just a matter of time." She closed her eyes, fighting back the nausea her poor head was causing her.

Liz sniffled and raised her damp eyes to meet his. "I guess I just didn't realize stopping to help that woman fill her tire would lead to something like this. I had no idea the magnitude of what we were dealing with."

He observed Olivia with serious eyes. He could see the exhaustion and pain she was desperately trying to hide. It was obvious she was maintaining control by a thread. However, despite her distress, he could see a deeper layer of resolve in her eyes. She may have just had a setback, but she hadn't given up, not yet.

He looked back at Liz. "Olivia's right. Probably even more right than she even knows. I apologize. I shouldn't have gone off like that."

Brad had been watching the whole reunion and exchange intently. Now he stepped forward. "Olivia, we *will* get this man. It's just a matter of time before he makes a mistake." He turned towards Mason. "If you have some new information, I'd appreciate it if you'd share it with me."

Mason regarded the officer with grave concern. "About that, I may have some details that are relevant to the case, and I'm hoping to have more by tomorrow morning. I'm just waiting for the results of a few tests that could help illuminate exactly what kind of person we're dealing with. Under the circumstances, it may be best to let her rest for a bit. May we please pick this back up tomorrow?"

Brad cast a look at Olivia and noticed the way her shoulders were hunched over, her hand still holding the ice pack over her eye, and sighed. The officer in him wanted nothing more than to get the details he needed from her, but as her friend, he could see she'd reached her limit. Resigned to waiting until the next day, he stepped towards her and placed a hand gently on her shoulder.

"Okay, I have enough to get started, at least. I swear to you, this is a personal priority for me. We will not stop until we get this guy." Olivia's one good eye swiveled up at him. It pained him to see her like this. He turned towards Mason and gave him the go ahead. "We'll put a unit outside her house tonight, just in case. All the same, guard her closely."

"With my life." Mason growled.

"I'll stop by tomorrow morning to take her statement and get any other information from you." Satisfied, Brad turned and made his way back towards the chaos halfway down the block.

Mason wrapped his arm gingerly around Olivia's shoulders to steady her as she lowered herself down from the ambulance bay.

Liz rushed up and took her other arm. "How could it have come to this?" she asked Mason.

"Unfortunately, it's not unusual for these kinds of cases to escalate to the point of violence."

The three of them stood, but before they could head towards his truck, Olivia stopped. "Please. I need to get closer. I need to see…"

His first instinct was to protest. He didn't want her to have the images of her café looking like that in her head. Especially not after what she'd just been through. However, when he went to open his mouth, she just squeezed his hand and gave him a tired, understanding smile.

Resigned, the three of them rounded the corner of the building and turned towards the crowd watching the fire from across the street. They watched as the firefighters valiantly fought back the flames and tried to save the surrounding buildings.

Day had already begun to darken into the steely gray and blue winter hours of twilight. The large, plate glass windows in the front had been smashed, either by the heat of the fire itself or in order to grant easier access for the large hose the men had carried in.

At Olivia's shudder, he wrapped his arm more firmly around her shoulders. Liz snaked her arm around her waist from the other side, each doing their part to make sure she was supported. They both looked over her head and met each other's determined gaze, a silent understanding shared between the two of them.

Chapter Thirty-Three

I t didn't take them very long to arrive at the house, Liz following closely behind them in her Jeep. As they approached the
door, Mason paused. "Liz, why don't you stay out here, for a
minute, just in case? I want to go in and check around the house."

Olivia looked up, startled. "You don't think…?"

Leaning down, he took a moment to place a gentle kiss on her
cheek. "No honey, I don't. It's just a precaution, but I think we'd
all feel better for making sure."

Liz wrapped her arm around her sister and shot him a fearful
look before firming her jaw. "Don't worry, I've got her. Be careful."

He swung open the door quietly and cautiously, hesitating for
a moment on the threshold to listen to the sounds of the house
and get a feel of the place. Everything was quiet. It felt empty.

Taking a deep breath and wishing he'd thought to bring his
handgun with him, he slowly made his way through the house. He
stopped first in the kitchen to grab a knife from the butcher block,
just in case.

Meanwhile, the two sisters sat huddled and shivering on the
front stoop. The sun had finally gone down and the already cold
temperature edged towards zero without the light. They both
strained their ears for any unusual sounds. Liz had pulled her
phone out and was poised to call 911 at the first sign of trouble.

It took about fifteen minutes before he stepped back out and gave them the all clear. Liz walked Olivia to the kitchen and led her to one of the kitchen stools, then turned towards the stove. "How about some hot tea to help get us warm?" Briskly, she grabbed the cheerful red kettle from the stove and began to fill it up at the sink.

Mason moved towards Olivia and noticed the lost, vacant look in her eyes. He'd seen the thousand-yard stare before in other victims of violence. Cautiously, he wrapped his arms around her. He couldn't seem to get rid of the need to hold her, to reassure himself that she was still there and that, despite her injuries, she was okay.

She sighed and leaned into him. He gently rubbed her back, incredibly grateful that she seemed to feel the same way. "The minute I saw those flashing lights surrounding your café, I swear, I have never been so afraid in my life. If anything had happened to you…" His voice cracked as he fought to swallow past the lump in his throat. Reflexively, he tightened his arms at the thought of what could have happened to her.

She grimaced and flinched slightly. Instantly, Mason released her, remembering she was in pain. "Here, let me take a look at you." He spoke quietly as he bent down to assess her face again. He winced at how swollen her eye had gotten. Somewhere along the way, she must have set the ice pack aside.

"Ouch. That's gonna be a doozy of a shiner. We need to get some more ice on that."

Cautiously, she probed the puffy skin with her fingertips. "I think I may have left it in the back of the ambulance."

Liz opened the freezer and took out an ice tray. "Well, let's make you another."

"I wish I didn't need it. It's too cold to have ice pressed up against me." Just then she was wracked by a full body shiver. "I can't seem to get warm."

"That's probably due to a slight case of shock and the

adrenaline leaving your system. We should get you into a hot bath and changed into something warm and comfortable."

"A hot bath sounds heavenly right now." Olivia admitted.

"Would you like me to help you upstairs?"

Her lower lip trembled for a moment before she pressed them firmly together. "Actually, if you don't mind, I think I just need a moment alone."

Mason stepped back, keeping one hand on her shoulder to help steady her. "That's okay. I'll be right here if you need me."

Liz quietly handed her the baggie full of ice that she'd wrapped into a dishtowel, "Here, I know you probably don't want to deal with it right now, but you'll be happy you did tomorrow."

Olivia gave her sister a hug. "Thanks, Liz."

They both watched as Olivia left the room and listened as she made her way up the stairs. She knew they were both concerned for her well-being and doing what they could to comfort her, but she couldn't seem to explain just how rattled and vulnerable she was feeling at the moment. She needed to wrap her head around what had happened.

She needed a moment to think.

Her body felt sluggish as she entered the calm serenity of her bathroom and groaned in protest as she bent down and got the hot water running. After pouring some bubble bath in, she turned away from the tub and faced the full length mirror hanging on the back of the door.

She gasped. Now that she could get a good look at her face in the mirror, it was every bit as bad as people had been telling her, maybe even worse.

The large knot on her forehead had already begun to turn a deep shade of eggplant purple, with a nasty cut where the skin had broken. No wonder her head was still pounding so badly.

She turned her head to the side to get a good look at the way her right eye was beginning to swell. The entire cheekbone had swollen to epic proportions and was tender to the touch.

Being the first black eye she'd ever had, she'd had no idea her eye could get that big. Olivia remembered the makeshift ice pack Liz had handed to her and hastily picked it up off the bathroom counter where she'd set it.

With her one eye covered, she noticed flour covered her entire torso, lower back, and one side of her leg. *What a mess that was going to be to clean up…*

The thought stopped her in her tracks. *Her café!*

For one, brief, shining moment, she'd forgotten. A large mess of flour would have been so much more preferable than what she had to clean up.

A heavy blanket of depression descended around her. Dejectedly, she pulled her jeans down over her hips and stepped out of them. Slipping out of the rest of her clothes, she paused once more to note the map of violence catalogued along her flesh.

Shadowed fingertips gripped her bicep. Constellations of blue bruises scattered across her ribs and torso. A dark and angry black hole of a knot graced her right hip.

Olivia found she felt slightly removed as she took note of the damage done to her body. This was not who she was. She wasn't the kind of woman who would have something like this done to her. Was she?

Broken, she turned and checked the bath before turning the water off. Gratefully, she dipped her toes into the steaming, scented water and sank into the depths down to her chin. Maybe if she closed her eyes, she could forget everything outside of those four walls for a moment.

From behind her lids, an image of the smoke wafting up over the crowd of people entered her mind. She could see the glow of the flames reflected on their upturned faces, their mouths opened in sick, fascinated horror.

Water rippled and sloshed as she sat up abruptly.

Her café!

The place she had fed her very soul into. Where she had invested hours and hours of time, sweat, blood, and tears. The place that had helped her climb from the deep morass of depression overhanging her after her parents had died, and given her a means to support her sisters.

Gone.

That word—*gone*—cracked her composure like an egg. She didn't even realize she'd begun to break down until she gasped for breath on another sob. Clasping her hands over her mouth, she stifled the sounds of her despair as emotion welled up past her throat.

Olivia pulled her knees up to her chest and huddled in the hot water, instinctively reverting back to a fetal position of warmth and comfort, and released the valve on her emotions. After a few moments, the initial squall left her feeling exhausted and wrung out.

She slid down further into the water and submerged her head, enjoying the shield of muffled silence. Calmer, she reluctantly came up for air. Laying her head back, she closed her eyes and willed herself to regain some composure.

A light tap sounded at the bathroom door. "Olivia?" Mason cautiously poked his head through the threshold. "May I come in?"

Chapter Thirty-Four

Mason paused just inside the bathroom door, a cup of tea and a couple of ibuprofen balanced in one hand, and sucked in a breath at his first full look at Olivia.

Raw fury surged up and threatened to overwhelm him as he took stock of the damage to her beautiful body. For a moment, all he could do was stand there and clench the doorknob, the teacup rattling slightly in its saucer.

Silently, he wrestled with his rage, instinctively understanding that the last thing she needed was to be faced with more violence – even if it was on her behalf.

Controlling his initial reaction, he calmly moved to place the cup on the counter. Looking up, he caught her reflection in the mirror and could see the exhaustion on her face, despite her eyes being closed.

With a deep breath, he let the anger built up in him dissolve and slowly knelt down by the tub. Olivia opened her eyes and pierced his soul with the turmoil in their depths.

"Liz has taken off. She said she'll call you tomorrow. How are you feeling?"

"Tired, hurt…numb. I don't think it's fully hit me yet." She raised a hand to her black eye, and offered him a wry smile. "Sorry, poor choice of words."

Unable to resist touching her, he lifted a hand to brush a strand of damp hair back from her face. He pretended not to notice her slight, instinctual flinch when he did so, but inside his heart wrenched a little tighter.

"I'm so sorry this has happened to you." His voice cracked with emotion. Taking a moment, he struggled to compose himself.

Silently, she turned her cheek into his palm. Filled with tenderness, he leaned over and softly placed a kiss on her poor, abused brow. Olivia tilted her head up, offering her lips to his.

With a groan, he gently captured her lips, brushing across them tenderly, back and forth with his own until she opened them, inviting him deeper. He took a moment to delicately explore the sweet hollows of her mouth before pulling back.

Carefully, he took the bottle of scented shampoo lying on the ledge and poured a dollop into his palm. "Lean back and I'll wash your hair for you."

A spark of desire flared in her eyes before she complied with his request and slowly slid deeper into the hot, fragrant water. Taking care not to harm her bruises, he began to lift and lather her hair.

He enjoyed the way her eyes closed as his fingertips gently massaged her scalp and rinsed the suds from her strands. Slowly, he worked his way towards the back of her head and down her neck.

Her lips parted and she sighed, letting out a soft groan. Her neck was damp and exposed; the creamy skin beckoned to him. He watched as a single droplet of water traced its way down past the hollow of her throat and through the valley below.

Just the tops of her soft, round globes were exposed above the water, disappearing into a frothy line of sheer bubbles. Mason swallowed. He ached to follow the path of the water drop with his tongue and taste the scent on her skin.

"Mason…" Olivia's breathy voice cut through his fantasies and he looked up to find her watching him through shuttered eyes.

Sitting up abruptly, she gripped his shirt with wet fists. She paused for a moment and stared at his mouth before looking back up to his eyes. "Make love to me, Mason. Please. I *need* you to make love to me. Let me shut the world out for a while."

He liked to think that if it had just been desperation in her eyes, he would have had the strength to say no, but underneath the dark bruises and damage to her face, he saw the hunger and was helpless to resist.

Reverently, he traced her face, letting his fingertips trail down her neck and along the line of her collarbone. He could feel her begin to tremble at his touch. "Let's get you out of this water."

Standing, he helped her exit the tub and wrapped her in a plush bath towel. Being careful not to press too hard on her bruises, he began to gently dry her skin.

She stood there and patiently gave herself over to his ministrations as he methodically worked his way from her shoulders and down each arm, her breasts, torso, and the curve of her buttocks.

He knelt before her and dried down the long columns of her legs, and then looked up at her from his crouched position. She stared down at him. Water streamed from the ends of her hair as it hung in long curtains around her face, casting it in darkness.

Her burnished eyes glowed from the shadows, hot and wary and needy.

Standing, he took a moment to towel dry her hair, then lifted her gently into his arms and carried her to the bedroom. Carefully, he deposited her on the bed and, standing before her, began to remove his clothes. He took his time and watched the reactions flit across her face. His eyes silently promised that this would be all about her tonight.

He wanted—needed—to show her that a man's touch could be gentle. A part of him recognized he needed the closeness as much as she did.

Naked, he climbed up onto the bed and lay beside her, letting her feel the full length of his body touching hers. Olivia's eyes swam as she looked up at him and he caught a tear as it cut a salty path towards her temple.

"Olivia…"

She raised her hand and pressed a finger to his lips. "Shhh. These aren't bad tears." Her hand slowly stroked the side of his face, memorizing the curvature of his jawline. Her lip quivered as she gave him a watery smile. "It's just that you're so beautiful."

The look in her eyes had Mason's heart leaping. He may not be ready to acknowledge the gaze that passed between them, but his soul recognized it for what it was and rejoiced.

A fierce need to protect surged up in his chest and he was caught by the intensity of his emotions. Unable to put what he was feeling into words around the lump in his throat, he did the only thing left to him and endeavored to show her.

Olivia let out a sigh as Mason bent his head down to capture her lips. Softly, he nibbled at the corners of her mouth, carefully following its outline, and taking care to avoid the damaged skin.

He flicked his tongue into the sweet recesses of her mouth, teasing her with light kisses until she yearned to deepen them. As she moved to do so, he pulled back and began feathering his lips across her cheek, her brow, and down her nose, paying special attention to all the places violence had left its mark upon her face.

Gradually, he made his way down the slim column of her neck and to the arm that held the shadow of another man's hand. Holding her slender limb up, he paused at the inside of her elbow before kissing his way down to the fine bones of her wrist. Gently, he nuzzled her palm, carefully avoiding her ravaged fingertips.

She inhaled sharply at the feel of his mouth. Who knew her hand could be such an erogenous zone? She'd never had a man attend to her needs so tenderly.

Deliberately, with great care, Mason attended to all the sore points on her body, causing the pain to melt away until there was nothing but pleasure and heat and yearning.

Eventually, he made his way back to Olivia's mouth and sampled her lips once again before rising over her and positioning himself between her thighs. He could feel she was already slick for him and rubbed his tip along her entrance.

Beneath him, she writhed, now lost to the sensations Mason had built up in her. With a controlled push, he slowly began to sheath himself in her depths, groaning as he felt her inner muscles clench around him.

Desperate to take it slow and not worsen her injuries, he fought for control. He could feel the silky soft skin of her thighs as they slid along his hips. Watching, he noticed the way her nipples had turned to a dusky rose and couldn't resist bending down to suckle one between his lips.

Steady and sure, he filled her with pleasure, stoking the heat at her very core until she turned to molten lava around him. Her breathy whimpers and helpless panting set his blood on fire, but still, he forced himself to focus solely on her pleasure, ruthlessly denying his body the release it was clamoring for.

And then Olivia let out a high, keening sound and began to shudder all around him. With her back arched, her body began to tighten around his cock, sending him flying far beyond the edge of any control and reason.

Stunned in the aftermath of his orgasm, it took him a moment to gather his wits and realize the woman who'd given him such pleasure was looking up at him with a warm, glowing smile. He was relieved he'd kept the majority of his body weight propped up on his arms and hadn't crushed her or worsened her injuries.

He wasn't quite sure how he'd managed it.

Carefully, he pulled himself from her body and flopped down to the side of her. Limp and utterly content, she turned her head to face him.

"Thank you."

Mason nearly laughed. Wasn't it *him* that should be thanking *her?* But something about the solemn way her eyes held his had him stopping himself before he could give voice to his humor. Feeling more than a little privileged and humbled, he simply nodded and gathered her fully into his arms, pulling the blankets up around both of them.

"Shhh. Hush now." He stroked his hand down her back. "Why don't you relax and get some sleep? I'll keep watch over you and make sure you're safe."

He was gratified by the way she sighed and relaxed against him, yet it was a long time before he managed to nod off himself. And even then, it was with an ache filling his chest that hadn't been there before.

Chapter Thirty-Five

Olivia woke slowly in her bed and, for one brief moment, didn't remember any of the events that had occurred the day before. That is, until she made the ill-advised move of sitting up too quickly. Surprised, she froze as a wave of pain washed over her.

Inhaling sharply, she held her breath, waiting for the soreness in her body to ease back a bit. Her head, once again, began to pound, feeling like someone had taken a 2x4 to it.

Cautiously, she raised her hand and gently prodded the edges of the lump on her forehead, testing it for size and tenderness. It seemed to have gone down a bit, she was happy to note, and took it as an encouraging sign.

As she took stock of her physical status, she was reminded of the fact that not everything felt bad today. Mason's lovemaking the night before had given her a delicious soreness between her thighs that hadn't been there previously, and that wasn't at all a negative thing.

Memories came flooding back to her, both the good and the horrific, until her head begun to spin from too much thinking. Downstairs, she heard the faint trill of the phone before it was answered on the second ring. Mason's deep voice drifted up through the floorboards.

Groaning, she buried her head in her pillow and pulled the covers back over her. It would be so much easier to pretend the world outside her bedroom didn't exist.

A vision of the charred and hollowed-out shell of the café filled her mind and she thought of all she'd lost. Then she began to think about the man who had taken it from her. Had almost, literally, taken her.

Resolutely, she gritted her teeth and lowered the covers again. Slowly, she fought to get herself back into a sitting position, and then took a moment to catch her breath.

Every bone and muscle in her body ached in protest. She felt as if she'd been shoved into a dryer and set to tumble dry on its highest setting.

With more determination than panache, she managed to swivel her legs over the bed and plant her feet on the cool floor below. Cautiously, taking care with her poor, abused head, she turned and viewed the alarm clock across the room.

"Are you kidding me?" she muttered under her breath in shock. How on earth could she have slept past eleven o'clock in the morning?

With that realization, she slid her feet into her slippers and shuffled over to the bathroom. For a moment, all she could do was inspect her face in the mirror. Her poor eye was a dark black over the entire socket, up to the brow, to both corners, and all along the top of her cheekbone. The eye itself was bloodshot in the outer corner. It made her ill to look at it.

The large, goose egg of a bump in the middle of her forehead was hardly better. It was still very swollen and had also blackened. She suspected that was actually the culprit giving her the worst of her headache.

In fact, from about the middle of her forehead all the way down the left side of her face was one big contusion. Unnerved,

Olivia decided she'd seen enough and didn't even want to see the damage to the rest of her body.

Instead, she turned away from the mirror and headed out of the bathroom. On the way out of her bedroom, she grabbed her comforting, familiar robe and wrapped it around her like a cocoon.

The warm, homey smells of bacon and coffee greeted her as she opened the door. It was such a stark contrast to the damage she'd seen in the mirror that at first Olivia felt she must have stepped into another world.

Knowing Mason was in the house loosened a knot in her chest. She hadn't wanted to verbalize her fear out loud, or even to herself, but she wasn't quite ready to face an empty house this morning.

Joints and muscles creaked as Olivia padded down the stairs, protesting the abuse of the day before. She carefully made her way through the dining room, and then froze in the kitchen doorway, enthralled by the scene that greeted her. Mason stood in front of the stove, partially turned towards her, and was carefully folding a layer of egg over a bed of veggies.

She took a moment to let her eyes wander over his body, and admired the way his sweatpants hung low on his hips. She could see the muscles in his back ripple beneath the threadbare t-shirt he wore as he reached into the cupboard above him and grabbed the pepper.

Passion had her mouth turning dry, her body restless just looking at him. As she shifted her weight, one of the floorboards squeaked and had him turning to her.

"Oh, good. You're up. I was just about ready to come and get you." He moved to grab the pot of coffee and filled the mug he'd already set out on the counter for her. Dropping the pot back onto the burner, he reached into the fridge and poured her a small glass of orange juice.

Olivia moved fully into the room and awkwardly climbed up on the kitchen stool. It seemed her whole body was going to protest every little action she made today; she felt like she was moving as if she was a hundred years old.

"Ouch. You look like you're feeling sore. The coffee is probably still too hot to drink, but the OJ can help you wash down some ibuprofen. It should help cut the pain a little." He set two pills beside her.

"Thank you." She gulped the painkillers down. "Something smells really good."

He shrugged. "I figured you might like it if someone cooked breakfast for you, for once." He gave her a boyish grin and pulled a plate down from the cupboard. "I hope you don't mind that I kinda had to poke around your kitchen."

"Not at all. I'm glad you made yourself at home." She drained her juice and pulled the coffee towards her, hunching over and wrapping her hands around the warm mug. "I can't believe I slept so late!"

"You probably needed it." He placed the plate of food in front of her. "I hope you like omelets. It's one of the only things I feel somewhat confident feeding you."

Olivia picked up her fork eagerly and inhaled. "Are you kidding? This is perfect. Ooh, and home fries."

He turned back towards the stove and plated his own breakfast, then sat down beside her. "Yeah, I didn't think I could recreate Tom's amazing hash browns, but I can at least make decent home fries."

He watched her take her first bite and smiled when she dug right in. For a moment, the two of them ate quietly, taking the time to enjoy the meal and each other's company.

With the initial edge of her hunger appeased, Olivia sat back and took a sip of her coffee. She gave Mason a look over the rim. "Was that the phone I heard ringing earlier?"

"I'm surprised it didn't wake you up sooner. It's been ringing non-stop all morning."

"Really? Who has been calling?"

"Well, your sister, of course. Actually, both of them. Liz got a hold of Fiona and let her know what's going on. Jackie and Tom… Jackie was beside herself and completely distraught about leaving you yesterday…"

"But I insisted she go. There was no way either one of us could have known what would happen."

He placed a hand over hers. "I know. That's what I told her. But I think she'll feel a lot better hearing it come from you."

She nodded. "I need to call her."

"You do," he agreed, "but it can wait for a bit longer. Let's see, who else? Ah, well, your insurance agent tried to reach you. I took a message, but he said he would try back this afternoon."

Olivia sighed. "I haven't even begun to think about the insurance or how to tackle that."

"We'll work it out," Mason assured her. He hesitated. "I also got a very interesting and informative phone call from my captain that I need to tell you about, but I think it would be best to wait until Brad gets here."

"I'm assuming it has to do with Robert Mendez. Has it been confirmed?"

"We'll talk about it. Speaking of which, Brad also called and wanted to come over earlier this morning. I told him you were still sleeping. He said he'd be by around one or so."

Nodding, Olivia set her mug down and forced herself to take a few more bites of food, but all of a sudden she wasn't so hungry anymore. There was so much she had to do. Most disconcerting of all was the call from Brad. She really wished she didn't have to relive the events that had happened yesterday.

In fact, she dreaded it.

Sighing, she pushed her plate back. Mason watched her from the corner of his eye as he took another bite.

"Decided you didn't like my cooking after all?"

Olivia blushed. "No, it was delicious."

He set his fork down and turned more fully towards her. "Sorry, bad joke." Gently, he brushed his thumb along her cheekbone, then leaned over and feathered a kiss at her temple. "I know it feels overwhelming right now, but you have a lot of people who want to help you. We'll just take it one step at a time, okay?"

Nodding, she looked down at the counter. "I know. You're right. I know it sounds silly, but I'm actually more concerned about having to recount everything that happened yesterday for the report."

"I understand what it's like having demons. That's not silly at all. Just know that everything you can remember is going to help us catch this guy and make sure you're safe. Any detail, no matter how small, might make the difference between finding him quickly and you having to continue to look over your shoulder."

She leaned into him and sighed. "I know. I know. You're right. It's just going to be really hard having to relive it."

"I'll be with you the whole time." Mason cradled her face in his hands and looked directly into her eyes. "You can do this, Olivia. You're stronger than he'll ever be."

Nodding, she pulled back and stood up from her stool. "Well, if Brad is going to be stopping by soon, I'd better get myself pulled together."

"Good idea. I'll get the kitchen straightened up while you do that."

She wrapped her arms around his shoulders and took a moment to just stand in his arms. "Thank you, Mason."

She didn't see the pained and tender look on his face as she walked back up the stairs.

Chapter Thirty-Six

It didn't take Olivia very long to get herself ready. She pulled on some yoga pants and a tank top, and then crawled into her favorite sweatshirt. She briefly considered trying to put some makeup on to help cover the damage to her face, before concluding that no amount of cover-up could help the situation.

Besides, she had bigger concerns than what she looked like, at the moment. She couldn't be bothered to care all that much.

Tucking her feet back into her slippers, she headed downstairs and into the living room. Mason came in from the kitchen and found her curled up on the couch under a blanket.

"Would you like another cup of coffee?"

She looked at him. "You know, I'm already feeling a bit jittery. I don't know if coffee is such a good idea."

"How about some tea?"

She smiled as she leaned over and grabbed the remote. "That would be great, thanks."

Idly, she flipped the TV on and was surprised to find a reporter standing in front of the charred remains of her café. It was surreal watching them report on her life in such raw terms.

How many times had she watched someone else's misfortune fall from carefully lacquered lips, edited and choreographed to fit into a two minute news segment? The thought was unnerving.

Thankfully, a knock at the door gave her the excuse she needed to switch the box off. Before she could get up, Mason went to answer it. Olivia could hear Liz's voice at the door.

"It's so weird not being able to let myself in now," Liz said.

"Well, hopefully the extra security measures will only have to be temporary. This guy has already proven he can pick a lock. I thought it would be a good idea to get one of those safety bars installed, as well. That way, at least while you're in the house, you know you're protected."

"Oh, don't get me wrong, I think it's a great idea. It just stinks that it had to come down to this." Liz dropped her voice a little before continuing. "How's she doing?"

"I'm fine!" Olivia called out from the living room. "Mason is already spoiling me by cooking breakfast for me *and* doing the dishes."

Liz stepped into the living room and took a look at her sister, curled up on the couch. "Well, that sounds like a pretty good morning." She sat down next to Olivia and examined her face closely. "That's quite a shiner you have there, Livvy."

"Tell me about it. I don't think I'll be winning any beauty pageants any time soon."

Another knock at the door had both sisters looking towards the entryway. Mason turned to answer it from where he'd been standing in the archway, watching the two women exchange greetings.

"Brad, come in."

Brad stepped into the entryway, along with another officer who was holding a satchel. "Hi, this is our resident sketch artist, Officer Cynthia Carlyle." He paused. "I'm also going to need to get some photographic documentation of Olivia's injuries and thought having a female associate here would help."

She shook Mason's hand. "Please, call me CeCe."

Olivia winced when she heard why Brad had brought CeCe.

She was definitely not looking forward to that. Sensing her uneasiness, Liz patted her knee in commiseration.

"Nice to meet you. Olivia is in the living room."

As they came in, she struggled to sit up a little straighter.

"Hey, Olivia. It's okay, don't get up," Brad said, bending over to give her a brief hug. "How are you feeling?"

She gave him a small smile. "You mean other than looking like I ran into a couple of walls? I'm pretty sore, but I'll be okay."

"Hello, ma'am. It's a pleasure to meet you, even if it is under poor circumstances." CeCe shook her hand.

Olivia nodded at the two chairs, indicating they should take a seat. "Thank you for coming. CeCe, this is my sister, Liz." The two women nodded at each other. "I heard what Brad said in the entryway. Sounds like we're going to get to know each other intimately pretty quickly."

The other woman laughed. "I think I like you already." Noticing Olivia's discomfort, she continued, "I'm afraid it's a necessary evil."

"Would you like anything to drink?" Mason asked from the doorway.

"Oh, no thank you. I think we're fine for now," Brad answered.

They both sat across from Olivia while Mason finished making tea. After setting the mug down in front of her, he squeezed in next to her on the couch, sandwiching her between himself and her sister. Casually, he took hold of her slightly damp hand.

Brad took out a little recorder, as well as a pen and small notebook. "Do you mind if I record this?"

"That's fine, Brad." She shot CeCe a glance. "I mean, Officer Thompson." She gave him a frustrated look. "You know, I never know what to call you. It's so weird being on this end of things."

"Brad is fine, Olivia. Whatever makes you comfortable."

"Okay. I have to admit, I'm a little nervous. How do we do this? Do I just tell you what happened?"

"Yup, that's it. Just start from the beginning and tell me everything you can remember. I'm probably not going to ask a lot of questions at first, and just let you get it all out. Then, if I need any more details, I'll follow up. Okay?"

Taking a deep breath, she took a moment to wipe her palms on the blanket, then reached over and held Mason's hand again. "It was about 2:30 in the afternoon. I know this, because the café was closed and Jackie had been staying with me, waiting for Liz to arrive…"

It took her nearly an hour to go through the events of the day before. A couple of times, she'd gotten choked up and had to stop to collect herself, but overall, it hadn't been as bad as she'd thought.

"Okay, Olivia, you're doing great. Let's go back for a minute. You said you flipped the latch on the door when Jackie left, but then he told you the door had been unlocked. Was the door locked, or not?"

Olivia closed her eyes and replayed the moment in her mind. "No, I'm sure I locked the door. I was being extra cautious because of everything that's been going on."

Brad gave her an encouraging smile. "Okay, so I think it's safe to say he has some experience with picking locks. That would coincide with the home invasion, as well."

He glanced back down at his notes. "I'm confused about your statement of what happened after you hit him in the face the first time. You described it as if his whole chin was ripped off…"

"Yes."

"It seems like there would be a lot of blood involved."

She wrinkled her brow. "But I don't remember there being a lot of blood." She gave him an apologetic look. "I know that doesn't make sense, but I swear it looked like I knocked his chin clean off." She raised a hand to her temple. "Maybe I'm misremembering it, though. I did get knocked pretty hard on the head."

Mason had been quietly listening the whole time. "Well,

actually, that might be related to the news I had to share with you all. The Captain called this morning with the lab results he got back."

Brad glanced at him. "Lab results?"

"Yeah, I found a pile of cigarette butts outside Olivia's house yesterday morning and collected a few to have tested in Boston when I went for my appointment. That's where I was and why I was so late in getting back."

"Ah, okay. So? What were the results?"

"What I've feared and suspected for a while now. I'm not sure how it came to be, but Mendez is definitely here, and judging by the number of butts piled outside her door, he's her stalker."

Liz gasped.

Olivia's heart dropped at the news, but strangely, she felt an odd sense of relief, too. Now, at least, she could finally put a name and a face to her stalker. Before, it could have been anyone, and her imagination had been getting the best of her.

"Wait, I don't understand," she said. "How does that have anything to do with me thinking I ripped his chin off?"

"Well, Robert's been known to use disguises in some of his abductions. I have a feeling he may have been using prosthetic makeup."

CeCe leaned forward. "Hmm, that could make things difficult, but if it's all the same, I'd still like to try and put together a sketch."

"I agree. It couldn't hurt. Maybe we could even get the basics down and have you make a few composite sketches using different chins," Mason said.

She nodded. "That's not a bad idea.

Brad turned towards Mason. "Okay, so, now we know who we're dealing with, for sure. What can you tell us about him? This is the same guy that shot you, right?"

Absently, Mason rubbed at the spot where the bullet had

entered his chest. "It is, yes. That right there should tell you that this guy is not to be underestimated." He looked at Olivia and then back at the officer. "But, unfortunately, there's more…"

Mason explained how Boston had connected a previously unsolved murder of a woman to Mendez. "What this tells me is that he's taken the use of violence with his stalking victims to the highest level. Unfortunately, stalkers have a tendency to develop patterns. Which means, now that we know he's killed someone at least once, he'll have no compunction about doing it again."

His words had the same effect as a bomb being dropped in the middle of the room. All five of them sat in silence as they digested this new information and the ramifications. Liz sighed. "Oh, Livvy…"

A cold ball of fear sat heavily in her stomach. Her initial instinct was to curl up as small as possible and hide from the rest of the world forever. Agoraphobia was starting to look like a pretty good idea. Maybe she could become a hermit. Olivia worried her lip, frustrated with her options.

She didn't *want* to be trapped in her own life, dammit!

As she scanned the faces of the people around her, she found Mason looking at her fixedly. She could feel him willing his strength into her and found that it actually did help to steady her nerves.

Feeling fortified, she took a deep breath. "So, what can we do? I can't live like this indefinitely. This guy needs to be caught."

CeCe grabbed her satchel and stood up. "Well, let's get to work, then. Why don't we go into the dining room, set up, and we can start putting together a sketch of this guy?"

Happy to have something tangible to do, she nodded and got up from the couch. "Sounds good. How long does this usually take?"

"Well, it depends. Usually it takes two to four hours, but I've known it to take longer."

Olivia stopped in her tracks. "A couple of hours? I never realized it took that long." She looked longingly over at the dining room table. "I would really like to get started on this, but I still have to get ahold of my insurance agent and I've yet to go over to the café and look at the damage."

Struck by that thought, she turned back towards Brad. "That reminds me. When do you think we can get into the café?"

"I'm thinking tomorrow. Like I said, we've had the forensic guys in there to do the preliminary work, but the fire department still has to go through and make sure it's structurally sound."

Olivia sighed. "Damn. Okay, then."

CeCe placed a comforting hand on her shoulder. "As far as the sketch goes, I'm sorry, but it's important that we get to it as soon as possible. People's memories tend to fade over time. Especially if the event was traumatic. We may also need you to come down to the station and take a look at some mugshots. Is there any way you can reschedule with your insurance agent?"

Liz stood up. "I can call his office, if you'd like. I'm sure he'll understand, given the circumstances."

Resigned, Olivia gave her sister a nod and then turned back to CeCe. "You're right. Whatever is going to help catch this guy is more important."

CeCe gave her an encouraging smile. "Before we get started on that, I think we should go up and document your injuries first."

At Olivia's look of distaste, CeCe gave her a sympathetic smile. "I know, it's not pleasant, but it will help us build a case against him once he's caught." At this, she got a determined look on her face. "And he *will* be caught…"

She appreciated the other woman's attempt to reassure her. "Okay, then. You're right, whatever it takes." She started heading up the stairs. "Let's get this over with."

Liz hung up the phone. "It's all set. He said tomorrow will be fine. Would you feel more comfortable if I came up with you two?"

Olivia hesitated. "I don't know, Liz. You might find it disturbing. It's pretty bad…"

Liz gave her sister a bald look. "It's probably not any worse than what I've been imagining. When I think about what could have happened, I just…," Liz took a deep breath and tried to collect her thoughts. "I know you said it wasn't my fault for being late, but I just *need* to make it up to you, ok? Can I come up and give you some moral support?"

She smiled at her sister and gave her a hug. "Of course. You guys going to be okay down here?"

Mason looked at her. "We'll be fine. Do what you need to do."

With that, the three women headed up to the bedroom, leaving the men to their own devices in the living room.

"So, I take it you guys are definitely an item now," Brad said.

Mason turned to him. "Yeah. That's not a problem, is it?"

"What? Oh no, not with me. It's not like that between Olivia and me. I just hate seeing her have to deal with something like this. She's already been through a lot with her parents. Actually, I'm glad she has someone like you watching her back."

Mason nodded. "It's good to know she has a friend on the force that will be making her case a priority. She's going to need all the help she can get. Especially now that we know this is Mendez."

"Yeah, I'm glad a lab was able to collect some DNA from the samples you got yesterday. I had my forensic guys go over the crime scene at the café, but the fire destroyed any of the evidence we may have gotten from it. Judging by Olivia's account, it sounds like she got him pretty good. It would have been nice if some of that blood had been found."

"She's tough, that's for sure. I'm glad she could fight him off. But, you know, that's also part luck. The fact is, he underestimated her and she caught him off guard. Next time, he'll be expecting it."

"So, you think there will definitely be a next time?"

Mason leveled a look at the other man. "I do believe he will try again, yes. But I don't plan to give him the kind of opportunity that he had yesterday to get a hold of her."

"If you're sticking around her too closely, he may not make another attempt for a long time. Are you prepared to put that kind of time and energy into this situation? I was under the impression you were planning to head back to your old position after the holidays. Isn't that still the case?"

Sighing, Mason ran a hand through his hair. "Well, there is that. I haven't quite figured the logistics out for that yet."

"Look, I know it's not what either of us wants, but maybe we should consider setting a trap for him. Help expedite this process."

"You mean have her act as bait."

"Well, there would be a few advantages, if we did it that way. One is that we'd be able to better control the time and place she gets approached.

"Besides, you said yourself this guy could end up going to ground for a bit before making his move. In fact, the incentive is there for him to do exactly that. Especially now that his presence around here is known and the heat is on.

"You know how it goes with these kinds of cases. We can't sustain that level of interest in the public for long before people are looking to the next thing. Not to mention, it's the holidays and everybody's got happier times to be thinking about."

Mason sighed. "The point is, he can afford to wait me out."

Brad gave him a wry, twisted smile. "Basically, yeah. Not to put too fine a point on it, but you may not have the options you'll need to beat this guy."

Mason's hands balled into fists as he thought about what the officer had said. He knew Brad's reasoning was valid, but didn't want to face that possibility just yet. "Let's just give it a little time before we consider that step. Let's get through Thanksgiving first. Then, if nothing further has happened, we can try to bring it up to her."

Brad sighed. "I agree. That's probably the best course of action for now. CeCe should have something later this afternoon. She's the best, which is why I brought her. We'll work on circulating the sketch and getting the media attention on it, see if anybody has spotted this guy. Then we can go from there." He paused. "But, Mason, I want to make sure you're looking down the line on this. You need to figure out just how committed you are."

"You're right. I'll think about it."

Chapter Thirty-Seven

Hours later, Olivia, Liz, and Mason were following the two officers out of the house and locking the door. "Thank you for coming by to take my report, Brad," she gave the man a hug and then turned to CeCe. "It was very nice meeting you."

"You, too, honey. You did really well today. We'll get this to the media outlets as soon as possible. I think we're even in time to make the nightly news."

"I just hope it helps."

"It all helps." CeCe gently placed her hand on Olivia's shoulder. "You take care of yourself."

"Thank you, I will."

The three of them watched as the officers climbed into their car and took off. Shadows ran long in the fading afternoon light. Mason turned to the two sisters. "Liz, you sticking with us?"

She nodded. "If you don't mind. I haven't been back to the café, either, and thought I'd take a look at it with you guys."

They all piled into Mason's truck and headed into town. The ride was quiet and pregnant with tension. The closer they got, the more Olivia's stomach turned into knots.

Wanting to break the silence, Mason said, "Are you ready to see this?"

"The truth? Not really." She attempted a smile before turning more sober. "But it has to be done. I need to see what the damage is with my own eyes."

"Okay, I can understand that."

As they pull up from behind the building, she was struck by the bright yellow police tape that cut through the leftover, dingy snow, keeping the parking lot and the back door cordoned off.

She could see the black smoke marks snaking their way out of the doorway and staining the decades-old bricks. There was a hole where the roof had collapsed which must have been where all the smoke had been billowing from the day before.

Losing the restaurant was like a kick in the gut. She'd poured everything she had into it. In turn, it had helped her to support her family and had seen her through the darkest periods of her life. Other than the death of her parents, she couldn't remember when she'd ever had a moment where she felt so forlorn and alone. She had hoped never to feel such a poisonous mix of anger and despair again.

Mason continued down the street and turned the corner, parking on the other side of the road from the café. They all just sat there for a moment and took in the sight of the place. She was thankful when, after a moment, he reached over and took hold of her hand.

Liz sighed and opened the door. "Maybe it won't hurt so much if we do this quickly, like tearing a bandage off fast."

The two of them peered through the windshield at the café. They could see that the large plate glass windows had all been shattered, and even from this distance, it was obvious the place had been gutted. Olivia hesitated, not sure if she was ready to take a closer look at what lay within.

"I don't think anything is going to help, to be honest," she said under her breath to Mason. "But let's get this over with."

Just then, Jackie and Tom walked up and stopped at the police tape sectioning off the sidewalk in front of the café. With one final fortifying breath, she released Mason's hand and climbed out of the truck to join them and her sister.

Gasping at the damage to her friend's face, Jackie burst into tears and rushed to hug her. "Olivia. Oh, my goodness, I'm so sorry. I'm so, *so* sorry! I can't believe this has happened. Can you believe this happened? I can't *believe* this."

Despite the pain from being hugged too tightly, Olivia didn't let go of her friend, giving her the time to work out her emotions. She rubbed a hand down her back and reassured her. "I'm okay, Jackie. I'm okay."

"When I heard what happened, my heart just dropped to the floor. I would have come over to see you sooner, but Mason said you slept in this morning."

Releasing her, Olivia turned to Tom and was carefully enfolded into another hug. "Yeah, I guess I needed the rest because I actually woke up after eleven today." Her voice cracked with emotion as she turned to face the damage. "Look at our beautiful café. It's ruined."

Tom pulled back and quietly stared into her eyes. "The important thing is you kept your head about you, fought back, and managed to get away. This can be rebuilt. *Will* be rebuilt. You, my friend, are not so easily replaced."

Touched by the look in his eyes, she managed to calm down a bit. "I know, you're right," she whispered, "but seeing this for the first time is *hard*. I didn't realize I would have such a visceral reaction like this."

"It's a natural reaction to trauma," Mason said, walking up to the little group.

"Tom, I don't think you've had a chance to officially meet Mason yet," she said, introducing the two men.

They both quickly sized each other up, and unspoken communication passed between them as two warriors recognized and acknowledged the signs of past battles in each other's eyes. Mason reached out his hand. "Nice to meet you."

"Likewise. Olivia mentioned she's been having trouble with an unwanted suitor paying too much attention." With that, he shot her a reproving look. "You should have let me know the extent of the trouble you were dealing with. I had no idea it was this bad."

Chagrined, she apologized. "I'm sorry. It's taken me a while to accept the situation for what it is, and I didn't really want to concern everybody over nothing."

Tom looked over the burnt husk of the café and back into Olivia's eyes. "This is not 'nothing.'" After a moment, he sighed and gave her another hug, accepting her apology.

Turning back towards Mason, he said, "Jackie mentioned you might know who is behind all of this."

"We just got the results back from a DNA sample I had tested," Mason said.

Jackie's eyes rounded. "Has it been confirmed?"

At Olivia's nod, all three women took a moment to hold on to each other. Each of them wiped their eyes when they parted.

Jackie looked up at Mason with tear-stained eyes. "You were right, yesterday. You tried to warn us."

Liz interjected, "I was the one who was late."

Jackie gave Liz a hug too. "I was the one who left her, all alone...with that *madman!*"

Despite everything, Olivia laughed a little. "You two. No having a guilt-off. Neither one of you did anything wrong." She walked over and wrapped her arms around both of the two women hugging. "Please. I don't want either one of you feeling bad about this. The only person who is guilty of anything is Robert Mendez."

Mason smiled kindly at Jackie's red, splotchy face. "Honestly? He probably would have found a way to get to her at some point, regardless. There was nothing you could have done by staying. In fact, I'm happy you weren't there to get hurt, as well."

Tom's eyes turned to flint. "I'd kill him."

At that, Jackie gasped and slapped him on the arm. "Tom, really."

Tom just looked at her intensely. "That wasn't meant to be a joke, Jackie. If he laid a hand on either you or Abby, I'd hunt that man down and kill him."

Mason's barely controlled voice was edged in frost. "You'd have to get in line."

Tom gave him a measured look. "Well, as it is, he's already made my 'maimed' list."

Olivia rolled her eyes and threaded her arm through Jackie's. "Alright, you guys. We both get that you're a couple of badasses," she smiled to soften her words, "and we're very thankful that you would want to protect us like that, but I'm not looking for anyone to be killed. I'd be happy just to have this guy caught, so he can be out of my life and the women he's harmed in the past could get some measure of justice."

The five of them turned and faced the café, lapsing into silence and their own thoughts. After a moment, Olivia broke the quiet. "I wish we could go in and really see the damage that's been done in there." She fingered the police tape. "I wonder if there's anything salvageable."

"When did they say you can get in there?" Jackie asked her.

"Tomorrow, maybe. I'm not sure how long it's going to be before we can get things up and running, but I promise you, I will find a way to make sure you two are taken care of."

"I appreciate that," Tom said, "but you don't have to worry about that right now. Just concentrate on getting back on your feet, first."

"Well, still. I'm supposed to meet with my insurance agent tomorrow afternoon. I'll let you know how it goes." Olivia shivered. The afternoon light was quickly fading from the sky. "I can't believe it's already so late. I guess that's what happens when you sleep half the day away." Mason enfolded her into his arms.

"Did you want us to be with you tomorrow when you go through the place?" Tom asked.

Olivia shrugged. "Only if you want to be. Otherwise, I'm sure it'll be fine."

"Oh!" Jackie exclaimed. "What about Thanksgiving this week?"

"If you want, we can take over hosting the event..." added Tom.

"Hm, I hadn't even thought about it." Olivia took a moment to consider. Granted, she did have a lot on her plate, but... "You know what? No. I still want to host this year. I'm not going to let this guy ruin it for me. Besides, since I'm not going to be at the café, I should have plenty of time to do the shopping and cooking. That is, of course, if you don't mind accompanying me, Mason?"

He smiled. He had very fond memories of the last time Olivia had cooked for him. "Do you mind if I invite Melody over for the holiday, as well?"

"Absolutely. Of course she's welcome."

Liz piped up. "I can always come by and help you get ready."

Surprised, Olivia turned to her sister. "But what about your shop?"

"Oh, well, I talked to Paul and he said he'd take it over for a few days."

"Liz, you didn't have to do that."

She gave her sister a stern look. "Seriously, Livvy? You're my sister. Of course I did." She shrugged. "Besides, it's been awhile since I've taken some time off, and with the holiday this week, it's not too busy."

"Okay. So, Thanksgiving at your place, then. As long as you don't think it's going to be too much," Jackie said, with a smile. "I guess we'll all plan on seeing you in a couple of days."

Mason watched as Olivia shivered again from the cold. "Sounds good. We'll see you on Thursday."

Chapter Thirty-Eight

Robert knew he was taking a huge risk by being there, but he hadn't been able to resist seeing the results of his handiwork one last time before heading out of town. He surreptitiously glanced around the coffee shop to make sure nothing was amiss.

Nobody was paying attention to him.

With relief, he swiveled on his stool and focused his attention on the scene across the street. Olivia, her sister, and another couple were standing there talking in front of the police tape.

He'd seen how she had walked up and hugged them both. The problem, he realized, was she was in her comfort zone and surrounded by her friends in this small town.

He'd messed up. It would be even harder to isolate her now. Everybody would be on their guard looking out for her, especially the cop.

He watched as Mason walked up to the small group and put his arm around her. His face tightened in anger as he saw the way she leaned into him. Robert could imagine how her curves would feel pressed against him. A spear of jealousy shot through him thinking about it happening to another man.

"Hello there. Would you like a free sample?"

His attention was diverted by the young woman's inquiry. He

gave her a glare and curtly shook his head, turning back to the show before him. With a huff, she walked away.

What he needed was a way to separate Olivia from everybody else. Something that she wouldn't be able to resist. Something that she'd *have* to respond to.

He thought about it for a moment as he turned to scan the café, *think, think, think…*

His attention was caught by a young family as they all sat around the table, enjoying their beverages, the little boy and girl gripping their apple juice boxes.

Suddenly, the little girl started to cry because she couldn't get her straw into the box. Before the parents could respond, the older brother reached over and helped her fix her drink, then bent down and placed a kiss on her cheek.

Aww, look how precious the stupid brats are.

It reminded him of Olivia and her family. The key was going to be to get her separated from their protective comfort.

On the other hand, even though her family was her strength, he may be able to exploit that and have it become her weak spot. Then it hit him. Of course. The sisters! He'd already seen how close they were. No way would she be able to resist if she thought one of her sisters was in trouble.

The seed of an idea began to germinate in Robert's mind. Maybe he could make that work. The question was how to implement it.

He'd stayed long enough. There would be plenty of time to iron out the details once he got up to the cabin. With that thought in mind, Robert got up and exited the café. Let her have her holiday. The few days it would take for him to come up with a solid plan would serve to help her relax into complacency. The thought made him smile.

Chapter Thirty-Nine

"Happy Thanksgiving!" Melody chimed as her brother opened the door.

"Hey, sis. Glad you could make it," Mason gave his sister a warm hug and stepped back to let her in. "Here, let me get that for you," he added, as he took the casserole dish from her hands. "You can hang your coat up on one of these hooks, assuming you can find one."

She did as he suggested, then took a moment to really look at her brother. "Haven't seen you very much this week. How are you holding up?"

He paused for a moment to think about his answer. "Given the circumstances, I'm doing okay. I keep thinking I must have somehow led him to her…"

"There's no way you could know that," she interjected.

"No, I know you're right, but still. What if he followed me here and has been watching me this whole time. Would he have latched onto her if I hadn't started seeing her? What if it had been you, Mel?"

"What if she didn't have you here to watch over her? Have you thought about it like that?"

"She might not have needed watching if I hadn't been here."

"Then, Mason, some other woman would be in his sights.

Look, I get that you care about her, but you can't be playing this 'what if' game with yourself. The situation is what it is. All you can do is help her deal with it."

An outburst of laughter erupted from the kitchen and had her turning towards the sound. "Sounds like she's dealing with it pretty well. I should go in and say hi."

Mason handed her casserole dish back. "Why don't you take this in with you? I'm going to check on the fire in the living room."

"You mean check the score on the game?"

He gave her a cocky grin. "That too."

Laughing, she made her way to the kitchen, surprised to find so many people. A slim, athletic brunette with an edgy pixie cut was just stuffing a piece of bruschetta in her mouth, while a younger woman had her head buried in the refrigerator and was digging around in the veggie drawer. A dark haired man bouncing a young girl on his knee was sitting at the dining room table across from a petite blonde woman.

Olivia glanced up and spotted her. "Hi, Melody. Welcome."

"Hi, I hope you don't mind I brought a dish with me."

"Not at all. What'd you bring?"

Melody shrugged. "Just some Brussel sprouts. I found a good recipe a few years back and they seem to go over pretty well."

"I'm sure they're delicious. There's probably some space in the fridge, but you may have to rearrange a few things. Hey, Fiona? Can you help her find a spot in there?"

The younger woman stood up and turned to greet her. "Hi, nice to meet you. I'm Olivia's sister, Fiona. Why don't you hand that to me?"

Melody was struck by how beautiful all three sisters were as she handed her the casserole dish. "Thanks. You're the sister going to Bowdoin College, right?"

"Yup, that's me," she gave her an impish smile. "And you're

Mason's sister that owns the bed and breakfast I've been dying to go see."

Melody laughed. "Stop by anytime. I'd be happy to show you around."

During the exchange, Liz had a chance to swallow her bite. "Melody, did you want some wine?"

"If you don't mind. Wow, this platter of bruschetta looks great."

"Thanks. Help yourself." Olivia laughed, "I figured we could always use a little food before the food." She checked the timer on the stove. "The turkey will be done in about an hour; I decided to go traditional this year. In the meantime I put together this and a platter of antipasto to tide us over."

Melody thanked Liz as she was handed a glass of wine, then turned back to Olivia, "What do you mean 'traditional'?"

"Oh," Fiona answered, "Olivia likes to experiment with the concept of the Thanksgiving meal."

"Well, I think that's the best thing about this holiday."

"What's that?" Melody asked, confused.

"Here we go…" Liz said, with an indulgent smile.

Melody cast a bemused smile at her before turning her attention back to her older sister.

"Okay," Olivia said, putting her hands on her hips, "this holiday is all about giving thanks, right?"

"And honoring that first dinner between the pilgrims and the Native Americans," Fiona interjected.

"Well, that, too," she allowed. "But, this country is made up of people from all over the world, from all types of different cultures… and the best part is that everybody is welcome to join in and celebrate it. It doesn't matter what religion you practice, if you're a new American, or one that's been around for generations. We're all invited to stop and give thanks for what we have."

Melody thought about it and nodded. "Uh huh, okay, I get that." She took a sip from her wine. "So, basically, by alternating the different types of cuisine, you're celebrating the diversity of America?"

"Exactly!" Olivia said, beaming at her.

"Remember that year we had Indian food?" Jackie said from her spot at the table.

"Naan and curry for Thanksgiving…" Tom said with disappointment.

"Not your favorite?" Melody asked him.

"Oh, I like Indian food fine enough, but I guess I'm just a traditionalist at heart. Give me the classics: turkey, stuffing, mashed potatoes, green beans, and cranberries any day."

"You have to admit, my Peking duck turned out pretty damn good that one year, though," Olivia protested.

He nodded. "Okay, Peking duck can get added to the list."

"It's a pretty cool idea, I'll give you that." Melody said, impressed. She hopped up on the stool and helped herself to a piece of bruschetta.

"By the way, have you met Liz and Tom?" Olivia asked. Everybody smiled and made a round of introductions.

"Paul is in the living room with Mason. I'm guessing they're both watching the game."

"Yeah, Mason's idea of a traditional Thanksgiving is drinking beer and watching the football game," Melody said, wryly.

Olivia laughed. "Spoken like a true sister. Well, he's in good company with Paul and Liz, then."

Liz grabbed a handful of beers from the fridge. "Speaking of which, I'm going to head back in."

"Did you need help with anything?" Melody asked.

Olivia wiped her hands on her apron and glanced around the kitchen. "I think we're pretty much covered for the moment. You'll have to let me know when to put your dish in the oven to heat it up."

The doorbell rang. "Olivia?" Mason called from the other room. "Are we expecting anybody else?"

"I invited Brad over." She turned to Melody. "His parents just moved down to Florida this past year, so he doesn't have any family in the area. I figured he's been helping us out so much lately, he might like to come here for the holiday."

Melody felt her pulse jump a little at the mention of the officer. He'd stopped by on a couple of nights to check in on her while Mason had been staying at Olivia's. His kind eyes and deep voice had made him an object of her dreams on more than a few occasions since then. It hadn't hurt her fantasies that she'd found him incredibly attractive in his uniform, either.

"You remember Brad, right?" Olivia asked her, as she noticed the funny look on her face. "I thought Mason mentioned he'd asked him to patrol by your place, with everything that's been going on."

"Oh, well…"

"I certainly hope she remembers me," Brad's deep voice said from behind her. "Because, guaranteed, I remember her."

Melody blushed as she turned on her stool and let her eyes travel up the long, lean frame of the man who had just walked in. Her mouth turned dry as she realized he looked just as good in jeans and a sweater. "Hello, Brad. Nice to see you again. Happy Thanksgiving."

"You, too." Brad's gaze lingered on her face for a few moments. "Looks like we get to be the new kids on the block together at this grand Thanksgiving event Olivia likes to put on. I've heard it gets pretty epic."

He came around the island and gave Olivia hug. "Thanks for the invite." He looked down at her face and gently thumbed her cheek. "Looks like the bruising is getting a little better. You won't even be able to see it in a few more days."

She gave him a squeeze. "Oh, trust me. It still looks pretty bad. What you're seeing is the very careful and judicious use of makeup."

He lightly chucked her under the chin. "Well, hopefully it will be the last time you ever have to worry about something like this."

"Count on it." Mason said from the doorway. Brad let her go and turned to the fridge. "Mind if I grab a beer?"

"Not at all. Help yourself. Dinner should be ready in about an hour or so."

"I'm hungry!" Abby piped up from Tom's lap.

Jackie got up and started making a small plate of snacks for the little girl as everybody laughed. "Or less..." Olivia said.

For the first few hours, everybody managed to set aside the events of the past few days and just enjoy the holiday and each other's company. However, as they all sat back, satisfied after the amazing meal, conversation gravitated towards the one topic they'd all been thinking about.

"So, I haven't had a chance to ask you how your meeting with the insurance agent went the other day, Olivia," Jackie said, broaching the subject.

Olivia sighed. "Well, the insurance policy covers fire protection, but he mentioned they'll have to do a cursory investigation of whether or not it was arson. I guess a lot of fires are set for insurance fraud..."

"But, that's ridiculous." Fiona exclaimed. "*You* didn't set the fire."

She shrugged. "He led me to believe it was standard protocol for most fire incidents. They'll get the report from the fire department about the cause of the fire."

Brad leaned forward. "Tell him to come and talk to me if he has any questions about the fire and I'll try to help where I can. Of course, the stalker situation is an open case, so I won't be able to do much from that angle. But I should be able to talk about the fire as a separate incident."

She gave him a look of relief. "Thanks. Actually, I already

mentioned your name to him. You'll probably be getting a call from him sometime in the next few days. I hope you don't mind."

"Okay, so assuming they find that this wasn't some attempt at insurance fraud, what happens next?" Paul asked.

Mason watched as the emotions played across her face and reached over to hold her hand. "Assuming everything goes okay, I'll probably be given a decent chunk of money to get back on my feet." Olivia opened her mouth, and then shut it again.

Sensing her hesitation, Tom looked at her. "But…?"

"Well, I'm kind of at a loss about what I should do with it," she glanced guiltily at Abby, happily coloring at the kitchen island behind them, and then at Jackie. "I mean, one of the worst things about everything that has happened is how it's affected you and Abby.

"You know I was already thinking about taking the café in a new direction. I'm not sure if I want to use this money to remake what I lost or to potentially apply it towards something new."

A flash of disappointment crossed Jackie's face before she quickly concealed it behind a too-bright smile. "I know you talked about wanting to open the place up for dinner." She shrugged as her eyes began to well. "But I loved that little café. We — all three of us — put our blood, sweat, and tears into that place. I'd hate to see it left broken down like it is right now."

Having been quiet up until that point, Tom laid a hand over Jackie's. "Well, maybe we could find a happy arrangement for all of us."

"Oh?" Olivia said, confused.

"I never told you this, but I was thinking about trying to buy you out if you ended up opening another restaurant."

"You were?!" both women exclaimed, turning to him.

Slightly uncomfortable with everybody looking at him, he rubbed the back of his neck and explained. "I've been saving money for a long time." He glanced at Jackie. "You have to remember that up until recently, I've been a workaholic bachelor without a lot of people to spend my money on, and very few living expenses."

Olivia saw a look of hope light her friend's face. "So, you'd want to reopen the café?"

"It could work…" Liz said, joining the conversation.

"But what about all of the damage?" Paul said.

"Well, I was thinking about that. Olivia isn't responsible for the majority of the repairs to that space. The building's landlord is. Once he gets the place back to neutral, he'll be looking to lease the place, anyway. I can just take over and make it back into a café."

Olivia thought about it. "Really, Tom? You'd be okay with that?"

"Yeah, I think so," Tom turned to Jackie. "That is, if you're okay with helping me run the place?"

She beamed at him and flung her arms around his shoulders, smacking him on the lips. "Absolutely."

"Mommy! What's happening?" Abby hopped off the stool and ran over to the couple.

Jackie pulled her daughter up on her lap and squeezed her. "Tom just made me very happy."

Abby clapped her hands and bounced up and down. "Yay, Tom!"

"Yay, Tom!" He blushed as everybody around the table mirrored her actions and started laughing.

After a few excited moments, everybody settled down again. "Wow, Tom," Olivia said. "You just took a *huge* weight off my shoulders. I can't thank you enough."

"I guess now the question is – what's the next step to opening your new restaurant, Livvy?" Liz asked.

"Gosh, I don't know. I'll have to figure out how much money I'll have left from the insurance and then, I guess I'll start looking for a decent space to rent…"

"Well, actually…" Melody began, "I might have an idea about that, as well."

Everybody turned towards her, "You remember the conversation we had about putting a restaurant in that old barn on my property?"

Instantly, Olivia's heart leapt. "Oh my gosh. How could have I forgotten? There's so much potential for that space."

Melody beamed. "I've always thought so. What if we did something with all that potential and actually made it happen? I have more than enough money left in the trust fund to cover the costs. That is, if you don't mind being business partners with me. As it is, that part of my property isn't generating any revenue right now.

"Plus, maybe we could create a deal where my guests staying at the bed and breakfast get a discount or a dinner coupon. I could see that helping both of us out."

"That could really work." Fiona said.

The whole time Melody had been proposing the idea, Brad had been watching her intently. As she finished, he leaned over and said, "I think it's a brilliant idea." Olivia was surprised to see her new friend blush under his praise and watched as she took a sip of wine to help hide her pleasure at his words.

Catching the energy between the officer and his sister, Mason cocked an eyebrow at Olivia with a question in his eyes. She just gave him a little smile, confirming he wasn't the only one noticing the attraction.

"I can't believe all of this is going to wind up having a happy ending. I bet it's not what that bastard would have guessed." Liz said.

At the mention of the man responsible for the destruction, the group grew quiet and became more solemn. Fiona sighed. "How did he latch on to Olivia in the first place? What's this guy's deal, anyway?"

Olivia looked at Mason just as Brad turned to him and said, "Mason? Did you want to take this?"

As he looked around the table at each of the people who were important in Olivia's life, he realized that they'd become important to him, as well. They deserved to know what she was up against.

"Most of you may know some of what I'm about to tell you, but for those that don't, I'll start from the beginning. His name is Robert Mendez, and he's a stalker that preys on women. He's also the man who recently shot me and killed my partner."

There were various gasps heard around the table as people who hadn't known the connection took in the news. Jackie squeezed her daughter a little tighter against her body, while Tom sat up a little straighter and put his arm around her shoulder. Melody gripped the stem of her wine glass with a trembling hand and struggled to control her tears at the memory of her brother coming so close to death.

Leaning forward, Paul put his elbows on the table. "So, what the hell does he want with our Livvy?"

"And, more importantly, what are we going to do about it?" Liz added.

Fiona grew thoughtful. "It might also help if we knew a little more about him. I realize it may be painful to discuss," she glanced at Melody and gave her an apologetic smile, "but, can you tell us anything specific about him?"

Mason laid everything he'd learned about Mendez out to the small group, including his capacity for murder, and told them the story of his own encounter. Throughout his retelling, Olivia held his hand, knowing how difficult it was for him to discuss his partner being shot.

About halfway through, Jackie got up and took Abby into the living room to play. Melody stood up. "I'm sorry, I already know the story, and it hurts every time I think about what could have happened." She excused herself and went to join the mother and daughter.

After everybody was on the same page, the remaining people sat around the table silently for a moment. Brad stepped in to fill the quiet. "I know the situation is bad right now. We're dealing with a dangerous man who is threatening someone we all love." At that, he gave Olivia a little wink. "However, there are a few things we can do to help mitigate the danger until he's caught. First off, we need to make sure Olivia isn't left alone, especially in public."

As Brad took over the conversation, Mason felt residual anger and frustration sitting hot and painful in his chest. Telling the story of what had happened to him and Ryan hadn't gotten any easier. Needing a moment to get his bearings, he quietly got up and moved into the kitchen.

He was trembling as he opened the refrigerator and stood there staring blindly into the cool interior. After a moment, he managed to gather his wits and grabbed a beer before closing the door. Tom stood on the other side and gave him a long look.

He handed him the bottle opener. "That's a tough story to have to tell."

Mason took a hard pull from the bottle before replying gruffly. "Try living it."

Tom looked directly into his eyes. "I have."

Mason didn't know what to say to that. There had been a look in the other man's eyes he'd recognized from the moment they'd first met.

Tom opened the fridge and got a beer out for himself. "After the war, I spent months wrapped up in what happened over there. I felt that same mix of guilt, memories, and rage that you're probably harboring."

Mason didn't know how to reply, so he took another sip of beer.

Leaning against the counter, Tom looked at him. "It's not an easy combination to live with. Until recently, I still hadn't figured it out. Hopefully, it won't take you as long to come to terms with what's happened."

"How did you?"

He glanced towards the living room where they could hear

Abby being tickled and laughing unrestrainedly. "You find other ways to be grateful, and things worth living for. You do it knowing that by doing so you honor the men who died in your stead."

Mason looked over to see Olivia talking earnestly with her sisters and nodded at Tom. "I just didn't want any of this ugliness to touch her, and instead I brought him to her doorstep, got her beaten up, her café torched…" Unconsciously, he rubbed at the ache in his chest. "If I thought it would make her safer, I'd walk away from her right now."

"But you don't."

"Dammit, no, I don't." Mason drew a frustrated hand through his hair. "This guy isn't someone who just changes his mind and moves on. Once he's picked his target, he latches on and will stop at nothing to get ahold of her. In the cases we suspect he's been involved in, it wasn't just the victims affected. Family members were hurt and betrayed, cars were run off the road, there was even one victim whose parents had a bomb placed in their mailbox. This guy always managed to get his girl….and then they were never seen alive again."

He blew out a breath. "He's bad news, Tom. Big, ugly, bad news. And the worst thing about it is that I don't know if I can keep her safe."

And there it was.

The ultimate truth all his concerns boiled down to.

The one fear that was driving a spike into Mason's heart; he wasn't sure he could win against this guy.

Until a month and a half ago, Mason had always been confident on the job. Not cocky, but confident that he could do the work, find the clues, take the steps, and get his guy. For the most part, that's what he and Ryan had done.

All of that was before he was shot, before his partner was killed, and before he'd come to…well, if not love, certainly care very deeply about the woman sitting at the dining room table. The same woman now being stalked by the guy who'd shot him.

"Hell," Mason said, slightly under his breath. He put the beer down on the counter. It was probably better if he didn't drink too much. He needed to stay alert.

"I know Olivia and Jackie thought we were joking the other day," Tom broached cautiously, watching the thoughts flitter across Mason's face. "But my offer was sincere. If you need help taking this guy out, I can help."

Mason carefully searched the determined intent in the other man's eye, and then shook his hand. "I really appreciate it. To tell the truth, I may need another set of eyes and ears I can trust to do the job. I'm really hoping it doesn't come down to that, though."

Tom nodded. "We can hope. In the meantime, let's get back over there and come up with a plan."

The pressure that had been building up in Mason's chest eased a little. As the two men made their way back to the group at the dining room table, he realized Tom could wind up becoming a very good friend, indeed.

Olivia looked at him with concern in her eyes as he sat down next to her. "Sorry about that." He glanced around the table at everybody. "So, as I was saying, we need to come up with a good way to make sure Olivia stays accompanied by at least one other person. I hate to say it, but not having the café could help."

"Or, it might hinder us, since she now has an open schedule," Fiona interjected, giving her sister a little bump in the shoulder.

He gave her a quick smile. "I hadn't thought of it like that, but you may have a point."

Olivia rolled her eyes. "Sure, go ahead and joke about it now, but wait until you have to sit with me through all those boring meetings with my insurance agent."

Fiona scowled. "Ooh, I hadn't thought about that."

"Hey!" Olivia laughed. "At least you're not the one stuck with a babysitter 24/7."

"Well," Mason said, "for the most part, I should be able to stick with her. However, there will obviously be times when someone else will have to step in. The main thing is that she not be left alone. Not even for a minute."

"I learned that one the hard way." Jackie spoke from the dining room doorway. "I promise I will *not* be making that mistake again. Heck, I may even come into the bathroom stall with you when you go pee from now on."

Olivia laughed. "I don't think we have to go quite that far."

"Well no, maybe not, but she should be accompanied to the bathroom, at least," Paul pointed out.

"Ugh, as much as I appreciate that you're all willing to do this for me, I have to admit, the idea of being watched every minute of every day is going to wear thin very quickly. For all of us, I'd imagine."

"Well, unfortunately," Brad said, "it will be for the indefinite and foreseeable future, until we can get a bead on this guy. Nobody knows where he is now or where he may have been staying. There's already a BOLO out. I don't know how often you've watched the news lately, Olivia, but we also had our public relations office working with the local media. They gave them the details and the sketch you and CeCe came up with the other day."

Olivia grimaced distastefully and apologized. "I have to admit I've been avoiding the reports. I caught one of them on the first day, and I couldn't watch it. However, I'm glad that they're getting the word out about him."

"Well, that's understandable. I can't say that I blame you. At any rate, we've also been in contact with the Boston PD — thanks to Mason — and have been making sure both departments are aware of the situation and up to speed. They're looking into a few leads and should be getting back to me in a few days.

"The point is, we're on top of this and working hard to find him so you can get back to your life as soon as possible."

Olivia smiled at her friend. "Thank you. I can't tell you how comforting it is that you're taking the lead on this case."

"Well, I have to tell you, I almost got pulled off of it by my superior when he found out we're friends. It took some pretty fast talking on my part and a word from Mason here."

Before Olivia could respond to that, she felt a tug on her shirt, and looked down to find Abby pulling on it with her bottom lip pouting out.

"What's up, sweetie?"

"I want pie!"

Instantly, the tension in the room eased as everybody laughed. Olivia bent down and picked the little girl up, giving her a squeeze. "You do? Well, it's a good thing I made your favorite, then."

Melody came into the room and sat at the dining room table beside Brad. "Don't you wish you could be that age again and have nothing more to worry about than when you're going to get dessert?"

Looking pleased that she'd come to sit by him, he gave her a boyish grin. "Too bad we didn't realize how good we had it back then, huh?"

As if by unspoken order, the group got up and began to clear the table. Liz and Mason took over doing the dishes while Olivia cut and served pie. Fiona refreshed drinks, Tom made another pot of coffee, and the rest of the evening was filled with fun and light-heartedness, as everybody decided to set aside the big issues, at least momentarily.

Chapter Forty

Constant vigilance required an adjustment for everybody, but none more so than for Olivia herself. The following weeks were filled with errands, as Olivia and Mason met with the insurance agent a number of times and dealt with the café's building manager, as well as stayed in contact with Brad at the police station.

However, she was surprised that despite it all, she was actually enjoying herself. She found Mason to be funny, considerate, and easy to live with….not to mention incredibly sexy. It would be easy to imagine spending her life with him, if not for everything else happening around them.

She still mourned her café, especially in the mornings when she'd normally be getting up to open it. It never would have occurred to her that she could actually miss waking up so early.

Instead of focusing on the sting of loss, she decided to throw herself into the work of opening her new restaurant. In her off hours, Olivia began researching various styles of décor, and spent hours combing through different aesthetics on the internet and brainstorming the kind of atmosphere she wanted. She'd even made an appointment with an interior designer.

It came as a pleasant surprise to find Mason had definite opinions on what looked good, and was comfortable talking about paint colors and the pros and cons of different fixtures. She found his thoughts to be insightful and she liked that he insisted that form should follow function in his design choices.

The days could have been a lot worse.

Granted, it was still hard work. She worried Mason might be wearing himself thin. Luckily, Fiona was able to come home from school after her finals, and helped take over some of the time. She was also the main reason Olivia found herself on a holiday shopping excursion in the middle of a Saturday during one of the busiest weekends of the year.

Olivia looked at the front entrance to the mall and paused, taking a deep breath to help calm her nerves. It had only been a few weeks, but she was surprised at how anxious she felt being in a crowded area out in public.

Mason and Fiona stood on either side of her while she collected herself. Liz was well ahead and striding towards the doors before she realized everybody else had stopped.

"What's wrong?" she asked, walking back to the little group.

Olivia laughed self-consciously. "I know it seems silly, but I haven't really been around a bunch of people since the incident. I'm a little nervous. What if he's here?" A thought struck her. "What if he's watching us right now?" She swiveled her head around, trying to see if she saw any suspicious characters loitering nearby.

Mason placed a hand on her back. "Are you sure you want to do this?"

Determined, Olivia shook off her fear and nodded. "Yes. Fiona's right, I need to get Christmas gifts. This guy may have taken away my café, but he is *not* taking away my holiday."

"Right. Besides, you'll have us around you the whole time." Fiona reassured her.

Liz hesitated, and then began digging in her purse. "You know, I was going to hold off giving this to you until Christmas morning, but I think it may be more useful now.

"Why does everything you want always wind up in the bottom corner of your bag where it's the most difficult to find?" she asked rhetorically. After another moment of foraging, she pulled out an item with triumph. "Aha! Got it."

"What is it?" Fiona asked curiously.

Liz smiled. "I found this the other day and thought of you, Olivia." She revealed a slim, pink, sparkly cylinder with a black cap at one end and a keychain attached to the other side.

Mason began to laugh. "Is that what I think it is?"

Olivia took it from Liz's hand. "What the heck?"

"It's pepper spray. All done up in girly packaging and ready to be attached to your keys so you never forget it."

Fiona laughed and grabbed it from Olivia. "Cuuuuttee! Please tell me you got one for me, too."

Liz shrugged. "You'll have to check your stocking on Christmas morning." She winked at her younger sister before turning her attention back to Olivia.

"Pepper spray?" She never thought she'd be the type of woman to carry pepper spray around with her. Maybe even more surprising was how much it had instantly calmed her nerves.

"This is really thoughtful of you. Thanks, Liz." Olivia immediately began threading it onto her keys.

"It's not a lot," Liz cautioned. "It's basically good for only one surprise hit. Still, it might give you the opportunity you need to get away."

Nodding, she examined the little canister. Suddenly, she felt silly for her momentary weakness. Olivia sucked in another fortifying breath and began walking towards the mall's double doors.

"You know...I wouldn't complain if you wanted to change your mind..." Mason mentioned hopefully.

Olivia laughed, and felt the last of her hesitation leave, "I know. Melody told me what a big fan of shopping you are. I'm sorry, Mason, but I really do want to get a few things."

Stoically, he nodded. "Well, then, let's do this."

Two hours later, laden with bags, Olivia was feeling tired but satisfied. She gratefully snagged a table at the coffee shop and piled her bags onto the chair beside her. At some point, Fiona and Liz had split off to do a bit of shopping themselves, but they'd all arranged to meet up and to get coffee.

"I wonder where they could be."

"Probably just got stuck in a line somewhere," Mason assured her.

* * *

Halfway across the mall, the two sisters were weaving their way through the crowd when Fiona changed course. "Fiona! We can't go in there. We're already running late. Olivia is going to kill us."

"I know. I'm sorry. I just wanted to check the prices on the new Samsung," she said, stepping into the busy Verizon store.

"Why? You already have a perfectly good phone. Besides, didn't you just get an upgrade?"

Fiona cast a guilty look at Liz. "Actually…"

"Oh no, not again. I love you, sis, but sometimes your head can be stuck in the clouds."

She looked down. "I don't know what happened. I went out with a few friends to a bar the other night – you know, to celebrate the end of finals? I could have sworn I had it on me, but when I went to plug it in, it was gone."

"Don't you think she has enough on her plate right now? She's going to shoot you when she finds out. Isn't that the third phone you've lost? Those things aren't cheap, y'know."

"Which is why I haven't told her. I don't want her to feel like she has to replace it again. I was going to price them, and pay for it myself this time. If everything works out, I can have it replaced by Christmas."

"But what about until then?"

Fiona tried reasoning with her sister. "Who's going to call? I'm home for the holidays now, which means for the most part I'll either be with you or Olivia, anyway."

Liz hesitated. "I don't know…"

"Come on. You said it yourself – she has a lot going on right now. The last thing we need to do is add to her stress about something like this. I will take care of it, I promise."

Liz looked at her and nodded. "Okay, Fiona. But if you haven't had a chance to replace it by New Year's Day I'm going to have to say something."

"Fair enough." She scanned the store and noticed how crowded it was. The salesclerks on duty looked overwhelmed and frazzled by the amount of people needing help. She sighed. "Shoot. This place is a zoo. We might as well go to meet them; no way are we going to get helped anytime soon."

Relieved, Liz looked down the concourse as they exited the store. "Thankfully the coffee shop isn't too far away."

Minutes later they sat down beside Olivia and Mason.

"Whew! The crowds are crazy. I saw two women get in a fight over a stuffed animal earlier," Fiona said.

"Kind of goes against the whole point, doesn't it?" Mason said, drily.

"About fifteen minutes in, I remembered that I hate shopping," Liz said.

"But I think you have more bags than me." Olivia exclaimed.

Defensively, she shrugged. "Well, if I'm going to be here, then I might as well get everything I need all at once. Besides," she added, blushing, "there were some really good sales."

They all laughed.

"So, what's next?" Fiona asked.

"Well," Olivia hesitated and looked at Mason. "I still have to buy a present for you but, in order to do that, we're going to need to split up."

Mason got a stubborn look on his face. "I don't think that's such a good idea."

Liz and Fiona noted the way they both jutted their chins out and adopted a mulish expression, and exchanged a look with each other. Hoping to avoid a standoff, Fiona cautiously interjected. "I have a thought…"

Everybody looked towards her. "These bags are getting super heavy. In fact, I don't think I'd be nearly as exhausted if I didn't have to cart them around everywhere. If you're willing, Mason, maybe you could run all the bags out to the car and give us an hour to look around without you…"

Instantly, he opened his mouth to protest, but Fiona rushed to continue, "…IF we promise to stick by her side like glue."

Liz nodded. "Come on, Mason. It will be all three of us. I doubt he'd try anything. That's assuming he's even here. Nobody has seen or heard from him in the last week, right?"

His scowl deepened. "That doesn't mean he's not still lying in wait. Just because we haven't seen him or felt his presence doesn't mean we can get lax in our vigilance."

Olivia laid a hand on his. "You're right. And, we won't. Like Fiona said, we'll all stick together."

He sighed. "I don't like it, but okay. It shouldn't be too risky, since it's so busy, anyway. We can meet back here." He gave her a stern look. "One hour only, though, okay?"

Fiona cheered and clapped her hands as Olivia looked into Mason's eyes. "One hour only, I promise."

The three girls thanked Mason profusely and watched as he left with the mountain of bags.

Liz leaned across the table and asked, "So, where do we start?"

"I don't know." Olivia looked around for a moment, lost. "I've been wracking my brain, thinking about what to get him. He's done so much for me this last week and a half, and I honestly don't know what I would have done without his help."

"Has it only been him helping you? You guys looked pretty romantically involved when I came home the other day," Fiona asked.

Liz gave Olivia a teasing grin. "Ooh, sounds like there's a story in there."

Olivia blushed. "We were just kissing."

Scoffing, Fiona chimed in. "You call that 'just' kissing? It was so hot, you were out-sizzling the bacon on the stove."

"Woohoo!" Liz crowed. "Livvy's got her groove back!"

Olivia smiled, smugly. "As a matter of fact, I do."

"If things are going well, why are you so worried about what to get him?" Fiona asked, puzzled.

"It's just that, ever since we've gotten together, we've had this other thing hanging over us. I'm afraid it's creating a false environment. We've been under a lot of stress and spending a lot more time together than we probably would have under normal circumstances. However, if you were to look at a calendar, we haven't really been together all that long."

"You're afraid it's not real?"

"Oh, it feels real to me, but what if it's not the same as what he's feeling? I'm just afraid it may be going too fast for him."

Always pragmatic, Liz asked, "Has he been giving any indication that he feels it's been getting too serious too quickly?"

"Well, no. Kind of the opposite, actually. The other night he was so sweet and tender…and I almost told him I loved him. It practically fell from my lips."

"But you didn't." It was more of a statement than a question as Liz focused on the stream of emotions running across her sister's face.

Olivia raised her hands. "What if his feelings are due to the forced intimacy the situation has created? What if he doesn't feel the same after it's resolved? And he's already sacrificed so much of his time, when really he should be focused on healing enough to go back to the force. I don't want to trap him here or make him feel an obligation to me."

"Oh, Livvy…I'm sure he doesn't feel like that." Fiona put a hand on her shoulder.

Liz nodded. "I don't get the impression he feels stuck, but I can understand your concerns." She got a confused look on her face. "What I don't understand is how this has anything to do with what kind of gift you get him?"

"You know…do I get him something intimate, and maybe expensive, or go more for light-hearted and casual? What's the right note to hit?" Olivia threw her hands up. "Liz, it's not as if I've had a lot of relationships before, and never during the holidays." She looked at her sisters glumly. "I just feel awkward about how much to expect and what I'm doing. Throw in everything else, and I'm afraid I'm totally lost."

Fiona moved to soothe her. "Well, we don't have much time, so let's just pop into some stores and see if anything stands out for you, okay?"

Together the women walked through a number of department stores, but nothing seemed quite right. Realizing they were running out of time, Liz checked her watch. Exasperated, she said, "I still think you should have just gotten him that wallet."

"I didn't know. I was afraid it would be too personal. Besides, I wasn't sure if he preferred tri-fold or bi-fold." Olivia explained, again. They walked by a lingerie shop.

"What if you got something sexy to wear? I mean, you guys have already been intimate, so there isn't any question of whether it's appropriate or not, right?"

"Hm, y'know, that's not a bad idea." Olivia paused and shrugged. "We might as well go in and look."

The three women walked in. Olivia and Fiona were looking at a few nice pieces hanging on the display rack when Liz called to them from the back of the store. "Oh ho! I found the perfect gift."

Excusing herself from the salesclerk, Olivia wandered back to see Liz holding a pair of fuzzy handcuffs up in the air triumphantly.

Choking on a laugh, Olivia covered her mouth. "Liz, put those away!"

"What? Don't you think they'd go with *these*?" Liz whipped out a pair of hokey male boxers from behind her back.

Groaning, Olivia walked up and looked at them a little closer. "These have little Santas on them!"

Fiona came back to join them. "What the heck, you guys?"

Olivia reached over to the rack and flipped through a number of items hanging there. "Are you kidding me, who wears this stuff?" She paused. "Oh…wow."

She started giggling and lifted up a mini hanger with a male thong cut out in the shape of a reindeer. The absurdity of the item she was holding instantly hit her funny bone.

Fiona started laughing, which caused her to hiccup, which got her sisters started. Soon, all three of them were bent over in a fit of laughter, tears streaming from their eyes.

"It even has a red nose on the tip!" Olivia exclaimed, holding it up for further examination.

She felt buoyant. It was as if all that laughter had released some of the stress and tension she'd been feeling the last few weeks. "What do you think, Liz? Can you imagine the look on his face?"

Liz straightened up, still chuckling, and glanced behind Olivia. Her eyes widened.

"Sorry, that's not really my color." Mason's deep voice cut Olivia's laugh off as she spun around, instinctively hiding the garment behind her back. Instantly, her face turned deep crimson.

The look on her face had Mason shooting her a big grin and waggling his eyebrows. "Busted."

Sputtering, she hastily shoved the hanger back on the rack and pointed. "It was Liz's idea!" Realizing that didn't sound quite right, either, she added, "Uh, not what I meant. We were just…"

"Ogling Rudolph? Hey, I get it. Should I be worried about this strange new fascination with reindeer? Lemme guess, it's the antlers." Behind her, she could hear her sisters snicker. Olivia sent them both a quick scowl, but couldn't keep the grin off her face.

"I can't believe you didn't tell me he was standing right behind me. What happened to sister solidarity?" she admonished playfully.

"I honestly didn't see him until it was too late," Liz said, as she threaded her arm through Olivia's. "Besides, we would have missed that absolutely priceless expression." She stopped and pantomimed a mock look of shock and dismay, dropping her jaw wide open.

Giving her shoulder a light push for her teasing, Olivia turned to Mason, "Has it already been an hour?"

"Just about. I was on my way to get you when I noticed the three of you in the store, laughing. Of course, I had to come see what had made you all so happy." He cocked his head at her. "Should I be taking notes?"

As she walked towards the front of the store, she tossed a wicked look over her shoulder. "I don't know…maybe."

The little group made their way out of the shop. "Questionable undergarments aside, did you ladies find what you were looking for?"

Olivia twisted her mouth. "Almost. I still haven't found what I want to get you, but I've had an idea. I just don't think I'm going to find it here."

"So, does that mean we can get going?" Mason tried, but failed, to keep the eagerness from his voice.

"Yeah, I think we're done here." Fiona reassured him.

Liz had a look of relief on her face that matched his. "Thank goodness I only have to do this once a year. I think I'd go nuts otherwise." She turned to Mason and gave him a bawdy wink. "No pun intended, of course."

They all laughed as it was Mason's turn to blush.

Chapter Forty-One

Robert watched as the three sisters left the slut shop for whores. He'd heard their laughter from across the concourse, and could only guess what it had been about. Most likely something inappropriate.

Despite her sin, he had to admit, it felt good to be near her again. Although he'd been busy for the past week and a half, getting the cabin ready for her arrival, his fantasies had been nothing compared to seeing her in person.

He lifted the camera and took a shot of the three sister's standing just outside the store. Taking an extra minute, he zoomed in on the youngest sister.

She'd been so sweet and innocent when he'd chatted her up at the bar. He paused and fingered the slim phone in his pocket and grinned. Really, it had been like taking candy from a baby. He wondered how there were any women out there who could still be that trusting.

Then again, they didn't know the things he'd done.

Tempting as the youngest was, she was nothing compared to her older sister.

Robert watched as Olivia linked her arm through Mason's and headed towards the mall doors. He couldn't wait to finally get her all alone and show her the present he'd made.

She was going to be so surprised.

Chapter Forty-Two

Mason ended the phone call with his captain and looked at the date and time he'd written down.

"Who was that?" Olivia asked, as she came into the room.

He looked up at her distractedly. "Huh? Oh, that was my captain. He wants me to come down and have my first psych evaluation. He reminded me that he wants me to be able to 'hit the ground running' after the holidays."

"Do you think you'll be ready to go back?"

He sighed. "Physically? Yeah, I'm almost fully recovered right now. Psychologically is maybe a little more questionable, but one thing is for sure."

"What's that?"

He smiled and walked to her, enveloping her in his arms. "I haven't been having nightmares lately."

Blushing, she wrapped her arms around his waist. "Out of this whole situation, having you here with me has been the best part."

Mason looked down at her and thought about the last few weeks. They had been some of the happiest he could remember. So good, in fact, that the thought of heading back to Boston didn't sound as appealing as it should.

"Listen, Olivia...I know we haven't talked much about what

happens after the holidays, but I want you to know, I'm committed to keeping you safe. If Robert isn't found before I'm supposed to leave, I will arrange for more leave time."

Olivia reached up and brushed his hair back off his forehead. She nodded, but a small part of her heart broke inside. He wasn't going to stay because he wanted to, but only in order to keep her safe.

Silently, she admonished herself. She couldn't expect him to give up his whole career for her. It wasn't as if he didn't care for her. She knew he did.

She'd just been hoping for more.

Squaring her shoulders, she gave him a bright smile, determined to make the most of the time she had with him.

"So, when is your appointment?"

Mason grabbed the notepad. "Tomorrow afternoon, at two. Kind of late notice, but I guess he had a cancellation. We're going to need to find someone to come over and spend the afternoon with you. Do you think Liz can do it?"

"I don't know. I'll have to check. You know, Liz is right. We haven't seen or heard from Robert in two weeks. Are you sure he hasn't moved on?"

"As sure as I can be, yeah." He noticed the hopeful doubt in her eyes. "I'd rather not chance it, okay?"

Olivia paced a few steps away from him. "No, I know you're right. I just feel like a terrible imposition, constantly needing someone to watch me. It's growing tedious, Mason."

He gently tucked a strand of hair behind her ear and lightly traced his thumb down the curve of her jaw. "I know. I'm sorry it's come to this. Just hang in there a little longer, okay? If it lasts past the holidays, then we can try to reassess the situation and figure something else out."

She felt bad for complaining. She knew he had been bending over backwards to make sure she could get to all her insurance appointments, search for designers and engineers for the new restaurant, and shop for various fixtures. If anybody had the right to complain, it had to be Mason himself.

"Never mind. I'm sorry I said anything. I know you're doing the best you can. Everybody is. I don't mean to make it harder."

"You've been very patient, Olivia. It would be hard for anybody."

Trying to move past her feelings of restlessness, she suggested, "Why don't I give Liz a call and see if she can come over tomorrow?"

Moments later, Liz picked up the phone. "Tomorrow?" she responded, hesitating. She scanned the garage, looking at the row of cars waiting for her attention. "I don't know, Olivia. I wish I could say yes, but I'm swamped over here. Especially since Paul is planning on taking off tomorrow for his annual hunting trip. Have you tried Fiona?"

"Not yet, that was going to be my next call."

"See if she can do it. If not, I'll try to move some things around."

Olivia winced as she heard the doubt in her sister's voice. She knew things must be pretty hectic if Liz was hedging. "It's okay. Don't worry about it. I'm sure I can find someone else for tomorrow."

"Livvy, I'm sorry, it's not that I don't want to…"

She rushed to reassure her. "Hey! Really, it's okay. I get that you have a business to run. Besides, I think I've already had you taking off more days in the last few weeks than you have in the last few years. If you keep it up, you're going to lose all of your customers."

"Thanks, Livvy. It has been crazy around here lately."

"I'm going to give Fiona a call. I'll talk to you later, okay?"

It was only after she had hung up with her sister that Liz remembered Fiona mentioned losing her phone. She was about to call her back, when a client walked in. "Ma'am? I was wondering if you could take a look at my car. It's got a really strange knocking sound coming from the back right tire."

The thought forgotten, Liz turned from the phone and greeted the man at the counter. "Sounds like it could be the ball bearings. Let me check the schedule and see when I can take a look at it for you."

Olivia tried to reach Fiona, but got her voicemail. After leaving her a message, she decided to text her with the request.

Mason looked at her. "Well?"

"Liz is out, but I texted Fiona. Hopefully she'll get back to me quickly."

"If nothing else, you could probably head up to Melody's for the day. I'm sure she'd enjoy the company since it's the off season right now. I don't think she even has any guests."

"I'm sure we'll figure something out. Don't worry."

But the next day, when they still hadn't heard from Fiona, Mason was concerned. "I need to leave in half an hour if I'm going to make it to the appointment on time. I probably shouldn't be late to my own psych evaluation."

Olivia frowned down at her phone. "I'm surprised Fiona didn't get back to me. Do you think she's okay?"

"We probably would have heard from her if she wasn't. You said she went to stay at her friend's house for a few days, right? They probably had too much fun and she's hung over or something."

"That doesn't really sound like her style," Olivia said, doubtfully.

"She's a college girl. Of course it's her style."

She laughed. "Maybe you're right. I'm sure there are things she'd rather I didn't know about."

"Which is as it should be." He looked at the time. "We need to figure something out, though. I really need to take off. Let's go. I can drive you up to Melody's and head out from there."

"That's almost twenty minutes one way. You'll definitely be

late if you do that." Olivia grabbed her keys. "Why don't I just head up to Melody's?"

"By yourself?" He gave her a stern look. "I don't think that's a good idea."

"Come on, Mason. I swear I'll go directly from here to there. No stopping in between."

Hesitating, he looked at his watch. "No stopping, you promise?"

"I promise, and you can come pick me up later."

He hesitated until she gave him a look of exasperation. "Really. I'll be fine."

Not quite convinced, but seeing no alternative, he nodded. "Okay. I really do have to go." He gave her a kiss. "Stay safe. Lock the door behind me until you leave."

"I will. I'm just going to grab a jacket, and then I'll take off."

Mason walked out to his truck and stopped, taking a quick look around. Nothing seemed out of place, no strange pile of cigarette butts or unknown people sitting in their cars. Everything looked peaceful.

He was probably overreacting, Mason thought to himself. With his captain's words ringing in his ears, he made himself climb into his truck and pull out of the driveway. The sooner he got this over with, the sooner he'd be able to get back.

Olivia watched him through the window until he took off. Then, after making sure the door was locked and the alarm was reset, she dialed her phone as she headed upstairs to get a jacket.

"Hey, Melody, it's Olivia. Mason had to take off and I figured I'd call and let you know I'm heading your way."

"Great! I was just about to run down to the basement and grab a box of Christmas ornaments. You can help me decorate the tree. If I don't answer the door, just let yourself in, okay?"

"Sounds like fun. I should be there in about twenty minutes."

"See you then."

Olivia smiled as she hung up the phone. She was relieved that she and Melody had so much in common. Not only was she looking forward to being business partners with her, but even if things didn't work out with Mason, she knew she had a new friend.

As happy as she was to spend the afternoon decorating with Melody, it bothered her that she still hadn't heard from Fiona. She tried texting her again to tell her that Mason had taken off to Boston and, if she could, she was welcome to meet her and Melody at the bed and breakfast.

Wondering what was keeping Fiona, she prepared to leave for La Luna Vista.

Chapter Forty-Three

Robert looked at the rundown motel room with distaste. He'd been forced to stay there for the last few days, since coming back from the cabin. If his plan didn't work out soon, he was going to have to come up with an alternative. As it was, he had no way of knowing how much was left on the credit card he had stolen from the car's owner.

He felt the phone vibrate again in his pocket and looked down. Even though he hadn't been able to crack the voicemail code, he'd been relieved to find Fiona kept her phone unlocked. The text Olivia had sent Fiona yesterday had informed him that Mason would be in Boston today.

He read the new message and he realized this was his chance to get Olivia alone. He knew exactly where La Luna Vista was, having followed her there before. If he left now, he could be waiting when she arrived.

He dashed to his car, unable to keep the grin off his face as he drove along the winding road. Finally! His plan was going to be put in action.

Robert glanced in his rearview mirror as he approached the bed and breakfast, relieved that the road behind him was clear. Carefully, he drove by the driveway and parked his car on the shoulder of the road. The bend in the road hid his vehicle enough that it was barely visible to anyone driving up to the house.

Instead of walking towards the driveway, Robert traipsed through the woods and found a spot that had a clear line of sight to the door of the house. He positioned himself just behind the line of trees near the area where he knew cars parked.

Casting his eyes about, he found a good-sized rock. He wasn't going to underestimate her a second time. Silently, he sat in the shadow of the trees, occasionally shaking his feet or blowing on his hands to keep warm.

Just as he was beginning to grow impatient, Olivia's car pulled into the gates and began to slowly make its way down the length of the driveway. Robert was thrilled when she pulled her car almost directly in front of him. She hadn't even seen him sitting there.

The car chimed as she opened the door and reached across the seat to grab her bag. Seeing his opportunity, Robert rushed forward and wrenched the door the rest of the way open.

Olivia had just started to turn when he struck the back of her head. She fell limply across the seat. Dropping the rock, Robert reached in to hoist her dead weight. Grunting, he managed to get his arms around her back and under her legs and, as quickly as possible, carried her to his car on the other side of the trees.

Luckily, he'd had the foresight to have the trunk already open. Not only did it help block the view from any passers-by, but it made it a lot easier to get Olivia where he wanted her.

With a big heave, he dropped her into the dark trunk. Taking a moment, Robert raised his head and scanned his surroundings, relieved to find no one watching. Perfect.

Grabbing the roll of duct tape he'd tossed in the trunk earlier, he carefully bound her wrists and ankles. Robert knew from experience how well she could put up a fight. The last thing he needed was to have her jumping out of the trunk and attacking him.

Smiling, he stared down at her prone form lying in the

shadowy confines. Reverently, he traced his finger down the soft line of her cheek, marveling at the satiny texture of her skin, and sighed.

He wished he could do more, but he knew once he got started, he wasn't going to want to stop. Just a few more hours to get to the cabin, and then he'd have all the time in the world, he reminded himself.

They were going to have so much fun. He chuckled. Well, one of them would, anyway.

Hastily, he shut the trunk, and after shooting it one final cursory glance, climbed back into the driver's seat of the sedan. The DJ on the radio filled the air with his jovial voice. "You're listening to Charlie FM, where we're playing the sounds of the holiday nonstop. Thank you for joining us for the greatest hits of the season! Which list will you be on this year? Next up, have you been a good boy or girl?"

"You better watch out…"

Robert chuckled and turned it up. Santa Claus certainly was coming to town. Suddenly, Christmas was looking a lot brighter.

He grinned as he thought about his present lying in the trunk and began humming along to the Christmas classic, turning his car north.

Chapter Forty-Four

Olivia heard the dulcet tones of Bing Crosby dreaming of a White Christmas before she became aware of anything else. Gradually, other perceptions began to filter in. The low rumble of the vehicle. A voice, slightly off-key, singing along with the radio. Her body swayed gently with the rocking motion felt in a moving car.

Is that Mason singing? What a strange dream, she thought to herself.

Cramped, she shifted to see where the sound was coming from. Pain sliced through her consciousness, ripping her back into reality. The sticky and slightly sweet odor of gas fumes permeated her senses.

She raised her hands to rub her head and discovered they were bound. Horror began to slowly creep in along the edges of her consciousness.

Shivering, she opened her eyes, expecting to see something that would help explain what was going on, but all she saw was darkness. Why was it so cold?

Blinking rapidly, she tried to figure out what had happened. Think, think…the last thing she remembered was parking the car outside La Luna Vista.

There had been a man!

Struck by a sudden sense of urgency, Olivia instinctually tried to sit up and smacked her forehead on the inside of the trunk lid.

Bass drums pounded in her temples as she fell back. For a moment, everything else receded behind the agony ringing in her ears. Damn, her head felt bad.

He must have hit her on the head pretty hard to have knocked her unconscious. Unfortunately, she had a pretty good idea who he was, too.

Sucking in a breath, the full weight of her situation came into focus. Panic and pressure began to well in her chest as if her lungs had instantly forgotten how to work. Fear choked her throat, making it hard to breathe.

The dark confines of the trunk closed in on her, and for a full minute, it was all she could do to find a way to keep getting oxygen to her bloodstream. Frantic thoughts fluttered and beat on the inside of her mind, like birds caught indoors desperately trying to push their way to freedom through glass windows.

After a moment of writhing in fear, Olivia mentally forced herself to count to three on each inhale until she could breathe more normally. Pausing, she tried to calmly take stock of her situation. Judging by the motion and the smell, she'd already deduced that she must be stuck in the trunk of a vehicle.

Gingerly, she raised her bound hands until she could feel the metal contours of the lid above her. Fumbling with her fingers, she traced the edges up, over her head and along the seam. Didn't trunks usually come with a safety release?

When she couldn't find anything that felt like a handle up over her head, she bent at the waist as much as possible, and tried to follow the line of the trunk down towards her feet, which, she was dismayed to discover, were also bound.

Still nothing. Dammit!

There was a ball of lead in her stomach threatening to weigh her down as she determinedly fought back another wave of fear.

Okay, that would have been too easy, anyway, she consoled herself. He'd probably already prepared for that contingency. She reminded herself that she wasn't the only woman he'd ever abducted. Awkwardly, she ran her feet along the other side of the trunk, trying to discover anything that may be helpful.

Nothing.

Frustrated, Olivia stopped and tried to think out the problem logically. Obviously, the first thing she needed to do was get her wrists and feet free. With that thought in mind, she began to gnaw on the slick, plastic edge of the tape.

Fifteen minutes later, she'd barely managed to start a small tear in the material. She wasn't sure when the little whimpering noises had begun to escape the back of her throat, but forced herself to stop. If she was going to survive this, she needed to keep her wits about her.

Carefully casting her head to the left, she could just make out a faint red glow of the tail light through a small hole in the corner of the trunk. Maybe there was a sharp edge there she could use…

Methodically, she began searching with the tips of her fingers for anything that might help her cut through the tape faster than her teeth. She found what she was looking for in the shape of a small splinter of metal, but it was awkwardly located above her head and wedged into the corner.

Jackknifing her hips so she could get her arms at a better angle, she frantically began rubbing her wrists across the raw edge. It was an incredibly tedious process with only the barest of millimeters in each direction to maneuver.

The throbbing in her head kept time with her meager efforts, while her neck and shoulder muscles began to scream because of her awkward position. In fact, her whole body felt like a symphony of complaints.

Stubbornly, she gritted her teeth and continued on. Who knew how much time she'd have before they got to wherever he was taking her? She didn't even know how long she'd been unconscious. Trying to visualize the metal piece in her mind's eyes, she determinedly kept at it until she felt the first give in the tape.

Sobbing with relief, she redoubled her efforts. If she could just get her hands free, she was confident that she could liberate her feet quickly.

Another thread of tape gave way. Suddenly, Olivia realized she could shift her hands within their confines. Wincing at the ache in her arms from the uncomfortable position, she pulled them back towards her body and once again set to gnawing the tape with her teeth.

Straining with all her might, she finally - finally! - managed to get her hands free. Wincing, she took a brief moment to pause and rub her poor, chafed wrists. Sharp needles of pain stabbed her fingers as the circulation rushed back into them.

Reminding herself she was still in a bad situation, she maneuvered onto her side and tried to curl her body into a fetal position so she could reach her feet. The muscles in her neck ached from the strain, and she began to get a cramp in the back of her right calf, but she refused to give up.

With her nail, she carefully followed the surface of the tape all around her ankles until she found the end. *It's just like the scotch tape roll you use to wrap gifts,* she told herself as she started to pick at the edge. Gradually, she managed to grip a corner of the tape, and began to pull it apart. The heavy duty adhesive resisted, but she kept at it until the bind was loosened enough that she could use her feet to help.

By the time she'd managed to free herself, Olivia was panting with exertion. Exhausted, she lay back for a moment and fought to catch her breath. All the while, her mind raced.

She winced as she heard the first refrains of a song, wishing her a holly, jolly Christmas. *Yeah, right...*

This was too surreal. Impulsively, she gently pinched herself, hoping it was some type of lucid nightmare. A hysterical giggle bubbled up at what she'd just done. If only it could be so easy.

Man, I'm really losing it. Keep it together.

How could she have been *so* unaware? Mason had warned her that Mendez was probably still around. She should have stayed more alert.

The deep, throbbing pain of her head threatened to make her black out again. Gingerly, she took another moment and felt along the edges of the goose egg sized bump on the back of her skull and wasn't surprised when her fingertips were slightly sticky with blood.

He'd really hit her hard.

Gritting her teeth, she thought about what he might have planned for her. She absolutely *had* to get out of this trunk. With that thought in mind, her eyes automatically focused on the faint red glow again. On a TV show she'd watched, someone that was abducted and trapped in a trunk had managed to force the tail light out and wave through the hole to a car behind them. Maybe she could try that.

Once again, Olivia turned onto her side facing the trunk latch, this time trying to get her fingers through the little hole she'd found earlier in the taillight casing.

The small piece of metal that had been so helpful cutting the tape from around her wrists now sliced through the webbing of her fingers. Gasping in pain, she tried to find another way to reach the light, but to no avail. Her fingers simply weren't long enough.

Anger and frustration had her pounding her fists on the bottom of the trunk. Forcing herself to calm down again, she flattened her palms and took a deep breath.

Wait a minute, she thought as she felt the rough fibers of carpet along her fingertips. The bottom of this trunk was lined. Didn't older cars have a hidden compartment for the spare tire? Eagerly, she began to pry the corner of the trunk liner up, searching for any hidden latches along the way.

Sure enough, just under her hip, was a slight indentation. Olivia scooted as far over to one side as possible and pulled the carpet up underneath her until she could reach the little handle.

Unfortunately, there wasn't enough room to lift the lid fully, and it opened at an angle that left her behind the little top, but she could just manage to angle her arm in and make a light sweep through the compartment underneath.

Score! Her heart leapt as her fingers grasped the hard metal bar of a tire iron. It took some finagling, but she managed to get it out of the compartment.

Gripping the tire iron with both hands, she shoved the end of it into the hole she'd worked on earlier. The plastic gave a soft thud of protest but didn't give way.

Again and again, Olivia tried to get enough force behind the tire iron to pop the taillight out, but she was finding it difficult to get the right angle and enough leverage in the confined space. Exasperated, she let out a sound of frustration.

"Have yourself a very merry Christmas…" The cheerful words of the Christmas carol felt even more twisted, as if it were mocking her. If the stakes hadn't been so high, she may have been tempted to laugh at the absurdity of her situation. As it was, she doubted she'd ever be a fan of holiday music again.

Suddenly, the car stopped, causing Olivia's spine to smack into the back of the backseat. Her hands holding the tire iron were smashed up against the edge of the trunk lid. The pain caused was nothing compared to the sense of victory she felt when she realized the momentum had provided it enough force to pop the taillight out.

As the car once again picked up in speed, she could feel the cooler air making its way through the opening. Eagerly, she cast about trying to find something to fit through the hole.

Her sock!

Desperately, Olivia toed her sneaker off and reached down her leg, wrenching the fabric off her foot. It was a hassle, but she took another moment to grab the shoe with her toe and wrestle it back on. She didn't want to be without a shoe if she got a chance to run.

Cautiously, she fed the cotton fabric into the hole, nervous that she might drop it straight through. Instead, she ended up over-compensating and gripping the fabric tightly with the other hand.

Finally, the length of the sock was hanging out of the trunk. She jiggled it frantically, hoping the small, white flag would catch someone's attention and she'd get some help.

After all the effort it had taken for her to get this far, it was a little disappointing when she didn't get any results after five minutes. Disheartened, she kept at it, limply shifting the sock back and forth.

Her head was one giant ball of pain, and it was all she could do to keep her eyes open and focused on the task she'd set for herself. Tears welled up behind her eyes as the weight of her situation came back to the foreground.

What if no one saw her distress signal? What was she going to do?

She thought longingly of the little pink canister of pepper spray her sister had given her. Too bad it was attached to her keys, which were probably still hanging from the ignition in her car.

With one hand grasping her sock, she wrapped the other one around the reassuring weight of the tire iron. At least she'd managed to find some sort of weapon.

Her mouth firmed. The minute she felt the car stop, she would pull the sock back in and get ready to fight. He was not going to find her an easy target.

With that thought in mind, she felt slightly more comforted and lay her head on the pillow of her bicep. The best thing she could do right now was keep trying to get someone's attention and conserve her energy.

Minutes dragged on, blurring into each other. She tried to stay alert, but caught herself drifting off a few times. Her mind followed along with the lyrics of the newest song. *"I'll be home for Christmas, you can count on me..."*

She hoped she'd be home for Christmas, too. If she didn't get out of the trunk, though, she doubted she'd ever make it back home again.

Stop it! You have to stay positive! Silently, she admonished herself and fought to stay as aware of her surroundings as possible.

If it hadn't been for the cold, she probably would have fallen asleep a long time ago. Instead, with nothing but a light jacket, t-shirt, and jeans on, she was suffering violent, full-body shivers... which wasn't doing anything good for the throbbing in her head.

Every few minutes, she alternated the hand holding the sock and blew on her frozen fingertips. They must have been driving for at least a couple of hours now, hadn't they? Where on Earth was he taking her?

Just as the thought crossed her mind, the car began to slow down again. It was nearly to a stop when he took a sharp ninety degree turn to the right.

The tires beneath her rumbled as the car began to jounce up and down fitfully. Wherever this side road was, it was unpaved.

Olivia had seen lots of roads like this in Maine, especially farther north, where there was a whole lot of forest and very few people. That would also explain why her sock flag of desperation hadn't caught anyone's attention.

The ride got rougher as the road got worse, and she found herself using both hands just to keep from being tossed from one side of the trunk to the other. At some point, she realized she'd let go of the sock and it had fallen out of the trunk.

The water runoff from the previous snows had created a

washboard effect on the road they were on. It would help if the bastard would slow down a little, but it seemed the longer they traveled the faster he went.

Olivia wondered how close his destination was when one particularly bad bump had her smacking her head against the underside of the trunk lid. Her temple landed down on the end of the tire iron.

Pain and blackness enveloped her once more.

Chapter Forty-Five

Mason hopped back in his truck. He really wished he had thought about filling his tank up before he was running ten minutes late. Sighing, he adjusted his rearview mirror and was just about to pull out of the lot when a white Mercedes cut him off.

"Watch it, jerk!" He muttered under his breath, and then reminded himself to calm down. It wouldn't do to arrive in Boston stressed out.

He rubbed the back of his neck. The whole day, he'd been feeling a little off. Hopefully, it wouldn't affect him during the session. Hell, it was probably today's appointment that was causing him to feel so disconcerted.

Trying to shake off the eerie feeling, Mason cranked up the radio. With any luck traffic wouldn't be too bad and he could make good time. With that thought in mind, he floored the gas pedal. By the time he reached the city, he had barely enough time to park his car and rush to the office.

An hour later, he had a pounding headache and felt like he'd just been put through the emotional wringer. How many more times would he have to recount what had happened between him and his partner before he'd be able to do so without getting choked up? Mason strode down the hallway, the soles of his shoes squeaking on the linoleum floor.

The fact that the very same man was now stalking Olivia left him feeling raw and angry. At least now he had enough evidence that people believed him. It had been even worse when everybody thought he was jumping at ghosts.

He didn't like being this far away from Olivia with the situation being what it was. However, if he had to be in Boston he might as well see if there had been any new breaks in the case and make the visit worth something. With that thought in mind, Mason shifted directions and headed towards Captain Field's office.

Giving a perfunctory knock, Mason poked his head through the doorway and watched as the older man hung up the phone and waved him in.

"Mason! Speak of the devil. That was Dr. Patel. He said the meeting went well, and if your other sessions go as well as today, you should be set to come back first thing after the holidays."

The thought should have had him feeling a bit more excited, but Mason was surprised to find he felt vaguely ambivalent about it.

"Well, glad to hear it. Sorry for dropping in on you like this, but I wanted to talk to you about the case."

The captain gave him a knowing look. "Of course you did. How is Olivia holding up so far?"

Mason sat down in the chair across from the other man. "As well as one can hope. She's anxious and feeling antsy, as you would expect."

"Well, I can understand that. You let her know we're doing everything we can to find this guy."

"I'm glad to hear it. I have to tell you, I don't feel comfortable leaving her in this dangerous situation to come back to work, assuming he's still out there after Christmas."

The captain leaned back in his chair, the springs protesting loudly. He pinned him with a steely look. "Mason…"

Mason's jaw hardened and a determined gleam entered his eyes. He respected this man, and appreciated the amount of time he'd already been given, but this was too important.

Sensing an argument, the captain hesitated. He'd seen that stubborn expression on the younger man's face enough times to know a brick wall when he saw one.

"Look, let's cross that bridge if we get to it."

"'That bridge,' as you put it, is next week. Christmas is fast approaching and I don't see us making much headway," Mason pointed out.

The captain sighed. "The best thing we can do for her is focus on catching this guy before it becomes an issue."

Mason couldn't fault the logic behind that. "So, what have you got for me? Anything new?"

"Actually," he reached over and grabbed the omnipresent manila folder, "yes. I'm glad you stopped in before heading back up. Apparently, his mother owned a cabin in Maine."

"What? Why didn't we know this before?"

The captain raised his hands. "It was under her maiden name, so it took some digging. She must have inherited it from her father's estate when he passed away. We suspect that's where he's been holing up."

Mason began to get a tingling sensation on the back of his neck. This was the right track, he knew it. He stood up. "What's the address, sir?"

Captain Fields handed the folder to Mason. "Take this one, it's your copy. Well, technically, it's the Bath, Maine police department's copy. See that they get it."

Nodding, Mason gave the other man a terse smile. "Thanks. I appreciate all you've done for me regarding this case. Not a lot of people would have let me stay in the loop like you have."

His boss looked Mason directly in the eye. "Detective Ryan was a good man. He deserves some justice, and you deserve some peace. I expect to hear a report on whatever happens at that address, you understand?"

"Yes, sir."

"And, you *will* be coming back after the holiday, correct?"

"Assuming this is finished, you can count on it, sir."

Giving a harrumph at the equivocation, the captain accepted Mason's answer and nodded. "You should probably get going then."

Mason eagerly strode out of the office and down the hallway towards the parking garage. Now that they had finally found their first good lead on where this guy might be, he was anxious to get back up to Maine as soon as possible.

Mason had pulled into the small town about twenty minutes from his sister's house when he fished his phone out of his jacket and turned it on. He'd forgotten he'd turned it off for his meeting with the shrink. Surprised, he noticed there were missed calls from his sister, and from an unfamiliar number.

Melody answered immediately. "Mason, thank goodness. Where have you been?"

"What's up, Mel?"

"Didn't you get my message? I've been trying to get ahold of you all afternoon. Olivia is missing."

"What? She was supposed to go directly over to your place after I left."

"I know. When I spoke to her she was just leaving the house. I told her I was going to run down to the basement to grab some ornaments and she could help me decorate the tree this afternoon.

"Thirty minutes later, I still hadn't seen her. I tried to call, but she didn't answer. That's when I noticed her car was parked out front. Mason, the door had been left open and the keys were still in the ignition."

Fear balled in Mason's stomach and the drumbeat of doom

that had been plaguing him all day began to pound in earnest in his chest. He pulled to the side of the road and dug the address out of the folder sitting on the passenger seat beside him. "Have you contacted Brad?"

"Yes, he's out canvasing the area, but hasn't found anything yet. I called Liz, as well. She's here with me. I haven't been able to reach Fiona."

Aw hell. "Okay, I may have a lead on where Robert has been staying. He probably took her there. I need to call Brad and let him know what's going on. When was the last time you talked to her?"

"It was just after you left, so…a little after noon? Oh, Mason. What if that son of a bitch got ahold of her?"

"I think we can safely assume that's happened. I've got to go. Call me if you hear from her." Without waiting for a reply, he hung up and frantically plugged the cabin's address into the GPS. After looking at the map, he wrenched the steering wheel around and headed north out of town. With one hand on the wheel, he dialed the local PD and reminded himself to pay attention to his driving as he barreled down the highway.

"Bath Police Department."

"Is Officer Brad Thompson available? This is Mason Clark; it's an emergency."

"I'll patch you through. One moment please."

"Officer Thompson."

"Brad? Mason. I just spoke to my sister and found out Olivia is missing."

"Mason, I tried calling you, but your phone was off."

"I was in a meeting. I think I may know where he's taken her. I'm on my way there now."

"What? Where?"

Mason told him about the cabin they'd only just discovered. "I'm on the highway headed north now."

He heard a sigh on the other end of the line. "Technically, this is a police matter, and as much leniency as I've allowed, you don't actually have jurisdiction here..."

Mason opened his mouth to protest. "Brad..."

"I know. I'm going to inform my captain about what's going on and give him the location of the cabin. He'll contact the department up there and see if we can't get some eyes on the address. I'm right behind you."

He felt better knowing there would be a number of law enforcement personnel helping to find Olivia, but he still felt a grinding, raw sensation when he thought about her in that sicko's hands.

Brad heard the silence from the other man and realized what he must be thinking. "Don't worry, Mason. We'll get her back."

"That's not what's concerning me. I *know* we will. But what damage will be done before we do?"

"You can't think like that, man. It's not going to do anything but hurt you and interfere with your concentration. The best thing you can do for Olivia right now is focus on the task at hand."

"Will do." Mason hung up. Luckily, traffic was light. There was another storm slated to pass through later that night, and most people had scurried home early from work in order to be off the roads.

Driven by a sense of urgency, Mason gunned the truck and shot down the two lane highway. He only hoped he could get there in time. If his calculation was correct, then Mendez had nearly three hours on them by this point.

His phone's navigator indicated it took a little over two hours to get to the cabin, so maybe Olivia was still in the car, or had just arrived. There was still hope that he could stop her from being hurt.

Some part of himself that he couldn't afford to acknowledge was wailing at the thought of her in the hands of that madman.

The knuckles on his fingers turned white as he gripped the steering wheel and strained to control his urge to howl.

Night came early in northern Maine during the winter, especially with another snowstorm projected to hit the region the next morning. The few cars on the road already had their headlights turned on, and the woods on both sides of the road were shrouded in shadows.

Cruising down the road, Mason ran through the list of events again through his mind, wondering how any of this could have been prevented.

The shrill ring of his phone pierced his ruminations. "Yeah?"

"It's Brad. I spoke to my captain and he's aware of the situation. He said there's been a major accident and most of the officers up there are tied up dealing with it. I'm about thirty-five minutes behind you. I'm hoping my siren will help me catch up."

"Damn." Mason sped up a little more. "Look, I appreciate everything you're doing, and keeping me in the loop. But I want you to know, if I see something happening, I'm not waiting to go in."

Silence filled the air for a moment. "I wouldn't expect anything less. If Olivia is in danger or being hurt, you absolutely should go in."

A tone of authority infused Brad's voice. "But, remember, this isn't vigilante justice for your partner. I expect Mendez to be taken into custody."

Mason's gorge rose when he thought about the guy who had killed his partner getting a chance to live out his years in prison. Or worse, what if he got off on a technicality and walked free?

Sensing his hesitation, Brad continued. "You swore to uphold the law when you became a cop. The system only works if we all agree to abide by it. Especially the ones who are expected to enforce it. I need your word, Mason."

Mason knew the other man was right, even if he didn't like

it. He'd have to trust the system to give Robert the justice he deserved. "You have it. I will do everything I can to deliver him safely into your custody."

"That's what I wanted to hear."

Mason hung up the phone. He'd been pushing twenty miles over the speed limit, but began to slow down slightly as night deepened around him. The last thing he needed was to hit a deer out here.

Or worse, go flying past the turn-off.

Chapter Forty-Six

The first thing Olivia became aware of was the vise grip of the pain throbbing in her head. Her whole world was surrounded by the misery emanating from her skull. Even her groan of pain caused pain.

Her arms were stretched up above her and she could feel her fingertips tingling from lack of circulation. She tried to pull them down and realized there was something chafing her wrists, preventing her from doing so. With that, her eyes popped open and she moved her head to look up.

Big mistake.

Spears of agony split her head in two and skittered down her neck. The wave of pain was so intense it made her stomach roll. Carefully, she let out a breath and fought to keep the nausea at bay.

How was she going to be able to fight when she wasn't even able to open her eyes or turn her head?

Panic threatened to drown her as she thought about her options. If only she'd managed to stay conscious in the trunk, at least there she'd had a tire iron.

Tears seeped out from under her lids and ran down towards her temples. Even crying hurt. The pressure behind her eyes began to build and throb as she took a moment to wallow in her sense of helplessness.

Pull yourself together. You're not going to beat this guy simpering like that! The part of her that was a survivalist ruthlessly berated her tears and urged her to fight. After another moment, she took a deep breath and began trying to calm herself once more.

She knew that Mason had to have realized something was wrong. He probably had gotten out of his evaluation hours ago. He was probably looking for her right now.

The best thing she could do was keep her wits about her and look for an opportunity to get away. Barring that, maybe she could hold the bastard off long enough for someone to rescue her.

Carefully, she cracked an eye open, and waited for the ensuing pain to abate before taking stock of her surroundings. The view of a white popcorn ceiling rewarded her for her efforts. Without moving her head, she rotated her eyes to the right.

The room had wood paneling, and there was a musty odor in the air she hadn't noticed before. The only light came from a small bedside lamp emitting a dingy yellow light from the far corner of the room.

Gingerly, she tested her feet, and was discouraged to find they were also bound again. Even more disconcerting was the fact that her arms and legs were bare. Cool air caused her skin to break out in goose bumps. Well, that and fear.

She could feel some kind of silky fabric slide across her torso, so she knew she wasn't completely nude, but it definitely wasn't the comforting feel of cotton from the jeans and t-shirt she had been wearing.

That meant someone had undressed her and changed her clothes while she was unconscious.

The thought had her breath catching all over again, her heart beating an unsteady staccato. Each pulse caused her head to hurt. Her mind fiercely shied away from all of the possible things that may have happened while she'd been unaware.

Don't think about that! Her inner voice admonished.

Once again, she found herself mentally berating herself for falling into the trap. She may as well have served herself up on a silver platter.

Stop it!

That line of thinking wasn't going to help either. With another deep breath, she brought herself back to the situation at hand. She only hoped there would be enough time for self-recriminations later.

With her eyes closed, she started to listen for any clues to where she was. There was someone moving around in what sounded like the kitchen. Water was running in the sink. She thought she could hear the faint, tinny sounds of a radio coming from the other room.

She shivered as a light breeze came from the slightly cracked window to the left and above her. Outside, all she could hear was the rustle of wind in trees, and what sounded like water lapping.

Desperately, she strained to hear any other sounds of civilization. A car door slamming, voices, television…but there was nothing. *So, not in a town or city.* Her heart dropped. It felt like there wasn't anybody but her and the person in the kitchen around for miles. Probably why he'd felt safe enough to leave the window cracked slightly open.

What was she going to do, even if she did manage to get away?

Her heart sunk as she reached that realization just as the floorboards creaked. She could hear footsteps, treading down what she assumed was a hallway.

Quickly, Olivia shut her eyes. She struggled to remain still and breathe slowly and deeply, hoping he would think she was still passed out.

The door creaked slightly as it was opened and she could sense his presence as he loomed over her.

*Calm, deep breaths…nice and slow…*she forced herself to concentrate on the words, ruthlessly reigning in her need to panic.

Hot breath brushed across her cheek as he leaned down close to her, and inhaled deeply. Was he *smelling* her? Every hair on her neck stood up as he lingered there. It was all she could do not to flinch away or turn her head.

Keep breathing, nice and slow...

After another minute that felt like eternity, he stood upright. He hadn't said anything. Hadn't touched her, or hurt her. Yet, as she heard him sigh and walk out the door, Olivia had never felt so terrified.

She knew pretending she was passed out wasn't going to be an option for much longer. Cautiously, she opened her eyes, more frantic than ever to get out of her bonds.

Chapter Forty-Seven

Robert regretted not being able to play with his acquisition just yet, but he'd left the car in front of the cabin and needed to park it in the back and get it covered.

Besides, having her unconscious took all the fun out of the experience.

He put his coat and boots on and stepped out into the crisp, frigid air. Pausing on the front porch, he inhaled deeply, enjoying the scent of pine and snow. Night had fallen fully now, and he could see the diamond point stars from the clearing his cabin sat in. The lake had begun to freeze around the edges, but he could still hear the water gently lapping off in the distance.

It brought back memories of staying with his grandfather after his mom had died from her whore's disease. He remembered the nightly lectures about how his mom had been a sinner, destined to end the way she had.

All women were transgressors, he'd learned. They couldn't help it, being the vessels of original sin. It was man's obligation to show a woman the error of her ways and help her find a righteous path. If she refused, then it was his duty to discipline and guide her.

It had been a relief to Robert to discover his role in life.

The years spent with the older man had been austere and strict, but in the end, better than anything he'd ever known previously. If only his grandfather could see him now, and appreciate the level he had taken his teachings to.

Shaking off his musings, he trudged out to the car and pulled it around to the back. He laughed when he glimpsed the broken taillight again. That had been quite a surprise when he'd first arrived at the cabin.

He'd even hesitated for a moment before opening the trunk, not knowing what to expect. It had been amusing to find she'd managed to knock herself out with the very same weapon she'd undoubtedly been planning to use on him.

He was going to have to really watch this one. Breaking her spirit and getting her trained was going to be a real accomplishment. His heart beat faster in anticipation.

Clever, tricky girl.

With the car taken care of, Robert had a bounce in his step as he walked towards the front of the house. Before letting himself in, he took a moment to listen for anything unusual. Satisfied with the familiar night sounds around him, he passed through the doorway and headed back towards the bedroom.

Time for sleeping beauty to wake up.

Now that he had his wayward angel safely secured, he didn't feel the need to rush. In fact, he wanted to savor the moment and fully enjoy this first night with her. He felt confident that nobody would be able to find them there at the cabin.

Quietly, he made his way back to the bedroom and cracked the door again. Peering in, he admired the way her figure looked, stretched out and welcoming him. His eyes traced where the silk and lace curved around her body, revealing as much as it concealed.

Frustrated, he noticed her eyes were still closed. He let his gaze linger on her face, and with a sudden flick of his wrist, slammed the bedroom door shut. Satisfied, he watched as she jolted with the shock of sound. Aha, so she *was* playing possum. He'd thought as much.

Robert approached the bed and traced his hand down the center line between her breasts, enjoying the way she quivered under his touch. Fascinated, his eyes soaked in the swath of creamy flesh revealed as his hand slid aside the silky teddy he'd dressed her in.

He'd always known she'd be beautiful in emerald green. It really was the right choice. He'd have to make sure she wore more jewel tones. No more of those ugly, shapeless chef coats. Of course, nobody but him would be allowed to see her like this.

Looking back to her face, it didn't surprise him to find her staring. He'd like to think it was passion he saw there, but wasn't that delusional. He had seen the way she'd looked at that detective. Robert promised himself that she *would* learn to look at him that way and forget all about the other guy.

With bottom lip trembling, she opened her lush lips. "Robert, please...please, don't hurt me."

His eyes widened slightly when she mentioned his name, and then took on a satisfied gleam. "I see you already know my name. That's good. That means you probably already know what I can do, as well." He leaned in, forcing her to meet his eyes. "You're mine. The sooner you learn that, the better off you'll be."

He looked down her body distastefully and grimaced. "I can smell the stink of that pig on you. How could you have let him defile you like that?"

Her voice caught on a sob. "Let me go..."

Hot, fierce rage filled him instantly. Didn't she know how lucky she was? He was going to make her one of his chosen few. His eyes narrowed into cruel slits as his fingers squeezed her breast until she gasped in shock and pain. Desperately, she twisted her hips away from him, trying to dislodge his hand from her chest.

Robert grabbed her hair and pulled it back, causing her to keen in agony. Silver tears streaked down her cheeks and dripped from her chin.

He twisted her hair just a little bit more, reveling in his

dominance over her. "Look at me. You're MINE now. I will not allow you to be contaminated like that ever again."

The whole world narrowed down to the place on her scalp where he gripped her hair. Olivia's already throbbing head began to clatter and wail. Black spots floated across her vision and for a moment she was afraid she might pass out again. Every sensation, every nerve ending, blared in protest.

The feeling overwhelmed her as her mind grasped for a solution. She was afraid to say the wrong thing and get him even angrier. On the other hand, she hesitated to be too welcoming, either.

Robert let go of her hair in disgust. Breathing heavily, he stood with his back to her and made an obvious attempt to calm himself.

Olivia thought back to the conversation she'd had with Mason during dinner all those weeks ago. He'd said that most obsession stalkers grew irate when the person they'd been harboring fantasies for didn't act in the way they were supposed to.

Revulsion rose in her. She was acutely cognizant of her vulnerable position, splayed across the bed, her limbs spread-eagled. The thought of playing along sickened and terrified her.

Just then, he turned to her and raked his eyes across her body. Gulping back another sob and resisting her natural instinct to fight, she gave a shy, tentative smile, instead. "I- I'm sorry that you're not pleased. If you unbind me, I can go freshen up for you, if you'd like."

Suspicion and lust warred in his gaze as he looked at her shrewdly. Trying not to let her disgust show in her eyes, she held still under his scrutiny. Olivia barely curbed the urge to flinch as he raised his hand and gently stroked her hair, following the strands down to the side of her breast.

All the while, his eyes never left hers—testing her. "I like that idea."

Robert moved to undo the bindings at her feet, pausing to wrap his hand around her ankle and stroke her calf. Adopting a light, conversational tone, he continued, "I really hope this isn't a game you're playing. I think you'll learn very quickly that I don't suffer games."

Unsure of how to respond to that, she opted for the prudent path and stayed quiet. As it was, she could barely keep alert with the all-consuming pain in her head. No doubt she was suffering from a concussion by this point and wondered how much more her poor abused skull could handle.

After a moment, he resumed untying the knots around her ankle. He gripped her foot firmly in his hands once it was released. She lay there, uncomfortably aware of the fact that the slip he'd dressed her in was slowly inching up her thigh as he held her leg at an angle.

She could tell that he'd noticed it too by the way his glance strayed to the betraying fabric. He ran his fingers up her leg, along the inside of her knee, and began to slowly trail it up her thigh.

*No, no, no, no….*chanted in Olivia's head. Her other foot was still bound, her arms still tied above her head. There would be nothing she could do if he decided to go forward with the intent showing in his eyes.

Desperate to stop his questing hand, she cleared her throat. "N-n-no game, R-Robert. I promise. You said you could still smell Mason on me. I just want to make sure I'm pleasing to you."

At her reference to the other man, he got a dark scowl on his face. Angrily, he reached up and twisted her nipple. She yelped in pain and surprise, stunned by the casual viciousness constantly lurking just below his surface.

"NEVER say his name again. Don't even refer to him, do you understand me? As far as you're concerned he no longer exists!"

"I'm sorry, I'm sorry, I'm sorry!" her voice rose higher and higher in pitch as he dug his nails into her tender skin. He seemed to take pleasure in watching her beg and plead. With one final wrench, he released her.

Sobbing, she turned her face away as he lifted his hand to her cheek. Entranced by her reaction, he caught a tear tenuously dangling from one of her lashes and delicately licked it off his finger tip. Olivia closed her eyes. She couldn't stand to see the dark joy in his expression as he tasted her tears.

He caught her chin between his forefinger and thumb and forced her to look directly at him. The fear he found in her eyes must have pleased him, because one moment he was twisting his mouth cruelly and the next he was smiling gently at her.

"Let's finish getting you unwrapped so you can go tidy yourself up for me, shall we?"

Afraid of setting him off again, Olivia slowly nodded her head. Satisfied, he began working on her other foot. Thankfully, much to her relief, he seemed distracted from his earlier foray up her leg.

Once her limbs were free, he gently eased her up. He let her get her bearings for a moment, even helped to rub sensation back into her hands. She sat docilely on the bed and stared down at the top of his head as he squatted before her, rubbing one of her feet. She briefly considered trying to kick him in the nose and make a run for it.

He must have sensed her thoughts, because suddenly he was looking up and pinned her with a stare. "Are you going to be a good girl?"

It became readily apparent this wasn't a good opportunity for her to attempt escape. Not only was she slightly dizzy from having her head knocked about so hard, but he was much stronger and had a fifty pound advantage on her physically. One wrong move and she'd find herself trussed up like a turkey again. Or worse.

No, she'd do better to work up his trust in her, first. Maybe she could get him to relax his guard a little. She smiled tremulously at him. "Yes, Robert, I'll be a good girl. It's just that I've been laying in that trunk for hours, and my arms and legs can barely move."

He seemed pleased with her answer. She began to realize that he liked hearing her say his name, and mentally filed the information away.

Olivia kept her hands clenched down by her sides and struggled not to flinch when he leaned forward and kissed her directly on the mouth. She desperately hoped he wouldn't try to take things any further.

Thankfully, after a moment he leaned back and stood up from where he was crouched before her. For a split second, she hesitated before taking his proffered hand and allowing him to help her up from the bed. Her first instinct had been to bat it away and run.

Instead, she graciously smiled and accepted his assistance, reminding herself that she needed him to lower his guard. She cautiously moved to walk around him and towards the door. Logically, she knew he could force himself on her anywhere, but being in a bedroom with him felt too dangerous.

Just as she thought he'd let her move past him, he yanked her up against his body, running his hands down her back, and ground his pelvis against hers.

Reflexively, she closed her eyes, bit her lip, and cringed. She could feel he was already aroused, stabbing her intimately. The thin barrier of cloth separating their bodies was woefully insufficient, and yet Olivia found herself intensely grateful for its presence.

She tried to refrain from shrinking away further as he leaned close and smelled her hair. Every cell in her body screamed to knee him in the groin and dash out the door.

"You don't know how I've longed to hold you like this, my angel. Do you feel how right it is between us? You were meant for me." He pulled back to look at her, but whatever he saw in her eyes made his face darken.

Sensing the change in his mood, she rushed to say, "Forgive me, Robert. My head is still pounding painfully. I really think I'll feel better after I've had a chance to freshen up."

Holding her breath, she watched the tumult of emotions cross his face and let out a relieved exhale when his brow finally cleared.

Tenderly, he pressed another kiss to her mouth. "Oh, my poor dear. Of course, you're right. How inconsiderate of me." He led her down the hallway to a little bathroom on the right. When she reached for the door, hoping to close it, he stopped her. "I don't think that's such a good idea. You've just suffered a concussion, my angel. What if you fell in the shower?"

Her heart plummeted. There was no way she was going to be able to do anything with the door open. She stammered. "B-but, Robert, I can't use the facilities with the door open."

"Why not?" he asked suspiciously. She put her best flirtatious smile on and tried to remember what it meant to be coquettish. She had never been much of a flirt at the best of times, and this situation was hardly conducive to that behavior.

"A woman has to have a little mystery, don't you think?" Forcing herself to take a step closer to him, she ran her fingers along the buttons of his shirt. "How can there be any allure if you see me do my business? Let me get myself ready for you."

Reluctantly, he agreed to let her use the bathroom, cautioning her not to lock the door, or he'd 'take the whole thing off its hinges, mystery be damned.'

Demurring, she stepped into the bathroom and gently shut the door in his face. She pressed her back against it and stuffed her knuckles in her mouth, struggling to muffle the sobs that attempted to climb up her throat. Tears raced down her cheeks, silent banners of the overwhelming dread that threatened to crush her.

Robert pounded on the door, causing her to jump. "Don't take too long, Olivia. I *will* come in and get you."

"I won't!" Hastily, she swiped the tears from her eyes and squared her shoulders. There wasn't enough time to indulge in wallowing. She needed to take this opportunity to find a way to escape.

Chapter Forty-Eight

Mason raked his fingers through his hair for the hundredth time in an hour. What was happening to Olivia right now? His imagination was going crazy with all the possibilities, none of them good.

The glowing green numbers of the vehicle's digital clock mocked him. He resisted the urge to go faster than he was already risking. Even then, he estimated he'd shaved close to an hour off the usual drive time.

Dusk had finally given way to full darkness, and the last thing he needed was to run off the road. The only good thing he could say was at least there wasn't anybody on the road with him; the landscape was deserted.

However, because the area was so remote, he'd lost cell phone service about thirty minutes ago. Luckily, he'd plugged the address of the cabin into his navigator before he had lost connection, so even though it wasn't able to give him turn by turn instructions, he had a map of the surrounding area.

Grudgingly, he slowed down as he came upon another little town, his headlights cutting across the general store and gas station that made up the entire business district. In a lot of these places, a person couldn't blink or they'd miss the whole town.

He peered through the darkened windshield, straining to see

further ahead, hoping he wouldn't drive by the turn off. Much to his chagrin, soft, swirling flurries had started to fall about thirty minutes ago. Mason hazarded a glance at his phone. He should be coming up on the road pretty soon.

A flash of light from a pair of eyes caught his attention, and he just barely saw the deer in time to slam on his brakes. It stood there for a split second, it's dark, limpid eyes pooled in mystery, then bounded off to the right of the road….down what looked like an overgrown gravel path.

His pulse began to race. This was it. With a brief confirming look at the map on his phone, and a slight plea to the universe that he was correct, he turned the wheel and began to make his way down the road.

Mason could hear the tree branches scrape along the length of his truck as he slowly made his way further into the woods. The road — if you could call it that — was deeply rutted and pitted. Large banks of snow piled up on either side, causing him to weave back and forth across the narrow track.

It didn't help that he'd cut his headlights off, afraid of tipping Robert to the fact that someone was coming. Mason leaned forward and squinted through the windshield, straining to see through the swirl of flurries beginning to drift down in earnest. He could just make out the thin, pale line of snow-covered road erratically winding its way through the gap in the shadows of the trees.

Mason knew caution was necessary, but inside, he was screaming with impatience. Finally, just as he was losing control, the shadows of the trees opened up and gave way to a small clearing. He could barely make out the shadow of a roofline by the faintest remnants of moonlight filtering through the clouds.

Braking and rolling his window down, he sat for a moment with the heater off and strained to hear anything out of place. Here in the woods, the snow was still deep from the last storm, and every sound seemed muffled and faint.

Afraid the engine might be too loud in the soft tones of night, he turned the truck off. Gradually, he became aware of the breeze rustling through the branches overhead. Somewhere off in the distance, an owl hooted.

Leaning over, he pulled out his handgun and a mini LED flashlight, and then carefully climbed out of the cab. He gently clicked the door shut behind him and thumbed the light on. A sharp, thin, beam of light speared out into the shadows. Up ahead, a soft, warm glow peeked out from the cracks in the curtains hanging in the cabin windows.

Slowly, he made his way towards the cabin, making sure to stick to the trees as much as possible. The crusty snow lightly crunching under his boots and the ghost of his breath were the only signs of his passing. Mason skirted the perimeter of the small clearing surrounding the house. There weren't any vehicles parked in the front, so he decided to make his way around to the back.

This could just be a fisherman, a hunter, or even a couple out here looking for a quiet retreat. He didn't want to accidentally disturb anybody at this hour if he didn't have to…and there was no telling if this was the right cabin or not. There were a lot of cabins just like this tucked all around the remote areas of Maine.

As Mason came around the side of the house, he spotted the hulking shape of a car sitting under a tarp. Hunched over, he ducked through the shadows and made his way closer. He laid a hand on the hood, finding that the engine was still warm. The car must not have been sitting for very long. The broken taillight he discovered when he rounded the trunk of the car had his heart jumping up in his throat. Some part of him already knew this was the right place.

Mason crept back towards the back of the house, pausing periodically to make sure no new sounds escaped his attention. Even in the dark, he could tell the back porch canted to the side and was dilapidated. As he grew closer, he could see the shredded remnants of torn screens in the windows. Poking his head through one of the openings, he noticed the back door was boarded up with a bunch of two-by-fours.

Disappointed, Mason cautiously made his way around to the side of the cabin. There appeared to be only one window on the back of the cabin that might be large enough for him to climb through. It even looked like it was cracked open a bit. Stopping underneath, he strained to hear what might be happening inside. Try as he might, he couldn't hear Olivia.

He took a moment to inspect the window a little more closely. It was high enough up that he'd probably make a lot of noise trying to gain access through it. He continued to make his way around towards the front of the cabin and tried to get the lay of the land as he went, knowing it would be better to consider all his options before committing to anything drastic. Even then, he realized that if Olivia was actually inside, he was probably going to have to storm the cabin.

Chapter Forty-Nine

Robert stood and listened at the door for a moment until he heard Olivia start the water in the shower. Part of him wanted to walk in on her and see what she was really up to. Did she really think that line about mystery was going to fool him?

He'd learned a long time ago never to trust the words coming out of a woman's mouth.

Still, it was good to finally have her with him.

He headed into the living room. All the photos he'd taken of her over the past few weeks were tacked up on the walls, covering the entire surface area. Olivia cooking, Olivia talking, Olivia with her sisters, Olivia smiling…he'd carefully curated her day-to-day life.

He hated the fact that he felt nervous now that she was there with him. Methodically, he began to straighten all the images of her, making sure they were just right and in their proper place.

After finishing his task, he sat and eased back onto the couch. Letting his hand stray to his crotch, he idly rubbed himself, momentarily easing the discomfort she'd caused him.

He looked down the hall towards the bathroom door. She'd better come out soon, or he was going to start getting angry. Impatiently, he grabbed the remote sitting on the table in front of him, deciding to give her a few more moments before knocking the door in.

He clicked the television on, happy to find the local news reporting on the weather, and watched as the slim blonde woman spoke of another storm coming in. Glancing out the window, he could see flakes had already started to float by the window.

Good, he thought. Though the cabin was remote, it would make it less likely they'd be able to get to him, even if they did find it. Just then, the news segment changed. He watched as a photo of Olivia came across the screen. The anchorwoman began to report on a missing woman abducted from Bath, Maine and thought to be in the Penobscot Bay area.

Robert cursed as they switched to a copy of his mugshot. *It's okay, everything is under control.* He always knew they'd find a way to tie him to the area. Granted, it had happened a little faster than he would have liked. He wondered where he had slipped up.

Frustrated with the newscast, Robert quickly shut the TV off and glanced over at the closed door. What was taking her so long? He stood up and walked back towards the bathroom.

Chapter Fifty

Having dashed the tears from her eyes, Olivia scanned the bathroom. The cheap off-white vanity had begun to yellow and the sink was lined in rust stains. A dingy, puke green shower curtain hung slightly askew on its rod. Poking her head behind the curtain, she noticed the shower itself was little bigger than a closet.

There was only one disappointingly small window located just above the toilet. Walking towards it, she noticed that the latch had been painted over and knew the window wouldn't open. It didn't really matter. No way would she be able to fit through that.

Olivia quickly rushed to the shower and turned it on, hoping it would mask any sounds he might hear. With urgent, methodical purpose, she checked through the medicine cabinet and under the sink. Nothing, nothing, nothing. Dammit! Not even a handy toilet brush or plunger she could use as a weapon, just a threadbare cotton towel and a sliver of soap. What was she going to do?

Panic, never far from the surface, once again threatened to bubble up inside of her. Ruthlessly, she shoved it down. Staring at herself in the mirror, she forced herself to think.

Okay, so she wasn't going to be able to escape or help herself from the bathroom. She had to have faith that Mason would be coming for her. Surely, people would have realized she's disappeared by now.

Her best option, if she couldn't find a way to escape, was going to be to stall. With that conclusion, she quickly ducked under the showerhead and dampened her hair. Olivia ran her hands through her now wet hair and shivered with cold.

Goose bumps pebbled her skin and she could see the distinct outline of her nipples through the thin fabric that barely covered her. She'd give just about anything to have her t-shirt and jeans on instead of the chintzy negligee he'd left her with.

After taking one last deep breath, she opened the bathroom door. Letting out an involuntary squeak, she quickly took a step back, startled to find Robert right outside the door. He leered down at her, focusing on the way her breasts were thrust upward. "I was just about to come in after you."

Giving him her most brilliant smile, she barely resisted the urge to cross her arms across her chest. "No need, I was just coming out…but, I have to tell you, I'm famished."

Olivia looked up at Robert and watched his suspicious expression morph into desire. *Hmm, maybe the smile was a little too much*, she thought.

He lifted his hand and ran his fingers through her damp strands. She fought to stand there and not take a step back. Instead, she gave him a puzzled look. "Robert? Did you hear me? I haven't eaten all day."

As if coming out of a trance, he shook his head and focused on her face. "What's that? Oh, of course. You must be starving." His eyes drifted down her throat as he began to stroke the contours of her collar bone.

Olivia stood, frozen for a split second, unsure of how to proceed. If she encouraged him too much, he might try to take things further than she was willing to go. At that point, she'd have no choice but to drop the charade and attempt to fight him off.

However, if she didn't convince him to lower his guard, she'd never have an opportunity to make her escape. Hoping to walk that thin line, she stepped towards him. "Y'know, I *am* a chef. Why don't I make us a nice dinner?" She placed her hand gently on his arm and looked up into his eyes. "It could be romantic."

Robert's eyes turned hot and he bent down to nuzzle her neck. "You stir my appetite in more ways than one."

Barely able to control her shudder, she pulled back. "Well, let's see what you have in the kitchen, then." She gave him a limp smile and tried to skirt around him, but stopped when he reached up and gripped her arm tightly.

His fingers dug painfully into the flesh of her upper arm. "You better not be trying anything. I guarantee you won't like the way I discipline you."

Olivia stared up at him with wide eyes. She had thought she was succeeding at lulling him into trusting her, but his moods were so mercurial that it was hard to keep up.

He leaned into her face. "I will deal with any cutting. Don't think I've forgotten how handy you can be with kitchen knives."

A small ember of hope in Olivia's breast fluttered and guttered out. The possibility had been so remote that she hadn't even admitted it to herself, but the knives had been floating in the back of her mind all the same.

Gulping, she nodded up at him. "O-o-okay, Robert. I just wanted to make us a nice meal. I'm so hungry!"

Almost as if a switch had been flipped, the hand that had been gripping her on her shoulder, gentled, and he kissed her on the temple. "Well, then let's go make you some dinner."

Moments later, Olivia grimaced as she took a look in his refrigerator. There wasn't a lot to work with. "Hm, I'm not sure what I'll be able to do with these ingredients," she muttered, half to herself.

He scowled. "We could always skip dinner."

Not willing to give up that easily, she stood and opened the cupboards. It felt like she was in some reality cooking show, trying to see what she can make from a bunch of disparate items. "Oh, come on, now. What's the fun in that?" She pulled a can of spam down from the shelf and placed it on the counter, along with a pack of ramen noodles.

"Do you have any veggies?"

Robert stood leaning against the counter, following her progress with his eyes. Now he pointed with his chin at another cupboard. "There might be a can of something in there. I don't usually eat them."

Nodding, she reached up and found a dusty, old can of green beans. "How old are these?"

He shrugged. "Probably left over from my grandfather."

"This used to be your grandfather's cabin?"

Not answering, Robert just looked at her. Deciding she should stay busy, she started opening drawers and looking for a can opener.

"I'll do that," he grabbed the can out of her hand and gave her a warning look. Instantly she shot him her best, innocent smile. "Great."

Olivia decided she'd make a simple ramen dish with the spam and green beans. It wouldn't be her best meal ever, but maybe it would give her a little more time to stall him.

After some digging, she found a couple of pieces of beat-up and mismatched cookware. The stove was an old electric one and there was a crusty ring of grime along the edges. With a bit of experimenting, she discovered only one out of the four burners worked, and placed the pot of water on the burner first. Robert handed her the opened can of green beans, then again leaned back against the counter.

Trying not to let him make her any more nervous than she already was, she cracked open the ramen package and tapped the flavor packet into the water. As she waited for the water to heat to a boil, she popped open the can of Spam.

Casually, she grabbed the cutting board from the lower cupboard, but before she could go for the knife in the drawer beside her, Robert grabbed her wrist. "Don't push me, Olivia."

Pretending that she was going to ask him all along, she waved her hand. "Will you dice this for me?"

It took him another long beat before he nodded and bent his head to the task. She was a little surprised, and disturbed, by the deft way he handled the knife.

After checking the water, she cracked the ramen noodles and tossed them in. "Should we put these in the water, too?" Robert asked her.

"Um, no, I'm going to cook the noodles first, then fry them in the pan. Figured we could make a stir-fry out of them."

She checked the clock above the stove and was relieved to find ten minutes had already passed. She knew it probably wouldn't take much longer to prepare the meal. If she was lucky, she'd be able to stall for, at most, another forty-five minutes. *Come on, Mason, where are you?*

As she finished preparing the meal, he began to pace back and forth in the kitchen. She could tell he was already impatient with playing house and cast him a look from the side of her eye, trying to gauge his emotion.

Just as she was tossing the spam into the noodles, Robert suddenly turned to her, grabbed the pan, and tossed it across the room. Gasping, Olivia stepped back at the look of fury on his face.

He stalked towards her and gripped her arms. "Don't you think I know what you're doing?" He shook her until she could feel her brain rattle.

Yanking her up against him, he crushed his mouth down on hers, his teeth splitting her bottom lip with the force. Yelping in pain, Olivia began to struggle in earnest, turning her head away as he bent to lick the blood from her lips.

With a sound of disgust, he frog-marched her out into the living room as she stubbornly ground her heels in and fought him every inch of the way. With her first glimpse of the room, she froze in disturbed silence. Everywhere she looked, her own image stared back at her. Spinning around, she was dismayed to find all three walls covered from floor to ceiling.

Horrified, she turned to watch as Robert walked up to one of the images and traced her face with his finger. There she was, illuminated from behind, standing at the sink in her kitchen window.

Dread filled her stomach. She'd had no idea he had been there. Turning, she looked at another photo closer to her. She was sitting in her car and obviously singing along to the radio. He must have been in the car right beside her, sitting at a stoplight when he'd taken it. She noticed a number of them had been cut out where Mason must have been standing. Where he couldn't separate their images, he'd scratched Mason's face out, as if trying to delete him from existence.

Robert turned to gauge her reaction. She could see the glow of pride in his eyes and struggled not to show her own revulsion and fear at seeing herself in so many photos.

"What do you think?"

She started to open her mouth to respond, but something in her expression must have shown how she truly felt, because next thing she knew, his fist flew up and slammed into her jaw.

With a cry, Olivia fell to the ground. A high pitched ringing filled her ears as she struggled to get up to her hands and knees. Robert bent down and grabbed her by her hair, lifting her back on her feet like a marionette.

"I *know* when you're lying to me. Don't you think I know who you are? I've been watching you for weeks." He gestured towards the walls with his hands. "*THIS* is who you are."

Desperately, she scrabbled at his hand gripping her hair. He pulled her face close to his own. "The sooner you understand you're mine, the sooner we can begin the process of your redemption." With his other hand, he tore the teddy from her shoulders, baring her from the waist up.

An animalistic sound of anguish ripped from her throat. One of the flimsy straps snapped as she disentangled her arms from them, and with it went all thought and reason. She began to struggle in earnest, giving up any pretense. Forming a claw with her hand, she thrashed out at him, scraping her nails down his cheek. A sick sense of satisfaction rose up in her at the sight of his blood spilling down his jawline.

"You little bitch!" He screamed, spittle flying from his mouth, spraying her in the face. It didn't register. All she could think of was causing him pain and her own survival. Robert shoved her down on the floor and climbed on top of her, using his weight advantage to gain control.

Bucking her hips wildly, she screamed in frustration. Her heels drummed the floor as she tried to dislodge him from her, to no avail.

Chapter Fifty-One

Hearing Olivia's cry shredded the last of Mason's willpower. Realizing he couldn't wait any longer, he threw his body weight into the front door. Stumbling, he barely managed to keep his balance, caught off guard because it hadn't been locked.

The tableau before him flashed across his awareness. Roaring with anger at the sight of Robert sprawled on top of her, he grabbed the other man by the shoulders and threw him across the room.

Robert let loose his own guttural growl, like an animal fighting to claim his mate. Sobbing, Olivia turned over and began to crawl away.

Mason raised his gun towards Robert, aiming at his chest, but was startled when Robert didn't even hesitate to rush him. As they grappled with each other, the gun was kicked from his hand, and spun away under one of the chairs.

Robert swung a fist at his face, but Mason managed to dodge at the last second. The sound of Robert's shoulder popping filled the air as he was rammed up against the wall. For a moment, all Olivia could do was pull her knees up to her chest and huddle into the corner. Almost as an afterthought, she pulled the single remaining slip strap back up over her shoulder and watched the two men tear at each other.

Mason's shoulder injury began to twinge in protest. Despite

being trained in hand-to-hand combat, he was disturbed to find Robert a much bigger challenge than he'd anticipated. He'd recovered enough to do most day-to-day activities without much difficulty, but taking the last couple of months off the force had left him weaker than he'd thought.

Sensing his opponent's vulnerability, Robert shifted tactics and began to concentrate on the raw and sensitive spots on his chest and shoulders, the same places he'd shot Mason a couple of months earlier. Mason grunted with the body blows, struggling to keep his balance. Seeing an opening, Robert charged him, toppling him to the floor.

Horrified at the turn of events, Olivia dove under the chair where she'd seen the gun fall. With her hands shaking, she aimed at the two men wrestling on the floor. Helplessly, she didn't dare try to shoot, considering she had no experience with guns and they were so close together. The last thing she wanted to do was hit the wrong man.

With a sound of frustration, she let the gun drop to the floor and looked around for some other means of helping Mason. She couldn't just sit there. In a flash of inspiration, Olivia skirted the two men and ran into the kitchen.

Grabbing the knife off the cutting board, she turned back toward the living room. She may not be familiar with guns, but she knew knives. Her fingers wrapped comfortingly around the familiar feel of the handle.

As the men came back into view, she was shocked to discover Robert had managed to get his hands wrapped around Mason's throat. There was a sick sense of satisfaction creeping over his face as Mason's face started to turn a ruddy shade of purple, his hands clawing at the other man's grip.

Fury, raw and pure, filled her mind. She let loose with an Amazonian war cry as she raised the knife high above her head and drove the blade down with as much force as she could muster.

The point of the knife gave a sickening thud as it sliced through the meat of his back and lodged in the solid bone of his right shoulder blade. Some part of her registered that the sound would probably haunt her dreams for the rest of her life.

Arching his back, Robert bellowed in pain as he reached up and tried to remove the blade from his shoulder. Aghast, she tugged, trying to pull it back out of his body in order to stab him again. She was startled to find it was embedded too deeply into the bone. Robert whirled around and shoved her, and she lost her grip on the knife handle.

Letting go and taking his eyes off Mason had been a mistake. With his windpipe now clear, he took a deep breath in and slammed his fist into Robert's face. With another blow, he gained his feet. Robert quickly stood and stepped back out of Mason's reach.

The two men squared off, facing each other in a contest of wills, calculating each movement. Slowly, they began to circle one another, both of them breathing heavily. Robert lurched to one side because of the knife in his back. Mason coughed as his bruised windpipe protested.

Olivia looked up from where she'd fallen to the floor and once again spied the gun. Checking both men, she realized she was unnoticed by either of them. Seeing her opportunity, she furtively sidled towards the weapon. The solid weight of it felt like death in her hand, oddly reassuring to her.

Turning back towards the stand-off, she could see the exact moment the expression in Robert's eyes changed. Before he could charge towards Mason, she squeezed the trigger. A blast of firepower exploded the air of the small room. The heavy piece jumped in her hand as if celebrating the violence it had wrought.

Robert stumbled back. His mouth was frozen in a rictus of surprise. He stared down at his chest and the rapidly growing pool of red. Fury and pain intertwined in his gaze as he raised his eyes to connect with hers.

Olivia shook uncontrollably, frozen and staring at the finality of what she'd done. Everything else in her mind blanked as she watched him fall, first to his knees, then to his side on the floor. All the while, he never broke eye contact with her horror-struck gaze. Jolting at the soft touch of Mason's hand on her forearm, she finally pulled her gaze from Robert's prone body and met the warm, summer blue of his eyes.

"Shhh, shhh, let me get this for you." Startled to find she still clutched the gun in both of her hands, Olivia suddenly released her fingers in revulsion, letting Mason take over the weight of it.

She'd just shot a man.

Her eyes pivoted towards the view of Robert's back, where he now lay — face down — on the floor. She noticed his back was also soaked in blood from where she'd stabbed him. The knife's handle still stubbornly protruded from his shoulder blade.

She'd just *killed* a man.

The words dropped into her consciousness like pebbles into the dark depths of a lake. The ripples of them broke the surface of her mind, but the full implication of their presence sunk to places unseen. Some small part of her spirit cracked, causing the structure of her psyche to fissure. Mason watched as her face crumpled before him.

"Oh, Livvy." Instantly, she found herself wrapped in the comforting embrace of his arms.

After all the abuse and pain and fear Olivia had suffered in the last day, his kindness shattered what was left of her control. The raw, damaged sound she uttered came from her very soul, and caused Mason's heart to bleed. He held her as her strength finally crumbled and she sobbed into his chest.

Chapter Fifty-Two

Olivia wiped her eyes after the initial emotional squall passed, and realized she was sitting on Mason's lap. She leaned into his body and allowed herself another moment to enjoy the comforting rhythm of his hand gently stroking her back.

With a hiccup, she fixed her watery gaze on his. Slowly, with a tenderness that almost made her lose control again, he wiped a tear from her cheek and kissed her nose. A troubled look crossed his face as he glanced down and noticed she was clad in nothing but a silky, emerald green teddy.

He could see the violence that had been wrought catalogued across her face but it was another fear that clutched his heart in a vise grip. "Are you injured? Did he...hurt you?"

She looked down. Pausing, she tried to assess the extent of her body's damage. "I was passed out when he dressed me in this." She gestured at the flimsy garment with a look of disgust. "But, no, I don't think he hurt me in that way."

She raised a hand to her temple, her eyes squinting in pain. "My head is pounding, though."

Carefully, hoping not to cause her any further pain, he reached up and discovered the large lump on the back of her head, wincing at the size and definition of it. "You probably have a concussion. I really need to call Brad and let him know what's happened. He shouldn't be too far away at this point. Then we need to get you checked out by a doctor."

It hurt too much for Olivia to nod her acquiescence, so she leaned her head on his shoulder, instead. She couldn't seem to drum up enough energy to be concerned with the details just yet.

After another moment, she raised her head. Curious, she asked, "How did you find me, anyway? It feels like we're in the middle of nowhere."

Mason explained how he discovered that Robert's grandfather used to have a cabin in Maine when he'd checked in at his department earlier that day, but refrained from going into particulars. Instead, he helped her stand up.

Images and more images of her stared down from the walls as Olivia cast a final glance at Robert's dead body lying on the floor. She looked down at her caked and bloody hands and shuddered.

Noticing her look of distress, Mason gave her a hug and led her closer to the front door. "Don't move, wait here." Sounds of running water came from the kitchen and a moment later Mason was back with a damp paper towel.

He took first one, then the other hand in his and wiped the gore from them, carefully taking the time to clean between each of her fingers. Olivia stood there numbly and let his tender act wash over her, feeling his care seep into her, beginning to ease the terror and pain of the past few hours.

With that small chore finished, he leaned over and gave her a kiss on the forehead before heading back into the kitchen and throwing the paper on the counter. Instead of returning directly to her, he turned and walked down the hallway towards the back bedroom.

Another spear of red-hot anger seized him when he saw the restraints on the bed. Clenching his fists, he wished Robert could be killed all over again. This time, slowly.

From the front room, Olivia called out. "Mason?"

"Just a moment." He struggled to reign in his impotent temper, knowing its target was beyond his reach for good. "I'm trying to find pants for you to wear on the ride home." After a short hunt around the room, he found her jeans tossed on the floor in the closet, but noticed her top had been cut off of her. He crumpled the shirt in his hands and inhaled.

Too close. It had been too damn close this time.

Resolutely, he grabbed her pants and shoes and turned to head out of the door. At the last minute, he snatched the blanket from the bed, as well.

Back at the front of the cabin, he noticed Olivia hadn't moved a muscle from where he'd left her. She had her arms wrapped around her waist and didn't even seem to be aware of her own shivering.

He helped her get dressed in the meager layers he had found and draped the blanket over her hunched shoulders. Having done what he could, he opened the front door. Thinking better of making her walk out to his truck, he turned to scoop her up in his arms and carried her out of the cabin.

He could feel her eyes on him as he made his way around the hood of the truck. After climbing into the cab with her, he turned to meet her eyes.

"It's really over now, right?"

Mason gently brushed her cheek where the shadow of violence was already starting to darken. "It's really over. You won't have to worry about Robert ever again. You have your life back, Olivia."

She held Mason's gaze for a moment longer, almost as if she didn't dare believe it to be true, then nodded, and leaned her head back on the seat.

She had her life back. Finally.

Mason cranked up the heat and made sure the vents were directed at her. "Are you going to be okay sitting here for a moment? I need to call Brad and let him know what's happened.

I would have thought he'd be here by now. Maybe he missed the turn-off. It was pretty hard to spot."

She would have nodded, but her head was too sore. Instead, without opening her eyes, she just waved him away. He got out of the truck and pulled his phone out.

Olivia stared out the window, grateful for the way it cooled her forehead. As he talked outside, she let the words he'd said earlier sink into her being. Sure, she had her life back, but so much of it had changed in the last two months – in the past year, even. Her sisters were still moved out of the house. Her café was still burned to the ground. Olivia wasn't sure what even a normal version of her life looked like now.

She wondered how Mason's psych evaluation had gone and what his plans were. They hadn't really discussed where the relationship was heading, but it had always been understood he was going back to Boston after the holidays. Now that he was mostly recovered and the stalker was officially out of the picture, there wasn't anything preventing him from moving on.

With a sigh, she closed her eyes again. It was too much to think about with her head pounding. She just needed some peace and quiet from her thoughts for a while.

Chapter Fifty-Three

Mason glanced at Olivia out of the corner of his eye as he paced outside the truck. Recounting everything to Brad, and seeing the damage from the events written across her face, had him clenching his teeth all over again.

"I missed the turn-off. I'm about fifteen minutes away. The local guys just wrapped up that bad accident on the other side of the county. They'll probably get there after me." Brad paused. "Is she okay?"

Mason choked past the rage, but didn't know how to answer the question. "Well, if you're asking if she's alive, yes. However, I don't think we can really know how she's doing. She got banged up pretty badly and I'm positive she has a concussion. She needs to get looked at immediately."

He could hear the other man's sigh over the connection. "Okay, I'm not sure when the paramedics are going to make it. Why don't you take off and get her to a hospital? The closest one is in Ellsworth about thirty minutes from here. I'll be there soon and will take care of it."

"Are you sure?"

"Yeah."

"Thanks. We left everything exactly as it happened. You'll find him dead in the living room. The gun is on the floor beside him."

"And you said Olivia did it? It wasn't you, Mason?"

"Honestly, she probably saved my life. The guy was not going to be taken in."

"Okay, we'll have to get statements and file all the reports. It's going to be a clusterfuck, given it's not even my jurisdiction." Mason knew there were going to be a lot of questions. Especially once people realized his history with the dead man. He couldn't bring himself to care. The world was a better place without Robert Mendez in it.

After hanging up with Brad, he took the road out incredibly slowly, wincing every time the truck bounced in the ruts. The pace picked up slightly once they reached pavement, but not by much. By then, the storm had started in earnest and it was obvious that the plows hadn't made the lonely stretch of road a priority. The delay was probably another factor why nobody else had managed to show up at the scene before everything went down.

Thankful that his truck had four-wheel drive, he kept a slow and steady pace through the drifts. They passed the lights of a couple of cruisers heading in the opposite direction. He had a pretty good idea where they were headed.

Mason hazarded a glance at Olivia and wondered what she was thinking about that caused her to sigh like that. Her eyes were still closed, making him hesitant to ask her. Reaching over, he turned the radio on, hoping it would help take her mind off the previous events.

Just as he recognized the first notes of Silent Night, she jerked, leaned forward, and snapped the radio off. Startled, he gave her a look, but she'd already resumed her position, leaning her forehead against the window. Shrugging, he resigned himself to a silent ride home.

Snow swirled and glowed in the headlights before flitting off into the darkness, similar to the thoughts in his mind. No amount of thinking could negate the fact that Robert had fixated on her because of him.

Silently gripping the steering wheel, Mason berated himself. He should have taken that bastard back in Boston to begin with. The fact that Robert had managed to get ahold of Olivia…he shuddered. What would he have done if he had succeeded in hurting her more than he had? What if he had violated her while she was passed out? Or worse, killed her before she could be found?

A deep sense of regret sat heavy on his heart. This was exactly why he'd never allowed himself to get too close to anyone or harbor any hopes of having a serious relationship. He couldn't ask someone like Olivia to deal with this kind of risk. Being with him, who knew what sickos he would attract? His job was dangerous. Mason had accepted that going in. Hell, even *he* had reconsidered his choice when he had paid a higher price than imagined with the loss of his partner.

But Olivia? She never signed up for this. In the two months he'd been with her, she'd had to fight against an attacker, had her café burned down, had her freedom and movement limited by having constant escorts, been abducted, nearly raped, came close to being murdered, and had to kill a person. She didn't deserve this.

What was worse was that he couldn't guarantee something like this would never happen again.

He looked over and noticed she'd fallen asleep. The glow of the dashboard lights washed her in a soft green light. Her head was tilted back, her hand lying limply across her lap. She looked so beautiful, so vulnerable to him in that moment. He didn't want to have to disturb her. "Olivia, honey? You have to stay awake for me."

She shifted her head to look at him through bleary eyes. "What?"

"I know it's hard, but you need to stay awake. You have a

concussion. I'm taking you to a hospital now, but you can't fall asleep yet."

Nodding, Olivia struggled to sit up in her seat a little more and turned back to look out the window.

Mason sighed. Although it was silent in the cab, he couldn't quiet the thoughts running through his head. The best thing he could do was distance himself from her. He was expected to resume his position back in Boston anyway, now that the holidays were almost over. Robert had been stopped and he had recovered enough to perform his duties. It was time.

Rubbing his chest, he tried to ease the heavy ache that came with the thought of leaving her. His heart may have doubts, but his head was resolute. He'd rather have Olivia safe at a distance than close and constantly in the line of fire. This would be for the best.

Gently, he reached down and threaded his fingers through hers. Soon, he would need to begin distancing himself. A clean break — quickly made — would probably be easiest on both of them. Mason savored the few minutes remaining to the hospital, lightly stroking the shape of her hand in his.

As the first sign of Ellsworth came into view, he carefully extricated his fingers from hers, girding himself for what he must do.

Chapter Fifty-Four

Olivia blinked her eyes rapidly as the doctor held a light up to them. "Well, I don't think there's any doubt about it; you have a concussion. I'd like to keep you overnight for observation."

"Where is she? It's our sister. You have to let us in!" The loud voices had both her and the doctor turning towards the door. Mason, standing by the entrance, let the two women in.

"Oh, Livvy! Are you okay?"

"We got here as fast as we could." A huge weight lifted from her heart as both of her sister's rushed into the room, the frazzled nurse right on their heels. "I told them she was in the middle of an exam, but they refused…"

"It's okay. I want them here." She turned to the doctor, her eyes pleading. "Please, let them stay."

The doctor watched as the two beautiful women enfolded their older sister in a warm hug. "Well, we're nearly wrapped up here, anyway. Why don't I let you take a moment together? I'll have a nurse give you something for your headache. Remember, ladies, not too long. She needs her rest."

Fiona pulled back from the embrace, tears streaming down her cheeks. "Livvy, I'm *so*, so, sorry I wasn't there for you." Her voice cracked as she broke down. Olivia struggled to soothe her, trying to keep the pain in her head from showing in her eyes.

Liz wrapped an arm around Fiona's shoulders and made eye contact with Olivia. "We were out of our minds with worry. Thank goodness Mason got to you in time."

"I don't understand. What happened to you, Fiona? I tried to call and text, but couldn't reach you. Where were you?"

Hiccupping, Fiona struggled to catch her breath and answer. "I told Liz that I had lost my phone while we were shopping at the mall the other day, but I didn't want to tell you because I knew you were under so much stress and, besides, I really wanted to replace it myself. In fact, that's where I was this afternoon. I went back to the mall, shopping for a new one."

Another piece of the puzzle clicked into place for Mason. "That would explain why Brad just texted me saying they found your phone on the scene, Fiona. We were trying to figure out how it got there."

"He must have stolen it when I was at the bar with my friends. That's when I lost it. This is all my fault!" She wailed.

"No, no sweetie." Olivia tried to comfort her sister while she thought back to the texts she had sent to Fiona's phone. The first had let him know Mason was going out of town; the second had let him know she was alone and where she was headed. It all made sense. Talk about bad luck.

Liz saw her Olivia's ordeal painted on her skin in deep blues and purples, but it was her eyes that seemed the most wounded. Turning to Mason, she gave him a small nod of thanks. "We owe you so much. Thank you for saving her."

He cleared his throat in embarrassment. "She wouldn't have ever had to deal with Robert in the first place if it weren't for her association with me."

Olivia disentangled herself from Fiona's arms and turned to look at Mason, standing by the doorway. She didn't know why, but ever since the ride in his truck, it had felt like he was a million miles away. Oh, he'd been unfailingly kind. He'd even stayed close throughout the examination when she'd asked him to, but something was different. Perplexed, and a little hurt, she reached toward him, but he kept his distance.

Sighing, she let her arm drop back to the bed. "You don't know that. The fact is, he was a very sick man, and would have latched onto someone again eventually. You can't blame yourself for this." She gestured up to her swollen, abused face. "It's Robert's doing, not yours. You saved me."

Her sisters cast each other glances as the tension in the room became more palpable. "Um, I think Fiona and I are going to go grab a cup of coffee. We'll be back in a few minutes."

Both of them headed out the door, brushing by Mason. Fiona stopped and gave him a comforting pat on the shoulder. "Don't be too hard on yourself." She leaned up and gave him a small peck on the cheek before walking away down the hall.

Touched, he lifted his fingers to where she'd kissed him. He turned to Olivia and in a raw voice haunted by demons said, "I'm glad you're safe. I- I- don't know what I would have done if he'd managed to really hurt you." Almost against his will, he moved towards her bed and stood beside it. "I can't bear the thought that I lead him to you."

Olivia didn't know how to answer him. Instead, she just leaned into his chest and soaked in his strength and comfort, inhaling the musky, masculine smell that was Mason.

He stroked a strand of her hair back and tucked it behind her ear. Unable to resist, he leaned down and kissed her mouth tenderly, taking care not to disturb her split lip. He knew what he had to do, but every fiber in his being ached with the knowledge. Reluctantly, he pulled back. "I need to go. You'll be alright here with your sisters."

Startled, she gave him a puzzled look. "Mason?"

He ran a hand through his hair. "I'm sorry. I need to get ahold of Brad and see where they're at with processing the scene. Then I need to contact my captain and let him know what's happened." He looked down at his torn and blood-spattered shirt. "Plus, I should probably try to get myself cleaned up."

Everything he was saying made sense, but she still got the impression that wasn't why he was leaving. Cautiously, Olivia acknowledged what he'd said. "Okay. I'll see you later?"

Mason stopped in the doorway and looked back at her. She looked so small and vulnerable lying in the hospital bed, surrounded by machines and white walls, her face a mottled mural of black and purple bruises. Without giving her a verbal commitment, he nodded and stepped out into the hallway. Seeing her look so confused and alone would haunt him for a long, long time.

Chapter Fifty-Five

O livia shuffled through the front door of her house and breathed in a sigh of relief. Between being woken up every few hours, hearing the hum and beep of the machines around her, and smelling unfamiliar stale air, she hadn't gotten much rest in the hospital.

Then, to make matters worse, she'd gone directly from the hospital to the police station and had spent hours giving her verbal account. The room she'd been sitting in was empty and cold, and she'd been constantly aware that every word she said was being recorded. Even though the officers had been kind and sympathetic to her situation, it had hurt to go over everything so soon after the incident. Olivia knew her voice had cracked going over some of the details.

She felt like her whole being had been put through a wringer. Every bone in her body felt brittle and old.

Liz watched her sister stand in the foyer, looking as if she were lost, her eyes cast in a thousand-yard stare. Her brow wrinkled in concern. "Hey, Livvy?" Liz reached for her, but Olivia jumped and flinched, startled. Quickly, Liz pulled her hand back.

"I was thinking – why don't you turn in for the night? You still look pretty tired."

Nothing in the world could have sounded better to her than

doing exactly that. Well, unless it was being able to curl up in Mason's strong arms while she did so. With the thought floating through her mind, she glanced out of the entry window, yearning to see his truck in the driveway.

No such luck.

With a sigh, she turned to her sister. "Yeah, I think that sounds like a good idea. I know Jackie and Tom called, but can you let them know I'll talk to them later?"

"I will."

Olivia made the trek up the stairs and stepped into her bedroom. She toed her shoes off, but didn't bother removing the rest of her clothes. Instead, she crawled under her covers, pulling them up over her head to make a cocoon. It didn't even take a minute before she had escaped into a mercifully dreamless sleep.

The next morning, she lay in bed and watched the sunlight chase the shadows on her ceiling. Swathed in the soft, downy warmth of her comforter, it was hard to believe the last two days hadn't been some ugly, horrible nightmare. For one moment, she thought maybe it *had* all been her imagination.

Just then, there was a light tap on her door and Liz poked her head in. "Oh, good, you're awake. I wish I could let you relax in here longer, but Brad called last night and is going to be coming by in about an hour. I thought you might like to get up and put yourself together before he gets here."

Olivia groaned and sat up. She rubbed her eyes. "What time is it?"

"A little after 11am."

"What? I can't believe I slept so late."

"I think you really needed it."

Honestly, she probably could have slept the rest of the day away, Olivia thought. "Okay, I'm getting up. I'll be ready in about half an hour. Have you heard from Mason?"

Liz's mouth twisted. "No, not yet. I'm sure he's been kept busy running around trying to coordinate what happened between the three departments. Since it was so far out, the county sheriff has gotten involved now, too. Brad mentioned the other police districts weren't too happy about getting there after the fact."

"Oh." Olivia tried hard not to let her disappointment show. It sounded like one big mess. Still, it would have been nice if he could have at least called to check up on her.

"I hate to leave you, but I need to head into the garage for a few hours. Fiona is here and will stay with you."

"Okay," she said, still distracted by her thoughts of Mason.

She hadn't heard from Mason all day yesterday. She had known he was planning on heading back to Boston and his job after the holidays, but she hadn't expected things to end so abruptly. Resolutely, she shoved the covers aside and sat on the edge of the bed. It was what it was. If this was the way he wanted to move on, then it was better if she accepted it now.

She was just putting the final touches on her makeup when she heard the doorbell ring downstairs. Turning her head to the side, she gave a satisfied nod, happy that the bruises weren't nearly as noticeable. Taking a shower and changing clothes had gone a long way towards lifting her spirits and making her feel halfway normal again.

Olivia made her way down the stairs. Fiona opened the door, and she could see Brad in the doorway. Mason stood just behind him. "I thought I'd bring Mason with me. I'm sorry I've been taking up all his time and keeping him away for so long. I hope you don't mind."

Fiona smiled at him. "I can't thank you enough for saving my sister." She turned back to include Brad in her gaze. "Both of you."

Mason gave her an odd, indecipherable look. "Of course." He spotted Olivia standing at the bottom of the stairs as he crossed the threshold. Their eyes caught, but it felt like there was a universe of distance between them. She fought back the urge to turn around and go back upstairs.

Instead, she straightened her spine and plastered a smile on her face. "Brad," she gave her friend a hug. He pulled back and lifted her chin, taking note of the careful way she'd applied her makeup.

"Heya, Livvy." He asked, gently, "How are you hanging in there?"

Tears welled in her eyes, but she stubbornly firmed her jaw before they could fall. She nodded up at him. "I'm doing okay. Why don't we all sit in the living room? We'll be more comfortable in there."

"Would anybody like something to drink?" Fiona offered. "I was just about to make some tea."

Letting go of Brad, she turned to her sister. "I wouldn't mind a good cup of coffee." She grinned for her sister's benefit. "The swill they call coffee at the hospital is disgusting."

Smiling in return, Fiona turned towards the kitchen as the other three moved into the living room. Olivia took her usual place, curled up in the corner of the couch, and pulled the throw around her legs. Ever since she'd been rescued, she hadn't been able to shake the feeling of being cold.

Brad sat down in the armchair and leaned his elbows on his knees. Olivia watched as Mason stood by the mantle of the fireplace. Her heart squeezed. She'd been hoping the space she'd felt between the two of them had been her imagination, and that he'd come and sit down next to her like he'd always done before.

Unconsciously defensive, she pulled her knees up and wrapped her arms around them, then turned back towards Brad. "Olivia, I wanted to go over a few things and give you an idea of what to expect going forward. I know we have your testimony and signed statement. At some point, they may ask you to go back to the station for a follow-up. But, more than any of that, I just wanted to check on you and see how you were doing."

Fiona came in to join them and sat down next to her. She was glad for her sister's comfort and support. It had begun to feel very lonely sitting on the couch by herself. Olivia answered Brad. "I think I'm still in shock, but for the most part, I'm just glad it's over." She looked directly at Mason. "I know I'm going to be okay."

Sensing some tension between the two, Brad said, "Mason, moved heaven and earth to get to you on time. He was a mad man on a mission. I'd like to think I could have done it as quickly, but the fact is I don't have any experience with something as large scale as this. It makes me even more thankful to be sitting here with you."

"Thank you, Brad, for everything you've done." Impulsively, she got up and gave him a hug. "You're a good cop, and a great friend."

Blushing a little, Brad turned to the other man before letting Fiona walk him to the front door. "I'll just be in the car."

Mason looked at him. "I'll be right out."

They both stood in the sun-filled living room, looking at each other. She found herself trying to imprint the look of him into her memory. The light was coming through the windows at just the right angle to turn his eyes into glowing sapphires. "So…"

With a soft curse under his breath, he strode up to her and took her mouth in a heated, passionate kiss - leaving her breathless. Dazed, she looked up at him with desire and confusion warring equally in her eyes.

He leaned his forehead against hers. "I'm sorry." His eyes stared into hers and then moved on to search and scan her face, as if he was trying to memorize every detail. She opened her mouth to ask him why he was acting so strangely, but he shook his head slightly.

Bending down, he brushed his lips lightly across hers one last time. With that final touch, Mason straightened and headed out the door.

Stunned, Olivia was left standing in the middle of the room, wondering what had just happened.

Chapter Fifty-Six

The next week, Tom and Jackie invited Olivia and her sisters to spend Christmas Day with them. Olivia found she was more than happy to let Tom cook the Christmas feast. Instead, she relaxed and enjoyed watching Abby's excitement opening her presents. Even hearing Christmas music again hadn't been so bad.

The entire day, she tried not to let her thoughts wander back towards Mason. She had gotten him concert tickets to see The Black Keys in Boston. His Christmas present had sat in an envelope in her top drawer up until Christmas Eve. She had been hoping he would stop by, but finally ended up giving them to Melody to give to him. It seemed like a shame to let them go to waste.

Weeks passed, and gradually things got back to some semblance of normal. It had taken a few days for Olivia to feel comfortable walking around by herself again, but eventually she grew more confident. It helped that she lived in a small town where she was familiar with, and loved by, the people in her community.

She'd had to go down to the police department and give additional details for her statement, but for the most part, it was an open and shut case. Robert Mendez had been implicated in at least one other stalker case—the woman who'd been rescued by Mason and his partner—and one murder in a different state. Knowing how badly things could have turned out troubled her for a number of sleepless nights, but thankfully, even the nightmares had begun to fade.

Although she hadn't heard from Mason directly since that day after "the incident," she had run into him on occasion during the debriefings and legal events that followed. It was hard for her not to resent the way he was unfailingly polite, but always slightly removed. What was even worse was that she couldn't help wondering how he was doing back in Boston.

Melody had gotten in touch with her and asked if she was still interested in developing the restaurant by her bed and breakfast. It had been awkward for both of them at first, but they'd managed to come to an understanding. Melody stated that she thought her brother was being an idiot. Olivia couldn't help but agree, but just smiled and said she hoped he was doing well. After that, they let the subject of Mason drop.

Olivia was happy and relieved to find that she really liked Melody and could be friends with her, despite the weird way things had ended with her brother. She admired Melody's sense of design and style, and relied heavily on her input as they made plans for the look and feel of the restaurant.

Thankfully, the renovations at the café hadn't taken very long, and Tom and Jackie were able to take over the business there. By the end of February, people were once again enjoying Tom's famous hash browns. They had changed the name to "Abby's" after Jackie's daughter. Olivia had never seen her best friend so happy, and had been glad to hear the café was once again doing brisk business.

Fiona padded down the stairs and stopped in the doorway to watch her sister wistfully staring out the window, a book of paint samples lying forgotten on the counter in front of her. She frowned. Ever since that day, Olivia had been much more quiet and pensive than usual. It was hard to tell whether it was due to her experiences with Robert, or the aftermath with Mason.

Olivia sighed and turned around, and then started at finding her sister staring at her. "Fiona. How'd you sleep last night?" She moved to get up. "Would you like me to make you some breakfast?"

"No, no, it's fine." Fiona took a good look at her sister, noticing the bags under her eyes. "I'm worried about you. Are you sure you won't make an appointment to talk to somebody?"

Laughing, her older sister shrugged it off. "Fi, I don't want a therapist. I just want to get this restaurant up and running."

Fiona walked up and wrapped an arm around her, laying her head on Olivia's shoulder. "You know I'm here for you, right? Liz and I both are, if you ever want to talk about it. Or about Mason…"

Olivia shook her head. How many times in the last two months had she caught herself staring into space, thinking about him and wondering what he was doing? The other day, hearing The Black Keys on the radio, she had automatically been transported to that first day in his car. How was it possible to miss someone so much and still be so angry with him?

Because, if she was being honest with herself, she was angry! Angry that he'd left her. Angry that he hadn't even given her a chance to talk things out. Angry that he'd be willing to give up something so damn good — especially knowing how bad life could get.

She shook her head again and forced herself away from that train of thought. No good could come of it, and she just didn't have any more time or energy to spend on it. Instead, she squeezed her sister back. "I know. Thank you. Maybe in the future I'll take you up on that offer, but for now, I think I just need to work some things out in my own mind. Does that make sense?"

Reluctantly, Fiona nodded and released her, turning to make a fresh pot of coffee. "Okay, whatever you need, let me know."

Olivia looked at the clock and jumped. "Oh! What I need right now is to go. I have a meeting with the contractor. I'm hoping we can break ground soon."

"How exciting! I can't wait when it's all finished."

"Me too. It feels good to know at least one good thing came out of all the bad that has happened. It kind of feels like giving a big middle finger to the memory of Robert." She shot her sister a wicked smile. "I don't know, maybe it makes me a bad person, but I can't help but feel satisfaction from that."

A short time later, Olivia pulled up to the large double doors of the barn and parked her car by the truck already waiting for her. As she climbed out of her car, she thought about how things would look completely different this time next year.

As she walked in, she spotted a man already taking measurements. When he shifted, she grinned in recognition. "Alex? Alex Weston?"

The tall, blond man turned at the sound of her approach and broke into a large smile. "Olivia, it's so nice to see you."

She shook his hand. "What an unexpected surprise. I didn't know you're a contractor. When did you come back to town?"

"Just recently. In fact, you'll be my first job for this company." He grew more somber. "I don't know if you heard, but my dad isn't doing so well. I came back to help him make final arrangements and figured I'd stick around for a while. How are your sisters doing? Is Eliza still a little grease monkey?"

For some reason, he always referred to Liz as Eliza. Olivia suspected he did it to tease her. She smiled. Most of the time, it worked.

Alex used to be the most popular guy in school; he'd been a couple of grades behind Olivia. He was the kind of guy they made high school movies about — a quintessential golden boy. The football captain who always had girls hanging over him. Until his father had suddenly decided, without warning, to ship him off to boarding school. He hadn't been seen much since.

"They're both doing well. Liz took over partnership of the mechanic shop and spends most of her waking hours there. Fiona is going to school at Bowdoin College."

"And you want to convert this old barn into a restaurant, huh?" He turned to look at the shadowed interior of the huge barn.

"I do. Think you can handle it?"

He took a moment to consider. "I think it will turn out amazing, actually. Hell yeah, I can handle it."

Rustling through her bag, she pulled out the portfolio she'd been putting together and handed it to him. "Here's kind of what I'm going for. You can see the atmosphere I want. High-end, but still warm and cozy. Maybe a little eclectic…" She walked over to the wall facing the cliff. "I was hoping we could change this wall into floor to ceiling windows to take advantage of the magnificent view."

Alex nodded and walked with her, taking notes as she talked. They spent a little more than an hour going over the site. Before leaving, he turned to her. "I think I have a pretty good idea of what you're after. Why don't I head back to my office and start working up some plans? We can talk about any changes in a week or so."

"I'd like that. I'm so happy we'll have a chance to work together on this."

He looked down at his former schoolmate and grew serious. She'd grown up to be a beautiful woman, but he could see the shadows in her eyes, belying the calm exterior she presented. "I heard about the troubles you've had recently. I'll do everything in my power to get you up and running as soon as possible."

Touched, she gave him a hug. "Thank you, I appreciate that."

He tucked her portfolio and his folder of notes under an arm and then gave her a brilliant smile. "Okay, I'll give you a call after I've managed to draw something up. Give me a few days."

"Sounds good." Already lost in her daydreams of what it would look like once it was finished, she turned to walk further back into the barn as Alex began to make his way to the double doors.

Chapter Fifty-Seven

Mason watched as Olivia embraced the other man, and felt the ache in his heart crack into a full-blown fissure. He was too late. What a fool he'd been to ever have left in the first place.

Absently, he rubbed his chest as the feeling of loss deepened. His eyes followed the tall, blonde man as he made his way towards the door. Wariness and distrust entered the other man's eyes. *Well, at least he's protective of her,* Mason thought.

"Can I help you?"

"Looks like you've already helped yourself." Mason couldn't quite manage to keep the grumble of discontent out of his voice. It hurt knowing he could be replaced so easily, when he had been tossing and turning every night for nearly three months.

Some small part of him realized he was being unfair. Olivia, of all people, deserved to be happy. Hoping to make a better impression, he extended his hand. "Sorry, I'm Mason."

Mason looked the other man up and down, noting that he wasn't much shorter than him. "I probably shouldn't have come."

Alex cocked his head to the side. "Mason? The cop that saved her, right?" He laughed at the other man's startled expression. Well, at least she'd mentioned him. Alex dispelled that comforting thought with his next statement. "Small town, news travels."

"Ah." Mason looked glumly down at the floor.

Finally, Alex took pity on him. "Well, I was just taking off. She's hired me as the contractor for her new restaurant and there's a lot to get started on. You should go see if you can do something about dispelling the shadows from her eyes."

Mason's gaze shot up and met the other man's. Alex just winked at him and kept walking toward his truck. Mason looked back toward Olivia, taking in the new information. She'd walked further into the shadows. Her head was tilted back, looking at one of the large rafters spanning the length of the barn.

He had missed seeing her profile and that look of intensity she got when she was concentrating on something. Although the angle was wrong, he could practically see the furrow that she'd have across her brow and the way she was probably biting her bottom lip.

Melody had informed him of her plans for the barn, of course. They had sounded great, but at the moment, Olivia concerned him more than construction plans. He couldn't seem to take his eyes off her. Suddenly, as if sensing she was being watched, she turned to him.

He watched as her eyes rounded in surprise and imagined that if they were in the light, they would look like two gold medallions. A shutter closed over her face, but not before he had seen the emotion there. A spark fluttered in him. There was still hope.

He walked across the expanse of the barn and stopped just before her. He found himself staring into the very same honey-colored eyes that had been haunting him for the past few months. Every morning, he had woken with her face in his mind. He only hoped he hadn't messed things up beyond repair.

A look of confusion and hurt crossed her face before the curtain guarding her emotions fell back into place. Well, what did he expect? That she'd greet him with open arms after such a long absence?

"I've missed you so much. You look good."

Her shoulders tensed. All the hurt and frustration that she had been harboring for nearly three months seemed to grow in her chest until it was hard to breathe. "You've missed me?"

She let out a short bark of laughter. It was a bitter sound he didn't recognize coming from her. "No. I'm sorry, Mason. You don't get to say that to me. Not after all this time. After you left me like that. Broken, hurt, scared, and alone in the aftermath of everything that happened. Now you want to come here and tell me you 'miss me?!'" Her voice cracked on the last word and she stopped, afraid if she went any further she'd burst into tears.

Olivia clenched her hands down by her sides and fought for composure. "What are you doing here, Mason?"

He took another step closer, but stopped again when she took a defiant step back. The foot of space between them was a chasm of regret. His hands lifted of their own volition, subconsciously reaching for her, pleading with her, before he let them drop back down to his sides again.

"What am I doing here? The real question should be, why did I ever leave? How could I have possibly thought it would be better?" He raked his hands through his hair and let out an explosive sigh. "The fact is, there hasn't been a single minute I haven't thought about you. I see you everywhere I go."

Calmly, she kept her eyes trained on him, the look of suspicion still clearly evident. Was it just his own wishful thinking that he thought he saw something else flickering there, as well? She folded her arms across her chest. "Why did you? Leave, that is."

Again, he found his hands palms up in supplication. "I didn't want my job, and the danger that surrounds me, to impact you again. Impact your life and dreams… You never signed up for the risks that I take on a daily basis. I had hoped, by leaving, I could keep you safe."

The tone of her voice softened. "That wasn't only your choice to make. You never even *asked* me how I felt, or what I wanted."

He half-turned away from her, revealing the inner battle he was waging. "I know. You're right. And, dammit, it's selfish of me, but I can't live without you."

Mason once again pinned her with his searing blue eyes, eyes that were raw, and open, and haunted. "I love you, Olivia."

Olivia heard his words, but they hardly registered. It was what she saw in his eyes that really drove home the message. All the fantasies, all the fairy-tale endings she had barely let herself have, were coming true in this one, precious moment. It was as if the roof had opened up and the sun was shining down upon her.

"Please." He whispered, brokenly. "Please, say something. Tell me I'm not too late."

The odd sound of a half-sob bubbled up and caught on the lump in her throat. "I- I- thought maybe it was because I killed him. That somehow you felt I had been tainted by my actions."

His heart fractured and shattered at her feet at what she'd just said. That she would even think he could feel that way. That he'd allowed even the hint of that impression to enter her mind. "What? NO! Never! Olivia, you are so precious to me. You're not tainted by what you had to do to survive." His voice cracked with emotion. "You are the strongest, most beautiful person I know."

He couldn't stand the space between them any longer. Taking that last step, his arms wrapped warmly around her shoulders and he pulled her tightly to his chest.

Leaning down, he barely heard her mumble. "Well, it's about time you figured it out, you foolish man."

Mason kissed the crown of her head. "I'm so sorry."

She looked up at him and managed to give him a tremulous grin through the tears.

"Oh baby, don't cry. Please, please, don't cry." Mason bent

down and kissed her damp cheeks, her eyes, her temple, trying to ease all the places he had caused her pain.

"You're going to have to make it up to me, y'know."

"I will. I promise. If you'll let me, I'd like to spend the rest of my life finding ways to make it up to you." He felt her sigh and lean into him. Finally, her arms wrapped themselves around his waist. Gratified, his whole being filled with love, and the tight knot in his chest began to ease.

It felt like coming home.

Note from the Author

I hope that you enjoyed reading my debut novel, Secret Hunger. If you did, please consider leaving a review on Amazon and Goodreads!

Reviews are vital to me, especially as a new author. They increase my visibility and help to convince other people to take a chance on reading my book.

Secret Need
The Harper Sisters, #2
by Satin Russell
Coming August 22, 2017

Liz may be forced to entrust her life to Alex, but can she trust him with her heart?

Liz Harper is a woman in control of her life. As the owner and mechanic of the best garage in town, she is strong, confident, and in demand. It's a far cry from her high school days spent as the social outcast. Then she runs into the boy who harassed her as a kid, only now he's the good-looking man who is showing interest in her. Despite the attraction, she's determined to keep her distance.

When Alex Weston returns to Bath, Maine to care for his ailing father, the place feels exactly the same. Everything except the awkward girl he used to tease. Liz Harper is all grown up and her transformation is the most intriguing thing about this place. If only he could convince her to give him the time of day.

Then fate throws them together and they discover things are more complicated than they seem. Big secrets lurk in the shadows of this small town. Caught up in a world of drugs and murder and accused of crimes they did not commit, they're now on the run. They must learn to rely on each other if they're going to survive.

Liz and Alex will return in Secret Need

About The Author

Satin Russell was a financial advisor for many years up until she decided to pursue her dream of becoming a writer back in April 2013.

It took her a full year of saving and planning before she was able to commit to her goal full-time. Secret Hunger is her debut novel and was published in April 2015. She looks forward to writing many more.

Satin lives in Massachusetts with her husband. Other than writing, she loves reading, supporting fellow authors (especially self-published ones,) traveling, and photography. She's also partial to a good whiskey every now and then.

Satin loves to hear from her readers. You can visit her website at www.satinrussell.com or email her at satinrussell@hotmail.com.

If you liked this book, please consider leaving a review and supporting Satin as a new author.

Thank you!